THE UNCANNY KINGDOM COLLECTION, VOLUME ONE

FAMILIAR MAGIC | SPECTRAL DETECTIVE | MAGIC EATER

M.V. STOTT

DAVID BUSSELL

BECOME AN INSIDER

FAMILIAR MAGIC

M.V. STOTT

1

It was the absence of magic that first got me, hitting me like a punch in the gut.

I shuffled forward along the scuffed cobbles of the alleyway, my legs threatening to unhinge and drop me to the ground.

My name is Stella Familiar. I belong to the London Coven, a trio of urban witches, and I had just arrived home to find the door of our home hanging off its hinges. The entrance was dented and scorched, as though someone had blasted their way inside, which was impossible. I stood there, looking at the remains of the door for a few seconds, dumbfounded. *Impossible.* And yet, there it was.

The London Coven is in Hammersmith, West London, just a few streets away from the Underground station. It's situated down a blind alley, the only building at the end of a short cobbled stretch. It's called a blind alley because only those who know it exists can see it; a simple but effective layer of perception magic that makes the alley invisible to most, even when looking directly at it.

But back to that impossible lack of magic...

The coven and the blind alley that lead to its door should

have been noisy with arcane energy. Should have been alive with boiling, agitated power; great churning fractals of the stuff. It was home to my masters, Kala, Trin and Feal, the three most powerful witches in England, and every inch of the place was infused with their sorcery. On top of that, there were the spells of protection; hundreds of them. Anyone that wasn't meant to be within the coven's walls could find themselves stepping into a patch of superheated air that melted the flesh from their bones, or perhaps they'd blink, and just before their heart gave out, find themselves wearing their insides on the outside. There were any number of ways it could happen. Any number of creative deaths to discover. With so many things of the dark seeking to slither inside and do us harm, the coven had to be locked up tight. It was impossible for anything to cross the threshold that wasn't invited, and yet...

The door—

That lack of magic—

I tucked a stray lock of raven-black hair behind my ear, swallowed hard, and ducked through the gap created by the half-off door, straightening up slowly on the other side. A corridor stretched before me; walls of bare grey brick, floor made of exposed hardwood boards. A few doors stood either side of the corridor. Straight ahead was the coven's common room.

The place was dead.

There wasn't a whisper of magic to be heard anywhere. To be felt. To be tasted.

It was impossible.

I know I keep using that word, but that's because it was true.

Every building, every street, every hill and river and grain of sand contains some residue of magic. It's all around us every day. We swim around in it; an invisible sea of Uncanny energy. Even if this place hadn't been a coven, hadn't housed three of the most powerful magical creatures in the country, the very fact of its existence meant it should emit trace levels of magic.

But there was nothing.

I reached out with all of my senses, desperate for anything. For a ghost of some ancient incantation.

I came up empty.

'Kala? Trin? Someone, please answer me.'

Silence.

I stepped into the first room; Kala's reading room, piled high with trashy paperback romances. It was empty, but there were signs of a struggle. 'Kala?' Chairs lay on their sides, broken glass scattered across wooden floorboards. The coven smelt the same despite the lack of magic; that strange mix of cinnamon, freshly-cut grass, and lavender that seemed to permanently drift about the place, no matter which potion was cooked up, or what meal was prepared. The smell of my master's witchcraft.

I turned back and stepped into the hallway again. 'Intruder, my name is Stella Familiar and you will show yourself or I... or I will...'

I pressed a palm against the wall to steady myself and swallowed, my throat dry. The emptiness was getting to me, giving me the shakes. All magical beings are connected to the power that radiates from the natural world, but few more are more connected than my kind. As a familiar, I feed on the magic that naturally occurs, soaking it in like a sponge, night and day, without even thinking about it. It sustains me, makes me stronger, gives me the energy to cast spells. But now, in this place, this empty coven, I was like a junkie whose supply had been cut off after a lifetime of indulgence, my slim but powerful body trembling. I was going cold turkey, and it really, *really* hurt.

It was disturbing how quickly I was affected. A minute had passed, tops, and I was already a shaking, sweaty wreck, struggling to resist the urge to run from the coven, from the blind alley, so I could get a good, strong hit.

I grunted, straightened up and tried to get my shit together. This was no time for weakness, no time to fall apart. My home had been attacked.

'Intruder, my name is Stella Familiar, and you will show yourself to me!' The words roared out of my mouth with a strength I didn't feel.

There was no reply.

I placed a hand on the door to the coven's common room and pushed.

I tasted death before I saw it; a metallic tang on the tongue that twisted my stomach and told me what I was going to see before my eyes had been given a chance to catch up. A taste like a gun barrel in my mouth.

The room was mostly as I'd left it: a few comfy chairs, a bookcase, a couch, and a long wooden table with ancient texts spread across it. A small cauldron hung in a fireplace, and beside that sat a television on a TV stand. Always the same. Except on this day, some extra items had been added.

There were three bodies on the floor.

Three bodies, but more than three pieces.

Kala, Trin, Feal—my masters, my creators, my coven's high witches—had been torn to pieces and scattered around the room.

Eyes wide, hand to my mouth, I stepped inside.

'No...'

Blood was sprayed across the grey brick walls and splattered across the floorboards, collecting in congealing red pools. It was a horror story. A world gone mad.

This couldn't be happening.

Nothing was capable of doing this to the witches of the London Coven. Together, when connected, the three of them wielded enough power to crack open mountains, to turn the oceans into sand, to make demons weep, and yet my shoes were soaking in a pool of their collective blood.

I crouched and placed a hand on a hunk of meat that could have belonged to any one of my masters. It, like the coven itself, was empty. Not just of life, but of magic. Of power. Something had broken into a place it was impossible to plunder, bypassed the magical safeguards it was impossible to survive, and torn to...

...and murdered my masters. Murdered three creatures of immeasurable power. And then, to finish things off, they'd drained every last drop of magic from the place.

Impossible on top of impossible on top of impossible.

I stood, angry. Angry that I'd allowed fear to infect me. I hadn't been created to feel fear, I'd been created to *instil* fear, and to bring about justice. I cradled the anger and blew upon it, igniting it like the first spark of a new fire. It didn't matter that this was impossible, it had happened. It didn't matter that the kind of power needed to have achieved any one of the unimaginable things done to this coven would be enough to turn me into a puddle of bubbling goo.

None of it mattered.

All that mattered was that the coven had been breached, and my creators, my mothers, had been murdered as though they were nothing. As though they were less than nothing. They'd been ripped and shredded and tossed aside. My nails dug into my palms and drew blood, but I didn't flinch. It felt *good*.

I was going to find out who was behind this and do something impossible myself.

I was going to get bloody, horrifying revenge.

I was nothing but a lowly familiar, but I swore to every god I knew that I was going to avenge my slaughtered coven.

'Listen to me,' I hissed, 'and listen closely. You have made a grave mistake. My name is Stella Familiar, and what has happened here today will be met with a fury you cannot even imagine. Do you hear me? I know you can. Whoever did this, I *will* find you, and when I do, I will rip your beating heart from your chest.'

A noise—

A movement in the corner of my eye—

I wasn't alone.

And I was in terrible danger.

2

Whatever it was that was inside the coven with me, it was taking its time. It was trying to scare me. And it was working.

Normally in this sort of situation—with an unknown assailant stalking me, ready to leap out and tear my throat from my neck at any moment—I'd draw upon the surrounding magic and cast a spell that would turn the creature into confetti. Sling a spell first, ask questions later, that was my usual way of dealing with threats. But there was no surrounding magic. I extended my senses as far as I could, invisible tendrils firing out in all directions, desperately searching for a hint of the Uncanny to draw upon, but everything out there was cold.

This was a dead place, in more ways than one.

The creature unleashed a low, rumbling growl that shook the floor beneath me. I was in deep trouble. I tried to ignore the blood, the chunks of my dead masters, and I reached out again to try and make sense of what I was up against.

A voice—

A single word, repeated staccato—

Kill Kill Kill—

The words rolled in my head as I came upon the thing stalking me. It was a slippery creature, hard to get a clear grip on, but it was obvious it wasn't the person behind this attack. No, this creature was a booby trap.

Time to take stock.

I had no magic to draw on, only the weak power I already had stored inside of me, and even that was dulled by my surroundings, as though my magic was shrinking back in confusion at the emptiness around me. Did the creature keeping just out of view know that? Did it realise I was running on empty? That I'd brought a slap to a gunfight?

No, I didn't think so. It was just toying with me; that's the only reason it hadn't already pounced. It wanted to make me scared to death before death actually came calling.

'Whatever you are, this is already getting boring. Show yourself, but know that I have enough juice in me to make your head go pop. Understand?'

A bluff, but I sold it as best I could. From what I could sense, it was a simple attack beast, left to take care of anyone who stumbled into the dead coven. To take care of *me*. Whatever this creature was, it was the monkey, not the organ grinder.

'Do you hear me, you dumb beast? Show yourself or get the hell out of my house.'

A growl and the floor shook—

A wall in front of me exploded—

A creature erupted into the room, busting through brick and plaster as though they were matchsticks and spit. The horned monster dog bore down on me, eyes burning with red fire, its slavering maw a jumble of razor-sharp teeth. It raised its great head, drool dripping from its mouth and splashing on the floor, mixing with the spilled blood of my masters.

I had to choose my next words carefully. 'There there,' I said. 'Good dog...?'

No, not ideal.

A thought struck me: this monster was created by magic, which meant it must have magic available for me to feed on. I ignored the fact that I should have already been able to sense any magic in my vicinity, and tried to reach out to it, to draw in some of its power, but whoever had created this thing was no idiot. Some sort of extra spell had been cast upon the beast that made my mental feelers slide off it, like I was trying to push two magnets of the same pole together. So that was why I hadn't been able to sense its presence, or its magic? The thing was shielded from me. Whoever had ripped apart my witches and left this booby trap didn't plan on making things easy.

The demon dog took a step forward, a floorboard cracking beneath one of its heavy, cloven feet.

'Stop. Stay there. Don't take another step or you're done for.' I raised a hand by way of a threat and formed a weak cloud of sparks that swam around. I could only hope the monster took it for the beginnings of something more powerful. 'You will tell me your name, beast, and the name of your master, or I will—'

I didn't get to finish the sentence. The creature snorted and began to charge, drool trailing from its mouth. I flung the weak defence spell I'd conjured in the creature's direction as I turned and bolted from the room. I wasn't sticking around to check for damage. I knew the energy I'd unleashed would present the beast with about as much of an obstacle a cobweb.

I ran some more, arms pumping. A second more and the thing would be on top of me. I stopped sharply and threw myself through the open door to my left, causing the monster to tumble past me, unable to halt its momentum.

I landed on the floor, shoulder jarring, but I didn't have time to register the pain. I rolled on to my knee and turned to the open doorway. I could hear the thing scrabbling to stop and turn. I looked around for anything in the room I could use, a weapon perhaps, then realised I'd jumped into Trin's gallery, which was swamped with easels and canvases and little else. I didn't have time to run back out of the door and head in the other direction, which left me only one option: the window.

My only hope was to get out of the coven and away from the blind alley. Either the thing wouldn't follow me—conjured to stay within the confines of the coven—or it would give chase. If it followed, then my one shot was to make it out of the blind alley and into the street before it caught up with me. After that, I'd pull whatever magic I could from the surroundings to do... whatever I could. I'd have at best seconds to power up, and I already knew that wouldn't be long enough for me to gain enough energy to destroy the thing, but I was out of options.

The corridor's floorboards crunched as the beast headed back to the doorway, back towards me. Its giant, snarling head came into view, and its burning, hellish eyes looked at me. Looked at me with hunger, desperate to taste my flesh.

Okay.

It was now or never.

This was going to hurt.

'Here, doggy,' I said.

I used the last of my power to hurl a chair at the beast's face, hoping to slow it down for even half a second, then I turned, raised my arms over my head, and threw myself through the coven window.

3

Shards of glass swarmed me like angry bees as I burst from the coven and fell hard on the cobbles outside. I heard the beast, its roar barely muffled behind me.

'Get up!' I yelled, and pushed myself to my feet, hands criss-crossed with livid cuts from the shattered window, the leather jacket I wore protecting me from too much more damage.

I'd made it outside, now I just had to make it another twenty metres to the end of the blind alley, to the streets beyond with their wash of background magic that I could pull on. I could do it.

Maybe I could do it.

No, no; I *had* to do it.

I had to survive, because no one else was going to get revenge for my coven. No one but me. If I died, this would go unpunished. I couldn't let that happen. Wouldn't.

I took a step and my knee almost buckled beneath me. The adrenalin was pumping so strong that I hadn't realised how hard I'd come down during my escape. I staggered and managed to keep just about upright, even if I did step more sideways than forward.

'Come on, you can do it.'

I gritted my teeth and kept moving. I had to make it to the street before the animal took me down.

'Well, look at you.'

The new voice came at me from all angles. I span around looking for a source, still moving forward, still heading for the street.

'Such willpower. Such determination. I find myself admiring you.'

'Show yourself!' I yelled, though, in truth, I hoped whoever was addressing me didn't deliver on the demand. I was as weak and empty as I'd ever been. A kitten could have knocked me down.

'Keep going, Stella. Don't make it easy for me. I want you to struggle and hope and strive. It makes the inevitable all the sweeter.'

The voice seemed to change from word to word, making it impossible to pin down. Impossible to work out who it might be. I knew every sorcerer, every member of the Uncanny that passed through London; if I heard their true voice, I'd know who it was in an instant. Another trick. More powerful magic, used to evade and disorientate.

'Why have you done this to my coven? Answer me!'

'No,' said the voice. *'But you should know... they screamed for mercy, Stella.'*

'Shut up.'

'Oh, they begged me for it. Even as I tore strips of flesh from their bones with my teeth. They tasted... weak.'

I stopped in my tracks, rage clouding my senses. 'I'll find you! Whoever you are, I will find you and I will kill you!'

Mocking laughter swirled around me, only to be replaced by the crashing of the coven wall as the beast leapt through and into the blind alley.

Bashed-up knee forgotten, I turned and ran. The creature howled and gave chase. I wasn't going to make it. I could feel the ground shaking beneath me as the animal grew closer with each bound, feel its hot breath beating against the back of my neck. Five metres to go until the end of the blind alley, until the street and its magic welcomed me.

It would be about four metres too far.

The beast reared up on me, claws cleaving the air. I screamed and hurled myself to the side, crashing into the wall so hard it's a wonder I didn't dash my brains out. The creature tried to stop, but stumbled and rolled out of the alley, roaring in frustration at having come so close. The beast was vicious and strong, but not gifted with brains.

I pushed myself back up and ran for the street, grinning madly I stumbled out of the blind alley, and the dead veil—the absence of magic—was pulled away from me. While the shoppers of Hammersmith High Street screamed and ran from the insanity, I inhaled a great gulp of power. My every nerve ending tingled as the magic, weak as it was, washed over me and soothed my jangled nerves. So dizzying was the rush that I closed my eyes, a beatific smile spreading across my face, and almost forgot about the giant devil dog about to feast on my guts. My eyes opened again and I took up an attack pose, legs spread, arms up and outstretched, ready to unleash whatever spell came to me.

I didn't have time to consider my attack.

The animal was already just metres away, teeth bared, the fire in its eye sockets raging hot and red. As it leapt for me, I felt a weakness in my knees. I always thought, when death came for me, that I'd be able to face it boldly, but there I was, shaking like a coward. Unable to form a clear thought as six or seven half-formed invocations formed a knot in my head, and the certainty of death seized my heart.

I'd failed.

I would die, and my witches' murders would go unpunished.

I closed my eyes and braced for the end.

4

After five or six seconds, I began to wonder why death was taking so long.

I opened my eyes to find myself looking not into the furious, twitching face of a monster hell-bent on tearing my skin off, but into the face of a man. He looked to be in his mid-thirties, with short, messy, dark brown hair, and was wearing an expression of utter surprise. In his hand he held a spoonful of cereal, which had suspended its journey to his gaping mouth.

'Hello,' I said.

'How did…' he started. 'I… I mean, where did…?'

Somehow, I'd jumped from standing in the street, about to be chewed on like the favourite squeaky toy of the Godzilla of dogs, to being laid out on my back in a strange man's kitchen. It was odd, but given the circumstances, far preferable to the former option.

I sat up sharply and took in my surroundings. The man jerked back, losing his spoon, which fell into the his cereal bowl with a milky plop.

'Have you seen a big monster devil dog thing?' I spluttered.

'Have I *what*?'

I pushed myself to my feet and looked around. The kitchen was cramped, with dirty dishes piled high and a tile floor that clearly hadn't been cleaned in months, if ever. I darted for the kitchen window, trying to see if the thing had managed to tail me.

'There's a monster after me. Have you seen it?'

'Of course I haven't seen a bloody monster!'

'Good. It was about to kill me and is probably very, very angry that it's not crunching my bones between its teeth. A thing like that doesn't like to skip a meal.'

'Doesn't it?'

'Well, of course it doesn't, it's the whole reason they're created. Think it through... um...' I gestured with one hand, 'name?'

'What?'

'Your name, what's your name?'

'David.'

'Oh, I knew a David once.'

'Most people do.'

'He was eaten by a bear. Well, a powerful sorcerer pretending to be a bear. Well, a demon pretending to be a powerful sorcerer, pretending to be a bear.'

'Right. Of course. We all know people like that.'

I was babbling, my brain spinning. I turned from the window, satisfied that the devil dog wasn't about to leap through the wall at me. My heart was still beating a hundred miles an hour, and I realised I'd been saying things to a normal that they weren't meant to know. But then, this wasn't a normal sort of a day. Someone had murdered the witches of London.

'So are you going to, I don't know, tell me what you're doing in my house or—'

I raised a finger and pressed it to his lips. 'Shh, David.' Closing my eyes, I extended my senses out as far as they would go, searching for any hint of trouble. Any sign that I'd been followed. There was nothing. All I felt was the normal background magic of the place. I was safe. Well, safe for now. Which meant I hadn't failed. Not yet. And as long as I was alive, I was going to do everything I could to exact revenge.

'I don't know how, but it looks like I shook the thing. Best guess I have is that the half-formed spells that sprang into my head as it leapt at me must have combined, formed some weird cocktail, and snatched me away from danger, dropping me, well, here. Where is *here*, by the way?'

'Can I talk now?' asked David, lips smushed by my finger still.

I pulled it away. 'Go ahead.'

'Thank you. My name is Detective David Tyler, and you just broke into my kitchen. Not the smartest of moves, what with the whole detective thing I just mentioned.'

My first thought was to raise my hand, conjure up something devastating, and toss it in Detective David Tyler's direction. Then I realised that was a bit rude, especially considering I'd just appeared from nowhere and interrupted the man's breakfast. On top of that, with the danger having passed, it suddenly hit me how weak I was. The fight, the strange lack of magic in the alley and the coven, the death of my witches... my masters... it was all too much. It was crushing me.

'Okay, so I want you to start answering a few questions now, or—'

He cut off as my knees buckled and I collapsed to the floor.

'Whoa, hey, sorry, are you... okay?'

'I'm fine,' I said, attempting to stand, only to find myself curling into a ball on the floor.

'Hey, you can't just—'

'Please. Help me. I'm in danger.'

'From what? And please don't say a monster.'

'I don't know. I heard a voice. Lots of voices.'

'A gang attacked you? Is that what those cuts came from?'

'I need a place to rest, just for a little while.' My limbs were wet noodles. I was ready to pass out.

David pinched the bridge of his nose. 'Oh, this is a stupid, bad decision I'm about to make, I can feel it. I've made enough dumb decisions in my life to know. I once dyed my hair blonde. Did not suit me.'

'I can stay?'

David crouched down beside me. 'Okay. But I'm locking the door to your room.'

He must have carried me, because I found myself in a bedroom I didn't remember walking to. I lifted my head from the wonderful softness of the pillow to see David stood in the doorway.

'Thanks,' I told him. 'You're a good person.'

'Some might say "idiot", but I'll take "good" for now.'

I smiled and he smiled back. It was a nice smile, open and friendly.

'I must be mental,' he said, then lifted a key, waggling it back and forth. 'One night, then you're going to tell me the truth. That or I'm taking you on a guided tour of the police station. Right?'

'Right.'

'Good. Okay. I left you a glass of water on the side, there.'

'Thanks, David.'

My eyes closed before the door did, and sleep had its way with me. I heard the key turn in the lock, and then I was gone.

5

I opened my eyes.

I was in the common room of the London Coven.

Power rolled around the place in great waves. It coiled and it flowed and it sparked; every colour imaginable, strobing endlessly. It was beautiful, intoxicating, and very, very moreish. To most people it was invisible, but not to someone like me: a familiar, a creature of the Uncanny.

I spread my arms wide and washed my hands through it, watching as the magic danced and weaved around my fingers. Few places in the country were as soaked in the stuff as this place.

My coven.

It would be too much for some. An amateur sorcerer or fledgling magician that walked into this building would most likely find themselves drowning in the coven's magic, or at least driven insane by it. But then very few people ever came here. The coven was not open to visitors, and was protected from the outside world by layer upon layer of spells, hexes and wards.

Or, at least, it had been.

I looked down at myself. I was naked.

'This is just a dream,' I told myself. I always knew when I

was dreaming, and I'd had this dream often enough. It was the day I was created.

'Familiar, I name you Stella,' came a voice from behind me. It was Kala's voice.

'Why Stella?' came a second voice; Trin's.

'It was the name of someone who was kind to me once. Many centuries ago.'

I turned and looked upon them. My witches. My creators.

'Well?' said Feal, who had so far remained silent. 'Can you talk, or did we forget to give you a tongue?'

'I can talk,' I replied. I felt tears prickle my eyes and fought to hold them back. In reality, all three of them were dead. But not here. Not in my dreams. Here they'd be able to live forever.

'You are this coven's familiar, from now until your life is taken,' said Kala. 'Do you accept your fate?'

I nodded. 'Yes. I suppose I've nothing better to do.'

Feal snorted, amused. One of the highlights of any day was making her laugh. Now she'd never laugh again. Not really. Not outside of my dreams.

A familiar is created to serve a coven. Most witches don't like to step beyond their home too much, especially when their home is as heavily protected as this one. So they use their familiar—created by them, for them—to step out into the world and do their leg-work.

I fetched. I carried. I delivered warnings, and worse. Much worse. Anything my masters asked of me. Most familiars are not expected to last long. They are sent out into danger, they are not expected to always return. But I had, for sixty years, served them happily. But now... a familiar was not meant to outlast its masters.

I felt the anger rise in me again and clenched my fists. I would get whoever did this to us. Whoever it was that murdered my coven. I would track them down, and I would make them scream in pain.

'She looks angry,' said Trin.

'Can you blame her?' replied Feal. 'After what she let happen?'

That caught my attention, snapping me out of my anger. 'What? What are you talking about?'

'What are you talking about?' repeated Kala, mocking me.

'It's your fault—'

'Your fault—'

'Your fault—-'

They stepped towards me slowly, making me back up until I was pressed against the wall. Without thinking, I drew in additional magic from the air, ready to defend myself. The witches stopped and watched as the wash of power in the room flowed towards me.

'I-I...' I bit my lip, trying to calm myself so the magic would stop lapping towards me.

'You think you can attack us?'

'She means us further harm yet, even in death.'

'No! I'm your familiar! That's who I am, that's all I am. I would never do anything to hurt you! Not any of you, you know that!'

'You know that—'

'You know that—'

Mocking me again, but wait...

'What did you say?' I asked.

'It's your fault we're dead, familiar.'

'Your fault—'

'Your fault—'

Their voices...

It was only now I was noticing, or perhaps only now I was being allowed to notice...

The witches spoke, but not with their own voices. Each word came out as though a different person had spoken it, just like the voice I'd heard in the blind alley outside.

Another trick.

'I'm not a big fan of people attacking me in my dreams,' I

told the stranger, 'especially not when they use the bodies of my masters to do it.'

'Oh—'

'She catches on—'

'Took her long enough.'

I drew the magic toward myself, spoke the words, and threw an orb of energy that turned the three fake witches to ash.

Breathing heavily, trying to ignore the guilt gnawing at me, telling me that I'd just burned up my own coven despite what I knew, I stepped forward. I poked at the ash with my foot.

'Come on, you coward, show yourself.'

Silence.

Would it be as easy as that? Well, it was my dream after all; maybe it was giving me this simple victory. Building my confidence and—

A scream as a hand burst from the ashes and gripped my ankle. I yelled out in shock despite myself, and tried to pull away, but the alabaster white hand dug its ragged yellow fingernails into my skin.

'Get off me!' I cried.

I tried to pry the fingers free. They felt like ice. As I struggled, a second hand burst from the ashes, then a third, pulling me down. I raised my hands to form a spell, but more fists shot from the floor, striking like vipers, gripping me and pulling me into the floor.

It was just a dream.

Just a dream, that's all it was.

I tried to calm myself by repeating that over and over.

This is just a dream. A nightmare. It doesn't matter what happens to me here, I'm going to wake up in Detective David Tyler's spare room at any moment, covered in sweat, breathing heavily, but alive.

'Are you sure of that, Stella Familiar?'

'Are you sure?'

'Sure?'

The words, spat out in a hundred different voices, swirled around me, over and over, like a ribbon made of razorblades, and now all that was left of me above the floor, above the ashes, was my head. I closed my mouth to stop myself from breathing in my masters' remains.

'I'm waiting for you.'

'I'm waiting.'

'Waiting'

Any moment now, I would wake up.

I had to.

Any moment.

Any moment...

...now...

I closed my eyes tight as the ashes swallowed me up.

6

'How did you get out?' asked David.

I looked up from the bowl of cereal I was eating and did my best to offer a cheery smile. 'Morning.'

David was wearing jeans with a snug, dark green shirt, his hair still expertly tousled. He looked good.

'You haven't broken my door, have you?' he asked. 'That's a nice door. I like that door.'

'Had a bit of a bad dream.'

'Were you naked? I'm always naked in my nightmares.'

'Very naked.'

David sat down opposite me. 'Tell me more.'

'My masters tried to attack me, I killed them with magic, then I was dragged into the floor by a dozen arms that burst up out of their ashes.'

David nodded slowly. 'I see. My naked dreams usually involve me having to take an exam I didn't study for, but okay.'

I nodded and leaned back in my chair. 'Sorry I broke your curfew, but I couldn't get back to sleep after that, so I decided to make myself useful. There's coffee in the pot if you're thirsty.'

David narrowed his eyes then went to investigate, pouring himself a cup.

'Careful, I like it strong,' I said.

'Me too,' he replied, taking a sip. He coughed, and when he turned around, his eyes were watering. 'P-perfect.'

'Thanks for letting me stay. Not everyone would allow a woman who'd broken into their home to sleep over.'

'Well, I'm not every man. In fact, if my ex-girlfriend is right, I'm barely a man at all.'

I snorted. He was funny as well as kind. David took his place opposite me again, raising the cup of coffee to his lips, then thinking better of it and placing it on the table.

'Well, thank you anyway, I appreciate it.'

'So... my door?' he replied. 'Did you pick the lock, or...?'

'Oh, I just used a simple trick to open it. Apprentice-level magic. Kleptomancy. It's the kind of thing you learn on day one.'

David did his slow nod again. 'I see.'

'Do you?'

'Almost definitely not.'

'Oh.'

'Magic?' he said.

'Magic,' I clarified.

'And by 'magic', you obviously mean...?'

'Magic.'

'Got it.' More slow nodding, this time combined with a look in his eyes that said, *'Careful, crazy ahead.'*

For some reason, it felt right to fill him in on my world. Like I owed it to him. Like sharing my pain with him would make it just a little more bearable

'Look, Officer David Tyler—'

'Just David will do—'

'David, I know you're not of the Uncanny. To you London is just another place, full of people, and buildings, and noise, and fried chicken shops, and everything can be explained. But what if I were to tell you that everything you knew about London, about the entire world in fact, was wrong?'

'I'd say you and my ex would get along like a house on fire.'

I stopped and stared into his eyes, unblinking. 'I'm being serious, David.'

He leaned back in his seat and folded his arms. 'No, you're being a nutcase, and if you're going to continue being a nutcase, I'm going to have to take you down to the station for further questioning. I may be nice, but I'm not that nice.'

I stood sharply, my chair toppling to the floor. David rose, one hand out in a calming gesture, the other reaching to his pocket. I wondered what he had in there. Some sort of spray, or maybe one of those extendable batons?

'I'm not going to hurt you, David.'

'Good, getting hurt is one of my least favourite parts of the job. Though maybe I'd take it over all the paperwork, and the sandwiches they serve in the canteen. Awful.'

'I'm not going to hurt you,' I said, 'I'm going to show you. Show you that I'm telling the truth.'

David's hand retreated from whatever he had stashed in his pocket. Good. He'd given me a place to sleep things off, the last thing I wanted was put him down on his arse.

'Okay, you're going to show me that magic is real?'

I nodded.

'How? I'm sorry but I don't have a pack of cards on me, and as far as I can tell, you don't have a hat to pull a bunny out of.'

I snorted and shook my head. 'You normals, you see only one, thin slice of reality. You're looking at the world through a crack in a door.'

'Okay, did you or did you not break my door?'

The background magic of David's house washed around me, but I didn't need to draw on it for this little demonstration. My own natural power would be more than enough to prove my point.

'Ready?' I asked.

'Oh, completely. Let's see this magic then. Unless you're talking out of your bum because you're insane.'

'Detective David Tyler?'

'Yes?'

Ancient words ran through my head as I reached out one hand and pushed them towards him. 'Shhh.'

I watched, amused, as David waited for something to happen, for the fireworks to begin. Perhaps disappointed, perhaps satisfied that I'd been lying all along, he smiled and opened his mouth to say something—

Only no words came out.

'It's no use trying,' I said, as David's eyes opened so wide they were in danger of falling from their sockets. He gripped his throat, pulled at his tongue, walked around in a little circle of panic, all the time trying and failing to speak.

Finally, he stopped and turned to me, mouthing some words, wide and slow.

'*What have I done?*' I repeated. 'I cast a spell on you. Just a little one. It's called the Spell of Silence and it robs anyone it's cast on of their voice. For a short time anyway, or until the spell is reversed.'

I pictured the words in my head again, but this time reversed them, before reaching out to him: 'Speak.'

'—uck is going on? I...! Wait... I can talk! Hello? Hello? This is David.' He looked up at me, immensely relieved. 'I can talk!'

'Yes, congratulations, you're neck and neck with a two-year-old.'

He stopped rubbing at his throat, and the relief began to drain from him as a horrible reality dawned.

'That was... was that...?'

'Magic?'

'Yeah. That was magic, wasn't it? I mean, sort of, magic-magic. David Blaine, but not tricksy bullshit.'

'Your face has gone very pale.'

'I'm just going to sit down and tremble for a moment or two, if that's okay?'

'Okay.'

David sat down at the kitchen table and placed his head in his hands. 'This is insane. This is all completely insane. It's the job, isn't it? It's all those times I got bashed over the head chasing criminals, finally catching up with me.'

This happened a lot when normals were confronted with magic. With *real* magic. They tried to shrug it off, to make sense of it in a way that didn't shake their world view to rubble. One demonstration would not be enough.

'Would you like to see more?'

David looked to me, eyes wide, and shrugged. 'Can't hurt. Unless it can, in which case... still yes.'

I smiled and got ready to blow his mind.

7

'Is that... that's me!'

David hopped to his feet and backed up, staring with a mixture of confusion and wonder at the replica of him I'd made appear between us. This David—this simulacrum of David—glimmered with colour, with magical sparks that popped and fizzed around it. It wasn't solid, it wouldn't fool anyone into thinking it was the real thing. This conjured David was see-through, like a ghost. It took more power than I knew how to cope with to create a true double; a double that could replace someone and fool even the closest of their friends.

'Officer David Tyler, meet Officer David Tyler.'

The copy smiled and waved to him. 'Hey there.'

'Okay. Okay, that is very disturbing. Also, I am at least an inch taller than that, and my shoulders are a lot broader.'

'Afraid not.'

I passed my hands through the double and he began to break apart, drifting apart like smoke.

'Bye, David,' said the simulacrum, 'it was good to meet you.'

David waved to his double as it faded from view. 'You too...'

'Well?' I asked. 'Feeling convinced yet?'

He looked to me. I knew what he was feeling. Bewildered, excited, terrified; I'd seen the emotions pass over more than a few normals in my time working as the London Coven's familiar.

'Stella.'

'Yes?'

'What did you put in that coffee?'

I sighed and dropped my chin to my chest.

'That's all this is, must be. You put something... something illegal in my coffee and now I'm seeing things. Hallucinating. Tripping off my tits. That's all there is to it.'

'Nope.'

'No?'

'Definitely not.'

He put his hands on his hips and huffed for a second, searching for what to say next. 'Well... I'm still getting that coffee tested.'

'Stop. You know it's not true. You know what I showed you was real, admit it.'

David's breathing slowed as he calmed down and took a seat again. 'Okay.'

'Okay?'

'Look, I'm not completely closed-minded,' he said. 'I'm open to the idea of, you know, the supernatural. Aliens. All of that spooky shit. But... look, this is just a lot to wrap my head around this early in the morning, okay?'

I sat opposite him and reached out, placing a hand over his. I thought he might pull away, but his hand remained under mine. 'You've no need to be scared of me, David.'

'Who said I was scared?'

'Your hand is trembling,' I replied.

'Okay. Maybe a touch, you know, terrified, but definitely not scared.'

'Magic is real. I use it to help people. I suppose you could say I'm the magical equivalent of you.'

'So, you're a what? A magic detective? Harry Potter with a badge?'

I smiled. 'Sort of. I'm the familiar to a coven of witches.'

A long pause.

'Okay,' said David. 'Witches. Coven. I'm following.'

'London is a hub of the Uncanny. All kinds of magical sorts run around these streets. If they were left to do whatever they wanted, it would be chaos. It's my coven's job to try and keep things under control.'

'So these witches, are we talking big floppy hats, broomsticks, black cats, giant warty noses?'

I laughed and shook my head. 'No, I'm afraid not. They look more like a group of middle-aged women at a knitting circle. Well… *looked*.'

'Looked? As in, past tense?'

I pulled my hand away and closed my eyes, hoping for dark, but instead seeing that room, empty of magic, covered in the blood and torn flesh of my masters. My creators. My friends.

'They're dead. Murdered.'

'Murdered? Okay, I need to call this in, the police can—'

'No. The police can't do anything, this is way beyond their, you know, *remit*. This wasn't a simple break-in. Nothing can get into my coven that isn't invited. Believe me when I say that place is locked up tight. If you'd tried to wander in and we didn't want you there, your heart would have exploded out of your ribcage before you took a second step.'

'Right. Okay. Gross, but cool. Go on.'

'Whoever did this to my coven is…' I shivered despite myself, 'they're powerful beyond anything I've ever come across before, and they're going to come after me. They already tried, that's how I ended up here. Somehow. Not sure of the specifics, but I'm grateful for the end result.'

'Look, if what you're saying is true—if someone just murdered a bunch of women—I'm not going to look past that. I don't care how high and mighty the killer is, I'm involved now, end of discussion.'

'You already helped me. Kept me safe.'

'That's my job, Stella. I don't take a lot seriously, but the oath I took? That I do.'

I sighed and nodded. 'Okay. So I owe you the truth, and you're probably not going to like it.'

'Well, today's the day for surprises that make me want to poop myself, so go ahead, what is it? You're not best buds with the Loch Ness Monster are you?'

'We've met, but no.'

'Okay, I'm probably going to want to circle back to that another time, but go on.'

'Here's the thing, David, by helping me, you might have placed a big, neon target on your back.'

David did one of his slow nods again. 'So, some almighty magic man is probably going to try and murder me?'

'Yes. Sorry about that.'

David sighed and rubbed at his eyes with the heels of his hands. 'I've only been up twenty minutes...'

8

Murder, magic and mayhem were a lot to take on an empty stomach. I'd finished off the last of David's cereal, and seeing as the only other food in his wreck of a kitchen was a bowl of rotting fruit, we made our way to a nearby cafe. It was the sort of place that stank of the last decade's fat and cigarette smoke, with sticky, plastic table cloths and chipped, stained tea mugs.

'I'll pay,' I said.

'Oh yeah, you're definitely paying,' was David's reply. Which, given the circumstances, was fair enough.

We sat in silence as David ate, the quiet giving me a chance to think things over. And over and over. The witches were dead, so where did that leave me? What was I without them? I only existed because they decided I should. My entire purpose for being was to do as they commanded, but now nobody was left to command me. I wasn't even a person, was I? Not really. So what did that make me now? Now that I was just me.

David finished his pile of bacon, sausages, beans, and mushrooms and pushed his empty plate aside, patting his stomach and reaching for a napkin.

'You didn't have to have the most expensive breakfast on the menu,' I said.

'No, I think I really, really did.' He turned his head to the counter and waved his hand, 'Garcon! Another round of your very whitest toast once you've got a mo.'

The woman behind the counter looked up with hangdog eyes and grunted.

'Well, at least you're talking again. For a moment I thought I'd accidentally unleashed the silence spell again.'

'Not funny, Stella. Not funny at all.'

'A bit funny.'

David eyed me, then broke, smiling and shaking his head. 'You know I should have you in cuffs already and be dragging you down to the station. This is insane.'

'I'm not the one who should be in chains.'

'Okay, let's say I believe what you're saying. Magic is everywhere and there's a freaky underworld that only super woke people like you know about. What makes you above the law? You walk the streets as the rest of us, or at least, I'm assuming you do. Unless you fly. Ooh, can you fly? Can you make *me* fly?'

'We're not above the law. And no, I can't fly.'

'Aw.'

'There's just a different kind of accountability in my world.'

'The London Coven.'

'Exactly. We keep the peace. Or we did.'

A plate piled high with pasty toast and butter pats was dropped between us with a distinct lack of hospitality.

'Thanks, Nora.'

Nora grunted and shuffled away, her body wobbling like a bin bag full of mayonnaise.

'So,' said David, 'it seems to me like someone didn't like being told what to do by your lot, and decided to do something about it.'

And that "something"—ripping apart the people I loved

and turning them into hunks of dead flesh—was going to get them killed.

'Maybe. They could be acting on revenge, I suppose. The reason isn't important, I just need to find out who was behind it.'

David slowed his toast buttering and looked up, serious for a moment. 'And what happens then?'

'And then I'm going to take them down.'

David nodded, took a bite of his toast, and sank into thoughtful chewing for a few seconds. 'You know that's against the law, yes? Like, properly, incredibly, illegally against the law.'

'Well, when I'm done, you can arrest me. Or try to anyway.'

David stopped and eyed me for a second, then broke into a grin. It might have sounded like a joke, but at this point I really didn't care. What had been done to my coven... revenge was all that mattered. Cold, violent revenge. What happened to me after that was beside the point, just so long as whoever committed the murders screamed in agony at my feet first.

'Toast.'

Another plate piled with more white bread was plopped into the centre of the table by Nora.

David looked up at her. 'Nora, I think one extra round is enough... Nora?'

The strange tone in his voice caught my attention. I looked up to Nora expecting to see her sagging face and hangdog eyes, but instead I saw something else.

Something terrible.

Her face was twisted and distorted, like someone had torn it off and glued it back on in the dark. Her mouth was a crowded mess of yellowed fangs, and her eyes were missing, leaving two dark hollows.

'Jesus...' said David, his voice a trembling hush.

'David, run, she's—'

The movement was so swift I didn't see it coming. Instead, I found myself sliding across the floor on my back, my right cheek throbbing from the back of Nora's hand.

'Stella, watch out!'

Shaking the stars away, I lurched to my knees, only to find Nora eating up the distance between us.

Around us, chairs were falling and people were screaming, a mad rush for the only door and away from this sudden explosion of violence.

I needed to make sure Nora kept her sights on me and not on any of the fleeing bystanders, so I did the stupid thing and ran directly at her.

It felt like a head-on collision with a truck.

I bounced off her into a wall, the back of my head connecting so hard I almost passed out.

The cafe was empty now apart from me, David, and whatever the thing was that had possessed Nora. Time to get to work.

I staggered up and drew in some extra magic from my surroundings, ready to—

Nora's hand gripped my throat, and my handle on the magic words was lost. The palm of her hand burned my flesh.

Lifting me as though I weighed no more than a bag of sugar, Nora picked me with one hand, slid me up the wall, and regarded me with a drooling, lopsided grin.

Any second now, she was going to lean forward and sink those teeth into my face. I needed to get my shit together. To stop letting pain and fear cloud my thoughts, and find the right spell to—

The hand around my throat opened and I dropped hard to the floor.

'My name is Detective David Tyler. Step away from her and put your hands behind your head.'

Nora turned from me, revealing a livid gash on the side of her head. David was stood, extendable baton raised, other hand out, warning Nora to keep her distance. He must have struck her with the thing. He'd more than likely saved my life, at least for a moment or two longer.

'I said my name is Detective David Tyler. You will surrender yourself or I will use further force. Now get on your knees, hands behind your head!'

I got back to my feet, throat throbbing, and circled wide towards him.

'David, no, you can't talk a thing like that down. Hit it as many times as you like with your little stick, it'll only keep coming.'

'*Hey, David, thanks for saving me from being choked to death a few seconds ago*,' he said. 'Oh, don't mention it, you're welcome.'

Nora laughed with a sound like metal twisting. 'You will both die now. Die like those stinking whore witches.'

'So I take it good ol' Nora here has been possessed by something magical and evil?'

'You catch on fast, Detective.'

'Well, the fangs, the empty eye holes, the super strength, they teach us to look out for these little clues at police preschool.'

'Nora is dead. Whatever has claimed her is all that's left now, and we are in a lot of danger.'

The Nora monster shambled towards us. 'I will rip and I will tear and I will grind your bones between my teeth.'

'Oh, Nora, we used to share such sweet pleasantries.' David raised his baton and charged forward.

'David, no—!'

Nora grabbed his arm mid-swing and tossed him across the room like a rag doll. He came to a crashing halt out of sight as he flew over the serving counter.

'David!'

'I will kill you first, familiar. Send you to the dark pit your creators now dwell in.'

Okay. It was time to put a stop to this. 'You know Nora, you're kind of big-headed for a lowly pit demon.'

Nora stopped, head cocked, confused for a moment. That moment was all I needed. The cafe was old. The building had stood for over two hundred years, and was chock-full of ancient, strong magic.

I pulled it into me and pictured the correct order of words. It took only moments, and then, screaming with fury, I punched a fist toward Nora and unleashed the spell.

It surged from me, a golden lasso, dripping like molten metal, and swamped Nora. Her empty eye sockets widened as the lasso tightened around her midriff, strangling her like a boa constrictor.

'Catching on now, Nora?'

She staggered back, clutching her head as it began to swell, the bones of her skull cracking, skin tearing. Any second now it would be over. Nora knew it too. She lowered her hands from her rapidly inflating cranium and looked at me, smiling, even as death came to claim her.

'That's good, familiar.'

'Who are you? Tell me your name. Tell me!'

'And where would the fun in that be?'

She laughed.

And then her head exploded.

9

When something like that happens in public, it's best not to stick around too long.

I grunted as I propped David against an alley wall ten streets away from the cafe. Leaning back on the opposite wall, I inhaled slow and deep, trying to catch my breath and rub some life back into my muscles. I was in good shape, but he was heavier than he looked.

So, that was attempt number two on my life. Whatever it was that destroyed my coven, it hadn't forgotten about me. I was a loose end it intended to tie up. But how had it found me? I did a quick check on myself, trying to locate any magical prints left on me that would help it zero in, but came up with nothing. Nothing that I was able to sense, anyway.

'M-my name is... I am a detective police man and you...'

I squatted down on my haunches next to David as he came to, his bleary eyes gradually coming into focus as they locked on mine.

'Hello, David.'

'Hello, magic lady woman.'

'Careful there, you took a bit of a knock.'

He rubbed his head, confused. 'I had the weirdest dream

that old Nora at the cafe became possessed by some sort of monster and tried to kill us.'

'Yes, sorry, that wasn't a dream.'

'Oh, I was afraid you might say that,' said David, using the grimy alley wall to find his feet

'Careful, you've been out of it for almost six minutes.'

'Don't worry, I get hit on the head a lot. So, what happened to Evil Nora?'

'I cast a spell on her.'

'A nice spell, like the hologram one you showed me?'

'Afraid not.'

'A wild stab in dark, but is it connected to all the blood you have across your face and dried in your hair?'

I nodded. 'Yes, I sort of made her head explode.'

David's eyes went wide as he made to speak, stopped himself, and then threw up noisily. After breathing in a few times slowly, then wiping his mouth, he looked up at me again. 'That was down to the bash on the head, not the... you know...'

'Me exploding someone's head.'

'Oh, God, I'm making small talk with a murderer.'

'I didn't have a choice. Nora was already dead, I told you, and we would've been next.'

'Right, yes. Okay. This is just, you know, tricky, for me to get to grips with. I went to bed last night and everything was semi-understandable, and now there's magic, and demons or ghosts or whatever, taking over the body of my favourite cafe owner and trying to murder me.'

'The good news is, things aren't going to get any better for a while.'

'Yes, that *is* good news.'

I smiled and helped him back up to his feet.

'Right, if you don't mind, I might just head off to work now and pretend none of this ever happened. Just really lovely to meet you though. Let's not keep in touch, deal?'

I grabbed David by the sleeve as he tried to walk away, yanking him back. 'You can't go.'

'Oh, yes, I really can.'

He pulled himself free and carried on walking. Seemed like we were going to have to do this the hard way. The words flashed through my mind as I extended my arms towards David and unleashed the command. There was a *whoosh*, followed by a slightly strangled yelp, and David found himself pinned, upside down, against the alley wall.

'You know this is assault, right?'

'You can't go. Well, you can, but not without me.'

'Are you holding me hostage? Because no one is going to pay a ransom. My family are very, very cheap.'

I smiled and released him, slowly, so he slid into an undignified heap on the ground. 'I told you, there'll be a target on your back now, too.'

'So now whoever it is that murdered, your, you know, witches, is also going to kill me?'

'Very probably.'

David stood. 'You know, I'm starting to not like you very much.'

'The thing that took over the cafe owner, it knows you're with me. It will try to use that. Interrogate you, torture you. Pull your limbs off one by one to try and get to me.'

'Okay, I think I get it. That's enough detail, thank you.'

'The only chance you have of getting out of this alive is to stay by my side until it's all over. Believe me, I'd much rather be on my own, too, but if I let you walk away, that's another death on my conscience.' I pictured my witches, torn to pieces on the floor of the coven, and shivered.

David sighed and kicked at the ground. 'Fine, okay, but you're going to listen to me. I'm not a passenger, I'm a detective. A good one.'

I arched an eyebrow.

'Well, not a terrible one, at any rate. I'm a solid six-and-a-half out of ten. Seven, on a good day. You can use me.'

I went to argue, then stopped and sighed. He was probably right. It wasn't my usual job to find clues and piece together a case. Up until now, I'd been told what to do and where to go by my masters. They'd say *go there and do this to that person,* and off I would go. I was a blunt instrument. A delivery service. Not the brains. And now I was alone, I was going to need all the help I could get.

'Um, Stella?' said David, pointing over my shoulder with a strange look on his face. 'Are you seeing her, too?'

I turned to see a remarkably tall woman, standing seven-feet high at least. Her head was shaved and her dark skin shone as if lit by an inner light.. She was dressed in brown sack-cloth robes. 'Familiar, you are required,' she said, her voice deep and certain, then she turned and walked out of the alley.

'A friend of yours?' asked David.

'I don't have friends,' I replied, then followed after the woman.

'No? I'm making a shocked face here,' said David as he jogged to catch up, 'turn around and look at my shocked face.'

I didn't turn around.

10

The Monk—because that's what she was—sat cross-legged and eyes closed on the floor of the tube train as it hurtled towards Greenwich. No one noticed her, no one pointed, or took pictures of her with their phones. No one ever saw her. The Monk radiated a spell that allowed her to remain invisible to any bystander she didn't want looking at her. To step around her without even realising there was anyone to step around. I could see the spell weaving around her in brilliant, coiling ribbons of gold.

'She's a big one, eh?' said David.

'She is tall, yes. Are those the detective skills you were bragging about earlier?'

'Har-de-har. So what does she want?'

'Did you hear her say another word after we left the alleyway?'

'No.'

'Then you know just as much as I do.'

'Yeah, I very much doubt that. So who is she?'

'A Monk, a keeper of the Sorcerer Tree.'

David did one of his slow head nods to indicate that he had absolutely no idea what I was talking about.

'Don't worry, if we're heading to the church in Greenwich, you'll see it for yourself soon enough.'

As the train continued to speed through the dark tunnel, I thought about my witches and hoped this diversion wouldn't keep me too long. As it turned out, it wasn't a diversion at all.

The Church of the Sorcerer Tree is an ordinary looking three-storey house sat in the centre of a residential street. At least, that's what it looks like to anyone passing by outside, and to any neighbours. They had no idea that it housed a spiritual order who watched over an ancient wonder.

The Monk paused at the door as she opened it, and looked back at me. 'You might want to prepare, the Church may still feel barren.' She turned back and bent low so she wouldn't hit her head on the doorframe.

'This doesn't look a whole lot like a church,' noted David.

'You'll see.' I replied.

I stepped across the threshold, followed by my companion.

'What in the...?' said David, looking around in disbelief. We had not stepped into a corridor, nor a room that you might expect to belong in a house like the one we had been taken to. No, this place was much larger, much different, to what the outside suggested. It was more like we'd stepped into an immense, gothic cathedral.

'Well, that's not normal,' said David, his voice echoing as he gazed around at the space he'd found himself in. At the stone columns that stretched up and up, to a ceiling that was out of view.

The dark stone of the walls were broken up by giant stained-glass windows and immense tapestries that colourfully displayed images from throughout the Uncanny world. Historic images and depictions of myth. Images of a giant beast, whose skin was fire, the Magic Eater, striding across the country. Pictures of wizards battling great packs of werewolves. Depictions of a dark angel, trapped within a cage of glass.

But most of all, there were pictures of the tree. The Sorcerer Tree.

The actual tree dominated the building. It burst up from the centre of the church and stretched high above, its upper branches lost from view. The Sorcerer Tree was as wide as six people laid head to toe, and its huge branches jutted from the great trunk at broken arm angles, bare of leaves.

David stepped out of the Church and into the street, bewildered, then stepped back in again. 'How is this possible?' he asked, looking around him in wonder.

'The Church doesn't exist inside the house, the house is just a portal to another place. To this place.'

'So you're saying the door of the house is sort of a magic door?'

'If you like.'

'Okay, right, gotcha. Magic door. Just a bloody magic door, that's all, of course it is.'

As I walked further into the Church, it was clear why the Monk had issued me a warning before stepping inside. It was also clear that this journey had not been a diversion, but part of the same case I was already investigating.

The Church's background magic was muted.

It wasn't like the Coven—where it had been drained entirely—but it was still enough to be a shock to my system. I had been inside the Church just once before, almost thirty years previously, and it had throbbed with magic, fed it by the Sorcerer Tree. But today its magic was weak, and the Sorcerer Tree looked different. There was a giant, ragged split right down its trunk, almost splitting the thing in two. It looked like a giant had struck down at it with an axe.

'It's been here,' I said.

The Monk nodded. 'When I arrived, the Church was

entirely empty of magic, the Tree desecrated. The Church should already be full of magic again, but since the attack, the Tree is weak. Look...'

She placed a finger to my temple, and for a few seconds, I saw the tree as she did. On my first visit, when given this insight, I'd barely been able to look directly at the Tree, such was the ferocity of the magic exploding from it, but this time... this time it was muted. A hazy wash lazily rolling out from the Tree, its wound a black, throbbing void.

'Bless the Tree.' The Monk pressed a fist against her forehead and bowed before the tree, then straightened up. 'Follow,' she said, and walked towards one of several arched corridor openings that lead off from the giant main antechamber.

'What, exactly, is that super, big, crazy tree?' asked David.

'The Sorcerer Tree,' I explained. 'The Monks believe it gave birth to the very first people capable of seeing and using magic. That it is a God, of sorts. It radiates a kind of pure, old magic that nourishes them. Or it did.'

'So that tree is God? Makes about as much sense as anything else, I suppose.'

The stone corridor opened up into a small chamber. Inside, was a thing from a nightmare. There was a man, stretched out on a simple cot. He was trembling, his eyes closed. He'd been skinned. Completely. His entire body was slick and red raw, all blood and exposed muscle and veins.

'Oh my God,' said David, turning away, a hand over his mouth. I'd like to say it affected me in the same way, but I'd seen the same and worse in my many years.

'How is this person still alive?' I asked.

'Force of will,' replied the Monk, as two others gently dabbed at the skinned man with damp rags.

'Tell me what happened,' I said, not able to look away from the horror movie in front of me.

'Half of us had been out foraging at the back of the supermarket,' the Monk replied. 'When we returned, the Church was empty of magic, the Tree desecrated, and all the monks who had remained behind were dead. All but this one, who was barely clinging to life.'

'Has he been able to tell you anything?' asked David, shielding his eyes still. 'A description maybe of who did this?'

The Monk shook her head. 'They cling to life as they wish to tell us. To tell us who defiled the Sorcerer Tree. But their damage is too severe and they are locked in this unconscious state, death creeping towards them, unable to give voice as they are desperate to.'

Apparently, the Coven and my witches were not this bastard's only target. It seemed like they were attacking any great seat of the Uncanny in the city. Draining it of magic and murdering all who stood before them. But why? What was their end game?

'What do you want me to do?' I asked the Monk.

'We cannot seek direct retribution, it is against our beliefs. But you can. And must.'

'I plan too. But if he can't speak, he can't help me.'

The Monk nodded. 'That is why I brought you here, and why we have been keeping our brother comfortable enough to cling to life until I did so. I can make him speak, but it will be the end of him. His body and mind are too far gone to withstand consciousness for more than one brief occasion.'

'Do it,' I replied.

'Woah,' said David, 'didn't you hear what she just said? It'll kill him. Maybe we should get him to a hospital or something.'

'He's already dead,' I replied, 'the only reason he hasn't stopped breathing yet is because he wants to tell me who did this to him. Who did this to my Coven. Understand? This is what he wants.'

Bug-eyed, David ran his hands through his short hair, then waved the Monk on. 'Sure, fine, whatever you say.'

The Monk clapped her hands together, and somewhere in the Church a great gong was struck. The stone chamber began to shake, dust falling down from the ceiling like ash into a grave. The Monk kissed the palm of one hand and placed it against the mortally wounded monk's forehead. His eyes snapped open and he lurched up, a shrill scream escaping his lipless mouth.

'Easy, fellow, easy,' said the Monk, as the man fell back on his blood-soaked bedclothes, his body shaking violently.

'Death, death is here,' said the man, the sentence escaping from his rasping, gurgling throat, a red-raw and fat tongue struggling around each word.

'Who did this?' I asked, stepping towards the dying man as his fingers clawed at the air, chest struggling for breath. 'Tell me while you can. Who did this to you? Who desecrated the Sorcerer Tree?'

The man's gurgled gasps ceased, and his hands stopped their twitching as he turned to me. 'Like nothing. Like... ancient. So old. So... pow... so powerful...'

'Show her what came here,' said the Monk, taking the man's wrist as I knelt down at his side. She pressed the man's hand to my forehead. 'Show her what did this.'

He nodded, blood dribbling out of his mouth. He didn't have long left.

'Show it to me.'

'I can... show you... I can... show...'

Cold rushed over me and the room shook again, then cut to black. I was in the man's mind's eye. In his thoughts, his memories. He was showing me what he could.

I walked into the black. Slowly, light began to weave into the dark, and I could see a man in sackcloth robes stood before me. It was the dying monk as he had looked before the attack.

'What is its name?' I asked.

He shook his head.

'What happened?'

'I do not know how it arrived into the Church,' he said. 'Suddenly, there was only screaming and death.'

Images flashed around us; memories rushing around the dark. Monks running, screaming, dying.

'Show me what did this. I need to see it!'

The memories warped and faded as the monk peered into the dark. 'It is here. It is here with us. Look!'

He pointed into the black, his finger trembling. Something was moving out there. A patch of the dark that was even darker than what surrounded us. Fear was not something I usually entertained, but as the thing crept slowly towards us—indistinct, giggling—I realised my hands were trembling too.

'It took my skin slowly,' said the dying monk. 'I was unable to move. It nibbled with its teeth, then dug its fingers in, tearing strips away, whistling while it worked.'

The shape in the dark began to whistle, and the monk staggered backwards. I turned to see he was now like he was in reality: skinless, grotesque, dying. He fell to his knees, coughing up a mouthful of blood that splattered on the ground and dripped down his chin.

'It eats... eats all. It hates... so... much hate...'

Time was almost up.

I ran towards the dark, quivering, whistling shape that was creeping towards us, desperate to see it clearly before the connection broke, before the monk died.

'I'm coming for you!' I said, but no matter how fast I ran, I never seemed to get any closer to the intruder. Just black on black, twitching and whistling.

A scream, and then I was pulled away.

I was back in the church, the monk dead on his cot. I stood slowly, worried my legs might give out beneath me.

'He's dead,' the Monk said, quietly. She lifted her brother's sheet and covered him with it.

'Did you see who did this?' David asked.

I turned to him, eyes wide, jaw moving without speaking.

'Hey,' he said, gently taking me by the arm, 'it's okay, you're okay.'

'Who did this?' asked the Monk, turning from the dead man.

'I don't... I couldn't quite see. Something of the dark. Something terrible. I think... I think the memory itself knew what he was doing and killed him before I could get a clear picture.'

A burble of loud voices from down the corridor caught our attention as a young monk rushed into the chamber. 'The Tree! The Tree!' she screamed, then turned and ran back down the corridor.

We rushed after to find the main church room in chaos.

The Sorcerer Tree was burning.

'No,' was all the Monk could say as she looked up at the flames ravaging the Tree, tears pouring down her cheeks.

The other monks were stood in a circle around the blazing tree, trying to use their magic to douse the flames, but it was clear it was having no effect. They were not ordinary flames, they raged with blues and coppers and purples, and grew more fierce with each spell poured upon it.

'Leave,' said the Monk.

'We should call the Fire Brigade,' said David, reaching for his phone.

'No use,' said the Monk. 'Go. And Stella, find it. Stop it. Kill it.'

I took hold of David's sleeve and pulled him towards the exit as the Monk joined her fellows in their circle of power, singing in exaltation of the Tree as the powerful, magical flames that ravaged it began to spread. Great jagged cracks appeared in the stone floor, the columns trembled, and the stained glass windows melted and ran as liquid from their frames.

'Get out! Everyone get the hell out of here!' said David as the flames crept towards the unwavering monks, but they continued to sing to the Tree as it died, and as death came for them, too.

'They won't. They can't,' I replied. 'But we can. Come on.'

The cool air from the street hit us like a bucket of ice water as we ran from the Church of the Sorcerer Tree, and the door to the simple house that lead to it slammed closed behind us. To walk down this street, you would have had no idea of what was going on beyond that door, beyond that portal. There would be no evidence of the destruction, of the death within.

That creature—that patch of twitching darkness—had destroyed my coven, and now it had killed the Sorcerer Tree. Destroyed its church, its followers, and I was still no closer to understanding what it was, or how I was going to stop it.

How many more would suffer while I fumbled in the black like a clueless child?

11

Every city in England has a place like The Beehive: a place for Uncanny types to socialise, to drink, to gossip, to mingle in a neutral setting. Outside there were rivalries, jealousies, even vendettas, but inside, all of that was expected to be left behind. Under The Beehive's roof, we could relax in peace and be ourselves, away from the prying eyes of normals.

At least, that was the idea.

Because someone had murdered the coven of witches that maintained the peace in London, and today, the Sorcerer Tree —which had stood for millennia—was burning. I would tear apart the city looking for the beast behind that, even if it meant upsetting the patrons of The Beehive.

'I already told you, there is no street up here on the left, it's a line of old shops and then a dead end.'

I strode on ahead, despite David's complaints. 'That's because it's hidden from the likes of you.'

'Um, the likes of me?'

'You know, *normals*.'

'That sounds a lot like racism, Stella.'

I stopped in front of the blind alley. Much like the street the

London Coven was situated on, the alley that led to The Beehive was hidden from all but those who should know of its existence.

David stopped by my side and stared blankly.

'What?'

'We're here.'

He looked ahead, then back to me. 'Oh God, you're mad, aren't you? Magic and mad. That's quite the cocktail.'

'Look, David.' I pointed down the blind alley.

David followed my finger.

'Oh, I see it!'

'Really?'

'No, of course not.'

The correct phrase entered my head and I released it towards him. 'David, look now...'

He shook his head and looked in the direction I was pointing once again. 'I told you, there's nothing over... wait... wait a second, where did...?'

I smiled as I looked at his handsome features hanging slack, eyes wide. 'Come on, you can buy me a drink.'

I strode into the blind alley, David trailing behind, arms outstretched as though it was all some trick, and he was about to walk into a wall.

At the far end of the alley stood the pub, just as it had done for hundreds of years now, its wooden sign with a faded picture of a beehive, gently creaking in the breeze. Pushing the door open, I stepped into The Beehive and felt the thin skin of a protective spell part around me, like I was stepping inside a giant soap bubble. The Beehive had a few pretty decent protection spells placed on it, one of which dampened the worst kinds of magic its patrons might choose to throw at one another. Like I say, the rules were clear about violence staying outside of the premises. The Beehive was meant to be a safe zone, but the place sold alcohol, and wherever you found alcohol, you were liable to find bloodshed.

So, the spells of protection.

They didn't rob patrons of their abilities entirely, but they deadened magic to the degree that nothing lethal could be chucked about. Fist fights still broke out of course, just like any other pub, but spill a short-tempered wizard's pint, and you weren't going home in a body bag.

'What is this place?' asked David, looking around at the old-fashioned pub, straw scattered on its dark, uneven floor. 'Why don't I know it? I know all of these streets.'

'You only think you do. There are many streets that people like you would swear don't exist, but they do. London is full of them. We call them blind alleys: streets hidden from all but those who know they're there. Now you've been to this place, you'll always be able to see it.'

David stopped suddenly. 'Wait a second... a year back I was chasing a guy, murder suspect, and he legged it into a side street. I took the corner and suddenly he was nowhere to be seen. We checked every house, and there were no streets he could have ducked down, nothing. Could he have...?'

'Probably. Sounds like you were chasing someone with magic. You should be grateful he found a blind alley, if you'd caught him, it probably wouldn't have ended well.'

David shook like a dog throwing off water. 'You know, this is all more than a bit creepy.'

'You get used to it.'

I scanned the early drinkers, recognising many of the faces. Most were friendly, but some had felt the wrath of my masters through me. Upon seeing me, they turned away, looked at the floor, their drinks, the wall. Word travelled fast in the world of the Uncanny, and a tale as juicy as this one would have been around the city a hundred times by now.

The witches of the London Coven were dead.

'So what are we doing here, then?' asked David.

'This is The Beehive. Anyone who is anyone, high or low,

passes through here. If someone knows who or what is behind all this, they're probably sat in this pub right now.'

David scanned the bar. 'How many of these people could make my head pop like you did Evil Nora's?'

'Oh, at least half of them, but not in this place. The worst they can do here is break a stool over your skull.'

'Good to know. Okay, so here's what we're going to do: I'm going to announce that I'm a police officer, and you're, you know, a magic police officer, or whatever, and tell them we want to talk to them all, one by one. Just ask a few questions, nothing heavy. Deal?'

'Okay.' I turned from David, picked up a chair and launched it across the room. The wall on the far side of the bar brought it to a crunching, splintered halt. 'Listen to me,' I bellowed. 'You know who I am and you know why I'm here.'

All eyes were on me, then the nearest exit, but the only way out was behind me. No one was going anywhere.

'Consider this a lock in. Someone in here knows what happened to my witches, and I will beat each and every one of you into a bloody pulp if they don't start talking.'

'Or,' said David, 'you could ignore me completely and do that. Either one, really.'

12

My fist met Razor's face with a satisfying crunch.

'Tell me what you know!' I demanded.

He looked up at me, a red river running down his chin, and spat something solid on the sawdust floor. Rage growled inside of me. It felt good. Good to unleash my pain on someone else's face.

'You shame your dead masters by acting this way,' he hissed.

Now he was really asking for it. I grabbed him by his thick neck and shoved him, making his head snap back and bounce painfully off the wall.

'Stella, stop!' cried David.

'Don't worry, this piece of crap has done far worse to far too many. Isn't that right, Razor?'

Razor was an eaves, and looked like a mole that had grown up into a man. He was squat and thick-limbed, and had a mouth full of small, sharp teeth that could bite through a man's finger as if it were candy floss. An eaves traded in information; all of their kind did. They collected news and hearsay, and would pass it on for a price. The cost? A taste of magic. They were limited in what they could actually use magic for, but it fed them, and allowed them to conceal their homes from anyone bearing a grudge. This was a particularly useful talent for an eaves like Razor, who was about as nasty a piece of work as you might find in London, and had collected a wealth of grudges.

'I've just made my way here from the Church of the Sorcerer Tree,' I said.

'So?'

'Whoever killed my witches just burned the Tree to the ground, and the monks with it. Now you're going to tell me everything you know about that, or I'm going to beat you inside out.'

'I ain't heard nothing.'

'I know you've heard something, Razor, so tell me now and maybe I'll make your pain brief.'

He smiled, exposing a recently-broken tooth. 'You think now your masters are gone that you can do whatever you want, Familiar?'

I punched him in the gut by way of an answer, causing him to crumple to the floor at my feet.

'Stop this,' rumbled a deep voice.

The owner of The Beehive lumbered into view. Lenny was a mountain of a man, with caterpillar-thick eyebrows and a grizzled beard. Everyone respected Lenny—respected what he could do with his coal shovel-sized hands—but not me. At least not today.

'Stay out of this, Lenny,' I urged, 'you know what's happened.'

'I do, but this is my gaff, and there's no fighting here.'

'Listen to him, little familiar,' said Razor, a giggle sliding out of his busted mouth that scraped across my skin like a blade.

'I know you, Razor. I know the kind of grim corners you hang out in. I'm going to give you one more chance to tell me something useful, and then I'm going to start breaking bones.'

David put a hand on my arm. 'Stella, come on, this isn't the way you conduct an investigation. Well, maybe in the '70s, but not today.'

I turned to him angrily. 'Don't tell me how to do my job. Someone murdered my masters, my family, do you understand?'

'I understand—'

'No you don't!'

'Normal, you need to get her out of here,' said Lenny.

'Oh sure, I'm going to drag the head-popper out of here. Good plan, Andre the Giant.'

They argued back and forth, but I tuned them out. Turned them to static. My focus was trained on Razor and that bloodied smile of his. He knew every piece of scum that hid in the shadows of London. Either he started being helpful, or I was going to kill him.

'You wouldn't. That's not how you do things,' said Razor, reading the look in my eyes.

'Maybe. But things have a way of changing.'

I grabbed Razor by the collar and dragged him towards the exit, throwing him out the door and into the blind alley.

'Oh, shit,' said David.

I marched after Razor, cutting off his escape, and exiting The Beehive's magic-dampening bubble as I did so. I felt my powers sharpen, felt the surrounding magic rush into me.

'You can't do this!' yelled Razor, cowering against the alley wall, spittle flying. 'You have no right!'

'Yesterday someone pulled the witches of London apart, piece by piece. Plucked bones from sockets, tore flesh, and worse. That means, today, I can do anything I want.'

I formed the words in my head and thrust my hands toward Razor, unleashing a ball of flame. He screamed and hurled himself out of its path, the fire singing his leather jacket.

'Stella,' said David, emerging from The Beehive. 'Stella, come on, this isn't you. I mean, maybe it is you, I barely know you, and you did make an old woman's head explode, but I like to think I'm a pretty good judge of character. It's one of the few things I know I'm good at, and everything tells me that you're not, well, a violent psycho.'

'Listen to him, Familiar! This isn't the way. This is not how your witches would want you to treat me! I helped them plenty over the years! Fed them all sorts of information!'

'You think you can speak for them, Razor?' I punched out another spell that snapped his head back, cracking it against the bricks behind him and sending him down to his knees. My fist erupted in flames. 'Tell me what I need to know or I swear I'll turn you into a grease spot.'

'Stella, come on, stop,' said David. 'I've seen a lot of bad coppers in my time on the force. Coppers who take bribes, and bully to get what they want. You don't want to be one of them, trust me.'

I turned to David and looked into his eyes, ready to unleash a fresh stream of justification, but something about the way he looked back made the words freeze. I suddenly felt small, weak, vulnerable.

'David... David, they're dead. Someone came into our home and murdered them.'

My flaming fist sputtered out, and David took my hand in his. I wanted to pull away. Wanted to turn back to Razor and beat him with my fists until my knuckles broke. Make him scream. But I didn't. I stood still, vision blurring as tears prickled my eyes.

'I don't know your witches, but I know the law and I know real justice. You don't get that by turning into one of them,' said David, aiming a finger at Razor. 'You need evidence. You need to know. Need to know for sure. And then...'

'And then?'

'And then you make them pay.'

I turned to Razor, who was crouched on the ground still, cowering. 'Please, no more,' he begged.

'Tell me what I need to know.'

'The Den Club. Go to The Den and ask Anya why she and her kind were heard laughing about the attack. Toasting it. Patting each other on the back like they had a hand in it. Go ask them. Go ask at The Den.'

I stepped back as the news sunk in. If The Den had a hand in this...

I stepped aside as Razor took the opportunity to barge past and go flailing from the blind alley.

'Should we go after him?' asked David. 'No is a response I'd be more than happy with.'

'Let him go. He told us what we need to know.'

David leaned back against the alley wall, clearly relieved that was all over. 'Well, that was all more than a little intense.'

I frowned as I looked at the scorch marks my magic had left on the alleyway's brick walls. I was getting out of control, I knew it, but I didn't feel like reigning myself in. Not yet. Not until whatever had crept towards me in the black of the skinned monk's memories was dead.

'Are you okay?' asked David, cutting into my brooding.

'This is my life, David. Always has been, for longer than you've been alive. I'm fine.'

'If you say so.' He didn't sound convinced, and I couldn't bring myself to meet his eyes. 'So what's next?' he asked.

'Next?' I said. 'You heard Razor; next we need to walk into The Den and talk to a succubus.'

'Right. You know sometimes how you regret asking a question...?'

13

The Den hunkered at the end of a street in Soho, its neon sign burning like the lure of an angler fish, pulling unwary prey into its hungry belly.

'So when you say we're going to talk to a succubus, I take it that's not a euphemism?' asked David.

'Correct.'

'Great. Remind me why I can't just forget all of this, head back to the office, and investigate a nice, old-fashioned stabbing or something?'

'Anya and her family are succubi,' I explained. 'They feast on pleasure. Pain. Anger. On any heightened emotion.'

'Monks worshipping giant God trees, secret streets, witches... this is insane. You do realise how insane this all is, yes?'

'No.'

'No, I suppose you probably don't, what with you being a big chunk of insane yourself. No offence.'

I stood by and watched as the patrons of The Den furtively filtered inside. Apart from the neon sign announcing its existence, the facade of the club was simple, nondescript, and there were no windows to give a glimpse at what might lurk within. Just a door and the sign, and that was all.

The Den made dreams come true; the sort of dreams you kept to yourself. The club offered all sorts of illicit delights, from gambling, to sex, to bare-knuckle fighting, to bondage, to… much, much worse. It wasn't just a place for a succubus to hang out and indulge their ways—everyone was welcome. Be they Uncanny or otherwise, all types of people would hear whispers of the place and find themselves drawn inexorably towards it. None of them would have heard of it, or even noticed it, until that whisper in the dark. Only then would they walk by and see it, and once that had happened, it would be all they could think about. There was some magic to it that neither I nor my witches had ever quite been able to crack. Inside those walls, pleasure waited. No judgment; whatever was desired was supplied. Even the most strong-minded of people could find themselves bewitched by the place. Obsessed with it. And then Anya, the head succubus, had you. Owned you.

I turned to David and saw how he looked at the place. A curiosity, a hunger.

'So anything goes in there?' he said. 'Anything you could want?'

'Clear your perverted mind, Detective.'

'What? I wasn't thinking about anything. Almost anything. And certainly not naked, peach-bottomed women covered in jelly, if that's what you're thinking.'

'I wasn't. At all.'

'Well. Good. Me neither.'

'The Den leads people astray by offering them what they want; which means you're definitely going to need protection.'

'Like what? A shooter?'

I closed my eyes as I placed my hands on his head.

'What is happening now?' he asked. 'I'm not sure a head massage is really appropriate at this point.'

'You know, you really do talk a lot.'

'Yeah, you're not the first person to tell me that. Hey, that sort of tingles.'

I opened my eyes and took my hands off him. 'I've just placed a protection spell on you. It should stop the worst of the place from getting its hooks into you.'

David frowned and massaged his temples. 'Oh, thanks. Come to think of it, that jelly idea doesn't seem half as appealing now. Not that it ever did, of course.'

'Of course.'

'Now, custard on the other hand...'

I resisted—very hard—the urge to slap the grin off his face. 'Come on, follow me and stay close. They can be civilised, but the monster is only a blink away. Don't trust them for a second.'

'Don't trust the succubus monster people, got it.'

I strode towards the entrance to The Den. Two large doormen stuffed into bulging suits eyeballed us as we approached.

'Well what do we have here?' asked the first. He was seven-foot, twice my width, with a glistening, bald head.

'Just what I was thinking, mate. What do we have here?' His partner in thuggery, almost as tall, equally as bald, with a nose that had been flattened so many times that breathing through it was no longer an option.

Jack and Jake had been the doormen for The Den since before I was created. I'd never found out exactly what type of Uncanny they were, but one thing was for sure: they'd lived a hell of a long time, and they enjoyed nothing more than someone stepping out of line. Then they could punch, head-butt, and kick that unfortunate person way, way, way out of line. So far out of line that being able to walk back into line was extremely unlikely.

'Jack, Jake, always a pleasure,' I said, in a way that I hoped clearly communicated that it wasn't at all.

'You know she don't like you in her place, Familiar.'

'Yeah, you know that.'

'She knows that.'

'Exactly.'

'Hi, I am also here,' said David, raising a hand. 'Detective David Tyler. In the immortal words of Judge Dredd: I am the law.'

'Don't show them your—'

'Here's my badge—' David pulled it out and brandished the badge with a clearly practiced flourish that might, in other circumstances, have received the desired reaction.

I sighed and turned to the doormen, offering them an apologetic look.

'Not looking for trouble, lads,' said David, 'we'd just like to step inside your sex-house and ask your boss a few questions.'

Jake and Jack scanned at the badge, looked up at David, then at each other, and burst out laughing. It was the kind of laughter that ran deep, bending the pair double as they grasped at each other for support, tears streaming down their knuckle-scarred cheeks. It's not the sort of thing that fills you with confidence.

'Ooh, a detective, Jack!'

'A detective, Jake!'

'Oh, I'm so scared!'

'Absolutely terrified!'

Fresh hysterics gripped their giant frames as David put away his badge with all the dignity he could muster. Which wasn't much.

'If you two have finished,' I said.

'So, you want to talk to Anya, huh?'

'Anya's who you're looking for, is it?'

'Yes, and I'm pretty sure you know why,' I replied.

They nodded as one.

'The witches of the London Coven are dead, said Jack.'

'Witches are dead, that's what I heard,' said Jake.

'That's what I heard, too.'

'Yup.'

'And how do you know that, guys?' asked David. 'Wouldn't be a little inside knowledge, would it?'

The two doormen shot David a look of such cold-blooded doom that he had to take a step back.

'You're gonna want to keep your normal on a short leash, Familiar.'

'A very short leash.'

'Cos there's nothing we like more than playing with a normal, is there Jake?'

'You got that right, Jack.'

'Hey, don't think you can intimidate me, pal, okay? I'm the one with authority here,' said David. Jack stepped forward and looked down at him, smothering him in his shadow. 'Just so long as that's clear, David continued, his voice barely audible. 'Over to you, Stella.'

'We're going inside and we're talking to Anya. If either of you two think you can stop us, please, take your best shot.'

The doormen turned to me, their eyes hooded and dark. I drew in the surrounding magic as it looked as though things might explode. I'd had to grapple with the pair before, but they were strong and could take a lot of magic being thrown at them, and still keep coming. Wherever possible, it was wise to avoid taking them head-on.

The pair broke and laughed again, Jack opening the door. 'In you go little familiar, and your pet detective, too.'

'Yeah, in you go. Anya was expecting you anyway.'

'Expecting you, she was.'

'The guilty always do,' said David.

'What was that, normal?'

'Nothing,' David replied, his voice high and sharp. 'Shall we go in then? Stella?'

I shook my head and followed David inside.

14

It was warm inside, uncomfortably so. The interior of The Den was all shadowy nooks and private booths with red velvet curtains. All around us, naked bodies writhed and squirmed. People were led around on dog leashes, chained women were whipped until their flesh ran red, and men pummelled each other into unconsciousness. We saw other things too; things you don't even want to think about, because they'd come back to haunt you later.

'How is this place even open?' asked David. 'None of this is legal. Especially what that woman over there is having that horse do.'

'I think that's a donkey.'

'Well, pardon me.'

The place stank. The cloying taste of sweat and blood mixed with other bodily fluids, assaulting my senses, making me dizzy. It may have been the afternoon outside, but it was always three A.M. in The Den, and the echoes of screams and moans never abated.

'Just stay close, will you? I said. 'There are some bad people in here.'

'Really?' David replied. 'That lady over there using a cheese grater on a man's testicles seems just super.'

Stella...

I ignored the voice, I knew it was only in my own head. We walked into the belly of the club, heads turning briefly our way as we passed, before returning to whatever depravity they'd gone to The Den to indulge in. Some of the faces you might recognise: politicians, athletes, even royalty. Everyone has something they want—something they're ashamed to want—and The Den was the place to get it. A place without shame, that was impossible for most to resist.

'Wait a second, that's... is that..?'

'Yes,' I replied.

'How does none of this end up in the papers?'

'This is the place you go to do whatever's in the dark recesses of your mind, because you know it never leaves these four walls. It never leaves these four walls, because the place belongs to Anya and her succubus family. To spread what you saw—to try and make money out of it, to blackmail—that gets you a home visit. A one-time and very final home visit.'

'Ah...'

I nodded. 'The only people allowed to make use of what goes on in here are Anya and her family.'

Stella, you let us die—

Let us die, Stella—

The voices of my dead masters, needling at me. I knew what it was of course; it was this place trying to find a weakness. A desire that I would give in to and indulge. Do that and I'd be in their hands. I'd been here on several occasions and had grown to manage the power of the place. To cope with it and ignore it. Or at least, that's what I thought. Of course, I'd never walked in there with any real, overwhelming desire before. I wasn't created to desire. But this time I had one.

Revenge.

'We need to go downstairs,' I said, 'to Anya's office, right now. That's where she'll be.'

David was looking at me funny. 'Are you okay there, Magic Lady? Hope you don't mind me saying, but you look a bit like a junkie who's about to pull a knife on me.'

'I'm fine!' I heard how loud my voice was, how fierce. I closed my eyes and tried to breathe. I needed to give myself a little of what I gave to David outside.

Don't ignore us, Stella—

Revenge—

Kill for us—

Spill blood for us—

Now!

I'd been stupid, arrogant. I needed to cast a protection spell upon myself before—

'Hey, I heard those bitch witches is dead, huh?' I turned to find a wall of flesh before me, a pair of horns twisting up from his forehead, a sneer upon his flattened face. 'Sounds like the good times are here at last!'

And then my brain seemed to implode.

I drew the magic in the room toward me and thrust my hands out, unleashing an explosive force at the man that smacked him across the room. He collided with the far wall, his head cracking like an egg, his body dropping to the floor unconscious.

'Stella, whoa, calm down—'

Without a second thought, I flicked my wrist and David corkscrewed away from me—

No time to stop—

No time for restraint—

Only for anger and violence and bloody, awful, wonderful revenge on...

On who...?

Everybody!

I drew the magic into me again, wallowing joyfully in the

screams and the panic, cheered on by the voices in my head as I unleashed spell after spell, and bodies were tossed around the place like pieces of discarded laundry.

I wasn't going to stop.

I was going to make everyone in the place cower in fear and pain before I gave them the release of death. Then I'd find the others; the other dark Uncannies revelling in the deaths of my masters. I would make them all cry in terror. I would make them scream and bleed and die—

'Oi, little familiar—'

I swung around in a rage, teeth bared, ready to sink them into flesh. Jake, one of The Den's doormen, waved at me.

'That's right, look at me, Mister Distraction, over here. Go on then Jack.'

'Right you are, Jake.'

Jack's voice came from behind me. I only had time to turn halfway around before something solid struck me on the side of the head, then out went the lights.

15

I came to, my head throbbing from whatever it was that had cracked me over the skull. I didn't open my eyes at first. Instead, I tried to let my senses spread out and tell me where I was without giving myself away. Unfortunately, my play-acting wasn't fooling anyone.

'Awake at last, Stella.'

I recognised the deep, sultry voice that seemed to caress my skin. Anya. Owner of The Den, and the head of London's succubus family. The game was up. I opened my eyes.

'Tell your doormen that if they try to knock me out again, I'll turn their spines to jelly.'

I uncurled from the floor and attempted to hide my unsteadiness as I pushed myself up to my feet.

'Always so feisty. It's why I like you, Stella.

She tossed a wave of thick raven hair over the shoulder of her emerald green dress and leaned forward to show off a generous décolletage. 'Why I don't just sit astride your chest and suck you dry, I have no idea.' She licked her perfect, bee-stung lips.

Jack and Jake were nowhere to be seen. Someone as strong

as Anya didn't need bodyguards, it was other people who needed to be protected from her.

'Before you ask, I'm having a really wonderful time,' said David, who was chained to the far wall, his eye swollen.

'Who attacked him?' I asked, spitting the words in Anya's direction.

'Yeah, that would be you, remember?' said David.

I thought back to the moments before I'd been knocked unconscious. To the fury and bloodlust that had raged through me, and to a rather startled looking David Tyler, as I'd smacked him across the room. I was relieved to find that The Den's grip on me was gone, and that I was in control again.

'It seems you misbehaved in my club, Stella. You know I don't take kindly to those who interrupt the serene debauchery of my clientele; it's bad for business. I want everyone to know this is a safe space for them to do very unsafe, nasty, cruel things, and I can't have the likes of you giving the establishment a bad name.'

I snorted at that. A *bad name.* There were few worse places than The Den in the whole of the Uncanny Kingdom. The only reason my masters hadn't closed the place down long ago was because they needed to keep the succubus family happy, busy, and contained. Sometimes diplomacy means letting awful things slide for the greater good. I'd learned that the hard way.

The office I was in was luxurious and expensively furnished, with a large antique desk at its centre.

Anya strode across the parquet floor to a drinks cabinet, her curves rippling beneath the thin satin dress that clung to her like a second skin. She poured something red and thick into a crystal glass and drank it slowly as she moved towards David, running her fingernails down his cheek. Not hard enough to break the skin, but hard enough for him to think she might.

'People will know if I go missing,' said David.

'Shut up,' I said.

'I'm just saying, I'm a detective. The last thing a place like this wants is the police sniffing around. They'll have you down the nick before you know what's hit you.'

Anya laughed. It wasn't a pleasant sound, and it made me tremble despite myself. She gripped David's jaw. 'Such mean words from such a pretty mouth.'

'Okay,' said David, his words coming out slightly garbled. 'Maybe we could stop right now before this all goes too far. What do you say?'

Anya smiled. 'I say that I am curious as to what it is that hides in the dark crannies of your tiny mind. There's something in there, isn't that right? I can see it. Something bad lurking inside, waiting. I can always see the dark, no matter how hard it tries to hide from me. What do you long for, Detective? What makes your blood boil, your loins twitch? Don't be shy....'

'Stella, anytime you're ready to lend a hand.'

I stepped forward, fists clenched. 'Anya, stop, now!'

Before I had time to think, she bounded across the room and pinned me to the wall by my neck, her eyes completely black.

'Stella, darling, tell me why I shouldn't break you over my knee and feast upon the emotions of you and your new pet?'

I pulled the magic in the room towards me, ready for a fight—

'You dare?' asked Anya, and with a scream, she threw me across the room. A wall brought a sudden halt to my flight, the thickly-carpeted floor catching me.

'Leave her alone!'

I heard David yelling as I scrambled up off the floor, head swirling. Anya walked towards me slowly. She wasn't scared. What reason did something as powerful as her have to be afraid of a lowly familiar like me?

'Isn't that sweet? The normal tries to stick up for you. The damsel in distress.'

'Yes I... wait, is she the damsel, or me?' asked David. 'Don't answer that. Look, I understand you're very powerful and scary and sexy, but I am an officer of the law. I don't care who or what you are, and you will respect that.'

Anya turned to David, licking her lips.

'I mean... if you want to.'

'Such bravery for something so vulnerable. I almost admire the sorry thing,' said Anya.

'Don't pay him any attention, focus on me, Anya. I'm the one you have to reckon with.'

'I heard about what happened to the witches,' said Anya. She turned her back on me, a sign of power. Of contempt. She knew that nothing I could do could trouble her. That she could take me any time she wanted.

'My masters were always good to you,' I said, trying to hide the quiver in my voice.

'Only because they had to be. You know as well as I do that if they could, they'd have chased every succubus from England, never mind London. But even they had their limits, so we came to an... understanding.'

I took a step towards her, ready to throw a spell if I had to. 'Did you have anything to do with their murder?'

Anya stopped and turned to me, one eyebrow raised. 'Who has been whispering such nasty ideas into your ear, Familiar?'

'So you don't deny it?'

Anya sighed and walked across her office, taking a seat behind her desk. 'Now, what possible good would it do me to kill the witches of the London Coven, hmm?'

'Because no matter what horrible stuff you get up to, you're still living within constraints, and that must burn you up inside.'

She smiled, leaning back in her chair. 'I won't deny that, on occasion, it has vexed me. The knowledge that we could be doing so much more. That we could turn the whole of this city into one big, writhing, pleasure palace. But I respect the witches. Let me rephrase that: I *respected* them.'

The word stung. They were gone. Past tense now. The fragile peace between all the different stripes of the Uncanny that stalked the streets of London hung in the balance, and I was the only one left holding it all together.

'So you're denying all knowledge?'

Anya shrugged, picking up her glass and taking another sip of the dark liquid it held. 'The first I heard about it was when Jack and Jake passed on the news. Said everyone was talking about it as they came in the club.' She stood and walked over to David again.

'Hey there, Miss Head Succubus Lady; sorry about all that police talk earlier. Please don't do anything horrible to any bits of me. Especially to my main bits.'

Anya turned to me, smiling. 'You know, I like your little poodle. He's funny.'

'Oh, thanks,' said David, giving her two thumbs up.

Anya opened the locks on his chains, and David warily stepped towards the door.

'Okay, well, Stella, perhaps we should, you know, get the hell out of here before our fine host changes her mind and decides to make our insides our outsides. What do you say?'

I wasn't ready to go yet, I hadn't got an answer that felt right. 'You look me in the face, Anya, and you promise me you had nothing to do with this.'

Anya walked towards me. I stood my ground, ready to stare her down. 'Hear these words, Familiar. I had nothing to do with the murder of your masters. In all honesty, the idea that something, anything, could enter your coven and do that to the witches of London terrifies me.'

I searched her eyes and saw nothing but the truth. Another dead end.

'Come on, David, let's get out of here.'

'Best news I've heard all day. Though to be honest, that wouldn't be hard, it's been kind of a bad news-heavy sort of a day.'

David opened the door and hopped outside. As I reached the exit, I paused. 'If you hear anything...'

'You would talk to me as though I'm an eaves? I should kill you just for that.'

'I mean it. I need to know.'

'I am not your informer. I make no promises to anyone but myself and my family. But know this, Familiar... you are in terrible danger. A thing that could do that to the witches ... I'm not sure what power could stop it.'

I shivered as I stepped out of Anya's office.

16

We exited The Den, ignoring some snide remarks from the doormen, Jack and Jake, as we passed by them. Part of me wanted to turn around and unleash some frustration on the pair; get into a real knock-down, drag-out fight. Maybe that would have made me feel a little better. Or maybe Anya would have joined in and left me an emotionless smear on the paving stones.

'Well, that was one of the most terrifying places I've ever been,' said David, as I silently brooded at his side. 'But at least we got some good info. If you believe her, anyway.'

I stopped and turned to him, confused. 'Good info? In what way was any of that *good*?'

'We can scratch a suspect off the list. Okay, it's not as good as finding out who did you wrong, but every name we can dismiss narrows things down. That's police work. If things keep on like that, it's only a matter of time before the culprit finds themselves under a spotlight.'

I snorted and carried on walking, but he was right. It didn't make me feel any better though. I didn't want to go about this on the slow path, I wanted the monster behind this in front of me right now so I could throw my fist in its direction.

'Uh, I think we might have taken a wrong turn,' said David.

'What?' I'd been lost in my thoughts. When I looked up, I saw the streets of Soho no long stretched before us. In fact, no streets of any kind. We were in the middle of a rural landscape, on the side of a steep hill with long grasses being teased in every direction by a swirling wind.

'A really, really wrong turn.'

To the left of us was a set of worn stone steps leading up to the hill's summit.

'I know where we are,' I said, and headed for the steps.

'Great. Care to share?'

'We've been summoned by The First,' I replied.

'Not any clearer, Magic Lady,' said David, as we began to scale the steep set of steps.

'The First Witch. This is her place.'

'Is it Yorkshire? It looks a bit like Yorkshire. Apart from that lake of boiling tar down there.'

'It's not Yorkshire. It's not anywhere you or any other normal will have heard of.'

I'd never been there. There was no reason why The First would want to talk to a familiar. At least, there hadn't been a reason for her to bring me here before. Now there was. The London Coven had fallen.

'So The First Witch, is she a nice, non-scary sort of a woman?'

'I don't know. I've never met her and I've never been here. I only know where I am because of what I am. It's in my genes. My bones. I look around and I just know where and who.'

After more than two hours of scaling the steps, the summit never seeming to come any closer, no matter how high we climbed, the ground suddenly evened out to reveal the entrance to a cave.

'Christ,' said David, gasping for breath, 'I hope we don't have to run away screaming any time soon, because my thighs are buggered.'

'It's okay, we're safe here,' I said.

'What now then? Do we go in for a chat?'

'Yes.'

'Okay.'

David stepped forward, but I pulled him back. 'Just me. She won't want you in there, tainting her dwelling.'

'Tainting? I know my aftershave is a bit on the strong side, but that's just rude.'

I smiled, just slightly, then left David behind.

'Okay. I'll just stay here then. Pining for you.'

I stepped into the inky mouth of the cave, the sound of outside world cutting out instantly. I shivered as I edged forward, the dark licking at my skin. A light flickered in the distance, and I moved towards it. A fire was burning, and an old woman sat cross-legged before it, prodding the flames with a metal poker.

'What's the weather out?'

'It's warm,' I replied.

The First nodded and spat into the flames. They shot up as though vodka had been poured on the fire.

'Sit,' she said. I lowered myself to the ground and watched The First as she continued to tend the fire. She looked ancient. She *was* ancient. Her hair long and thin, her face gnarled like old bark, limbs like sticks, but her eyes... her eyes looked young. They seemed to glow with life, with mischief, with knowledge.

'So,' she said at last, 'you let your witches die?'

'I didn't... I wasn't there to—'

'I've no time for excuses, familiar,' she spat on the fire again and a tongue of bright purple flame burst from the logs. I felt my heart quicken as faces seemed to dance within these new purple flames. Three faces; the faces of my dead masters.

'Pity. Good girls, those three,' said The First. 'Always good for a giggle.'

I nodded and felt a tear rolling down my cheek.

'Ach, now, now, enough of that. Unseemly for a familiar to cry, especially when there's revenge still out there, waiting for you.'

'I don't know who did it,' I said.

'No. I've had a poke around, asked the fire to show me, but...' she frowned and shifted. 'It shows me nothing.'

Sighing, The First stood, her joints cracking, and shuffled over to a table that had not been there moments before. On it, stood a large jug and two clay cups. 'Coffee?' she said, lifting the jug.

'No. Thank you.'

'Suit yourself. I like a pick-me-up cup at this time of day myself.'

She sipped the coffee, smacking her lips in appreciation. 'Yours is not the first coven to fall,' she said.

'This has happened before?'

'Hm? Oh, no, not like this. I'm just telling you it happens. Covens fall. Not anything that can be done about it sometimes.'

'If I'd been there...'

'You'd be dead too. Think you, a thing of spit and will, could do something that those three witches couldn't?

'I'm all that's left.'

'You are that.'

'I'm not good enough.'

'Right again.'

'So what should I do?'

The First shuffled back to the fire, standing beside me. I felt her long, bony fingers begin to stroke my hair.

'Do your best, I suppose. There's no replacements coming any time soon. Not the way it works. Oh, they'll come eventually—a new three for London—but not for a few hundred years at least. That's how long it takes for a new witch or three to appear. Not born, not created, one day they just shuffle out of the dark of my cave and join me by the fire. But not yet. Not for a long, long time. So you're it.'

'But I'm just a familiar, created to do their will. Created to wear out, to die, to be replaced. I'm not even supposed to last as long as I have.'

'Oh, you love to bellyache you, don't you? It's not you that's kicked the bucket, remember, so smile a little.'

'Why have you brought me here?'

'To look at you proper. Get the measure of you. To see whose hands London is in now.'

'And what do you see?' I asked, afraid of the answer.

The First wandered back to where she had risen from earlier, and lowered herself back down. She sipped at her coffee and resumed her tending of the fire with the poker.

'I see... potential.'

'Enough?'

The First's warm, glowing eyes darted from the flames, looking into mine for the first time since I'd arrived. 'Perhaps.'

I wanted to ask more questions, to ask what I should do next. Tell her that I was confused and didn't know which move to make. Didn't know if I *had* any moves worth making. That I was lost and angry and afraid. But before I could, The First spat upon the fire again and the flames swelled like a dying star, blinding me. By the time my eyes had cleared, I was no long sat in her cave.

17

I sat at David's kitchen table as he made himself busy with the kettle.

'Do you take sugar?'

'No,' I said, running my hands through my hair, feeling more tired than I should have. A cup of tea was placed before me and I wrapped my hands around it, warming myself. *Potential*. That's what she'd said. I had potential. But what good was that? Potential wasn't enough, not at that point, not to find and take down a thing capable of doing what this bastard had done. I needed to be an expert, not a novice. Not something that *could* become something useful one day.

'All in all, I'd say it's not going well so far, eh?'

'No.'

David nodded and blew on his tea. 'Still, now I know there are creatures like that Anya woman walking the streets of London, I can live the rest of my life in a state of blind terror. So that's something.'

I smiled despite myself. I kind of admired the way David could keep a bright face on things, despite the world-tipping situation he'd found himself in. Before I arrived, he thought he knew what the world was. It was simple. And now there was magic. And hidden streets. And monsters. And here he was, making me a cup of tea and trying to cheer *me* up.

'What now then?' said David, taking a sip from his mug, then jerking back with a hiss as the too-hot tea burned his lip.

'I don't know,' I replied. And the truth was, I really didn't. I wasn't used to picking up the clues myself. I did what I was told. I carried out instructions. I had no experience of putting a case together, of solving a mystery. I was out of my depth and it made my stomach churn. The knowledge that I was the only one who could find out what had happened to my masters and bring about justice, and yet I didn't have a clue as to how I was going to go about it.

I'd hit a dead end.

I was a failure.

The witches of the London Coven had been murdered and I wasn't up to the job I'd vowed. To take revenge upon whoever had slaughtered them. Rage rushed over me and I screamed, throwing the cup of tea against the wall.

'You know, my mum bought me that mug.'

I glared at him, then broke. 'I'm... sorry.'

'Hey, no biggie,' he replied, smiling softly.

'You know, what you did back at The Den... what you said to Anya... that was very brave of you.'

'*Stupid* might be a better word for it.'

'It's never stupid to be brave,' I replied.

'That's definitely not true, but I'll take it. So what's next?'

I shrank in my chair. 'I don't know.'

'Right, well, okay, let's just have a little think about this. What we're carrying out here is a murder investigation, right?'

I nodded.

'Okay, well it seems to me that we've missed a step.'

'What step?'

'Any good investigation starts at the scene of the crime.'

I felt myself grow cold. I closed my eyes and saw the

common room of the coven again. The blood, the destroyed bodies, the lack of any magic whatsoever.

'Hey, what's wrong? What is it?'

'I don't think... I don't think I can go back there.'

'I understand it's not pleasant, but—'

'No! You don't understand. You don't understand at all!'

'Hey, come on, calm down—'

'That was my family, David! My family! They brought me into this world and I let them down! And now I've got nothing and nobody!'

I kicked the chair away from me and turned from him, ashamed to realise I was crying like a baby.

'You're right. I don't understand. I've never lost anyone I loved. Even my gran is still up and kicking. But you want to do right by them, yes?'

'Yes.'

'Then we have to go back there, no matter how tough it is. No matter how scary. Because if we don't, the bad guys are going to win. And you never let the bad guys win.'

I felt his hand gently touch my arm, and I allowed him to slowly turn me his way. I didn't want him to see me like this. For anyone to see me like this. Tear-streaked and vulnerable. I was strong. I was created to be strong. But in that moment, I felt like I had nothing left. No fight, only empty, bewildered fear.

David smiled and rubbed at my tears with his thumb.

'It's okay, Magic Lady. I may be an idiot, but I know how to carry out an investigation. This is my thing. Trust me.'

I put my hand over his and nodded, breathing long and slow to get a grip on myself again. 'I'm sorry.'

'It's okay. Your family died yesterday, those tears just mean you're not quite the robot I'd started to take you for. Maybe there's even a real person with annoying emotions in there, too. Something besides rage would be nice.'

We stood for a second, just smiling at each other, then I pulled away and dried my face. It was time to get serious. 'It might be dangerous,' I told him. 'In fact, it almost certainly will be. Last time I was at the coven, there was a monster there waiting for me.'

'That's okay. I believe in you, Stella Familiar. You won't let anything bad happen to me, or to you. And together, we're going to find out who or what murdered your family. And then we're going to bring them to justice.'

I nodded, and for the first time I felt glad—really glad—that he was with me. He wasn't a burden, an annoyance standing in my way. He was my friend. Together, we were going to solve this thing.

18

The blind alley opened up in front of us. At its far end, sat the London Coven.

My birthplace.

My home.

'I take it you're not just staring at a brick wall, right?' said David.

'See it,' I said, pushing the spell towards David.

'I'm not ever getting used to that. One moment, it's a wall, then I blink, and suddenly there's a whole other place I can walk into.'

I stepped into the blind alley with David on my heels. I realised with relief that the alley had already begun to refill with background magic. A least I didn't have to deal with the withdrawal symptoms that had left me so weakened last time.

'This alley,' said David. 'The cobbled road, the stone walls, this is older than the last one. How long has your coven been standing here?'

'A long time.'

'Not quite as specific as I was angling for there, Stella.'

'This was my masters' home and seat of power for over three-hundred years. But the London Coven itself has stood for longer, they just took it over from the people who looked after London before them. My witches should have continued here, continued to serve London, for several hundred more years. Now they're gone, and this place doesn't have a successor to take their place.'

'What about you? You're still here.'

'I'm no witch. A witch has more power in a single thought than I have in my whole being.'

'What does that mean for London?'

'Nothing good, David.'

'You know, you really have a way with an unnerving answer, Stella. It's a gift, I mean that.'

I trailed one hand along the brick of the alley wall as we walked, feeling the history, the residual power that throbbed from stones that had stood for so long. I tried to draw in that power to bolster myself, to make me stronger than I felt. I needed it. Because as the coven grew closer with each step, my lungs would barely pull a breath. A childish fear had overcome me, as though I were cowering under a blanket from the bogeyman. Something terrible—something that I had never come across in my decades of service—had walked into my home and done the unimaginable, and I was scared to face it, no matter how much I knew I had to.

I felt a nauseating sense of unease, a sense that I was way out of my depth, that I hadn't been able to stop it, that I still hadn't been able to do anything about it. A terror at the fact I was about to see those dead, ripped-apart bodies again. The bodies of my family that I had abandoned and left to rot. Would they have started to smell? Would their putrefying odour infiltrate my nose, my very being? Would I taste it on my tongue? I feared I would carry that smell with me for the rest of my life. A phantom stench that would cling to me forever more. A constant reminder of the horrors that had fallen upon our house.

'Are you okay?'

I turned to David, realising I'd stopped walking.

'It's all right,' he said. 'You can do this.'

I nodded, but I couldn't reply. I worried if I tried to that only a childish whimper would come out. I felt David's hands on my arms.

'Hey, hey, listen to me, Stella. Don't let them do this to you. Don't let the bastards who tore your world apart win. You owe it to your witches, and you owe it to yourself.'

'I let them down, David. I let them—'

'Stop. A bomb's gone off in your life, but you're alive, and as long as you're alive, you've got to stay strong and stay determined. You don't get to break down until whoever did this to you is brought to justice, okay?'

I somehow managed to sketch out a smile as I straightened up and shook off the worst of it. 'Okay.'

'There we go. Let's get in there and do our job. Show them they messed with the wrong familiar.'

'Yes, let's do it,' I replied, trying to force all the authority I could into my voice. Somehow I managed to make my feet move again, and the two of us walked towards the coven, boots crunching over the broken glass that littered the cobbles from my desperate escape.

'David?'

'Yes, Stella?'

'Thank you.'

'That's okay. Feel free to return the favour when you get a moment, because I am seriously shitting it right now.'

ease tell me that throwing your voice is another of talents?'

have you taken their bodies?' I demanded, turning searching for some sign of the monster.

d all of the meat and bones to my dogs. My "devil dogs", hem. They chewed them up, yum-yum.'

shed a blast of energy in anger, not even realising loing it. David ducked and scrambled to the side as 1ook.

e! If you're so powerful then stop these stupid games ourself! Look me in the eyes and see if you can take

e best idea to encourage a psychotic murderer,

the normal, Stella. Maybe you'll live a little longer.'

ment in the corner of my eye—

d in time to see a shadow step from the open

iere!' I ran for the door, my only thought to catch, to kill.

wait!' David screamed, though the words sounded ath the sound of my heart boom-booming in

ied for the right words, strung them together, and f power wash through my arms and into my hands, unleashed. *Begging* to be.

ning for you!' I burst out of the coven, ready to go ng.

19

The bodies were gone.

All of the ripped up pieces of my witches had been taken, leaving only dark, dried blood rusting the floor. Part of me was outraged that they had been removed, that they weren't here waiting for me to give them a decent burial. A larger part of me was glad I didn't have to relive the carnage that had become of them. Did that make me a coward?

'What's that smell?' asked David.

I breathed it in and the corners of my mouth twitched up momentarily. 'Cinnamon, freshly cut grass, and lavender. The smell of home.' Not just of home, of life. For me, it was my first real memory. Before I had even opened my eyes for the first time after being created, I'd inhaled once deeply, through my nose, and the smell of this place had become part of me. Now it just reminded me of what I'd lost.

'So, whoever was behind this must have come back for the bodies?' said David, walking the room gingerly, studying every square inch for anything even remotely resembling a clue.

'There was a creature here waiting for me when I got back. A clean-up service in the form of a giant, devil dog that was left to mop me up when I walked in. It's what I jumped away from when I found myself in your kitchen.'

'Well, that's something.'

'What is?'

'Whoever is behind this can be sloppy. Or too sure of themselves. Probably both. That means they have weaknesses, and weaknesses can be exploited. Sooner or later, we'll find something that leads us to their door.'

I found a little fresh hope sprouting inside of me. Was David right? Because it was true, leaving a mindless beast behind to finish me off rather than seeing to the job personally, rather than making sure, had been an error. They had left a survivor behind at the Church of the Sorcerer Tree, too; at least for a while. Yes, whoever had done this was strong beyond measure, but far from infallible. They had a weak spot. Everyone and everything had a weak spot, an achilles heel, it was just a case of finding it.

David scratched at his chin. 'You said when you came back that the place was drained of magic, right?'

'Completely. That shouldn't be possible. Especially not here. Every street, every building, every blade of grass emits some trace of background magic, but somehow whoever did this sucked the whole place dry.'

'Tell me more about the coven's security measures.'

'I told you, the witches had layer upon layer upon layer of protective spells. No one but those three and myself were able to walk in or out unscathed. And only us four would be able to remove or even temporarily nullify them.'

'Could those be "sucked dry"? David asked. 'The magic of the protection spells, just like what happened to the background magic of the place?'

'No, that's different. The spells, they were fixed. Removing them would be like trying to suck a bowling ball through a drinking straw. The only way to get rid of them fully is if you know what they are, the name they've been given, and how to

mute them. That's the only way i
to be stripped away.'

David stood up from where h
the blood splatter patterns acros
know what that means then?'

'What?'

'It means someone must have
spells.'

I bristled and marched toward
very careful what you say next, norr

'Hey, hey, chill your boots, Ste
evidence so I can piece together t
what you say is true, then whoever
security of this place must have figu
Which means either someone told
they, I don't know, overheard one of y

I snarled and turned away, stomp
room before I gave in to the impulse
and squeeze. *An inside job.* There we
could have told them, and three of t
left me.

'I didn't say anything to anyone.'

'Hey, did I say that, Miss Hair-Trig
know: they found out somehow. If yo
that might be, then we have a thread
work, Stella. This is how you get thing
the facts because they make you unco
gather, you make connections, and yo
tions all the way down the line until
And then you win.'

I sighed and turned back to h
what now?'

'Now you die.'

That voice... no, *voices.* Each of th
spoken by a different person.

'Um,
your mar
'Whe
in a circl
*'Oh, I
as you ca*
I unl
that I wa
the room
'Face
and sho
my life!'
'Not
Stella.'
'Liste
A m
I tu
doorwa
'Ove
confron
'Ste
dull be
my hea
I se
felt a ti
ready t
'I'm
down f

19

The bodies were gone.

All of the ripped up pieces of my witches had been taken, leaving only dark, dried blood rusting the floor. Part of me was outraged that they had been removed, that they weren't here waiting for me to give them a decent burial. A larger part of me was glad I didn't have to relive the carnage that had become of them. Did that make me a coward?

'What's that smell?' asked David.

I breathed it in and the corners of my mouth twitched up momentarily. 'Cinnamon, freshly cut grass, and lavender. The smell of home.' Not just of home, of life. For me, it was my first real memory. Before I had even opened my eyes for the first time after being created, I'd inhaled once deeply, through my nose, and the smell of this place had become part of me. Now it just reminded me of what I'd lost.

'So, whoever was behind this must have come back for the bodies?' said David, walking the room gingerly, studying every square inch for anything even remotely resembling a clue.

'There was a creature here waiting for me when I got back. A clean-up service in the form of a giant, devil dog that was left to mop me up when I walked in. It's what I jumped away from when I found myself in your kitchen.'

'Well, that's something.'

'What is?'

'Whoever is behind this can be sloppy. Or too sure of themselves. Probably both. That means they have weaknesses, and weaknesses can be exploited. Sooner or later, we'll find something that leads us to their door.'

I found a little fresh hope sprouting inside of me. Was David right? Because it was true, leaving a mindless beast behind to finish me off rather than seeing to the job personally, rather than making sure, had been an error. They had left a survivor behind at the Church of the Sorcerer Tree, too; at least for a while. Yes, whoever had done this was strong beyond measure, but far from infallible. They had a weak spot. Everyone and everything had a weak spot, an achilles heel, it was just a case of finding it.

David scratched at his chin. 'You said when you came back that the place was drained of magic, right?'

'Completely. That shouldn't be possible. Especially not here. Every street, every building, every blade of grass emits some trace of background magic, but somehow whoever did this sucked the whole place dry.'

'Tell me more about the coven's security measures.'

'I told you, the witches had layer upon layer upon layer of protective spells. No one but those three and myself were able to walk in or out unscathed. And only us four would be able to remove or even temporarily nullify them.'

'Could those be "sucked dry"? David asked. 'The magic of the protection spells, just like what happened to the background magic of the place?'

'No, that's different. The spells, they were fixed. Removing them would be like trying to suck a bowling ball through a drinking straw. The only way to get rid of them fully is if you know what they are, the name they've been given, and how to mute them. That's the only way it would be possible for them to be stripped away.'

David stood up from where he'd been crouched studying the blood splatter patterns across the hardwood floor. 'You know what that means then?'

'What?'

'It means someone must have shared the names of those spells.'

I bristled and marched towards him, my head hot. 'I'd be very careful what you say next, normal.'

'Hey, hey, chill your boots, Stella, I'm just following the evidence so I can piece together the most likely scenario. If what you say is true, then whoever stripped away the magical security of this place must have figured out a way to bypass it. Which means either someone told them—an inside job—or they, I don't know, overheard one of you.'

I snarled and turned away, stomping to the other side of the room before I gave in to the impulse to grab David by the neck and squeeze. *An inside job.* There were only four people who could have told them, and three of them were dead. That just left me.

'I didn't say anything to anyone.'

'Hey, did I say that, Miss Hair-Trigger? Look, here's what we know: they found out somehow. If you can think why or how that might be, then we have a thread to pull at. This is police work, Stella. This is how you get things done. You don't ignore the facts because they make you uncomfortable. You look, you gather, you make connections, and you follow those connections all the way down the line until you find out who did it. And then you win.'

I sighed and turned back to him, anger fading. 'So what now?'

'Now you die.'

That voice... no, *voices.* Each of the words like they were spoken by a different person.

'Um, please tell me that throwing your voice is another of your many talents?'

'Where have you taken their bodies?' I demanded, turning in a circle, searching for some sign of the monster.

'Oh, I fed all of the meat and bones to my dogs. My "devil dogs", as you call them. They chewed them up, yum-yum.'

I unleashed a blast of energy in anger, not even realising that I was doing it. David ducked and scrambled to the side as the room shook.

'Face me! If you're so powerful then stop these stupid games and show yourself! Look me in the eyes and see if you can take my life!'

'Not the best idea to encourage a psychotic murderer, Stella.'

'Listen to the normal, Stella. Maybe you'll live a little longer.'

A movement in the corner of my eye—

I turned in time to see a shadow step from the open doorway—

'Over there!' I ran for the door, my only thought to catch, to confront, to kill.

'Stella, wait!' David screamed, though the words sounded dull beneath the sound of my heart boom-booming in my head.

I searched for the right words, strung them together, and felt a tide of power wash through my arms and into my hands, ready to be unleashed. *Begging* to be.

'I'm coming for you!' I burst out of the coven, ready to go down fighting.

'Stella, come on, this is crazy, look at the size of those things!'

I didn't have time to argue. A flick of my head and David—his eyes wide with surprise—was lifted from his feet and thrown through the air and back into the coven. I heard him land with a thump and a grumble as I shut the door on him and willed it to remain so.

'Well,' I asked the air, asked the hidden puppet master, asked the devil dogs, 'are you going to do something, or should I just get on with it and start killing?'

The first dog bolted towards me, claws tearing up cobbles, jaws trailing long, toxic ropes of slaver. I let fly a scream and a surge of magic erupted from me in a great, gushing stream, ripping into the beast's hide. It screamed like a puppy as the magic tore up its left flank, causing it to careen to the side and into a wall, so hard I could hear the crunch of its bones.

I laughed. 'Did you think this would be easy?' I'm Stella Familiar of the London Coven, you dumb mutt.' I roared a war cry as I threw out my right arm and a torrent of fire welled forth from my palm and turned the broken devil dog to ash. I didn't wait for the next attack; I turned on my heels, both fists cocked and ready, and sprinted toward the two remaining dogs. They came at me as one, but froze mid-step as I swung out my left hand and sent a lashing orbit of white light spinning their way. I heard a yelp of confusion from one of the dogs, followed by a blink of its eyes before it fell apart in two halves, cleaved down the middle, its organs landing with a wet slap on the cobbles.

'Very impressive, Familiar,' came the many voices.

I ignored them, turning my attention instead to the final, still-frozen dog. As I stopped before it and stared into the twin fires of its eyes, the simple thing suddenly understood what was about to happen. What it was about to lose. I could taste its fear.

And it tasted *good.*

I thrust my burning hands into the monster's chest, blasting through bone and tissue to tear out its giant pulsating heart. The dog huffed once then toppled to the ground, and I threw away its heart like the rubbish it was.

'That's it. They're done. If that's all you've got for me, then you're in big fucking trouble.' I felt the devil dog's blood on my hands, warm and sticky, and almost felt like licking my fingers with satisfaction. 'Well? Why won't you speak now? Are you done? Did you run away?'

The devil dog with the missing heart twitched on the ground before me. I stepped back into a boxer's stance, hands up, power pulsing from my fists.

An arm thrust out of the corpse. And another. Something was pulling itself out of the dead dog and into the blind alley. Something with long black hair, coated in gore. Then the same happened with the devil dog I'd split in two. Viscera-painted women crawled towards me, leaving a bloody slug trail behind them. I should have dispatched them immediately. Should have already unleashed the power swelling in my hands, but I was frozen to the spot. I recognised the women. They were my masters.

'Your fault.'

'Your fault, Familiar.'

I staggered back as their dead, empty eyes bored into me with raw hatred, all the power I'd built drained from me.

'Please, I didn't know, I couldn't help, I didn't...'

My witches screamed in unison as they crawled jaggedly towards me, their mouths opening wider and wider still until it seemed their entire heads were one huge black hole, ready to swallow me down into the darkness.

I backed into the alley wall, and the damp cold of its brick-work soaked into my back and snapped me out of my panic. This was just a trick. A deception. That's all it was. All it could be.

They were almost upon me as I pulled in the magic around

me and—with tears in my eyes—screamed and unleashed all the power I could on the witches. My masters. The blood-coated lies created to break my spirit

And then the screaming stopped.

The only sound now was the wind and my own heartbeat throbbing in my ears. Nothing was left of the witches—the lies—not even ashes. I drew what magic I could back inside of me as I stepped forward, my knees ready to give way, but I knew that I was alone. Whoever it was that was behind all this had already gone. It had done what it set out to do. It had poked and prodded at me, made me shake and scream with fear, tested my limits, my strength of will. It was playing games, and it was enjoying itself far too much to take me off the board just yet.

'David—' I waved my hand across the coven door, allowing it to be opened again. 'David, come out, it's safe.'

Silence.

'David, come on.'

The door didn't open.

My eyes widened.

No...

I was running before I really even understood why. I threw open the coven door, hoping, dreading, knowing. David wasn't waiting for me. The only thing greeting me was a pool of fresh blood on the floor.

David's blood.

21

The door to The Beehive swung inward, smashing back against the wall under the force of my boot.

'Where is he?'

I stepped inside, feeling the pub's magic-dampening bubble part around me as I entered. It meant I couldn't make anyone's head explode with a few well-chosen words, but that was okay. I wasn't looking for anything that fast. My fists were all I needed.

I'd reached out for David, trying to sense him, trying to find out where the many-mouthed creature had taken him. I'd been with David long enough that I should have been able to recognise his, for want of a better word, "scent"; the impression he left in the magic that surrounds everything. He'd been stolen away from me mere seconds before I'd found the pool of his blood, so I should have been able to sniff him out without much difficulty.

And yet, there was nothing. No sign of him. Not a trace.

I'd searched the coven from top to bottom, chased along the blind alley, run wildly around the streets of Hammersmith. I must have looked like a total head case as I sprinted around, goggle-eyed, taking random turn after random turn, hoping to see or sense something. Anything.

But he was gone.

And that's when I realised I'd been played. Whatever was behind all of this, whatever was hiding behind those hundreds of voices, it wasn't trying to kill me. It was distracting me. Prodding at me; throwing obstacles with giant teeth in my way until my anger took over and I pushed David out of the way. Then, with my back turned and fists throwing fury, it had been free to take him. First it murdered my masters, the only people I was close to. Now, the first person that came into my orbit, the first person I had taken under my wing and allowed to get close to me, had been snatched away, leaving nothing but a scarlet reminder on the floor.

But no body.

No corpse.

No shredded pieces of flesh this time, waiting to greet me as I entered my coven. And that was the only thing that gave me hope. Gave me the sense that maybe, just maybe, David was still alive. That this thing wasn't done playing just yet. That it was going to keep David alive because it wanted me to come and find him. To try and fight and take him back. At least, that's what I had to tell myself, because what else did I have?

I'd dropped into David's life and turned it upside down. Exposed him to the kind of darkness and danger that no normal should ever have to know about. It was my fault he was who-knows-where with who-knows-what, his life hanging by a thread. So this wasn't just about revenge anymore. I had to find this thing and I had to beat it, otherwise David's death would be on my hands. Annoying, brave, strong, funny David. I couldn't let that happen.

I wouldn't let it happen.

'Razor! Get out here, now!'

I stalked towards him, causing the other patrons of The Beehive to part before me. They moved back, relief washing over their faces as they heard me call out for someone beside themselves.

'Stella—'

I shot Lenny a look, a look that told him all he needed to know. He nodded and turned away.

'Razor!'

The door to the bathroom squeaked and Razor stepped into the bar. At first, he didn't notice me. Instead, he looked at the nearest few tables of drinkers, saw the way they were hunkered down, shoulders hunched, ignoring everything.

'What's going on?'

He turned and saw me, saw the smile on my face that didn't reach my eyes.

'You've been a bad boy, Razor.'

'Shit—'

The only exit was behind me, so Razor spun on his heels, almost falling over in his hurry, and bolted back through the door towards the bathrooms. I gave chase, shoving the door open so it cracked against the wall as I ran through. I stepped into the Men's room, the sharp stench of piss burning my nostrils as I padded towards the closed cubicles.

'Get out here, Razor.'

'What d'you want with me? I didn't do anything.'

I stopped in front of the closed cubicle door Razor was trying to shield himself behind. He may as well have been hiding under a sheet of wet paper for all the good it would do him.

'You lied to me, Razor. You know that's not a good idea.'

'Lied to you? I didn't lie to you. I mean, I have done, of course I have, I've lied to you lots of times, but not recently.'

I grunted as the sole of my boot connected with the cubicle door and turned its lock into shrapnel. I found Razor squatting inside, quivering, his feet on the toilet seat.

'I came to you looking for information, Razor. Information about what happened to the witches of the London Coven.

Information about the piece of shit that murdered them. And you spat up a lie.'

'What?'

'You sent me on a wild goose chase. And now my friend has been taken.'

'What are you talking about? You're crazy. Someone help me! Lenny! Anyone!'

I grabbed Razor by the throat and squeezed until his eyes bulged out on their stalks. He beat at my face with his fists but I barely felt the blows.

'You're going to give me something I can use, or you're going to die in here, Razor. Die in a toilet. Do you hear me?'

With a roar, I twisted and threw him across the bathroom. He crashed into the mirror and fell hard into the sinks. I smiled as he groaned, rolling and falling to the dirty tiled floor. I was strong. I was born strong. Right now, with the anger and adrenalin coursing through me, I was unstoppable.

'Please... please, I don't know what you're talking a—'

I landed a boot in his side and heard a rib crack. It made me smile.

'Wait, please, just wait—'

Razor winced and slid back until he was pressed against the wall, one hand to his busted side.

'Give me a name, Razor. Give me something I can use.'

'I swear, I didn't send you wrong.'

I grimaced. Even now he was trying to feed me lies. He saw what was about to happen and lifted his hands to try and placate me—

'Stella, wait. Just... just wait a second. Look, okay, I heard about the witches, and this might surprise you, but I'm not happy about what happened. I'm not. This city without the witches? Chaos is coming! They held all of this together! Stopped the whole of London from falling to bits.'

'I'm not hearing any names, Razor...'

'I didn't lie to you, or whatever you think I did—'

My fist met his jaw and blood spat from between his busted lips.

'Stella, I haven't spoken to you in weeks!'

What was this? A game? Did he think he was being funny? Did he think I was stupid?

'I came in here and I beat a name out of you Razor.'

'What are you talking about? No, you didn't!'

Enough. I grabbed him by the collar and threw him back against the mirror again so that his head left a fresh crack and a spray of red. He screamed as he fell, tried to make for the door. Bad idea. I took hold of him and threw him back until the side of the first toilet cubicle halted his momentum, crumpling like cardboard under the force. I couldn't kill him with magic inside The Beehive, but I could toss him around like a rag doll until he stopped moving.

I stalked towards him as he coughed up a fresh glob of blood.

'Stella... Stella, I'm telling you the truth. It was playing a game with you. That's all.'

I stopped. *A game*. That rang true.

'Go on.'

'I swear, Stella. I swear on everything my clan holds dear, I did not feed you any false intel. I haven't seen you since this whole thing started. It played you. The thing played you. It pretended to be me and sent you running after nothing.'

I crouched by the destroyed cubicle and gripped Razor by the balls. He screamed long and high as I twisted.

'Give me a name!'

'I don't know any—'

A twist, more savage this time.

'You always know something, Razor! Always! You swim in the filth all day; you taste a piece of every dark thing that goes on in this city!'

'Please, I can't, I can't—'

'I'll tear these things off and choke you with them, Razor.'

He screamed again, his animal howls bouncing off hard tile.

'Please-please, it'll kill me if it knows I said anything—'

'And I'll kill you if you don't. Give me a name.'

Razor's chest was rising and falling spasmodically, his eyes pinned open as though they were about to pop out. He was terrified. Beyond terrified. Of me, I could see that, but not just of me. He knew who had killed my witches, knew who had David, and it terrified him.

'Please-! Please don't make me—!'

I grabbed a shard of the broken cubicle wall and jabbed it into the meat of his thigh.

He screamed.

I laughed.

I twisted the shard in his thigh—

'Mr. Trick! Its name is Mr. Trick!'

22

True names hold power.

In the right hands, a true name can be a useful thing. But was Mr. Trick a true name, or just another part of the game? Another sleight of hand. A tripwire to send me sprawling to the ground, to be laughed at once again as I dragged myself up out of the dirt. To be stomped on and made an idiot of, yet again.

I left Razor bloody but alive in a puddle of his own—and various other peoples'—urine. I had work to do; a friend to find and a monster to strike down. But first I needed to find him, and to do that meant crossing a line. I'm only a familiar, and I don't have the knowledge or capability to do the kind of magic that I needed. Black Magic. Bad magic. The kind of spell I needed was forbidden. It latched on to an Uncanny's essence to pinpoint them, to show the user where they were. I might be too lowly to grapple with such spells, but I knew of a man ancient and powerful enough to do whatever he liked.

I pushed open the door to L'Merrier's Antiques, which sat snugly down a side street off Portobello Road. A stale fug wafted over me as I crossed the threshold, and motes of dust danced in the ensuing breeze, illuminated by the few shafts of light that managed to penetrate the shop's dim interior. Every inch of the place was covered in curiosities, large and small. Some were what you might expect from an antiques shop: old lamps, bits of furniture, ceramic ornaments, the usual. But the usual stood side by side with the unusual. Artefacts of bygone eras, antiquities spawned from the country's mysterious underbelly, the Uncanny Kingdom.

I could see, half-hidden in one corner, the partial skeleton of an angel wing, its feathers long since decayed. Sat on a shelf between an original first copy of the *Complete Works of Shakespeare* and a football signed by the 1966 England World Cup, jutted an actual Unicorn horn. All these wonders and more lived in this place.

'L'Merrier...'

'I have lowered my protections and allowed you to enter my establishment, little one. Be thankful for that.' Giles L'Merrier's voice rolled from the shadows like silk as he moved into view. He wore a floor-length gown over his bulky frame, covered in ancient symbols. Despite his girth, he moved gracefully, seeming to glide rather than walk.

Despite what he's told me, I didn't feel the presence of any warding spells when I entered. 'I didn't notice any protections,' I said.

He smiled and interlocked his fingers, resting his hands on the bulge of his large stomach. He stopped in a shaft of light that bounced from his large, bald head, almost dazzling me. 'A lowly familiar such as you? Of course you did not feel it, creature. I create spells of protection on a much higher plane than a familiar could ever hope to exist in. You are a bug. An ant scurrying underfoot, unaware that at any moment I could bring that self same foot down to crush you.'

'I get it, you're super powerful. Can we move on?'

His smile twitched into a frown, but just for a moment. 'Do not test me, little one. I have not taken the life of an Uncanny in many years, but I will not hesitate to do so if you disrespect me again.'

He was trying to scare me, and I don't mind saying it was working. He may not have killed in years, but everyone in London and far beyond knew of his history. Of the stories. The true stories of Giles L'Merrier; the man who once strode the globe as though it belonged to him. Who had gone to war with the most fearsome black magicians of the age, and had never walked away the loser.

'I came here to ask for you help,' I said.

A smile quirked his lips. 'No doubt you have come to buy a trinket for your coven. A set of silverware, perhaps, or maybe a nice Toby jug? I can do you a very good deal.'

He knew very well that wasn't why I was there. The smugness he radiated made me ball my fists, made me want to give him a hard smack to the jaw. That wouldn't have been my wisest move.

'My masters are dead.'

'Ah, yes. 'Tis a shame, it's true. They served London well for many centuries.'

'The Church of the Sorcerer Tree is gone, too.'

'Pah. Pious ninnies worshiping bark. I am sure we shall all miss them greatly.'

'Someone is attacking great seats of the Uncanny in London, L'Merrier.'

'Perhaps. Though if that were true, would they not have come directly here? Where else radiates power as strongly as my little shop?'

L'Merrier was renowned for his enormous self-regard, but he wasn't exaggerating when it came to the power he possessed.

'I need you to do something for me.'

'Oh, I do not do requests. I'm sorry to say I am not coin-operated.' He turned from me and began to glide back into the shadows. 'You know the way out.'

'You owe my coven a debt!'

He paused, his giant head turning to look back at me. 'Is that so?'

'My witches helped you a decade back and they never called in the debt.'

'And now you are?'

I swallowed and nodded, my heart fluttering.

L'Merrier laughed. 'The London Coven is dead, with no witches in place to take the reins. The debt is gone.'

'No. The London Coven lives on in me.'

L'Merrier turned fully towards me now as he arched an eyebrow. 'You?'

I nodded and tried to make myself look big. And less terrified.

'Oh little one, that is adorable. But I think not.'

'I will carry on my masters' work. It is my duty. What I was made for.'

'You are a trifle. A marionette moulded from dirt, spittle, and force of will to do the bidding of others. Of great women. You are the monkey, not the organ grinder. My apologies to monkeys everywhere for that dreadful slur on their kind. Now, if you do not wish to make a purchase, you will leave.'

'No, I came here to—' I blinked and found myself outside, looking at the door to L'Merrier's Antiques. Grunting, I pulled some magic towards me and punched forward, allowing the power to unleash and throw the door open, smashing the handle into the wall and leaving a divot in the plaster. I strode back into the shop, L'Merrier was waiting, his face slightly redder than moments before.

'You dare, familiar?'

'The debt stands and will only be paid when you do the thing I want you to do.'

L'Merrier sighed and swatted one hand back lazily. I braced myself as the spell caught me and lifted me from my feet, pinning me to the ceiling, my head cracking back and throwing spots in my vision.

'L'Merrier, please—'

'Begging now? My, my. You come into my shop and make demands. Tut-tut, little one. I should dispatch you at once you for showing such arrogance. Pluck your limbs from their sockets one by one. What say you? Shall we begin with an arm? Left or right, hmm?'

'L'Merrier, the witches of the London Coven are dead! Murdered in their own seat of power, and it is my duty to get revenge! Do you want their deaths to go unpunished?'

He wavered, considering my words. 'They were good women, 'tis true. For witches, that is.'

'My masters did a lot for you, even in the short space of time I was their familiar. Do you not want their killer found? If they could take down the London Coven, who's next? Who's safe? Maybe they'll pay this shop a visit.'

He twitched his hand and I fell to the floor, my head jarring as the wooden floorboards caught me. I groaned and rolled on to my back. L'Merrier gliding into view as he leaned over me.

'What is the animal's name?'

'His name... his name is Mr. Trick.'

23

We were standing in the basement of L'Merrier's Antiques, or at least that's where I thought we were. In truth, he hadn't allowed me to walk there, he'd simply clapped his hands and there we were. For all I knew, his inner sanctum was located inside a mountaintop in Tibet, or underneath a betting shop in Ealing.

The sanctum was dressed simply. A desk and chair was set against one wall and a rug sat in the room's centre, upon which L'Merrier stood. I could see neither a window or a door. No evidence of a way in or out.

'Stay within the circle,' said L'Merrier. I looked down at the brass ring that was inlaid into the stone floor in one corner of the room. 'It is unbroken and infused with magic. As long as you do not step out of it, you will be safe.'

'What about you?' I asked.

'This is my sanctum; the sanctum of the mighty Giles L'Merrier. The things of the dark would not dare to touch me within this place.' He puffed out his already considerable chest. 'Familiar, understand this: using a name to locate a member of the Uncanny Kingdom is of the black arts. I am friends with the Nether, but you… you may be upset by some of the things you are about to see.'

'I can take it,' I replied, trying to ignore the prickle of cold sweat on my neck.

'Very well, then we shall begin.' He clapped his hands and it sounded like thunder, shaking the room.

'Ruma-Chk-Ella-Ruma-Chk-Ella—' His voice rolled out, deep and powerful.

The temperature in the room immediately dropped twenty degrees, and I shivered as my breath fogged in front of me.

'Hear me. Know me. Know what I want. What I can do with a single thought. Know what I demand.' On and on he went, around and around, repeating the mantra.

Something skittered across the floor, just out of view. I almost stepped back in surprise, in fear, at which point my foot would have broken the circle of protection. My magical senses began to recoil at the unnaturalness flooding into L'Merrier's sanctum. My first instinct was to pull in the magic surrounding me, ready to defend myself, to attack, but the room was no longer bathed in ordinary magic. It was flooded with black magic. Corrupt magic. If I soaked that up, there was no telling what it might do to me.

'Chk-Ella! Chk-Ella! I, Giles L'Merrier, the wonder of mankind, have a name for you. A true name!'

There was a shape in the room. It looked almost like a person, but wrong. Stretched out. Bent. Its flesh was crisp and blackened. It didn't have a face, just a giant mouth, full of teeth. A snake's tongue slithered out to lick at the air. Two horns curled and wound from its forehead.

'I am here,' it said, its voice a harsh whisper that turned my stomach into a fist.

'I seek the whereabouts of a stranger,' said L'Merrier. 'I will give you a name, foul beast, and you will reveal him to me.'

The creature wasn't listening. It was looking at me. 'I know you, little thing. Yes I do.'

It stepped towards me, its movements twitchy, unnerving, as though I were watching a film with frames clipped out.

'Beast, I command you!' cried the wizard, but the demon wasn't listening.

The whole of my back was slick with sweat now. I wanted to run, but the moment I did, I would be outside the protective magic of the brass ring, and the thing would chew my bones to dust.

'You don't know me,' I managed to say, my voice a childish stutter.

'Do not speak with the thing, familiar,' roared L'Merrier, setting his jowls wobbling.

'Oh yes I do know you,' whispered the creature, speaking to me. 'I have. Have yet to. Will. We all will. The dark knows you.'

A sonic boom as L'Merrier clapped his mighty hands together once more. The demon winced and turned from me, its attention recaptured.

'Yes, look to me, thing.'

'The magic man seeks our council once again,' snarled the creature, its mouth oozing black ichor.

'I have a true name in my possession, and I demand you show me the man I seek.'

'Why should we bend to you?'

'Do not play games or speak falsely with me, foul creature. You know me. You know this sanctum, the shapes I have drawn, the words I have spoken. The magic that flows through this place is without question. In here, with me, you are bound to tell me answers.'

The creature raised one ragged nail and drew it down its cheek. Thick, black blood oozed from the wound and the beast giggled. 'Go ahead, ask and ask and ask.'

'The name of the person we wish to find is Mr. Trick,' I said.

'Ah yes. The one who did slay the witches of London.'

L'Merrier's turned to me, eyes blazing, then back to the demon. 'Ignore this insect. I am the one who asks, the one who is in control. The one who—with a few well-placed words—could turn you to ash.'

'You would threaten a thing of the dark?' asked the creature, tipping back his horned head and regarding the wizard with hooded eyes.

'And more besides,' L'Merrier replied, coolly. 'You know me. Know what I have done. Do not think that your destruction is beyond my power.'

The creature giggled again, and my knees shook.

'Very well,' said the demon, 'look...'

The beast's hand shot towards L'Merrier, gripping his broad forehead in its filthy hand. The wizard threw open his arms and screamed as the ground threw up a sheet of flames around him.

'L'Merrier!' I screamed, shielding my face from the heat, from the blinding burst of light. Had the thing killed him?

And then the blanket was lifted. The dark magic was gone. The flames were dead. On the floor, sat L'Merrier, head in his hands. He was trembling. That might have been the image that scared me most of all about this whole thing. The mighty Giles L'Merrier, quivering like a child.

'Is it over?' I asked.

He looked up to me, his eyes wide. 'I know where the thing you seek resides. But... it is like nothing I have ever...'

He stopped, stood, and strode across the room, grabbing a pen and paper and scribbling down an address. 'Here.'

I took the piece of paper and read it. I knew where it was. Knew where the monster that had murdered my family was hiding. Knew where David, my friend, was being kept.

'Now get out!' demanded L'Merrier.

'What if we take on Mr. Trick together? I am only a familiar, as you're always keen to remind me. Maybe together we could—'

He rounded on me, eyes full of fire. 'The debt is paid, familiar. More than paid. Do not come to me asking favours again.'

'Wai—'

But before I could even spit out the word, I felt an outdoor chill cool my skin. I was stood outside of L'Merrier's Antiques again, only now the sign on the shop door read CLOSED. I looked at the address on the piece of paper, then stuffed it into the pocket of my leather jacket.

I knew where the thing was.

The thing that had succeeded in frightening even Giles L'Merrier.

And I was going to kill it.

24

I felt my stomach turn over as I lowered myself through the manhole and into the sewer. It's amazing how often my line of work dragged me sloshing through these subterranean, waste-clogged tunnels. The dark Uncanny hid in these disgusting places knowing that the upstairs world wanted nothing to do with them, but that had never stopped me paying them a visit.

I let go of the ladder and my boots splashed down in something horrendous. I grimaced and wafted a hand in front of my nose.

'Fresh.'

In an instant, the smell of piss and shit was masked by the fragrant aroma of a summer meadow. I knew it wasn't the wisest move to close off one of my senses while I was hunting, but I was so full of fear and anger that I was worried—if I didn't—that the stench would overpower me and have me chucking my guts up.

I slid my hand into my jacket pocket and felt the crumpled piece of paper that bore Mr. Trick's address. Who knew how long the thing would remain at that location? I wanted to go straight there and confront whatever it was, but knowing what it had been able to do, and having seen the look in L'Merrier's eyes, I knew it would be a mistake to go rushing in head-first. I was a weak Uncanny compared to many, so to even stand a chance, I needed to be as powerful as I could possibly be. To be topped up with enough magical juice that it was practically leaking out of my ears. And that meant paying a visit to the fairies.

I looked back and forth down the sewer tunnel, stretching out my senses as far as they would go. I made a choice, turned to my right, and set off.

One way or another, I knew this thing was almost over. Mr. Trick would be where the piece of paper said he was. I felt it, deep in my gut. And the way things had been going, I was sure he already knew I was on my way. That he would have felt L'Merrier stretching out into the dark to locate him. He wanted me to find him. Wanted a final confrontation. I felt like I understood the thing, its motives. It wanted to play with me, like a cat with a wounded mouse. But not forever. Letting me know its whereabouts meant it was tired of playing. Now it wanted to take me off the board and start a new game elsewhere.

A flicker in the distance, a stuttering pinprick of white light in the stinking dark. *Here we go.* I chased after it, filthy liquid exploding from my footfalls as I ran, soaking into the bottoms of my jeans.

What was I doing underneath London, chasing a fairy through a shit-smeared tunnel? I was there because real fairies aren't the whimsical creatures they're depicted as in kiddie books. Think of them more like flies, feasting on waste, passing on infections. Dumb animals that live only to breed, and the way they do that? By laying their eggs in a host. Generally a human host. They're not above sneaking into your house after dark and filling you full of eggs while you sleep, but for ease of access, they mostly prefer a passed-out, homeless person. Here's how they operate: they extend what looks like a stinger from their rear ends and sink it deep into the unconscious person's stomach, injecting hundreds, sometimes thousands, of eggs. The infected person will wake up the next morning with a stomach-ache, but they won't suspect anything. Why would they? Fairies aren't real.

In a few short days, the host will find their stomach horribly distended, but they won't look for help. Instead, the infection tricks the victim's brain into seeking out a place to hide. That's when they find their way to the sewer. Down there, out of sight, they will writhe in agony for up to a week, until, finally, their stomach splits and tears apart, ending their misery. Then, from out of the host's cored husk, pours a cloud of new fairies, ready to repeat the process all over again.

We Uncanny people do our best to cull their numbers to stop the normal population from plummeting, but the fairies do have their uses. The creatures are chock-full of magic. Magic that can be extracted and devoured. Many use it as a sort of drug. There are dens all over London in which Uncanny people lounge about on beds, drinking down the magic from a freshly-dead fairy, getting drunk on the hit of magic coursing through their system.

So that's why I was here. Stalking through a fairy-infested sewer. I needed to power up for a fight.

The fairy I was following was so fast I was beginning to lose sight of it. As I ran, I reached out a hand—

'Here—'

I placed the magical words together in my mind and felt energy fly from my palm, catching the fairy like the sticky tongue of a lizard, and drawing the thing into my grip.

'Got you, you little monster.'

It wriggled in my hand, squealing in its high-pitched but unintelligible voice.

'Take me to your home.' The creature went still and blinked rapidly in confusion as the spell took hold. 'Well?' I insisted.

The fairy nodded and I unfurled my fist, allowing the creature to hop into the air and take flight on its dirty wings. It flew away from me, slow enough that I could jog and keep up.

One fairy holds a nice amount of magical juice, but not enough for the fight that lay ahead. To win that, I'd need to find a whole nest of the things and take my fill.

Ten minutes later, the fairy pulled to a stop and hovered mid-air, allowing me to catch up. It pointed eagerly into the gloom, and when I squinted, I saw it: a large nest stuck high to the sewer wall, writhing like a blister full of spiders.

'Thanks,' I said, patting the fairy on the head, then I tore it in two and sucked out its innards. I gasped, my eyes opening wide as the magic filled me, warming my innards like I'd downed a triple whiskey.

'More.'

I threw what was left of the fairy to the ground, then reached up and thrust a hand into the nest, snatching out a fistful of fairies.

'Stop wriggling,' I said, then filled myself so full of magic I thought my body might go supernova.

Okay.

Nothing else to do.

No reason to put it off any longer.

It was time to finish this.

'I'm coming, David.'

I left fifty fairy corpses swilling around in the watery filth before I made my way to the nearest manhole, praying to everything I held dear that David was still alive.

25

It was an ordinary street in Ealing, West London; a nice stretch of three-bedroom houses, tucked safely away from any busy roads. The sort of street that nice families with money lived on. People who went abroad three times a year and left the kids with a live-in nanny.

Ever since I'd read L'Merrier's scribbled-down address, I'd been confused. I'd expected Mr. Trick to be lurking somewhere sinister, somewhere barren. Somewhere he could hide away from prying eyes. But here I was, in a densely-populated and well-to-do street, tracking down a monster.

I walked forward, down the broken white line of the road, my senses on high alert, searching for any sign of an ambush. Any magical booby traps that might turn me inside out in a heartbeat. I didn't think for a moment that this monster was going to make things easy for me.

I was so full of bubbling, raging energy from the fairy banquet that it took me a minute to notice something familiar: just like the blind alley and the coven when I'd discovered my witch's bodies, this street was completely empty of magic. Not even a remnant, not a wisp of smoke twisting in the breeze. Just like home, just like the Church of the Sorcerer Tree, the impossible had happened, and every ounce of the area's magic had been removed.

Is this how it liked things, this Mr. Trick? Liked to live in the empty? A barren place scorched clean of magic?

I still had no idea how that was even possible. It shouldn't be. Mr. Trick was unlike anything I'd ever taken on before. Maybe not like anything *anyone* had taken on before. There were plenty of creatures that could feast on magic, suckle on it to feed themselves or to grow in power, but I knew of none that could scrape a place clean of any trace of it.

I figured this was what Mr Trick did to disorient any Uncanny who came his way. A means of putting them on the back foot before a confrontation, making them easy pickings in a fight. I imagined Mr. Trick liked to watch as his victim began to sweat, twitching like junkies, gasping for magic. Good. Because unlike last time, I didn't feel withdrawal. I was so hopped up on fairy juice that it cancelled out the effect of there being no surrounding magic. I wasn't weak and I wasn't scared. I was ready.

'Who are you?'

The voice came from behind me. I whirled on my heels, hands instantly alive with power, ready to unleash. What I found was a small boy, maybe six years old, looking at me from the door of one of the houses. He was dressed smartly and had neat hair, like he was on his way to church.

'Looks like it might rain,' said the boy, his voice flat, empty of emotion.

'Where is he?' I demanded. 'Where's David?'

'If it rains, we shall get wet.'

Was this Mr. Trick? This skinny boy? Could it really be? Or was this just a puppet of his? A part of the thing's game. A bauble to distract me with, to keep me off-kilter and guessing.

'I said, where is David? You'll tell me or I'll take your head clean off.'

'Dead. Or alive. Here or elsewhere. Up or down, a smile or a frown? It's so hard to keep track in this day and age, don't you find? And lose? And find again?"

I began to walk towards the boy. His eyes stayed fixed on mine, an empty smile on his rosy-cheeked face.

'Don't think talking in riddles is going to stop me. Either you tell me what I need to know or I'll beat it out of you.'

The boy laughed, the sound coming out in a multitude of voices at once. I clenched my right fist, the energy burning, desperate to be unleashed.

'Nice of you to come and visit, familiar.' The speaking voice had changed now, shifting into the style I'd heard before, as though a different person were speaking each word.

'I know your name, Mr. Trick.'

'Mr. Trick, will come to town, and all of the Uncanny shall fall and frown.'

'Is that what you want? To kill us all?'

'So many dead and worse besides. Dead fairies, floating in filth under the streets of old London town; oh, what a dreadful sight to see. You know, when I was last here, the city was nothing but a huddle of wooden buildings. Even then, the stink of magic tainted the place.'

The thing was crazy. Had to be. Some sort of self-hating Uncanny? That was a new one.

'I'm only going to ask you one more time: where is David?' I threw a line of molten power that exploded from my palm like a lava lasso, scorching the brickwork to the boy's right.

'Your temper is a terrible thing, familiar. It'll get you killed, or worse. If you want David, just come along inside and find him. Mother said it's okay, you're expected.'

The boy turned and disappeared into the house. I paused for a second, aware that I was almost certainly walking into a trap, but I didn't see what other option I had.

I paced forward and stepped through the open doorway, my breath now rapid and short.

I stopped in the entrance corridor, the temperature inside a good ten degrees colder than the street outside. The house I found myself looked perfectly ordinary. A cosy, middle-class place, with plush carpets, a vase of brightly coloured flowers on a table against the corridor wall, and pictures of a smiling family on the wall.

I turned and looked back to where I'd come from to see the front door swing shut of its own accord, cutting off the view. Cutting off the exit.

And then the door vanished.

I ran to it and felt around but couldn't find any sign of the exit, just rough brick, solid, like it had been that way for years. Like it had always been that way.

'Stella...'

I raised two glowing fists and whirled around to see the boy skipping out of view at the other end of the corridor.

'I'm coming for you!' I screamed, hurling a ball of energy in front of me to show I meant business, crisping my own hair as I sprinted through it. I rounded the corner to find the corridor ahead empty, a staircase to my right.

'Pssst, familiar—'

The boy was crouched at the top of the stairs, looking down at me through the banister.

'Enough with the messing around, Mr. Trick. Are you going to stand and fight, or are you going to keep hiding behind this boy?'

I felt it before I heard or saw anything; a prickle on the back of my neck that told me I had to get moving. I turned to my right, just in time to see the glint of a large knife, its blade embedded in the banister where my head had been just moments earlier. Still holding the knife's handle was a woman in her late thirties.

'Drat,' she said, 'you weren't supposed to move, you were supposed to get stabbed.'

'Oh, I don't think Mother likes you at all, familiar,' said the boy, as Mother yanked the blade free and swung it in an arc, only just missing my neck as I threw myself backwards, landing with a crash on the floor.

'Mother knows best,' she said, and stamped on my knee. I cried out in pain and reflexively tossed up a ball of flame that engulfed the woman. Her hair caught fire, then her whole head, but the woman didn't flail or fall or even yell out as her flesh broiled. Instead, she giggled.

'What are you?' I asked, as the boy appeared at her side, holding her hand.

'We're bad and bad and bad all over,' he said. 'Isn't that right, Mother?'

'Right as rain,' she replied.

They stepped towards me, the flames dying and revealing the woman's blackened face, flesh scorched, eyeballs running down her cheeks like slug trails.

'Where is David?' I kicked back across the floor and tried to scramble to my feet, my knee sharp with pain.

'Already hurt?'

'Already?'

'You're even less sport than your bitch whore witches.'

I snarled. 'You made a mistake coming into my city. Into my coven. If you think you're going to walk away from this alive, you're wrong.'

I didn't stop to think; I found the right words leap into my mind and unleashed a concussive wave of energy, sweeping the pair aside and depositing them in the kitchen. I ran for the stairs, taking them three at a time, any pain in my knee forgotten. I moved from room to room, searching for any sign of David, until there was only one door left. I turned the handle and shook the door, but it refused to open.

'Who is that?' said a voice from inside; David.

'David, it's me, are you okay?'

'Just great, apart from being kidnapped by a creepy mum and her even creepier son.'

It was so good to hear his voice.

'Step back.'

I placed my hand over the lock, placing the correct phrase together in my mind. The lock clicked as it opened, the door swinging inwards. I found David tied to a chair in the centre of the bedroom.

'David!'

'Well, you took your bloody time.'

'You're welcome. Now come on, I'm getting you out of here and then I'm coming back to finish this thing.'

I pulled a knife from my jacket and sliced through the ropes, letting David shrug them off.

'I knew you'd come,' he said. 'Well, hoped you would. You or Superman. I'm glad it was you though, as Superman isn't real.'

'David, we don't really have time for your babble.'

'Right, imminent danger, consider the babble stopped. But thanks. Thank you for not letting me die. That would have been really shit.'

I smiled and just about resisted the urge to hug him. David followed me as I made my way back to the stairs, trying to ignore that tickle that was telling me this had all been far too easy. This couldn't be the end of it. They weren't going to let me just run out of here with him, were they?

I soon got my answer.

'Stay close to me,' I said edging forward, my right hand ablaze, lighting the way.

'If I was any closer you'd be giving me a piggyback, Magic Lady.'

They were waiting for us downstairs. We were going to have to fight our way out. As I reached the top of the stairs, I took a breath to ready myself. I turned to David, 'Are you ready for this?'

He opened his mouth to reply, but then his eyes widened as he looked past me.

I didn't have time to react.

A flash of something whistled past my head and the knife found its target, entering David's throat up to the hilt.

He looked at me with confusion, unable to understand what had just happened. I think he tried to speak, but all that came out was blood, coughed up in a violent spray.

'No—' I put my hands to my mouth as he stepped back, then stumbled, then fell to his knees. He reached up and took hold of the knife and pulled it from his neck along with a torrent of blood.

'David...'

He looked at me one last time, then fell to his side, blood pouring from his throat and forming a scarlet pillow around his head.

I walked towards him in a daze, unconcerned about any threat to myself. I fell to my knees.

A corpse before me.

I'd failed.

First my masters, now David.

What good was I?

What was I if I couldn't keep those around me safe?

The boy and his mother were holding hands as they stepped from the stairs and into the corridor.

'Mr. Trick has been a bad boy, hasn't he?'

'Hasn't he?'

'Hasn't he?'

I couldn't think straight, couldn't fight.

'No more,' I said. 'No more.'

I felt all the anger, the fear, the despair, and the shame boil up inside of me like a storm. It met the still untapped reservoir of magic I'd drunk down, and without thinking, without putting any magical form together, I stood and threw back my head, arms outstretched, and screamed. Power exploded from me, rampaging down the corridor, around the house, like I was a volcano erupting, destroying everything in my path. The walls cracked, the windows shattered, everything around me was turned to ash.

I couldn't tell you how long it lasted. Perhaps a second. Perhaps an hour. Then, like a switch had been flicked, it was over and I fell to the blackened floor.

26

I'm not sure how long it took me to get back to the coven, or how I even got there. Maybe I walked, maybe I took the tube. The world was a daze, a dream, an awful lie. I found myself back in my room, curled up on the bed I hadn't slept on since this whole thing had started. I felt weak, drained of energy. Whatever I had unleashed back in that house in Ealing had completely sapped me.

I'd thought that I was walking into the final confrontation. That whatever happened between me and Mr. Trick, that one of us wasn't walking away. One way or another, I was going to save David. It didn't matter what happened to me, I just had to stop Mr. Trick from taking that one life.

And I'd failed.

Mr. Trick had no intention of attending the grand finale. He'd just lured me in to make me suffer once again. To take something that had become dear to me, and not even give me the release of death. No, he had more in store for me yet.

I couldn't remember seeing him, seeing the boy and his mother, or anyone else—not after I'd unleashed all of my pent-up magic. Their bodies had been completely destroyed by my outburst, David's too, but no part of me thought it was over.

Those things weren't Mr. Trick, they were just playing pieces being pushed around the board. Testing me, seeing what I had.

I could picture that look in David's eyes as I tried to close my own. The incomprehension. Had he even known what had happened? That there was a kitchen knife embedded up to the handle in his throat?

I should never have involved him in this thing. He was a just a normal. No, that's wrong, he wasn't *just* anything. He was a brave man, full of light and kindness, and I'd been too wrapped up in my own thirst for revenge to do the right thing. To realise that involving him in a mission against the most powerful Uncanny I had ever known was only going to end in calamity.

My body felt heavy. This was different to what had happened to my masters. They could handle themselves. They didn't need my help to keep them safe. They were always safe. Well, always had been before Mr. Trick came to town.

Mr. Trick will come to town, and all of the Uncanny shall fall and frown.

Uncanny and normal alike. He wasn't fussy.

A noise from the corridor.

A floorboard creaking as though someone had shifted their weight upon it.

I sat up and stared at the gap between the door and the floor.

A shadow passed, something moving quickly away.

I didn't bother asking who it was, I already knew.

Mr. Trick had come to town.

It was time for this Uncanny to fall and frown.

But not without a fight.

I wouldn't fall without throwing everything I had left in me at the thing, no matter how ineffective it might be. I wouldn't give the monster the satisfaction of a meek shuffle towards death's door.

I drew the magic in the room towards me as I padded

toward the exit and opened it quietly, peering out into the gloom of the corridor beyond. No sign of anyone.

I opened the door just wide enough and slipped out of my room, my right hand fierce with magic; a raging lantern, leading the way.

I could hear the murmur of hushed voices drifting from the main coven room. I moved forward, and as I got closer, a chill crept across my skin.

I shivered and broke out in gooseflesh.

The voices became clearer:

'I told you.'

'Me too.'

'She was not ready.'

'How could she be, a thing such as her?'

'Spit and force of will.'

'Dirt and rags.'

No...

This was...

I knew those voices.

The power in my right hand grew weaker, then sputtered out altogether as I pushed the door open and stepped inside the coven's common room.

In the centre of the space stood three figures. Three women more powerful than any other Uncanny of London, even though to look at them you would assume they were nothing more than three middle-aged women attending their weekly knitting circle.

Kala, Trin, and Feal.

The witches of the London Coven.

My masters.

My creators.

'Look how she gawps,' said Kala.

'This isn't possible... '

'You think anything exists that could take us out? In our own coven? Our own seat of power?'

'This is just... just a dream, a nightmare, that's all. That's all it can be.'

'You really are pathetic,' said Kala. 'This was a test.'

'A test?'

'I told you she'd fail,' said Trin.

'Yes, but I never thought she would fail so completely.'

I fell to my knees as confusion overtook me.

'Well, fail she did,' said Feal, 'and you know what comes next.'

My masters nodded as one: 'We must destroy her.'

27

The world had become a nightmare.

Ever since I'd first walked into the blind alley that housed my coven, I'd felt things spinning further and further out of control. Further into unreality, insanity, and now...

I looked up again through tear-blurred eyes to see my masters stood before me, smiling. Mocking.

'I don't believe you,' I said.

'Why would we care about a thing like that? Like what you think? What is that to us? What is your opinion worth?'

'It is nothing.'

'Nothing at all.'

'You are just a thing.'

'A tool we created to take care of the drudge and the filth.'

'You're not a person.'

'Not a person.'

'Not even nearly.'

I stood and staggered backwards, angrily wiping away tears with the sleeve of my leather jacket. I reached out with my senses, searching for signs of the trick I was seeing, because that's all this could be. No matter how real it seemed, no matter how much my emotions boiled and told me it was true, this was Mr. Trick's doing. It had to be.

'Oh, that is cute.'

'You feel it too?'

'Of course. Her puny little magical tendrils eagerly snuffling around us like a retarded pup, searching for signs of falsehood.'

My senses recoiled as I failed to find any lies. They were alive, really alive. They didn't seem like some pretence. As far as I could tell, the three women in front of me were the trio of witches that had created me. The ones I had served without question for decades.

'She sees the truth of it.'

'Why? Why did you do this to me?' I looked at their smirking faces, and for the first time in my many years of life, I felt like I wanted to tear them to pieces. Wanted to draw in every scrap of magic and throw it at them. Wanted to knock them down and stamp them out like they were on fire.

'Your face flushes, Familiar.'

'Ooh, Trin, I believe she wishes us harm.'

'Us!' cried Twin. 'Her own creators.'

'You think something as worthless as you could harm a hair upon our heads?' said Kala.

They laughed, but there was no humour in it, only malice.

I sank to my knees. My fists were hot with energy, but I couldn't bring myself to do anything with it. Not just because they were right—me going against them would be like a fly taking on a T-Rex—but because, despite it all, they were my masters. My creators. For want of a better word, they were my gods. And what right did I have to attack a god?

I wasn't a person.

I was a thing.

A thing they owned.

'Just do it,' I said. 'Do it if you're going to.'

My head sank, eyes closed, as I waited for them to put an end to my long life. If this was who they really were, I didn't want to exist anymore. I thought about David again. About how I'd let him down. My own stupidity had got him killed. My failure to pass their stinking "test". Well, fuck it all. Fuck everything. Time to die.

And maybe I would have done. Maybe that would have been the end of my time, of this story. But then I noticed something. Or perhaps I should say I realised for the first time that I *didn't* notice something. I opened my eyes and a smile spread across my face.

'Why are you smiling, Familiar?'

'She has gone mad. Accepting the truth.'

'Accepting the end.'

'The end at our hand! Because we created her—'

'And so we will also end her!'

I began to laugh, loud and crazy. Crazy with relief.

'What is it?'

'What?'

'Answer us!'

I was a step ahead for once. I knew something he didn't.

'This was really good. I mean, *really* good. You almost had me. I was even sure it wasn't true, and yet you were still able to make me question my doubt. To believe this lie. But you made a mistake. Like David said, you're sloppy.'

'Do not talk to your masters like—'

'Oh, shut up. You're a lie. Another trick. You know how I know that?'

The three witches looked at me, dumbfounded, and I savoured the moment for several seconds.

'Tell us!'

I inhaled once, deeply, through the nose, then breathed out. 'You got the smell wrong.'

The witches looked at one other, not understanding what I was saying. It felt good.

'This place always smells the same. It's my first memory,

that smell: cinnamon, cut grass, and lavender. The scent of the London Coven. And you overlooked it. Even I almost did.'

It was time for this trick to end.

I pulled the magic towards me and unleashed it at them in a great, fiery torrent. They stood dumbly as my magic swirled around them in golden arcs of molten fire. Then the screaming began. They wailed and thrashed as the magic penetrated their bodies.

'Well played, Stella,' said Mr. Trick, many voices as one. *'You actually won a round, but I'm afraid the game isn't over yet.'*

I picked up a chair. 'It soon will be,' I snarled, and launched the chair at the squirming, screaming pretend witches. It turned them to ash on impact and carried on, breaking through the far wall. No, *tearing* through. The wall wasn't brick, it was paper. How had I missed that?

The entire room began to sag and collapse. I ran for the tear I'd created and leapt through as the pretend coven fell.

28

I was in the street in Ealing again; Mr. Trick's street. I'd never left. Never stumbled back to the London Coven after unleashing all of the raging magic I'd devoured. After burning everything around me.

It had all just been another trick.

Christ, was I tired of all this childish playing around.

He'd even filled the fake coven with enough magic for me to accept it. Now the illusion had wilted and I'd stepped out of it, I felt the emptiness of his street again. A street impossibly drained of all magic. It gnawed at my stomach like I was starving hungry, but I'd drawn in enough magic from the fake coven to feel some power inside me. To stave off the sweats and the shakes. But it wouldn't be enough. Not to face this creature. I was walking towards who-knows-what without the safety of the fairy magic coursing through my veins.

Who was I kidding? Even with that power inside of me, I didn't stand a chance. There was no difference between then and now. I was still walking naked into a pit of hungry lions. But it didn't matter. All that mattered was seeing this through, finally, to the end. To face the thing responsible for all of this and not back down. For the witches of the London Coven. For the monks who had peacefully dedicated themselves to the Sorcerer Tree. For David. Most of all for him.

I flinched as all of the doors in the houses that lined either side of the street shot open, and out stepped the same two people to stand and stare at me as I walked past. The same mother and child as I'd encountered last time, over and over, in front of every house, her arm around his shoulder.

'He's waiting for you,' they said in turn as I passed. 'Mr. Trick has come to town, and all the Uncanny, shall fall and frown.'

I waited for one of them to break ranks, checking over my shoulder every other second, eyes darting from door to door, but they stayed where they were, calmly watching as I moved along the centre of the road.

'It's okay,' said that familiar multitude of voices, *'It's almost over. You're almost done.'*

'Show yourself,' I commanded.

'I'm afraid I won't let you go easy. Oh, it's going to hurt. You're going to wriggle and scream and beg, beg, beg for me to stop. And I will look down at you, your blood on my face and my teeth as I smile, and I will say "no."'

His words itched at me. Invaded me. His words were fear and I was breathing them in.

'You want to see me? Really see me?'

'Get out here!'

As I walked, I began to notice something strange happening. The street was devolving. As I moved forward it was like I was actually moving back. Back in time. The houses, the brickwork, neat gardens, cars, were becoming wild grass, trees, forest. It should have been jarring, but somehow it seemed natural, a seamless flow.

Within a few more steps, the street was gone entirely. I looked back, but all I saw was a dirt road and trees, as though the street of houses had never existed. I didn't know what magic this was, even worse, I couldn't even *feel* the presence of magic. This was sorcery from a whole other plane. The kind a bug like me could never see or feel.

'Mr. Trick, I know your name, and I think I know what you want. To devour all magic. All magical practitioners. To scorch it all from the planet. To stamp it all out until there's only you left. So come on, stop playing games. Stop being a coward. Come out here and take my life from me. See if you can put me down.'

I didn't look into the tree line; I could sense things in there. Impossible, dark things. Maybe if I saw one of them clearly it would burst on to the dirt track and swallow me whole. Where on Earth was I? Was this place real?

'This is London, Stella. A small sliver of old London that refused to die. Isn't it beautiful?'

The voices came from everywhere, it was impossible to get a fix on him. I felt my hands burning hot with power, desperate to leave a mark on the monster before he snuffed me out.

'No people, no cars, no chemicals or magic tainting the air. Free of the stink of the Uncanny. Almost free...'

My heart hammered in my chest, like it might burst from my ribcage at any moment and make its escape.

'Why do you hate the Uncanny so much? You're part of it, you're the most powerful Uncanny I've ever—'

I was cut off as the unseen beasts of the forest screamed as one, drowning me out. Finally, silence fell again.

'Sounds like I hit a nerve there, Mr. Trick. Tell me, where did the evil warlocks, wizards, and witches touch you?'

A mighty crack to my right. I turned to see a giant oak tree falling in my direction and leapt out of the way, rolling in the dirt as the tree struck down by my side and shook the earth beneath me.

I pushed myself to my feet and staggered back, looking for a sign of any more trees about to fall, but all seemed calm again. He didn't want to kill me that way. Whatever happened, Mr. Trick wanted me dead by his own two hands.

'Nice try, but your aim was a bit off there.'

When I looked around I saw a large wooden hut in front of me, directly in the centre of the dirt road. Instead of a door, an animal skin covered its entrance, gently undulating in the breeze.

'Is this it? Is this where you're hiding?'

Silence.

He was in there. *It* was in there. I knew it. My every nerve ending was screaming at me that he was, and that I had to turn and run. I breathed long and slow, then reached out a hand and pushed the heavy animal skin aside, ducking as I stepped indoors.

The hut was dark and smelled like dirt.

I blinked several times and my eyes began to adjust to the dark.

There was a hunched figure crouched in the far corner of the room, draped in a thin blanket. It rose and fell rapidly as the figure sucked in short, sharp breaths.

My stomach churned, my senses retreated. Refused to interact with the person, knew I was in the presence of something beyond dark. Beyond horror. Beyond death.

Mr. Trick was waiting for me.

'I'm here,' I said, my voice a croak, my throat dry.

No response.

Hand trembling, I reached out to the figure, took hold of the blanket and whipped it away. The material was damp.

Still the figure didn't stand, didn't move.

I reached out again, took hold of the person's shoulder, tried to turn them-

'Mr. Trick, I'm here. Here to end—'

The figure twisted round, thrusting up to his feet, face rushing towards mine, teeth bared, eyes crazy—

I screamed and fell back to the floor, my mind refusing to believe what my eyes were seeing.

He stepped towards me as I pushed myself away across the floor—

'No-no-no—'

He leapt over me, grabbed me by the collar, laughing and pushing his face towards mine.

It was a leering, mad face, with wild eyes and a rictus grin.

And it was a face I recognised.

It was David.

29

Somehow I wriggled free and half staggered, half fell, past the animal skin door and back out onto the dirt path that led through the forest of London.

I stood to see the mother and son clones emerging from the surrounding tree line and applauding wildly as David stepped out of the wooden hut. He bowed and threw out kisses.

'David, how are you... I don't—'

This was a lie.

Another lie, that's all. Did he really think he could fool me again?

'Hello, Stella.'

The world tilted.

It couldn't be true.

That voice.

Two words, two different voices.

'My name is Mr. Trick, and I'm here to tear your city down.'

The unseen beasts of the forest stamped their feet. The trees shook and the ground trembled.

'Listen to them, Stella.'

This was just another trick, that's all. Like the witches, my masters; a lie inside of a paper coven. I just had to sniff out the lie again, find the mistake, and then all of this would warp and crumble, and the snake would slither out to be stamped upon.

'You're a lie. You're not Mr. Trick. You're just another puppet. Another playing piece.'

'Oh no, I can see why you would think that, but I'm afraid this really is the final act. Even the best of games has to end eventually, and this is where I take my trophy.'

The mothers and the sons clapped and cheered wildly before being silenced with a gesture from David. From Mr. Trick.

'I saw you die.'

'Oh, even eyes can betray. Sad.'

I felt fire in my hand and threw my arm out, unleashing a blast of magic. It hurtled towards David, who made no attempt to jump out of the way. Instead, he raised an eyebrow, and the ball of furious power stopped. It hung in the air, rippling with energy.

'And I thought we were friends, Stella. To think I let you stay in my home when you were hurt.'

'That was David. You're not him.'

He sighed and the ball of magic reversed and lurched towards me. I did my best to jump out of the way, but it struck my legs, corkscrewing me through the air, making my skin burn. I landed in a painful heap, limbs twisted.

'With you this whole time as you struggled and failed, failed, failed. What a nasty trick of me to play,' said David.

'Why?'

'Why not? Why should I let my devil dogs eat you up right away when there was so much more to be had from you. To watch you yell and run and search for clues like a good little Familiar. All the while with me at your side. You can be a brutal thing at times, can't you?'

Could it really be true? I remembered my confusion when I opened my eyes to find myself in his house. I'd been moments from death as one of Mr. Trick's devil dogs lunged for me, too flustered to string an incantation together, and then all of a sudden I was somewhere else. A nice, safe house, miles from where I had been, with a stranger looking down at me.

With David looking down at me.

Mr. Trick.

'I think she's putting it together. Finding the pieces slot neatly.'

The mothers and sons cheered once, high and sharp.

I realised with certainty that I'd entered another world—a mad world—and the last thing I wanted was to die there. I turned and ran, the people that lined the path laughing and pointing as I passed them by.

'Where are you going, Stella? The end is the end is the end,' called David. 'When Mr. Trick comes to town, all the Uncanny will fall and frown.'

A bend in the path, and David—Mr. Trick—was stood in front of me. I pulled up short and darted into the forest, batting aside tree branches that fought to slow me down. This was a mistake. This whole thing. Trying to face Mr. Trick, and now running off the path. Nothing good would come from running into a forest full of monsters.

'Stella. Stop. It's over. Now lie down in the dirt like the filthy creature you are and wait for the heel of my boot to grind against your eyes.'

There was no time for a pithy reply, all there was time for was running and fear. A real, primal fear. Mr. Trick, this place, this past London, it was like it had found the primitive part of my psyche and was jabbing it with hot pokers. In all my decades of life, I couldn't remember ever feeling such blind fear. The kind of fear I imagined a child might feel as it lay hot under the blanket in bed, trying to ignore the thing lurking inside the wardrobe.

I stopped to catch my breath. Where the hell was I running to? Was there even a way out? Was there a way back to London proper, or was I just sprinting further and further into Mr. Trick's nightmare world?

A scream.

No, *hundreds* of screams.

Human, but not quite; more animalistic, hungry.

I turned to see all of the mothers and sons, their faces masks of fury, mouths wide, teeth bared, running through the trees towards me.

No time for magic, for spells, I couldn't even think straight to put the right incantation together.

All I could do was run.

I heard them behind me, desperate to feel me in their hands, under their feet, between their teeth. They wanted to rip me apart, I knew it. I looked over my shoulder, they were falling over each other in their desperation to get to me. The looks in their eyes… I'd never seen anything like it. Anything so dark.

I yelled as I ran straight into something and bounced back, landing painfully on the forest floor. No time for pain, for stopping. I hopped up into a crouch, dimly aware of the sharp complaint of my ankle, and prepared for the first wave of mothers and sons to pile on to me—

But they were gone.

I couldn't see them, couldn't hear them. The only sound now was the noise of my own heavy breathing.

I wasn't going to get out of this. I couldn't run from him. Couldn't step out of old London and make it back to my coven and lock the door. What happened to my witches was proof enough that no one and nowhere was safe from this thing. Sooner or later, he was going to track me down.

I didn't want to die.

I especially didn't want to die at this monster's hands.

This twisted bastard.

But I was out of options and tired of running.

And yet, I refused to run another step. Refused to give the beast that satisfaction.

So I sat. I lowered myself to the forest floor and crossed my legs. All around me, always out of view, I could feel great, ancient creatures moving through the forest. The ancient fears made flesh that lived in this place.

'They are beautiful,' said Mr. Trick, stepping out of the shadows and sitting opposite me.

'Give David back.'

Mr. Trick arched one of David's eyebrows.

'I know he isn't you. He can't be.'

He tilted his head as he regarded me, then shrugged. 'Well, okay, you got me.'

'You're just a thing, hijacking his body. You've crawled inside him and used him.'

'But he's so warm and comfortable,' he replied, smiling. 'I think I may stay in here for a while, holding on to his spark. His soul. Squeezing it between my hands so it squirms and screams.'

'You're trying to make me angry. Make me frightened. I think I'm done with that.'

He nodded and reached forward, taking my hand in his. I tried to pull away, but found I couldn't. Without a word, he broke my little finger. The snap rang out like a rifle shot. He let my injured hand go and I clung to it, trying not to scream.

'You don't make the rules, familiar. I am the dark. The terror. I am the thing that frightens the monsters. I will make you feel any way I wish. And then... then I will devour you. Take your spark and store it inside of me, next to all the others. Next to your poor, poor witches. They're in me now, thrashing around. It tickles.' He licked his lips.

'Talk all you want,' I said through gritted teeth, the pain in my hand sharp.

'Sticks and stones, eh?'

I didn't respond. Part of me was screaming to get up and

run again, but sod that. 'If you're going to kill me, come and have at it. I won't go easy.'

'Isn't she brave?'

The monsters in the forest roared in agreement.

'Well, perhaps I can break you yet, before I swallow you down...'

I shivered despite myself, wondering what he meant. More broken bones? Or would he nibble off my skin, like he had with the monk? I could take it. I'd have to.

'Here,' said Mr. Trick, 'let me show you something to make you scream...' He reached out his hands and grasped me by the temples and...

...I...

...I could see...

...I was a fragment and...

...Don't let...

...I was lost, lost, lost, and...

The fog cleared and I was stood in a familiar place; the blind alley that led to the London Coven.

'What is this?' I asked, but my words were silent.

The door to the coven opened and I saw myself step out.

A dark shape rushed past me, towards my other self.

I tried to shout out to warn her, to warn me, but couldn't.

The shadow became a person of sorts, and it whispered in the other me's ear. And then I realised when I was.

I saw myself turn to the door of the coven and watched as my hands swept over and over again, forming ancient patterns as I spoke secret words under my breath.

No...

Oh God...

I couldn't have!

The other me stopped and turned away from the coven, walked down the alley, walked past me and turned out of sight. I looked back to the shadow figure and watched it push open the door and step inside.

It was my fault.

All those protection spells. Layers upon layers of magical protection that nothing could ever get through unscathed, and only four people knew how to take them down: my three witches and me.

I'd let the fox into the hen house.

30

Mr. Trick had done something to me, whispered some magic in my ear, and I'd unlocked the coven for him. Allowed him to step into the most protected place in London and tear my witches into bloody pieces.

'No!' My voice rang loud and high, suddenly audible again as I found myself back in the forest, curled up on my side, a child sobbing in the dirt.

Mr. Trick looked down at me, smiling. 'There's that pain. That scream. That delicious anguish.'

I wanted to believe it was a deception, but I knew that it wasn't. Now I'd seen it, it was like a door had been unlocked in my mind. I could remember it happening now. The strange compulsion to remove the protection. The satisfied feeling I'd had as I walked away. The confusion as I stepped out of the blind alley, and the knowledge of what I had done disappearing. I'd turned on the spot, wondering if I'd forgotten to take something with me. I'd almost gone back to the coven to check for the thing I couldn't remember, but shrugged it off and walked away.

My fault. My fault. My fault.

Just a stupid, weak Familiar. A weak spot that had been taken advantage of.

And now all of London was going to pay. Maybe all of the Uncanny Kingdom.

'What say you, Stella? A rum do and no mistake. Oh, I let them know you'd shown me the way in before I had my wicked, gruesome way with them. I think they were a little annoyed. Sorry.'

'You bastard...'

I stood and felt what magic I had surge through me and explode from my outstretched hands at Mr. Trick. It was no use. He swatted my best aside and stepped forward, grabbing me by the neck and hurling me against the nearest tree. My back hit hard and I fell to the ground, the wind punched out of me.

'Would you like to see how I finished them off? The fun I had? Oh, I took my time.'

'Please, don't.'

I felt his cold hands grasp my head again and—

I was in the coven's common room. My witches, my brave masters, were giving everything they had, but the creature I'd let in was too strong. It brushed each spell aside. It was a mouse playing with its scampering food. They were bleeding, exhausted, terrified. I had never seen them scared before. It broke my heart.

'Watch, familiar. Watch me play.'

'That's enough. Please, I don't want to see...'

I tried to close my eyes, tried to turn my head away as the dark figure rampaged through the coven, tearing flesh, opening wounds at will, but I could feel Mr. Trick's hands on me, holding my eyes open, keeping my head still.

'Watch me play, Stella. It's so, so beautiful.'

The attack was not fast. He blocked any chance of escape and took his time to break them down. To give them hope that they could turn the tables, then smack them down again. Near the end, the witches of London struggled to meet each other. Dragged their shattered bodies across the floor, leaving trails of dark blood behind them. I could see it in their eyes now, the certainty that this was it. They'd done what they could and it was all about to be over. I felt the tears rushing from my eyes, soaking my cheeks.

'Aw, it's almost over, Mr. Trick lamented, 'but don't worry, we can watch it again and again and again...'

'Please. Please don't show me...'

I wanted to die. For him to kill me at last and have it be over.

But then—

Oh!

Then I saw something. Something *wonderful*.

As I watched the dark shape in Mr. Trick's shadow play attack my witches, I saw them hold hands. They did not fight, did not run. Instead I saw their lips move as one, saying the same words. Words I recognised. Casting a spell only my witches could have created, and only when working together as one.

I began to laugh.

'Stop.'

I was hysterical now, howling. Shaking with great gales of laughter that hurt my stomach.

'Stop it!' said Mr. Trick.

The coven whipped away like a cloth being yanked from a table, and I was back in the forest. Mr. Trick rocked back on his heels, confused.

'Is this madness? Have I broken you so easily?'

'I'm sorry, it's just, you're making a habit out of this.'

'Of what?' He studied my face, my smile. 'Making a habit of what?'

'Well, first you let me live when you really should have taken care of me right away. Then there was the lack of smell in the pretend coven earlier. Not a details person, are you Mr.

Trick? A little too arrogant for that, too sure of yourself. But this one? This one is a big boo-boo.'

'What? Tell me!' His voice roared out, the trees shaking, my hair blowing back, but I didn't shield myself from it. I walked forward, walked towards Mr. Trick. Now I saw fear in *his* eyes.

'Don't you see? They left the door open for me to walk in.'

'Your witches? They are dead. Dead! I killed them, tore them apart, left them as nothing more than meat and rags on the floor! I swallowed them down, ate their spark! I did that! Me, me, me!'

'Yes, but not before they left me a gift; and thank you for letting me see it, because otherwise I'd never have noticed.'

Mr. Trick blinked slowly. 'What did they do? Tell me what they did.'

I smiled. 'It's something my masters created called the Achilles Curse.'

His lips twitched. 'No. No, no, no... that's not.... not possible.'

'A weak spot. A chink in your armour. Know where it is and even a fledgling sorcerer could take you down.'

Mr. Trick backed away. 'Where is it? Where?'

'Now, those who cast the spell can't take advantage of it,' I went on. 'Magic has rules, it can be a right bitch like that. But me? I can use it. They left it for me. One last job for the familiar.'

Mr. Trick screamed and raised his hands, ready to throw everything he had at me.

'Hush,' I said. He froze, unable to cast the spell that would surely have killed me.

I walked slowly towards him, savouring his terror.

'Now it's you that can feel fear. That can know what it's like to beg for your life. I feel you struggling against me, but it's no good. There's no point. I know where your weak spot is, and I'm focussing my magic on it. You can't stop me.'

'You think you can put an end to me? You think I can just be—'

'Oh, please shut up. I'm going to kill you now. For my witches, and for David. Goodbye and fuck you.'

I placed the right words together and a flaming sword appeared in my hand—

'No!'

'Oh, yes—'

I thrust the sword into Mr. Trick's chest and he screamed, his mouth growing ever larger until I thought his head was going to split in two. Magic erupted from him in great flaming torrents, forcing me to stagger back. He shook violently, like he was having a fit, and shapes began to burst from him, tearing his flesh open to escape and circle around us. These were the sparks he'd taken, the souls he'd eaten. It was clear he'd feasted often and for many years, and I knew my witches must be up there among them somewhere.

'I did it,' I said. I hoped they could hear me.

Mr. Trick's body fell to the ground and something dark and wet began to crawl out of him. Began to crawl out of David. This was Mr. Trick's true form. His true body. Dragging itself out of David's corpse. The form looked drained and withered, and was dripping with foul black goo. I wondered what it had been, how it had become such a horrific creature. It looked up at me, its face smooth and featureless apart from two giant yellow eyes that met mine, imploring.

'Beg all you want,' I said, 'you won't find mercy here.' I reached out my hands, fire shooting from my palms, and reduced the thing to ash.

Mr. Trick was dead and gone.

I'd done it.

Mr. Trick had come to town, and a lowly familiar had put him down.

I'd started this whole episode seeing impossible things, and now I'd done something impossible myself. I'd destroyed the most powerful creature I had ever met.

'Stella...?'

I whirled round to where David's body lay. He wasn't dead! Not quite, but he would be. I ran to him and cradled him in my arms, fussing at the open wounds that covered him, the giant gaping hole that Mr. Trick had crawled out of.

'David. Oh God, David, you're going... you're going to be...' I couldn't finish the sentence, because he wasn't going to be okay. His wounds were too severe. He was seconds from death. I thought he'd died once, but this time he really would. This time he was really done for...

...unless...

I looked up at the sparks still swirling around in a confusion of magic. It was forbidden, I knew that. It was the dark arts, black magic. It was especially bad for a thing such as me to use it, and maybe it wouldn't work anyway. But...

I stood and lifted my hands to the sky, head thrown back, looking up at all of the sparks rushing around like a tornado. All of those Uncanny souls. So much magic in one place, for this moment only, but would it be enough? Would *I* be enough? Would I be able to harness it and channel it correctly, or would it burn me up and leave me a husk on the ground?

'Sod it,' I said. 'Let's do this...'

The forms shaped in my head. The forbidden forms. I felt the energy in the forest change. I was a lightning rod, a thing of pure focus. I tensed and tried to ready myself, but as the first spark rushed into me, I heard myself scream. All the Uncanny sparks, the souls, entered me one after one. I could feel my bones burning, my flesh twisting. They were tearing me apart.

No-no-no-

'You will... do what I want... I... I control you... I demand it... I... demand...'

I felt the dark energy I was tapping into, and it terrified me. Whether it worked or not, there would be a price. A familiar like me couldn't play with this side of magic, not without paying a toll down the line. It didn't matter. I didn't care. All that mattered was winning; was pulling one life back from Mr. Trick.

Throat raw from screaming, I lowered my arms and looked at David on the ground before me. I knelt beside him, my body on fire, and I gathered him into my arms, his head lolling back.

'Stella...I think...I think I'm going to...'

'Shh now, David. Everything is going to be okay.'

I craned my neck, placed my lips upon his and I blew into him.

The power, the sparks, the dark magic, rushed from inside me and into him. He jolted from my arms and hung in the air in a brilliant ball of light, the trees around us catching flame, David at its centre. The whole world was screams and fire and blinding light, and it was too much, too much, too much—

And then it was over.

David fell with a thump to the ground, the sparks gone, the dark magic gone. All was silent. I slumped back, every part of me in agony, trying to catch my breath. I was alive. I'd managed to harness all that magic, tap into the dark plane, and somehow I'd survived.

But what about...?

'Stella?'

I rolled over and crawled towards David, my head coming to rest on his stomach.

'Yes?'

'That really, really hurt.'

I smiled. 'You're welcome.'

31

A month later, back at the London Coven, back at my home.

My body had just about recovered from everything, though I still walked with a bit of a limp. I'd stopped coughing up blood in the mornings too, so that was good. For a while, it had felt strange to return to this place. To decide I was going to live there still. But it was my home. I wouldn't let Mr. Trick win by forcing me out. This was where I belonged.

'Hey,' said David as I entered the kitchen. He put a mug of coffee down before me. He'd recovered much quicker than I had. All the dark magic that had saved his life had fixed him up pretty well.

I wrapped my hands around the mug and not for the first time wondered what the price would be for my harnessing such black magic. There was always a price. I looked up at David and knew I'd do it again in a heartbeat.

'Hey, have I thanked you yet for saving my life?' he asked.

'Only about ten times a day for the last month.'

He patted my shoulder and sat opposite me. He'd described what had happened to him as a sort of dream. He was aware at times that something was inside him, willing him to act in certain ways, but he hadn't been able to do anything about it. At other times, he hadn't known anything was wrong at all. Mr. Trick had only used him for brief bits of time, until he'd staged his disappearance. From then on, until Mr. Trick had crawled out of him, he'd been completely cut off and unaware of anything. As if he was in a deep, dreamless sleep.

'So today's the day?'

'Today's the day,' I said, nodding.

'You're sure? I saw you pretending not to limp when you walked in here.'

'London has been without its witches for too long. Without the protection and order of this coven. Well, I might only be a puny familiar, but I'm of here, and until someone better comes along, I'm going to carry on doing what I was created for: keeping the Uncanny of London in line.'

'With me by your side, right? Remember, this is my city too. Now I know all of the spooky stuff that goes on here, it's my duty to make sure people are safe. And you can use the intelligence I get through official channels. You know it makes sense.'

I smiled and nodded. Truth be told, I could do with the help, and he knew things that I didn't. People, places, ways to go about investigations. What to look for and how to fit clues together. I needed him. Not that I'd say that to him, he had a big enough head as it was.

Also, I didn't *want* him to go away.

I wanted him to stay with me.

'Stella Familiar and Detective David Tyler,' he said, 'taking on anyone who tries to upset our city. This is going to be fun. Me and you, a crime-fighting duo. Ooh, like Batman and Robin! Bagsy I'm Batman.' He whistled and began cracking eggs into a pan.

There was another reason I wanted David close by. Well, another two reasons. He'd played host to the most powerful creature I'd ever come across. Was Mr. Trick gone for good? Would David now become a weak link, the creature's way to crawl back into this plane? There was no way of knowing. And then there was the fact that I'd used black magic on him, and who knew what the long-term effect of that might be? No, I wanted to keep my eye on him. To protect him. Maybe protect others *from* him.

'It's not going to be an easy ride,' I said. 'The Uncanny world is a dangerous one, as I'm sure you're already very aware.'

'Hey, danger is my middle name.'

'I can't believe you just said that with a straight face.'

'I am pretty much shameless,' he replied with a grin.

'Oh, and David?'

'Yeah?'

'You're definitely Robin.'

The witches of the London Coven might be dead.

And I might not be a fifth of the Uncanny they were.

But it didn't matter. I'd walked into Mr. Trick's world and taken him out, and I'd do whatever it took to see off anything looking to take his place.

That was my job.

My whole reason for existing.

My name is Stella Familiar.

Created by the witches of the London Coven.

And this city will be protected.

The End.

SPECTRAL DETECTIVE

DAVID BUSSELL

1

It was half past midnight when the screaming started.

It came from the east bank of Regent's Canal, not far from Camden Lock. The person who called it in said they heard a commotion outside their narrow boat and pulled back a curtain to find a figure running along the towpath, screeching at the top of their lungs. The witness said they couldn't understand why the screamer was making such a racket, not until they slammed their palm against the boat's porthole and painted it with a big, red handprint.

The victim didn't have any skin.

They'd been flayed alive from head to toe, peeled like a prawn, yet somehow they still had it in them to be running barefoot—*literally barefoot*—alongside the canal.

The victim ran some more after that, but didn't make it much farther before they took a tumble over the bank and toppled face-first into the water. It probably won't shock you to learn that they were pronounced dead on arrival.

When I picked up the message from DCI Stronge that the Marine Policing Unit had fished a skinned corpse out of the drink, I took an interest right away. Things like that—bizarre, gruesome murders—they're right in my wheelhouse. All my life I've had a preoccupation with the macabre: the creatures in the shadows, the lurkers beneath the floorboards, the monsters in the closet. Believe it or not, back in a past life I used to be an exorcist (although obviously I'd prefer if you did take my word for it, otherwise this story is going to be a really tough sell).

I suppose I should introduce myself. My name is Jake Fletcher. I'm six-feet tall, I fill out a suit real nice and I've been told by more than one woman that I have—and I quote—"nice teeth." Oh, and I'm dead. Dead as a doornail.

Now, don't start giving me any of that, "Ghosts aren't real, Jake", bollocks, all right? You're just going to have to go with me on this. I'm dead, ghosts are kosher, and *Two Broke Girls* is the nadir of human accomplishment. These are the facts. Deal with them.

Where was I again? Oh, right, me being an ex-exorcist...

You're probably wondering how I wound up being one of those in the first place, right? I mean, it's not exactly your run of the mill, garden variety profession. My school careers advisor had me pegged as a newspaper reporter or an English teacher, but I guess I was always destined to work with the dead. I was born with The Sight, you see, a special sensitivity to the Uncanny. No one knows how it works exactly—whether it's a sixth sense, an overactive pineal gland, or just plain bad luck—but I have an ability to see the spirits of the dead. Ghosts, phantoms, spectres, whatever you want to call them, I can see the lot, and more besides. If I was to show you some of the "besides" that I've seen, you'd lock yourself in your house and soil yourself for seven days straight. It made for a challenging childhood—Jesus, it did—but it set me up just right for a career evicting spooks.

I spent a good few years doing the exorcist thing: screaming bible passages, waving burning sage about, cleansing haunted properties. That was until I died and became a spook myself. Yeah, I'm not blind to the irony. And don't worry, I'm not the bad kind of ghost who makes the walls bleed and writes threatening messages in the condensation on your bathroom mirror. Honestly, I wouldn't say boo to a goose, nor can I think of a single good reason for doing so.

Anyway, since I croaked, I've taken a bit of a U-turn on the whole "ghost rights" thing. Matter of fact, I've become something of an undead activist. *Rights not rites*, that's what I say. Because I learned the truth. The real truth about the consequences of what I was doing as an exorcist. But we'll get back to that later.

So... ghosts. Most of them end up marooned on the physical plane because they died a traumatic death and need closure to move on. Not me. I solved my murder – had my chance at the afterlife and passed it up. Well, that's not entirely true. The truth is, I did a runner from the pearly gates. I didn't feel I was ready to face the Big Man at that juncture. Not after the life I'd led. Not after the things I'd done. I had a feeling He wouldn't be too quick to hand me a gold card to the exec lounge, at least until I'd cancelled out the stuff I'd been up to while I was still alive. Of course, I hadn't known then that I was up to no good, but something told me ignorance wasn't going to earn me a pass with Him Upstairs.

So, I found my way back here, back to the physical realm, back to London. Now I live somewhere between the two worlds, tucked in the middle and out of sight, like a g-string up an arse crack. I move invisibly in this realm, a rumour drifting through a world of facts. Tell you what, let's stick with that last one—the rumour/facts line—it's got a bit more poetry to it than the arse crack thing.

So, you probably want to know how I wound up dead in the first place, right? Well, you know that expression, "Die young and leave a good-looking corpse"? I managed to get the "young" part right. The "good-looking corpse" part, that's a whole other story. The quick version: I succeeded in pissing off the wrong person and ended up cut into four chunks, so... not exactly good-looking. Unless a horribly mashed up corpse gets your motor running, in which case, hey, I won't judge you (actually, what am I talking about? Of course I will, that's messed up).

Anyway, my death's a story for another time – we've already got one sliced-up corpse bobbing in a canal, so let's not muddy the waters with another. The reason I mention it is to remind you that, as a bona-fide "goner," I don't have a body. Most of the time I do just fine without one, but seeing as I was about to meet with the police and they wouldn't be able to see me in my spook state, something needed doing. If I wanted to talk with DCI Stronge, I was going to have to make a quick stop-off.

2

I found him sat in the booth of a late-night bar with his arm around a woman. She was presenting enough chest to be charged with indecent exposure. He was ordering table service. Of course he was, he'd always been a wanker. His name was Mark Ryan and I'd known him since we were eleven years old. Since we were at school together. Since he left me with a scar that never healed.

Mark and me didn't run in the same circles back then. His circle was all sports trophies and Duke of Edinburgh Awards and hand jobs behind the bike sheds, while mine—thanks to him—was the kind of circle Dante wrote about. Fucking Mark Ryan. No matter what I did to avoid the guy, he'd always find a way to seek me out and give me shit: barging me into my locker, kicking footballs at me, tripping me over in the corridor. Boosting his ego at my expense. I tell you, Mark Ryan was the first person to really make my life hell, and I've been closer to the place than most.

One time, Mark brought a pair of handcuffs into Science class, and when the teacher went out of the room to fetch some lab equipment, he manacled me to a radiator. I know what you're thinking: that doesn't sound so bad, right? There are people who pay good money for that kind of treatment. Thing is, Mark wasn't in it for the kink, he just wanted to hurt someone. The first thing he did was over-ratchet my cuff, making it too tight, cutting off the circulation to my hand. But that wasn't what really hurt. The real hurt came when the heat from the radiator—which was set to warm a large room in the coldest part of winter—conducted through the metal cuff and into the bracelet I was wearing. That was a new kind of pain. Naturally, Mark and his crew did nothing to help me – just stood back and laughed like jackals, waggling the key at me as I thrashed around, howling in agony.

Even as a ghost, I still wear a scar on my wrist.

So yeah, Mark Ryan's not exactly top of my friends list, which is why I had zero qualms about making him my designated meat puppet; the physical form I use whenever I need to pass for living. At least this way he serves a useful function in life. Think of him as my toupee, except instead of hiding a bald spot, he hides the fact that I don't have a blood and guts body.

I looked over to Mark's booth and saw him peck his side-piece on the cheek.

'Back in a minute,' he said. 'Just going to siphon the python.'

He squeezed past the girl and headed to the Gents for a slash. Meanwhile, I breezed by the rest of the bar's punters unseen and phased through the bathroom wall to follow Mark inside.

When I got there, I found him stood at a urinal, phone in one hand, cock in the other. In case you were wondering, no, his downstairs department isn't anything to write home about. The guy might act like a swinging dick, but he has a knob like an outie belly button.

I sidled up and prepared to stake a pitch in Mark's body. Believe me when I tell you that it's no mean feat, possessing someone. It took me a long time to get the knack of that trick. For a while there I was just jumping into people and going arse over tit through the other side as they stood there oblivious. Meat is a very tricky medium. Most ghosts never get a handle on it to be honest, but eventually I figured out a way. If you asked me how, I'd tell you that my work as an exorcist gave me a qualified understanding of ghosts and their unique metaphysical properties. I'd be shitting you though. All I know for certain is that after a lot of trial and error, I finally sussed out how to inhabit the living. Well, at least for a little while. An hour, two at most, and a living body rejects me like an unwanted kidney. That's just the way things are, don't ask me to explain the science of it.

I invisibly manoeuvred behind Mark and smiled. It's funny, he used to get a big kick out of telling the kids at school that I was a "gay boy", but only one of us was getting a man inside of him that night.

I stepped into Mark's body and felt him jolt and recoil. Someone had flushed the toilet on his nice, hot shower, and he wasn't liking it one bit.

He went into spasms, fighting me, doing what he could to resist my intrusion. He needn't have bothered. A couple of seconds more and I was all moved in, boxes unpacked and making myself good and comfy.

Mark's body was mine. I sniffed the air and sighed. It smelled like piss and urinal cake, but the simple act of breathing was reward enough. I'm telling you, it's the little things you miss when you don't have a body.

I zipped Mark up, washed his hands—a habit of mine, not his—and checked my reflection in the mirror above the bathroom sink. He was a handsome bastard, I'll give him that; a swimmer's chest and the kind of face that gets you places in life. Too bad for him that his body was a timeshare property.

I headed through the bathroom door and back to the bar. I saw Mark's bit of fluff there, tucked up in her booth, sipping something tall and pink. Now, a more unscrupulous ghost might, when such an opportunity was presented to them, use

Mark's body to take his chesty young bint to pleasure town. Well, not me. I may, in many ways, be a bit of a bastard, but I'm not an *utter* bastard.

I strolled by her and made for the exit.

'Where are you going?' she screeched.

'Out,' I told her, and carried on walking.

Mark was going to have some explaining to do after I was done with him, that was sure. He wouldn't have much info to go on though. He has no recollection of what I get up to while I'm wearing him, I make sure of that. All he has is guesswork. Did he have too much to drink? Did he take a spill, knock his head and black out? Did the light from a full moon turn him into a werewolf? (those are real by the way, plus vampires, trolls and witches. No such thing as mermaids though. Mermaids are for chumps).

And look, in case you're left with some lingering wisp of sympathy for poor old Mark—some *moulded by a bad upbringing* guff—you should know this: on top of being a bully, a womaniser, and an all-round subhuman piece of shit, Mark Ryan is a hedge fund manager.

Yup.

So, I headed for the canal to meet DCI Stronge, my conscience clean and my spirit cosy inside of my meat puppet. A dead woman needed my help. A dead woman with a curious lack of skin.

3

I call myself a P.I.

The "P" can stand for "Private" or "Paranormal", that's up to you. Here's the main thing you need to know: I'm basically Magnum in that old TV show, except I wouldn't be seen dead in one of his shirts, and I mean that literally (full disclosure: I did attempt the moustache once but ended up looking like the type of bloke who hangs around school playgrounds. That 'tache was *sparse*).

As a P.I., I help tortured spirits find peace by solving the mystery of their untimely ends. Why do I do it? Well, I figure if I do enough good deeds in the time that I have left on Earth, I'll earn a spot in the Good Place. Thing is, right now I'm not so sure I'm on the guest list. Matter of fact, I'm more than pretty sure I'm not. If the Man Upstairs has a shit list, I expect I rank pretty high on the thing. Like I said before, I'll come back to that. It's a whole saga.

For now, let's get back to the task at hand.

Wearing Mark's body, I arrived at the crime scene at a little after one in the morning. The old bill had set up a secure perimeter around the canal, guarded by a couple of uniforms in reflective jackets and pointy hats. I flashed my ID at the constables and they nodded and let me duck the crime scene tape.

I made a beeline for Detective Chief Inspector Stronge, who was heading up the investigation. Kat, as she occasionally lets me call her, is a hell of an officer. A no-nonsense, work-horse of a woman with a sharp mind and the cheekbones to match. She's also the detective responsible for locking up my killer—with a little help from yours truly—but again, that's a story for another time.

Since putting my murderer behind bars, Stronge's been promoted to the rank of DCI and the pair of us have struck up a professional friendship. Of course, she has no idea that I'm a ghost inhabiting another man's body, or that I'm the same guy whose murder she solved five years ago. Reckon I'll keep that to myself for a bit. Maybe save it for our third date.

I work for DCI Stronge as a "psychic consultant". She took me for a piss-taker when we first met, but it didn't take me long to prove my value. Turns out I have an eerie knack for solving murders – finding clues, unearthing motives, fingering suspects (not literally). Of course, these things are easy to come by when you have the luxury of consulting the victim's ghost. Eighty percent of the victims I talk to already know who it was that killed them. I mean, it's usually someone they know. A friend. A spurned lover. A business associate. A rival. A lot of the time I just have to ask, *Who did it?* then find the best way to steer the law at them.

I saw Stronge across the way, illuminated by a tripod flood-light. She was dressed in a black quilted jacket and an entirely sensible pair of trousers. A huddle of forensics officers in boiler suits crowded around her, making her look like a black sheep among a flock of white.

I met Stronge in the doorway of an evidence tent, which had been set up to conceal the vic's dead body.

'Morning,' I said, and handed her a coffee I'd picked up on the way.

She gave it a sniff. 'It's not that castrated, decaff shit, is it?'

'Nope. Cup of lightning, just the way you like it.'

She took a sip and nodded a thank you. 'I was starting to think you weren't going to show.'

I widened my eyes theatrically. 'And miss all this?'

The faintest glimpse of a smile quirked her lips. God, I loved that smile. It was the hard-won type, the kind you had to chisel from stone.

She coughed and the smile was gone. 'Let's get to work.'

She nodded to the forensics officer inside the tent, who bent down and peeled back a tarp.

There it was, the corpse, female and naked—extremely naked—not even wearing her birthday suit. The woman's dermis had been expertly removed, stripped from the body like the skin from a rabbit. The blood on her exposed muscles shone slick and glossy under the LEDs of the surrounding lamps. It looked as though she'd been hung upside down and dipped in blood, like tallow into red wax.

'Jesus,' I muttered. 'She's going to need a hell of a dermatologist.'

Call me callous if you like, but someone had to let the air out of the room.

'Any news to share yet?' I asked.

Stronge shook her head. 'Early days. She has no ID on her, well, no *anything* on her.'

'She have her teeth still?'

'Yeah, but IDing her dentals is going to take time, and there's no saying we'll get anything anyway.' Stronge raked a hand through her bob. 'Well, what do you make of it?'

'Not sure yet. I'm going to need to do my thing – the ol' psychic bit, just me and the body.' I bent down to examine the corpse. 'Alone.'

A second plainclothes officer barged into the frame wearing a thick camel overcoat. 'Oh, you'd love that, wouldn't you?' he barked, spittle flying.

Ladies and Gentlemen, meet DI Maddox, Detective Stronge's partner and a royal pain in my dead arse. While his colleague is something of a paranormal sceptic, Maddox is a straight up heretic.

'Why don't you fuck off home and play with your ouija board?' he inquired.

I refused to meet his eye, choosing instead to stare at the top of his head, which was bald and shiny like an ice rink for fleas.

'Mr Fletcher is here under my invitation,' Stronge told him.

'What's wrong with you?' he asked her. 'Why do you keep entertaining this con artist? You know people back at the nick take the piss?'

Stronge shot him a look that could melt steel beams. 'I'm the lead on this case, Maddox. If you don't like it, I suggest you take it up with the Super.'

Maddox went to say something but thought better of it. He turned to me. 'Five minutes,' he growled, 'then you can piss off to the nearest graveyard and get your rocks off there.'

'I will, DI Maddox, your Great Granny's expecting me.'

He took a step at me, only for Stronge to move in front of him. 'Five minutes, okay?' she said.

Maddox stomped away.

Stronge turned to me. 'Do you really have to be alone with the body?'

'I'm afraid so, Detective.'

She shook her head and sighed. 'You'd better come back with something good for me.'

Stronge left, closing the flap of the tent behind her and retreating to a respectable distance. Only after the scene was clear did I turn to the presence that had been watching me since I'd arrived.

A ghost.

The phantom spirit of the body dredged from the canal.

She looked a lot better with her skin on: waif-thin and top-heavy, with one of those faces that looked like it was cut from something rare and expensive. She had husky-blue eyes, a beauty spot right where it should be, and perfect, Cupid's bow lips. Her glowing, blonde hair cast a halo about her head, making her look less like a ghost than an angel. The woman was stunning. Catwalk quality.

'Hello,' I said, letting her know I could see her but trying not to letch. 'My name's Jake. Jake Fletcher.'

'You're like me, aren't you?' she said. 'Inside.'

She could see through my meat suit to the man within. Us ghosts can do that.

'That's right,' I replied. 'I'm here to help.'

'I'm dead,' she replied in her perfect, cut-glass voice. 'How are you going to help a dead person?'

I get that a lot.

'I can help you get to the next place,' I explained. 'That's what I do.'

'The next place?'

'Take it from me, you don't want to get stuck down here forever. No, there's somewhere else you're meant to be, and it's my job to get you there. But first I need know what happened to you.'

I had five minutes to get what I needed, and time was running out.

Her face wrinkled and two perfect rivers of tears raced down her cheeks. 'Oh God, I'm really dead, aren't I? How can I be dead?'

'Look, I know it's hard but you have to tell me what happened. I can only help you pass over if you let me know who did this.'

'I don't know!' she said between sobs. 'He was wearing a mask. One of those... what do you call those things... the ski masks...?'

'Like Jason?'

'No, that's a hockey mask!'

'Oh, you mean like a balaclava.'

'Yes. A balaclava.'

'What else can you tell me? Anything at all, it doesn't matter how small.'

She nodded and got a hold of herself. 'Sorry, I'm just a bit, you know…'

'Hey, I understand, believe me. You've just been murdered, that sort of thing can spin you out a bit. But you have to tell me what you remember. Come on, you can do this.'

She nodded and pushed away her tears. 'He came at me from behind. He had a rag. Knocked me out.'

'Then what?' I asked.

'When I woke up it was just me and him in a dark room. I didn't see much before he came at me with the rag again. When I woke up that time he was gone. I wasn't tied up or anything, but I was woozy and I hurt all over. I felt like… like my whole body was a paper cut and someone had poured lemon juice into me. It wasn't until I looked down that I realised I was bleeding. Bleeding everywhere.'

I felt the human suit I was wearing grimace.

She went on. 'I ran for help but I only made it a little way before I passed out. Next thing I knew, I was looking down at my own dead body. That's all I know, I promise.'

I forced a smile. 'That's excellent,' I told her. 'Plenty to get me started.'

'Really?'

Well, no, but I wasn't about to tell her that, so I changed the subject. 'I just have a couple more questions…'

'Anything.'

I placed a hand over hers. 'Why don't we start with a name?'

She told me her name was Ingrid. Ingrid Vallens.

Yup, you heard right. Former supermodel and Nineties "it" girl, Ingrid Vallens.

I thought I smelled catwalk on her but I had no idea I was chit-chatting with the undisputed queen of lingerie models.

Some people are so famous your mind just can't handle it. It's like your eyes know the truth, but your brain tells you *no way*. *No way* can this be the girl from all those music videos and perfume ads. There she was though, *Ingrid frigging Vallens*. Model turned fashion consultant, Ingrid Vallens. Ambitious, enterprising, and filthy rich. The kind of woman Beyonce likes to sing about. Ingrid Vallens. And some sick bastard had stolen her perfect skin.

I played it cool. 'What else can you tell me about yourself, Ms Vallens?'

I got her next of kin, National Insurance number, home address, everything I needed to stick it to Maddox. I got her DoB too: 3rd February 1974. A bit of subtraction told me that put her at forty-two years old, which came as a bit of a shock seeing as she didn't look a day over thirty.

I jotted down her details and snapped my Moleskine shut. 'Thanks, Ingrid, that's a big help.'

'What happens now?' she asked.

'Now I start my investigation.'

Her brow knitted. 'So you're just going to leave me here?'

I forced a smile. 'I have to, it's the only way.'

'Can't I come with you?'

'You have to stay here, near the site of your... passing.'

'Then how come you get to go gallivanting about the place?'

'It's different for me, I know how to make the ghost thing work.'

In the five years I've been a phantom I've picked up a few tricks, not least of which is being able to stay anchored to the material plane. I'm a rare diamond though, most ghosts stay pretty rooted, but not me. My best guess is that it's something to do with me having had an inside track on the Uncanny before I snuffed it.

'If you were to go wandering from here you'd get lost,' I told Ingrid.

'I know my way around London, thank you.'

'Not that kind of lost. I'm talking about your soul. Drift too far from this point and you'd risk losing it for good, or worse.'

'What do you mean, *worse*? How could it possibly get any worse than this?'

I was hoping she wouldn't ask that. 'Sometimes instead of turning insubstantial, a ghost can turn... well, feral.'

'Like an animal?'

'Sort of. They're known as "malevolent spirits" or "shades". The kind of ghosts you read about in horror stories: your wailing, chain-rattling phantoms.'

Turning feral wasn't limited to her moving location either. The longer she spent trapped between this world and the next, the more likely she was to go full banshee.

'Okay then,' she said, casting her eyes to the ground. 'I'll stay here.'

'Good. Plant your arse for now, I won't be long.'

I could see Maddox and Stronge marching my way. My five minutes were up.

'Jake,' said Ingrid. 'Why would someone want to kill me?'

'I don't know,' I told her, 'but trust me, Ingrid, I'm going to find out.'

Maddox arrived wearing his trademark scowl. 'You're out of time, Fletcher. So tell us, oh mighty Oracle, what have you got?'

I tore a page from my Moleskine and handed it to him. 'Just a name, address and DoB. I only wish I could give you something useful.' I practically fluttered my eyelashes at the turd.

He scanned my notes. 'Are you taking the piss? Ingrid Vallens? As in Victoria's Secret model, Ingrid Vallens?'

'Yes. I'm sure there's a lot more to her than a nice body though.' I looked past him and gave Ingrid a sly wink.

Stronge took the scrap of paper from her partner and sighed. 'This seems a bit unlikely, Fletcher.'

Maddox put it more succinctly. 'You're a fucking con artist, mate.'

'Just run the details then give me a basket of muffins when you're up to speed,' I told him. 'I don't have time to piss about.'

As I turned and walked away, Maddox sang me a refrain.

'You're about as useful as a fucking magic 8-ball, Fletcher.'

I headed to the Camden Tavern for a breather and a pint. It was past closing time but they knew my face there (well, Mark's face), so they let me break the lock-in and come inside.

I ordered a tap beer and found a seat in the corner under an old print of two Victorian pugilists squaring off in a boxing ring. It felt good to take the weight off Mark's feet. I exhaust pretty easily when I'm forced to tote his big lump of a body all over the place.

Looking around, I watched the other patrons milling about, wasted, the lot of 'em, staggering to and fro as if the ground beneath them were the deck of a storm-tossed boat. I took a sup of my pint. It tasted like heaven. As a ghost, I don't get to drink, or eat, or even breathe. If I couldn't take control of a person's body from time to time, I don't know what I'd do. Those simple, earthly pleasures are everything to me. It's only the thought of sinking a beer from time to time that keeps me from going completely doolally.

A woman walked past me on her way to the bar; attractive, put together, a little stern-looking. She reminded me of Sarah, my ex-wife. The two of us were in love once, back when I was alive, before she went mental and started acting like a thing possessed. I didn't need that. Got enough of it from the day job, thank you very much.

I reached into my pocket, pulled out a Twix bar and unwrapped the packet. I took out one of the fingers and gave it a sniff. It's important to savour the good things in life, take it from a dead man. I sucked the chocolate off the Twix, right down to the biscuit. Jesus H Christ, it tasted good, but then I'm a man of simple tastes. When you're used to working the night shift, you tend to eat anything you can get your hands on, and that suits me fine. I've always been a Scotch egg in a service station kind of guy.

I finished off the Twix and drained the last of my beer. Mark's body was beginning to twitch around me, trembling like I was stuck in a meat locker. I always hated this part. It was time to give Mark his body back before it unceremoniously ejected me. Ordinarily, I'd leave him in the pub once I was done with him – stick ten empty pint glasses in front of the bloke and let him join the dots. Tonight I was feeling puckish though. Tonight Mark had a date with an alleyway, a dry bottle of White Lightning, and a condom tucked where the sun don't shine.

4

You know that Jon Bon Jovi line, "I'll sleep when I'm dead"? Well, it turns out the dead don't get that luxury, at least not if they ended up a ghost like I did.

I do have a place I go to when the working day's done, though. A place to spend my downtime. Somewhere I can put my feet up and pass the hours while the rest of the city snoozes. Since I don't need a bedroom, I set myself up in an office block in Chalk Farm. It's a bit dilapidated, but that's to be expected since no one but me works there anymore. Apparently the place is haunted. Awful business.

The building is a converted gin warehouse. It has a lift with a folding shutter door that takes you up five floors. The top one is where you'll find me. Actually, you won't, not since I'm invisible. What you will find—if you're nosy and brave enough—is one semi-furnished office with a panoramic view of Camden Town. I like to think of the place as my little patch of London. There's a desk there and an old office chair I sit on when I'm talking to clients about potential jobs. Potential "psychic investigation" jobs that is. I prefer to take bookings by phone as it disguises the fact that I don't have a body. People can be weird about that.

Aside from a simple office setup, the only other item of furniture I own is a TV/DVD player combo perched on a milk crate next to a pile of boxed sets and old movies. Changing the channel on the thing is a bitch. Even now, with all the practice I've had, picking up a remote is like working with a giant pair of Mickey Mouse gloves that keep turning into smoke.

With no small amount of trouble, I set the TV to AV1 and pressed play on a DVD. Movies are a great release for me, and the best way I know to chalk off some hours before the sun comes up. My favourite kind of movies are ghost movies, which I watch for the pleasure of yelling at them whenever I spot an inaccuracy. What can I tell you, a man needs a hobby.

The target of this evening's ridicule was the Patrick Swayze/Demi Moore vehicle, *Ghost*. I was only twenty minutes into it before I was mouthing off at the screen.

'Bullshit! A tunnel of light? As if!' I hollered, as Swayze turned down his ticket to heaven so he could chase around after his Grumpy Gus girlfriend.

Ten minutes later, Swayze was having it out with some hobo on the subway and I was calling foul again. 'He's a droopy-faced old man! Just give him a punch in the bracket!'

Next thing I know, Swayze's waltzing into the shop of some spiritual advisor. 'Oh yeah, right!' I cried, 'because Whoopi Goldberg's going to solve all your problems!'

Maybe it was the day I'd had. Maybe it was seeing what some scumbag had done to Ingrid Vallens, I don't know, but I was in no mood. I picked up the remote and hurled it at the TV screen, not hard enough to break it, but hard enough to give me some degree of satisfaction.

That's when something weird happened.

No, not weird, downright terrifying.

Whoopi Goldberg turned, looked right down the barrel of the camera, and spoke to me.

'You've been a naughty boy, Jake Fletcher,' she said.

I yelped and scrabbled away from the telly like the chick from *The Ring* had crawled out of it.

Was I dreaming? Of course I wasn't, I've already established that I don't sleep. At least try to keep up.

Whoopi went on as her co-stars stayed on pause. 'Your running days are over, Jake. We're coming for you. You have to answer for the things you've done.'

'Who are you?' I asked.

Something told me I wasn't really being addressed by the EGOT-winning actress and popular daytime television host.

'You drifted from His light, Jake. You revolted against God.'

It must be one of the Big Man's stooges, I thought. After five years on the lam, He was finally turning His attention to me. That didn't add up to anything good.

Thing is, like I hinted at earlier, I did some bad stuff back in my corporeal days, and it turns out He took them kind of personally. Don't get me wrong, I never meant to be a sinner, I was just... misguided. Like I say, I used to be an exorcist by trade—the only agnostic exorcist in the phonebook, thank you very much—and my job training was something I kind of pieced together myself. I thought I was doing the lost souls I dealt with a kindness, releasing them from their suffering and returning them to the Great Beyond.

Apparently, I was way off.

The fact is, I was obliterating those poor bastards. Annihilating them. Exorcisms, as it turns out, are for banishing malevolent forces, not for relocating fragile, earthly spirits. I didn't know it at the time, but I was throwing the baby out with the bathwater on a daily basis. So many souls just... gone. By the time I learned the folly of what I was doing, it was already too late. I was dead. Time up. Off to meet my maker, and I wasn't expecting him to roll out the red carpet for me.

So, here I am, a phantom on the run, trying to do as much good as I can to cancel out the bad before I'm made to answer for my misdeeds.

Whoopi glared at me through the TV screen, her eyes unnaturally bright – luminescent even. 'Well then, what do you have to say for yourself, Fletcher?'

'Listen, I did some bad things, okay? I hold my hands up to that. But I'm on the right track now, all right? Scout's honour.'

'Go on,' she said, cocking her head to one side.

'I have a case... I'm helping a lost soul find her way back home. Back home to *you*. That's got to be worth something, right?'

'You think that's going to save you, Fletcher? You think one, paltry soul is going to rescue you from damnation? From an eternity in Hell? After all the souls you turned to nothing?'

'It's the ghost of Ingrid Vallens,' I said.

That caught Whoopi's interest. 'As in noted lingerie model, Ingrid Vallens?'

'That's the kiddie.'

Whoopi stared at me for a second then turned to one side as though she was being talked to by somebody standing off screen. She turned back to me, muttering something under her breath. 'Very well, Jake Fletcher, you have bought yourself some time. But know this – if the soul of Ingrid Vallens isn't delivered to us in one week's time, I will come down there, and I will drag you back here myself.'

Suddenly, the light went out of Whoopi's eyes and she returned to her scripted dialogue.

I looked at my hands. They were shaking.

Five years it took them.

I was starting to think they're never find me.

But now they had my number.

5

Sun up, back at Regent's Canal.

Eager to press forward with my case, I'd chosen to follow the next stage of the investigation au naturel, using my ghost form to tag along with Stronge and Maddox incognito.

I was dressed in a black suit and tie, the same duds I was wearing on my deathday. That's the way it works with ghosts, we get stuck with the last look we had in life. Good news for those of us who dressed up nice for the occasion, bad news for the poor sods who drowned in the bathtub.

By daylight, the police had discovered a set of bloody footprints leading from the crime scene to the location Ingrid had taken flight from. The prints led into a disused warehouse along the wharf, one of the few in the area that had yet to be converted into luxury flats. The building was surrounded by a chain-link fence, but the blood trail led through a snipped out portion—likely the work of squatters—that Ingrid had managed to escape through.

I followed the police officers through the hole, across some broken tarmac, and into the warehouse. The interior was dark, dusty and mostly empty, save for a few wooden pallets, some empty shelves, and a clapped out forklift. The forensics team were on site already, dressed in protective clothing and shoe baggies, analysing blood spatter, collecting evidence, poring over the scene. I watched them drifting around in their white boiler suits and thought they looked more like ghosts than I did.

Stronge weaved between cordons and approached the Scene of Crime Officer. 'So, what do we have?'

The officer tugged down his face mask and pulled back his hood. 'So far we have hair, some soil samples, and a whole lot of blood.'

Stronge nodded. That much was to be expected. 'Fingerprints?'

'Nothing yet.'

Maddox chimed in. 'Anything else?'

'As a matter of fact, yes.'

I shadowed the officer as he led the detectives down a thin corridor marked by police tape. The space either side of us was a hub of activity, a crowd of CSIs performing fingertip searches, crawling over the scene like army ants. Having squeezed between them, we arrived at a cluster of evidence tags surrounded by a cordon of police tape. A photographer was leaning over it, taking snaps of what was inside.

There, drawn on the floor in lines of white chalk, was a pattern: a series of intersecting circles enclosed in a large square. The corners of the square were marked by candles, now just puddles of wax. I'd seen similar things in my former business as an exorcist. From the looks of things, Ingrid had been used as a blood sacrifice, an offering to win the favour of a demon.

Oh yeah, those are real too.

There's a whole world that exists beneath the surface of the one most people know. Us Insiders call it the Uncanny. Ever since I was a kid I knew it was there – knew there was more to the story than I was being told. I could see them, the things that shouldn't exist: the ghosts, the demons, the boogeymen. It wasn't until I died that I learned about the rest: the witches, the warlocks, the imps, the skinwalkers, and that's just the start of it. I'm talking hidden streets, sewers infested with fairies, even a succubus-run, anything-goes sex club in Soho that I may or may not poke my nose into from time to time. Hey, I may not have taken advantage of Mark's bit on the side, but I'm a ghost, not an angel.

The fact is, all manner of bonkers shit is going on in London that you normals don't know a thing about, but it's every much a part of the city as your local corner shop, and it's happening right under your noses.

Still, something wasn't right here. The realm of the Uncanny is meant to live alongside the world as you see it, not collide with it. It's not a free-for-all, with ghouls and goblins scampering through the streets of London Town. There are things that shouldn't be able to crash into the normal world, at least not without a great deal of effort. One of those things is demons. Demons belong in Hell, just like angels belong in Heaven. Even for the most skilled magician, drawing a demon into the physical world is hard work. Summoning a demon capable of skinning someone alive would be like trying to push a water balloon through a brick wall.

I watched a forensics officer take a scoop of chalk from the pattern on the floor and deposit it into a Sure-Seal bag. I felt a chill – the kind ghosts aren't meant to feel. If something like that could be pulled off, summoning a demon, what could that mean for reality as we knew it? Could it be that the barriers were weakening somehow? The stitches popping? Whatever was happening, long-term, it didn't fill me with rainbows and smiles.

I looked closer at the chalk pattern on the ground. It was a warding symbol: defensive magic to make sure the summoned demon was kept in check. A barrier to stop the guest murdering its conjurer before a bargain could be struck. So, we had a sacrifice, a ward, and a demon. Only one thing missing: a lure. A summons targeted at a specific demonic entity. Without one of those, the conjurer might as well throw his invitation into the wind.

While the authorities chatted among themselves, I scanned the area looking for the missing lure. It took me a while, but I found it a few yards from the site of the sacrifice, lodged under a rack of dented aluminium shelves. It looked as though it had been knocked aside, most likely by Ingrid as she fled for her life. The lure was a ram's skull with a sigil etched into its forehead. An infinity symbol with two evil eyes staring out from the holes.

There was that chill again.

6

I went to an old friend for her view on what I'd seen.

My friend goes by the name of Madame Olena, but I call her Jazz Hands on account of her being a magician. Jazz Hands is a serious woman with the wisdom of a million fortune cookies. She's also the proprietor of a premises called Legerdomain, a dusty little magic shop tucked away in a King's Cross back alley; stage props on the shelves, real magic under the counter.

I arrived at Jazz's shop in an instant. It's a skill I have. If I picture a place I'm familiar with and think about it hard enough, I can just kind of go there. In a comic book they'd probably call it something fruity like "translocation" or "teleportation". Like it was a superpower. Personally, I prefer not to think of it that way. Superpowers are for 'roided up beefcakes buzzing around in their jammies – I'm just a working class pleb with a couple of tricks up his sleeve. Superman doesn't know how easy he has it – just about everything is my Kryptonite. Being dead ain't all it's cracked up to be, you know? As a ghost, the simple act of kicking a ball about without my foot passing through the thing is a ball-ache. Plus, I'm invisible to anyone without The Sight, which is about as annoying as it is useful.

Oh, and like a London cabbie refusing to go south of the River, I can't cross large bodies of water either.

Still, being able to zap from one place to the next comes in pretty handy.

I appeared in the middle of Jazz's magic shop atop a Turkish rug that's more hole than thread. The surrounding decor was the same as ever, liver-red walls and bowed black shelves heaving with all manner of magical knick-knacks and doo-dads, all lit by the scant shafts of sunlight that managed the penetrate the store's grimy windows.

An entry bell tinkled, and the woman behind the counter sat up straight on her stool. I wouldn't have tripped an ordinary chime, but there was no getting one over on Jazz Hands. She'd rigged a bell with magic, ensuring that it sounded whenever a ghost entered her premises, or more accurately, when *I* entered her premises.

'Can I help you?' she asked, not looking up from her magazine.

'No thanks, just browsing,' I replied.

Jazz Hands closed her mag and sighed. It's funny, she acts like she spends all her spare time studying up on ancient grimoires, but every time I catch her, she's got her nose buried in a celebrity gossip rag.

She reached down for a pair of pince-nez hanging on a chain around her neck and perched them on her nose. Right away her eyes landed on me. See, as well as the early warning system, she'd also manufactured a pair of violet-lensed glasses that allowed her to see ghosts. I guess you'd call them "spooktacles", but only if you were an utter wanker.

Jazz addressed me in a croaky voice that told me this was her first conversation of the day. 'If you're planning a visit, I'd prefer you called ahead instead of appearing in the middle of my shop like a bloody—'

'Ghost?'

'Precisely.'

Since she was apparently entertaining guests, she checked her reflection in the blade of a trick guillotine and smoothed down her frizzy brown hair. Jazz Hands wasn't exactly what you'd call a looker, but with the right light and a bit of slap, she had a kind of schoolmarmish charm.

'Well,' she said, 'are you going to stand there like a lemon or are you going to tell me why you're here?'

She acts all tough and spiky, but she loves me really. Besides, she has her uses. What Jazz Hands knows about the Uncanny could fill an aircraft hangar.

'Got a new case,' I told her.

She reluctantly set her magazine on her lap. The graphic close-ups of celebrity cellulite and tales of Khloe Kardashian's troubled marriage would have to wait.

'Very well then. Get on with it.'

I brought her up to speed. The skinned supermodel, the black magic ritual, the contents of the warehouse. Everything.

'A ram's skull?' she said. 'A bit bread and butter, don't you think? Oh, for a wayward magician with a little imagination...'

'This one had a carving on it. An infinity symbol with two eyes inside.'

'Hmmm,' she replied, and pulled a dusty old bestiary from under the counter. 'Like this?' she asked, flicking to a tab and showing me the page.

I was presented with a black and white plate of a goat's skull. It was engraved with a collapsed 8 dotted with two pupils, and was a dead match for the one found at the crime scene.

'That's the kiddie,' I told her. 'So, I get what it's for, but what's it supposed to summon?'

Her expression turned grave. 'The lure calls on a demon said to be able to grant its summoner the power of everlasting youth.'

'Righty-oh. One of them Faustian pack deals; The Devil Went to Georgia and all that.'

'You should take this more seriously,' she said, and leafed forwards a couple of pages to point at another plate. 'Look...'

She showed me a woodcut of... well, I hesitate to call it a creature even. It looked like a skeleton, with a slippery layer of flesh covering a set of long, sinewy limbs. It had claws as sharp as steak knives and two smouldering eyes that burned with unholy malice. Real nightmare fuel, this thing.

'They call it "fuere epulone", Jazz Hands explained.

'In English?'

'The soul feaster.'

Nasty. 'Well, at least it's out of our hair now.'

'How's that?'

'Not to tell you your job, Jazz, but a demon returns to its realm after a bargain is struck.

Them's the rules.

She shrugged. 'Maybe, maybe not. Demons are tricky buggers. If this one managed to find a way to break through the summoner's ward, it could be out there still... and hungry.'

In case you didn't figure it out from what I said earlier, that's bad. Demons are meant to keep to their plane, not go running around London willy nilly. I remembered the strange feeling I had back at the wharf and suppressed another shiver.

'That doesn't add up,' I argued. 'If the demon had gone AWOL, we'd be looking at two dead bodies right now: the sacrifice and the summoner.'

'Not if the demon *ate* the summoner.' She followed the book's text with her finger, translating it from Latin as she read. 'The demon feasts on souls, but it also has a taste for human flesh. To remain on the material plane, it needs to consume both.'

She snapped the book shut, making it puff a cloud of dust.

If Jazz was right and the demon was out there still, things were likely to get pretty dicey around these parts. And bloody. Not to mention deathy. A runaway demon is not the sort of thing you take on lightly. Or at all, if you've got any sense in you. But this was my case, and I'd made a promise to Ingrid Vallens.

'Don't even think about it,' said Jazz, as if reading my mind.

'What?' I protested.

'This isn't your fight, Fletcher. There are beings in this city far more suited to taking on the things that go bump in the night.'

'I am a thing that goes bump in the night!'

'You know what I mean. This is too dangerous for you. Besides, you need to keep a low profile if you want to stay off *His* radar.'

Yeah, it was a little too late for that.

'I appreciate the concern,' I told her, 'but the walls are closing in. I was given a message last night – some emissary of God telling me that if I don't solve this case in a week, that I'm going back upstairs to answer for my sins. I can't have that, Jazz. Because call me a handsome ol' cynic, but I don't think there's anything good waiting for me up there.'

I had to solve Ingrid's murder, had to rub some of that red ink out of my account, because right now it looked like Carrie on prom night.

Jazz stared back at me, her mouth set in a hard line. 'You're an idiot.'

'You've got that right,' I said, 'so, are you going to help me or not?'

She shook her head and muttered something sweary under her breath. 'What do you need?'

I smiled. 'Let's start with the summoner. What can you tell me about the person who conjured this soul eater thing?'

'So long as you're determined to pull at this thread, I'd start your investigation with the Order of the Everlasting Flame. They're a group of magicians dedicated to the pursuit of eternal life. If you're looking to find someone desperate enough to summon the soul feaster, the Order would be a good place to start.'

'Okay. So where do I find these nutters?'

She shrugged. 'That I don't know.'

'What? I thought you knew everything about the hocus pocus in this town.'

'Not everything.'

'You managed to track me down easy enough, back in the day.'

'You were hardly a four-leaf clover.'

Fair do's.

It looked like I was going to have to get my intel from someone a bit more in touch with the streets. Thankfully, I knew just the man.

'Cheers for the help, Jazz,' I said, and prepared to make haste.

'Hold your horses,' she said, and ducked under the counter. 'I have something here that will help...'

She resurfaced with a ring.

'Jazz, this is all so sudden. But yes, yes, a thousand times yes!'

She looked at me like I'd crimped off a turd on her Turkish rug.

'Tough crowd.'

'Here you go, chuckles,' she said, holding out the ring.

I took it off her and rolled it over in my palm. Jazz Hands was a dab hand at enchanting, and had perfected a spell that made certain items tangible to me. Usually, solid objects pass through my body like a dodgy madras, but once Jazz had worked her magic, I could touch them, hold them, even wear them.

I examined the ring closer. It had a silver band and was set with an opal-like stone of shifting colours. I was *really* hoping for something I could use against a demon. A weapon, the more dangerous the better. 'What is this, some kind of mood ring?' I asked, squinting at the thing. 'What colour is "disappointed?"'

Jazz Hands shot me a wicked frown. 'It detects lies,' she said. 'Hold it up to the person you're questioning and it will tell you if they're being honest with you. If what they're saying is true, it will glow blue in colour. If it's a lie, it will turn red.'

'That's it? A voodoo truth detector? Can't you knock me up something with a bit more oomph? A demon laser or something?'

She blinked twice. Slowly. '*A demon laser?*'

'No?'

'You ungrateful shit.'

I laughed. 'Aw, you love me really.'

'I certainly do not.'

I held the ring up to her and it turned red. As a blush mounted her cheeks, the colour of her face was quick to follow.

'See you around, sweet cheeks,' I said, and disappeared with a wink before the swearing really started.

7

I went to Frosty for the low-down.

Frosty's a homeless guy I know, a victim of the Tories austerity measures. He used to get disability benefits for his gammy legs, but when the DWP declared him Fit to Work (despite him being no such thing), he lost everything. With no other way of looking after himself, he was forced to take to the streets begging. He didn't last long. There was a cold snap that winter, and Frosty didn't see the other side of it. The poor bugger froze to death on Camden High Street, and he lies there still, a ghost.

'What's up, feller?' I asked as I knelt down beside him.

He coughed and hawked up a blob of ectoplasm. 'What do you want, Fletcher?'

He didn't look well, but then he never did. Dying of hypothermia will do that to a man.

'I need to pick your brains,' I told him.

'You're out of luck,' he replied, 'I haven't had one of those in donkeys yonks.' He cackled as he poked a finger into his head, right up to the knuckle. The cackle quickly turned into a hacking cough that led to another delightful eruption of ectoplasm, spat just to the side of me. I shuffled away from the up-chuck as it trickled towards my shoes.

You might wonder why I'd choose to hang about with such a charmer, but Frosty is without a doubt the most useful ghost I've ever met. No one's more in touch with the streets than old Frost, and I mean that in every sense of the phrase. His pitch is a spot of pavement under a Sainsbury's cashpoint – a patch of pavement he's permanently frozen to. You'd think this would limit his power to know things, but you'd be dead wrong. See, where some ghosts can phase through solid objects and *ahem* *teleport*, Frosty has a different skill set.

From his vantage point, he's able to read the minds of anyone he comes in contact with. Even better, he's able to get a read on anyone that person has come in contact with, and the person they were in contact with before that, and so on and so on. It's a whole six-degrees of separation thing. Thanks to that, Frosty knows pretty much everything that goes on in this neighbourhood. After all, everyone knows something.

A short queue of people lined up at the ATM, oblivious to the two ghosts chatting by their side. As a young woman stepped up to the machine to withdraw a couple of twenties, Frosty stole a look up her skirt.

'Nice,' he perved. 'Have a butchers at that, Fletcher. No knickers, and she's shaved it into a little heart.'

'I'd love to take you up on that, Frost, but I'm a gentleman.'

He snorted. 'You're dead, live a little.'

'That's a hard pass.'

'Ooh, I'm so sorry, Your Majesty,' he growled. 'Look, are you going to get to the point or what?'

Business time. 'I'm looking for a cult calling themselves the Order of the Everlasting Flame. Got anything in the memory banks?'

'Maybe I have, maybe I haven't.'

'Have you?'

'Who's to say?'

'You. You're the one to say.'

'Perhaps I am, perhaps I'm not.'

I sighed and stood, play acting like I was about to walk away. 'Well, I'd best be off then, Frosty, ol' pal. Nice seeing you.'

'All right! I've got something, I've got something!'

Bingo bango.

'Tell me.'

'Hold your horses, sunshine. First things first, have you got anything for *me*?'

This wasn't my first time dealing with the cantankerous old sod – I knew what he was after. From my jacket pocket I produced a can of Special Brew. This was no ordinary bruiser juice though. Any regular lager would pass right through the wily old lush, but this one had been blessed by Jazz Hands and made ghost-friendly, just like my new ring. I can't say she was overjoyed at the prospect of blessing cheap beer, but she's always been a sucker for the old Fletcher charm.

Frosty snatched the can of beer from my hands and glugged it down in five seconds flat. He wiped the froth from his beard, along with a few stray icicles. 'That's the stuff,' he gasped.

'So, what can you tell me about this cult?' I asked.

'What, is that it? One measly can?'

'You know the deal, Frosty. I've given you a bit of what you want, now you give me what I want. Tell me about this Everlasting Flame lot. Where do they set up shop?'

He sulked for another minute or so, then he told me.

'No way!' I said. 'There?'

'Yup.'

It just seemed so... obvious. 'You're serious. You're not shitting me?'

'Cross my heart and hope to die.'

It was a weak promise coming from a ghost, but Frosty had yet to steer me wrong. 'Thanks for the tip, me old mucker. I'll catch you later.'

'One can? One? You rotten bastard!'

I smiled, lifted a second blessed can from my other pocket and rolled it across the ground into his grasping fingers. 'Don't drink it all at once.'

He drank it all at once.

'Mind yourself, Jake. There ain't many things that can do us ghosts a mischief, but magic's one of 'em.'

He was right about that. He was right about that and then some.

8

According to Frosty, the people I needed to pay a visit were operating out of the Magic Circle. Yeah, *that* Magic Circle. Stage magicians with silk scarves doing card tricks for hen parties. Believe me, I'm as surprised as you are, but according to Frosty, the top hat and tails stuff is all a front. Just like Jazz Hands, the Order of the Everlasting Flame like to hide in plain sight.

I arrived at the Magic Circle's HQ under the cloak of night. The address was a nondescript building not far from Euston Station. Well, nondescript so long as you weren't looking too hard. To the trained eye, the place stuck out like a sore thumb.

There was a cage around the building, a magical field that enclosed it from top to bottom. The cage throbbed with magical power, its bars strobing, spitting out purple sparks. It was as though the thing were electrified, but electrified with the Uncanny.

The cage presented a problem. Being a ghost usually makes it a piece of piss to get inside places—kind of like having an Access All Areas pass to the entire world—but this joint was strictly invite only. Anyone wanting to get in there had better know a thing or two about magic.

Thankfully, I knew plenty.

Back in the day, I studied it all: theurgy, thaumaturgy, tarot, Gnosticism, Enochian chants, the Quabalah, Left Hand occultism, and a healthy dose of Hitchens to balance out all the bollocks. While the rest of my friends were busy chasing skirt, I was reading ancient texts and learning about the pagans. When you're born with The Sight—with a connection to the Uncanny that no one else around you can see or feel—you make it your business to investigate the esoteric. By the time I graduated from art school and my peers were drifting into temp jobs, I'd started to practice magic. Nothing major, just a few cantrips and such. I stuck with it though, learned some new tricks along the way, and one of those tricks was getting into places I shouldn't be.

I spoke the words of disenchantment, took a strobing purple bar in each hand, and the felt the cage weaken in my grip, softening like boiled spaghetti. I continued to chant, forcing the bars apart until I had them at a shoulder's width. Continuing the mantra, I squeezed myself through the gap in the cage until all that stood between me and my intention was a helpless brick wall.

I Caspered my way through that and arrived in the building's lobby. Stood before me was an impressive spiral staircase planted on an illuminated zodiac symbol. Something sparkly for the tourists to gawp at while the real magic was practiced behind closed doors.

I strained my ears and heard a muffled conversation going on upstairs. I headed off in search of it, and at the top of the steps, on the building's uppermost floor, I found a door marked PRIVATE. Of course, no room is really "private" when you're a ghost, but it always gives me a thrill to break life's little rules. I'm only human after all. Well, sort of.

Passing through the door, I found myself in the Order of the Eternal Flame's inner sanctum. The windowless clubhouse throbbed with a low, ambient hum that made the motes of dust hanging in the air quiver and dance. Display cabinets piled with all manner of magical oddments lined the walls, and in the centre of the room, throwing light and shadow all around, was a hammered iron brazier containing a large, flickering flame. Surrounding this was an engraved pentacle three metres wide with four men stood at each of its five tips, leaving one spot empty. The men faced one another dressed in cowled robes to preserve their anonymity. I suspect they were going for menacing, but despite the fancy duds and spooky decor, the gathering had the distinct whiff of an AA meeting about it.

'Hello, my name's Merlin and I have a wizard problem...'

All that was missing was the smell of stale cigarettes and a half-eaten box of Krispy Kreme.

Spying on the conclave, I roamed the room invisibly to see if I could get a better look at the four magicians. There wasn't much to go on though; the only facial features I could make out were from the bottom of the nose down, which made the identification process a mite tricky. Still, I paid attention and took note of what I saw.

One had a waxed moustache.

Another a weak jaw.

The third a Ben Affleck chin dimple.

And the last a cleft lip.

Chin Dimple broke the silence. 'Where are they?' he asked, gesturing to the empty spot of the pentacle.

'We don't know,' replied Moustachio, the eldest of the group, with an air of authority that led me to believe he was running the show.

'Isn't it obvious?' said Glass Jaw. 'We've all seen the news.'

'The murder at the canal?' said cleft lip. 'You think they were responsible for that?'

'Obviously.'

'We can't be certain,' asserted Moustachio.

Glass Jaw snorted. '*Can't be certain?* It's all they ever talked about!'

'They talked about the *theory* of it. I made it perfectly clear that the Order wouldn't stand for one of its elders meddling with demonic forces.'

'And you think they listened?'

There it was. They were in it right up to their exposed chins.

'Forgive me, Brother,' said Chin Dimple, raising his hand like a kid in class, 'but why does the Order continue to enforce this draconian policy on demonic intervention? With the correct wards, the creatures of the Nether are our playthings, to do as we bid them.'

Why they all spoke like they were playing a game of Dungeons & Dragons was anyone's guess.

Moustachio took a calming breath. 'The reason we don't practice demonology, *Brother*, is because not all demons are alike.'

This time he and Glass Jaw agreed. 'The demon our colleague wished to strike a bargain with is a creature unlike any other. Forty years ago, the elders of this Order summoned the beast to this realm, and not only did most of them die for their temerity, so too did a string of innocents.'

Cleft Lip picked up the slack. 'The authorities were as powerless as they were clueless. They pinned the murders on some nameless cannibal. Spent months chasing their tails.'

'It fell to those of us who survived the demon's wrath to send the demon back to its realm,' said Moustachio.

'How?' asked Chin Dimple.

Moustachio's shoulders went slack. 'With the seraphim sword.'

'The seraphim sword?' parroted Cleft Lip. 'The relic we keep in the museum?' He cast a look to the ground, likely toward the sub-level where the item was kept. 'I thought that was just a ceremonial piece.'

Interesting. A magic sword. I quite fancied getting a butcher's at the thing, as soon as I was done earwigging on this little chinwag.

'So,' said Chin Dimple. 'Who did it? Who wielded the sword and banished the demon?'

Glass Jaw turned to Moustachio, who looked as though he was recalling some terrible memory. 'I did,' he said, and rolled up his robe's left sleeve. The arm beneath was plastic from the elbow down. 'It was a battle hard won.'

A one-armed magician, eh? Nice gimmick I suppose, but I can't imagine he booked many kids' parties.

I was mulling that over when I came to realise that the magicians had stopped talking. I turned my attention back to the hooded group, only to find all four of them were looking dead at me. I checked my rear, thinking something must be going on behind me, and saw a shadow stretching from my heels all the way across the floor and to the room's far wall.

The brazier.

The eternal flame that burned in the centre of the pentacle must have been witchfire: a magical element that casts shadows on the ethereal and the corporeal alike.

Bollocks.

I should have seen it. I should have sized up the situation the moment I walked in, but I'd been sloppy. Being a ghost breeds a certain cockiness. Once you get used to moving around invisibly and unobstructed, it's easy to forget that the world isn't your personal playground. Easy to forget that there are things out there that can harm even the dead.

It was Glass Jaw who raised his finger first. 'There!' he cried, pointing to my dirty great shadow. 'We're not alone!'

Yup, I'd been rumbled good and proper.

Moustachio uttered an incantation and made a somatic gesture that flooded the chamber with a blinding, magenta light. When I opened my eyes, I discovered he'd somehow rendered me visible.

'Hey, neat trick, how'd you do that? Because I've got to tell you, that would really come in handy now and again.'

Moustachio threw back his cowl, continuing to aim an accusatory finger at me. 'What are you doing here?' he demanded.

I offered an apologetic shrug. 'Don't mind me gents, I'll be out of your hair in just a second.'

Time to pull a disappearing trick. I closed my eyes and imagined myself boomeranging back to Jazz Hands' magic shop, but a strange thing happened.

I didn't budge an inch.

I felt my body judder, saw it blur, like I was dropping out of focus, only to snap back into sharp, HD clarity. I tried again, but got the same result. It was a little disconcerting, I don't mind telling you.

'You're going nowhere, phantom,' said Glass Jaw, who I could see now had cast his own spell: a bubble of undulating, purple energy that surrounded me completely. Apparently, these guys had a real stiffy for the colour purple.

The bubble was somehow interfering with my hopping out of that place. Those numpties might have looked like they were playing dress up, but they were no joke. I rapped a knuckle on the side the bubble and found it hard as frozen oak. I was trapped.

'Explain yourself,' ordered Moustachio, the words falling from his mouth like a curse. 'Or suffer the consequences.'

'I came to see some card tricks, fellas, that's all—maybe a rabbit from a hat if you were in the mood—but I can see you're busy. Anyway, if you want to drop the old magic forcefield job, I'll be offski.' I started to skirt around the room, attempting to find a weak spot in the spell. There's always a weak spot with these things. Well, usually.

'Halt!' said Moustachio

'You know you can just say "stop", right?' I replied, not pausing, never mind halting.

The four magicians joined hands and began to glow as they muttered arcane words under their collective breath. Whatever they were doing was probably not going to be good news for old Jakey.

I kept moving as the purple prison surrounding me exploded with sparks. I turned to see Mustachio pointing his free hand in my direction, just as a globe of violet, sparking energy burst from it and headed in my direction. I ducked just in time and the missile missed me by inches.

I hopped up again, hands out. 'Easy fellas, there's no need for this to get—'

I didn't even see the next missile coming it was so fast, but holy shit, did I feel it. It felt like I'd run right into a wall. A wall of electricity that had collapsed on top of me. I lay on the floor, twitching, writhing in agony. Being dead, it's not often I feel pain, or much of anything really, but whatever this spell was, it hurt like a bastard.

Once the effect had worn off a bit, I was able to push myself up slightly, vision hazy, and saw Moustachio nod to his fellow elders. The four of them held their arms in the air, hands splayed, swaying in unison. I had a feeling I wasn't going to like what came next.

I was not wrong.

The magicians blasted the outside of the bubble with their combined power, and my prison began to shrink until I was the only thing contained within it. Then it shrank some more. And more.

'Guys, I feel like we've got off on the wrong foot here. How about we chalk this one up to experience and I'll be on my way, huh?'

'Tell us why you have invaded our sanctum, ghost,' roared Mustachio.

'Not until you tell me how you grew that glorious lady tickler, because mine comes in patchier than a fourteen-year-old trying to convince a barman he's of drinking age.'

'Enough, fool! Tell us the truth or prepare to die for a second time.'

He wasn't overstating the facts. While I am immune to most things—bullets, knives, the mystifying appeal of Orlando Bloom—magic can really bugger me up. Lucky for me, the guys working the enchanted trash compactor weren't the only magicians in the room.

As I mentioned already, I've always dabbled with magic, but it wasn't until I died that I fully got to grips with the Uncanny. Before then I had a trick or two at my disposal, but since I croaked, I've managed to expand my repertoire. When you've got nothing but time on your hands, you get to really dedicate yourself to a thing. Being a ghost is kind of like being an alcoholic who ditched the booze; your days suddenly start running very long. If you don't find something to fill all those extra hours, you'll go mental in no time.

'Talk!' screamed Glass Jaw, but I wasn't about to spill my guts to some crusty old spell-slinger.

They began to lower their hands, and the bubble shrank further. If I didn't act fast I was going to end up the same place as all those souls I'd evicted during my pre-dead, exorcist years. Nowhere. Scrubbed from existence. A non-entity.

There was a way out though. There always is with these things. Like I said, every spell has a weak spot, it's just a matter of finding it; like picking a lock or turning a frog back into a handsome prince.

I placed my palms on the inside of the bubble and went in search of it.

Feeling for a glitch.

A chink in the amour.

Any vulnerability I could exploit.

The bubble pressed against my back and the top of my head, forcing me to crouch into a ball. I had seconds left at best. I began to panic, turning as best I could, searching, searching, searching for the way out. Where was it?

'You were warned,' insisted Moustachio, but I wasn't paying the man much attention.

I was concentrating on my prison still, hands scrabbling, desperately searching for that sweet spot—

—when suddenly I felt it.

There it was...

A fault.

A fatal flaw.

I think I laughed out loud with relief.

I took aim and pulled back my fist, or at least pulled it back as far as I could – the bubble was so small it was like being zipped up in a sleeping bag.

I summoned all the strength I had, offered up a silent prayer to a God who probably wanted to send me to Hell, and threw my fist forward with a scream of effort.

There was a crack, and my knuckles burst right through to the other side.

I expected it to pop like a soap bubble, but instead it exploded, shattering and pelting my captors with shards of raw magic.

The elders howled in protest and prepared to lob a return barrage my way, but they were too late.

'Nice meeting you gents,' I said, 'but I've got places to be...'

Abracadabra.

And like that, I was gone.

9

I decided to pay Ingrid Vallens a visit and bring her up to speed on the story so far.

I found Ingrid pacing the canal towpath near Camden Lock, just where I'd left her. She was very happy to see me, and the feeling was mutual. To be honest, after what I'd just been through, I was happy to see anyone.

'You came back,' Ingrid trilled.

'Of course.'

She gave me a glowing smile that melted my cold heart.

'It's been ages. I thought maybe you'd left and that I was stuck here alone. Alone and dead and, oh God, it's still really strange saying that. I'm dead. I was alive and now I'm dead.'

'Yeah, it takes a minute to get your head around. Well, a bit longer than that, actually. I'm still not completely there, truth told. But hey, at least we're still, you know, "around".'

Ingrid Vallens, ex-model, and ex-alive person, offered up another glorious smile and I drank it down like nectar.

This was only my second time seeing Ingrid, but I was already starting to feel a real connection to her. The kind of connection I hadn't felt in a long time. There's something about two ghosts coming together... something pure. When you take all the physical stuff out of the picture—the rutting, the hormones, the springs and the leaks—you're left with a different kind of appreciation. An ability to enjoy someone on a purely spiritual level. Honestly, I was starting to wonder if I even wanted to solve her murder – not if it meant her going away. Not if it meant her heading off to her final reward and leaving me stuck here.

But of course I would, it was the right thing to do. Plus, after last night's chat with Whoopi Goldberg, it seemed my own future depended upon it.

'Well then,' said Ingrid, 'don't keep me hanging, did you find out who did it?'

I told her what I'd learned at the Magic Circle: that she'd been used as a blood sacrifice – killed by a magician seeking eternal life. Naturally, she was horrified. Well, you would be, wouldn't you?

'I'm sorry,' I told her, 'but it won't be long now. I'm on the right track, I promise. I'll have the bastard who did this soon enough.'

She thanked me emphatically and came in for a hug, but I stopped her. 'We can't.'

'Why not?'

'I mean we literally can't. You'd pass right through me.'

It's a sad impediment of the corporeally challenged that we're not able to experience physical contact.

Ingrid nodded sombrely. I wish I could have hugged her. God knows I did. Hug her and turn that frown she was wearing into another of those glorious smiles.

'I have to get going,' I said.

Her voice came out crumpled. 'Where to?'

'To lay some bait.'

'What do you mean, *bait*?'

'I need to draw your killer out into the open,' I explained. 'That's why I'm going to set a trap in Highgate Cemetery; to make him show himself. Once he shows, I'll have the bastard.'

'Why there? Of all the places, why a graveyard?'

It was a fair question. 'It's home ground,' I replied, and I just feel safe there, don't ask me why. Must be a ghost thing.'

She smiled that smile again, the one that warmed my non-existent heart.

'Okay then, but don't be long,' she said. 'I don't like being here alone. It feels... cold.' A tear spilled from her eye and she quickly swiped it away.

'Don't worry, Ingrid. Soon enough this will all be over, and you'll be ready to move on to a better place. Just trust me, okay?'

'I trust you, Jake.'

We said our goodbyes, then I left, heading off to my next destination, thinking of Ingrid the whole way.

Maybe one day—once I'd cleaned all that red from my account and made good with God—maybe then, something could happen between Ingrid and me. I pictured the two of us meeting up on the other side, going on a date, getting serious, making angel babies (I don't know how things work up there exactly).

I smiled.

Dying might be the best thing that ever happened to me.

10

In order for my trap to work I needed to get a message to a rogue magician, and in this town, that meant a visit to The Beehive.

Every city in England has a place like the 'Hive – an old-fashioned boozer for Uncanny types. A place where we can relax, chew the fat, and get sloshed, away from the prying eyes of you normals.

I felt my mobile vibrate in my jacket pocket. The phone was a gift from Jazz Hands; another of her handy enchantments. I sighed as it buzzed a second time. I may be dead, but even ghosts don't get to escape the sticky tendrils of the modern world. There's no rest for the wicked, as they say, and I've been more wicked than most.

I plucked the mobile from my pocket and saw Detective Kat Stronge's name shining out. I smiled and answered.

'How's my favourite Chief Inspector?'

'Overworked and underpaid,' she replied.

'What can I do you for, Detective?'

'We've hit a wall with the canal case. Hoped you might have had another, you know, "insight", or whatever you call them.'

'It's always straight to business with you. Whatever happened to the art of conversation?'

'Jake...'

'I'm working on it, Kat. These things can take time to, you know, become clear.'

I heard her sigh on the other end. 'So you have nothing. Got it.'

'Trust me, I'll have better news soon,' I replied, and I even believed it.

'One thing that always bugs me about you, Jake—'

'—I know, how can one man be blessed with charisma, good looks, *and* a sparkling sense of humour, right?'

'No.'

'You're sure?'

'I want to know how you always talk the same but your voice sounds so... off, sometimes, and only over the phone.'

Ah, yes. A smarter person would have practiced doing Mark's voice when he wasn't in his body, but I was a lousy mimic.

'Isn't it obvious?' I asked.

'No.'

'It's to do with, uh, my "gift", I said, winging it.

'Your gift?'

'Yeah. It can play havoc with phones. And... other sorts of technology. It's a curse, really.'

'What types of technology?'

'Sun beds are a total no-go. Electronic toothbrushes – manual only for this guy. Toasters – I can't get an evenly browned slice out of one of those bastards for the life of me.'

'Sounds like a living nightmare,' replied Stronge, deadpan.

'Yup. Well, gotta go, Kat. I'll let you know as soon as something juicy jumps out at me from the spiritual ether. Toodle pip.'

I ended the call, pocketed my phone, and carried on towards The Beehive.

The pub is stood at the top end of Ealing Broadway, and has been for a century or more. Don't bother looking for it though, it's situated at the end of a blind alley, a hidden passageway, invisible to anyone not in the know.

I arrived at a nondescript door bearing the faded image of a beehive, and pushed through to the pub beyond. I felt the skin of a protective spell part around me as I stepped through the threshold. The Beehive had a rule—no spells in the bar—and in case anyone decided to ignore that rule, the dampening magic that permeated the place saw to it that disputes never got too out of hand. It didn't rob the patrons of their powers entirely, but it deadened any spells to the point of making them non-lethal. That way no one got burned to the ground for giving the wrong bloke's missus the eye. Which isn't to say that thrown fists were unheard of there. When you cater to the kind of crowd The Beehive does, all bets are off.

I scanned the lounge and a couple of heads turned toward me. Some Uncanny sorts can see ghosts, some can't. As far as I can tell, there's no rhyme or reason to it. For example, witches can see me, their familiars too. Fairies? Werewolves? Ogres? They toodle by on their merry way without ever knowing I was there. Like I say, the rules are a mess.

As I made my way to the bar, a distracted imp playing darts with a telekinesis spell saw his arrow go wide, and cursed in an ancient tongue as it buried itself in the door to the Ladies. It was barely lunchtime, but the place was already peppered with day-drinkers. I saw Lenny behind the pumps, the pub's proprietor, a grizzled mountain of a man who looked like he was born with bear DNA. He was tall. The kind of tall that casts a shadow on a cinema screen, even when he's sitting down.

He looked at me from head to toe. I wasn't a regular, but Lenny knew me well enough to know I was an Insider; someone who belonged in his establishment.

'What do you want?' he growled.

'I'm looking for someone,' I told him. 'A magician.'

'Lot of conjurers come this way.'

'This one belongs to a gang, or did before he went rogue. Order of the Eternal Flame. You know who I'm talking about?'

Lenny's face stayed poker solid.

I was about to dig a little deeper when I felt a hand on my shoulder, heavy as a trailer hitch. Not good. Whoever that paw belonged to could touch me, and in this place, that did not bode well.

I turned around to see a short, muscled creature dressed like a pile of dirty laundry. He had no hair and a mouthful of piranha teeth. The guy looked like the keynote speaker at a psychopath convention.

'You're not wanted here, phantom,' he spat.

I get this a lot. There's a certain breed of people who just don't like ghosts. I guess we must depress them or something. Remind them of their own mortality.

'Leave it,' said Lenny, cautioning the punter on my behalf. 'Haven't you had enough of being knocked around?'

It was only then that I saw the lumps and bruises on the little guy's face. He'd been in the wars all right.

I smiled back at him, all peaches and cream. 'What's your name, mate?'

'Razor. And I'm not your "mate".'

Now he was just getting on my nerves. I came to The Beehive for intel, not to get mugged off by some... whatever the fuck this thing was.

I squared up to the little scrote. 'What's your problem, pal?'

'You are. You stink. Stink of the grave. It turns my stomach.'

I tried one last time to lighten the mood. 'Hey, don't blame me if you can't handle your spirits.'

He pulled an expression so sour I thought he might sneer his face off. Apparently the lowlife was not a fan of wordplay.

I began to wonder if the attitude I was getting was about more than Razor was letting on. Had he overheard the conversation I was having with Lenny? Did he know something about the rogue magician I was looking for? Was he protecting him?

I held my magic ring up to Razor's face. 'Do you know where I can find the magician? The one from the Order of the Eternal Flame?'

'No,' he growled back.

The ring glowed blue. He was telling the truth. Damn it.

Then, quick as a flash, Razor snapped his knife-edged teeth at my hand. Thankfully, I was quicker, and just about managed to pull my hand back in time to keep my full complement of fingers.

'You dare use magic here?' he said. 'On me?'

He took a swing and chinned me, sending me sprawling through the bar.

'Oi, staff only,' said Lenny.

I rubbed my jaw and stepped back through the bar, narrowing my eyes at Razor, who stood ready, legs spread and solid like a boxer. Whatever Razor was, he knew how to throw a punch.

He chucked another one my way but I blocked it and gave him an elbow to the mouth for his trouble. Wallop. Couple of loosened fangs. Any more aggro and the next ones were going down his throat. I may not look like I'd be much use in a fight, but I'm not shy of a spot of fisticuffs. As a lad, I'd had it out on the cobbles more times than I could count. I was brought up in an all boys school in a rough part of town, and it could get pretty scrappy at times. Downright vicious in fact. My teenage years were no different; walk around small town Britain dressed like a goth and trouble has a way of seeking you out.

Razor sent another punch my way and it connected with my temple. I staggered backwards, my senses smudged. I realised I was actually smiling. Call me crazy, but when you spend so much of your life (well, afterlife) being about as solid as smoke, it's actually kind of exhilarating to feel something, even if it is a smack in the chops.

'That all you got, you stinking corpse?' he snarled.

Oh, it was on.

The bar's patrons gathered around, placing bets on the fight's outcome. Well, the ones that could see me did. The others just enjoyed watching Razor take part in a vigorous bout of shadow boxing.

Bets were called. The imp whose dart game I'd disturbed put a hefty wager on the home player. That really jabbed my fight button.

Razor came at me again. He delivered a fist to my stomach this time, hoping to knock the wind out of me. Fat chance of that happening, what with me not being a breather.

I stomped on his instep and cuffed him hard around the side of the head, disorienting him and leaving him with a hell of an earache.

He threw himself at me, raging. We slugged it out some more, careening about the place, overturning furniture, hitting each other with whatever came to hand. The bystanders cheered, yelling for more, howling for blood. It was bedlam.

I shouldered Razor to the ground, and when he came up, he had a bottle in his hand. He smashed it on the edge of the bar and came at me with the sharp end, making to glass me in the face. Jesus, only in a country this vicious do we use "glass" as a verb.

As I backed away, I accidentally lost my footing and went sprawling to the ground. No sooner had I hit the deck than Razor was on top of me, bearing down with that jagged bottle. Razor could touch me, but did that ability extend to the bottle in his hand? Would it cut my skin, pierce my flesh? I didn't fancy finding out the answer to that little riddle.

I managed to get a hand on his wrist, but he was surprisingly strong for a person of his size; a real pit bull of a thing.

The cheering bystanders reached fever pitch. I was beginning to get the distinct impression that none of them was rooting for me.

'You act like a hard man,' Razor hissed, 'but I see right through you.'

'Of course you do,' I told him. 'I'm a fucking ghost.'

I concentrated on my free hand, willing it to be even less solid than usual, and reached into his chest—right through his skin, right through his rib cage—and grabbed him by the heart.

He choked and froze.

'One twitch and you're a dead man,' I hissed, tightening my grip. 'So, what do you reckon? You wanna keep going at it, or shall we call this one quits?'

The kind of hocus pocus that could kill people was cancelled out by The Beehive's dampening magic, but that couldn't stop me from doing my ghost thing.

'I submit,' he gasped.

'Good boy.'

To make sure he didn't go back on the deal the moment I let go, I gave his ticker just enough of a squeeze to knock him out.

'Take a nap, mate,' I said as I rolled him off me, 'and don't feel like you have to wake up.'

I stood up and dusted myself down. 'He'll be fine,' I told the onlookers. 'Just needs to sleep it off.'

A shadow swamped me from behind. Lenny.

'Out. Now,' he growled.

I didn't put up a fight. I had no idea what kind of Uncanny Lenny was, but I knew better than to tangle with him.

'Sorry about the mess,' I said.

'Out!'

I called to the rest of the pub's patrons as Lenny's glare practically shoved me to the exit. 'Listen up, dickheads. Any of you knows the scumbag that killed Ingrid Vallens, you tell him to meet me in Highgate Cemetery at midnight. You hear me? Highgate Cemetery! I'll be ready with my fighting pants on!'

'That's enough,' said Lenny.

'You think they got the message?' I asked, wondering if I'd stirred the pot sufficiently.

Lenny told me not to worry. 'Don't you worry, the whole of the Uncanny Kingdom will want words with you soon enough...'

11

I stopped by Legerdomain to kill some time before the meet.

'You're telling me you walked into The Beehive and started a fight?' Jazz Hands screeched.

'No, he started it,' I corrected.

'You're like a child! Do you have any idea of the things that go on in that place?'

'I'm beginning to get an idea,' I replied, rubbing my jaw.

She marched up to me, gesticulating wildly. 'You could have been killed! Again!'

'Goes with the territory.'

'This isn't your territory, Jake. You solve murders, domestics, hit-and-runs, muggings gone wrong. Since when do you get involved with magicians and creatures from the abyss?'

'Hey, I was an exorcist once—'

'—who banished piss-weak pit fiends and mopped up projectile vomit.'

'Not exactly the way I presented it on my CV.'

She threw up her hands in dismay. 'Idiot.'

I folded my arms. 'Well, you've been a real ray of sunshine today. So glad I stopped by.'

Jazz slid back behind her counter and snatched up the handset of a telephone. It was an old-fashioned rotary phone with magical glyphs on the dial instead of numbers.

'Who are you calling?' I asked.

'I'm calling for help,' she said, jamming a finger in the wheel and giving it a swivel. 'I'm contacting the London Coven.'

'I thought you told me they'd been wiped out.'

'They left a familiar. A protector. Someone they built especially to handle this sort of thing.'

The London Coven was, as far as Jazz explained it, a kind of police force that kept an eye on the Uncanny of London, keeping them in line when the shit hit the fan. Except now they were extinct, and all that was left of them was a single familiar keeping the peace in the entire city. She must have been putting in a shit-load of overtime.

I turned my hand corporeal and placed a finger on the phone's hang-up button, cutting off the call.

'Listen,' I said. 'I appreciate you looking out for me, but the message I got from Heaven didn't say anything about bringing in a second party. I'm going to have to lone wolf this one.'

'Then let me help you find a way to hide,' she said. 'There must be some way to get you off His radar.' She began pulling old tomes off the shelves and riffling their yellowed pages.

'Give it up, Jazz. There's no hiding from this. Judgment Day is coming, and I'm going to make sure I show up for it spick and span. Anyway, aren't you the one who's always telling me I need to make up for the bad things I've done?'

'Yes, but—'

'So which is it? Do I carry on running from my fate, or do I get out there and atone for my sins?'

I had her there.

She hung up the receiver. 'Tell me why you're really doing this.'

'I just told you—'

'It's a woman, isn't it?'

'How dare you? I am doing this one-hundred percent because it's the right and correct thing to do! I am a ghost of honour, not driven by something as mortal as crotch-based lust.'

'How pretty is she?'

'Oh, off the scale pretty. I mean it is just *insane.*'

She sighed and buried her hands in her hair. If I didn't know better I'd almost think she was jealous.

'Look, Jazz, I have to do this. Not just to get the Big Man out of my hair, but because I made a promise. To the victim. To Ingrid.'

'*Ingrid.* Of course she's an Ingrid. What do you even know about this woman?'

'That she's dead and that she's in trouble and that she needs my help. What else do I need to know?'

Jazz drew a long breath. 'Tell me this, Jake... is she worth dying for? I mean, properly dying? No ghosting around, no playing detective, no anything. Just the void.'

I chose not to answer that one. Instead, I checked my watch for the time. Ten to midnight. Almost time for my rendezvous. 'I have to get going,' I said. 'Duty calls.'

I was about to make off when Jazz Hands held up a hand. 'Hold your horses.'

She walked away and went to the framed picture of James Randi that she kept behind the counter. Pulling it aside, she revealed a hidden wall safe, which she opened using a key she kept about her neck. Reaching into the safe, she produced a bundle of some sort and set it down on the counter. The contents of the bundle were wrapped in a silk handkerchief, which I touched and found solid. Whatever was under there, Jazz Hands had worked her magic on it.

'Go ahead,' she said.

I picked it up. It was cold and weighed heavy in my palm.

I whipped off the hankie and found myself holding a pearl-handled revolver.

'Cool,' I remarked. 'Is this the demon laser I asked for?'

'It's a gun,' Jazz Hands replied, flatly. 'You point it at the thing you want to kill and pull the trigger.'

Huh. Well, that'd work too. 'Thanks,' I told her, slipping the gun into the inside pocket of my jacket.

'Be careful,' she said, full of motherly concern.

'Always am.'

'A month ago I gave you an enchanted knife you could carry. Before you'd even vacated my premises you almost had an eye out.'

'You didn't let me finish. Always am... *since then.*'

I doffed an imaginary cap as Jazz Hands rolled her eyes, then I made haste.

A second later, I arrived at the rendezvous location, Highgate Cemetery. I held the pistol in my pocket, hand tight about its grip.

Would the rogue magician show, I wondered. I'd shouted my mouth off at The Beehive; surely word of my invitation must have spread by now. Someone was bound to have passed the news on to the guilty party, right?

So there I was, walking among the burial plots, using myself as tasty bait. Would the magician swim by and leave the worm on the hook, I asked myself, or would he take this opportunity to chow down and use me for fish food?

A light breeze rolled across a blanket of newly browned leaves, making the cemetery seem to whisper. There were no voices though; it was too late for the living and no place for ghosts. The graveyard was full of bodies, and yet nothing but empty.

Then I heard a noise. A commotion up ahead. I ran, wading through a sea of tombstones until I arrived at the source of the disturbance.

A man lay dead on the ground.

His chest sliced open.

His rib cage cranked apart.

I pulled out my gun and scanned the area, trying to get a bead on the killer. There was no one out there though, not as far as I could see. Whoever did this was long gone.

I returned my attention to the body and stooped down to see if I could ID him. His face didn't ring any bells. Sixty or so years of age, dressed like a school supply teacher, an upper crust whiff about him. One of those chinless wonders with a face that seemed to connect to his neck with nothing happening in between.

The old geezer's body was splayed out on a magic circle that had been painted in his own blood. This wasn't a ward like before though. This was weakening magic – a trigger spell to sap the life force of anyone foolish enough to set foot inside the circle's boundary.

The rogue magician had been here, that much was obvious. It seemed my visit to The Beehive had been a success, and that he'd gotten word I wanted a natter with him. So then why cut and run, and why leave me a corpse for a calling card? What was the message? Maybe it was a case of mistaken identity, could that be possible? Was this poor sod coming to see his departed old mum, only to end up joining her in great hereafter?

I looked down and saw something odd in the pattern of blood surrounding him. A spot of something breaking up the red. A spot of something tar-like. I crouched down to get a better look at it. It was black—a deep, deep, stygian black—and it gave off some truly unholy vibes. Was this blood too? The demon's blood?

Not wanting to touch the stuff, I took a sample by dipping the tip of my revolver into it. Maybe Jazz Hands would be able to make something of it.

But before I got to that, there was something else bothering me.

I began to look around the area close to the body, even peering behind a gravestone or two. I was stood three feet from a dead man, a man that had only recently been murdered, and yet there was something very obviously missing.

His ghost was gone.

The soul feaster had eaten well tonight.

12

A cemetery tour guide found the old man's body first thing the next morning.

The police transferred the body to St Pancras Mortuary for inspection, and Detective Inspector Stronge invited me along to attend the next stage of the investigation. I hitched a ride to the meet in Mark Ryan's body. I've spent enough time in the guy's skull now that I know his routine by heart, so finding the bloke when I need him is never a problem.

Stronge and her partner, DI Maddox (or Inspector Fuckwit as I prefer to call him), flashed their warrant cards at the front desk. Once they were let through, they led me down a series of antiseptic corridors until we reached the autopsy room.

Dr Anand was there, dressed in her customary blue plastic apron and scrubs. The two of us were intimately acquainted already, not that she was aware of it. Wait, that didn't sound great. Let me try that again....

If Dr Anand were able to see through my meat suit, she'd have recognised the real me. See, Anand was the coroner that dealt with Jake Fletcher's sliced-up remains—with *my* sliced-up remains—so she'd seen parts of me that even I didn't know about. Like I say, *intimate*. Anand was also a major asset in solving my murder, which made her A-OK in my book.

'Okay, let's do this,' she said, with just a touch too much relish for my liking.

While she snapped on a pair of powdered latex gloves and the rest of us rubbed oil of camphor under our noses, a couple of assistants fetched the corpse of the recently deceased. They rolled in a gurney and carefully lifted the bag containing the body on to the room's ceramic autopsy slab.

'Thank you, gents,' said Anand. 'Please close the doors behind you.'

The assistants did as asked and Dr Anand unzipped the bag. I noticed Maddox recoil slightly as she did it. Obviously this wasn't his favourite part of the job.

Inside, was the body of the old man, just as I'd left him, save for the relocation from the cemetery. The only difference was the toe tag.

Anand whistled when she saw the state of the corpse's chest, all opened up and flapping in the breeze. 'Looks like somebody got this one started for me,' she joked.

The three of us stood back while she did her job, delving around in the dead guy's chest cavity for clues.

Stronge leaned over and whispered in my ear. 'No coffee for me today?'

'Sorry,' I replied, 'I was in a rush.'

She smiled that rare smile of hers. 'Don't worry about it. We can always grab one afterwards.'

Interesting.

Not that she was talking coffee two feet from a mangled corpse—Stronge's always had a stomach to match her name—but that she was so obviously hitting on me. I'd always felt like there was a spark between us, and God knows I have a thing for ice queens, but this definitely seemed like an escalation.

'Sounds great, Kat,' I whispered back, 'but I can't.'

I don't mind a bit of flirting here and there, but going the distance in another guy's body? What can I say, I'm just not that kind of ghost.

Stronge pulled back. 'Don't get any ideas, Fletcher. I just wanted to discuss the case.'

Maddox heard her raised voice. 'Everything all right?'

'Everything's fine,' Stronge huffed.

Dr Anand broke the tension. 'This is interesting...'

'What is it?' asked Maddox, gingerly stepping forward.

Anand picked up a pen from one of the stainless steel counters and used it to point inside the cadaver's chest cavity. 'See that?'

'I don't see anything,' Maddox replied, wincing.

'Exactly. No heart. Somebody took it out.'

'Why?'

'Better to ask *how*. See the incision there, through the skin? See how clean it is?'

'Yeah.'

'Now look at what's going on inside the chest. See the aorta there? The pulmonary artery?'

Maddox hesitated, then leaned in for a closer look, green around the gills but keen not to show it.

Anand went on. 'Unlike the opening laceration, the internal wounds are imprecise. Sloppy.'

Stronge stepped in. 'I've a feeling this is leading somewhere, so can you please cut to the chase?'

Dr Anand arched an eyebrow. 'It looks as though the victim's heart was eaten from their chest cavity. Chewed out.'

'Jesus!' said Maddox, before sprinting to a bin and chucking up his guts.

I stifled a smile. Oh Maddox, you big Jessie.

'And that's only the half of it,' Anand added.

'What do you mean?' asked Stronge, covering for her partner while he ejected his breakfast.

'Neither of these wounds was caused post-mortem. Both occurred while the victim was alive.'

'So, something cut him open then ate his heart right out of his chest?' asked Stronge.

Maddox arched over behind me and up-chucked again.

I leaned into the cadaver. 'You're sure?' I asked Dr Anand. 'That the body was opened clean?'

'Sixteen years of medical training and a master's degree in criminology? Yeah, I'm pretty sure I've got this one, Mystic Meg.'

I walked right into that one. Still, what I didn't know about dead bodies, I more than made up for with my demon know-how, and if there's one thing I'd learned about this particular hell-beast, it's that it didn't eat its dinner with a knife and fork. The soul feaster would have stuck its head through the old fella's chest and gone at him like it was bobbing for apples, only this meal had been dished up. Served hot and presented like a waiter lifting the lid on a soup tureen. That could only mean one thing.

The summoner and the demon were working together.

But to what end? If the rogue magician had convinced the demon to grant him eternal life, what was he doing running errands for the thing? I've heard of some wasted lives in my time—I count mine as one of them—but this took the cake.

Stronge broke my concentration. 'The body, do you think there's any connection between this one and the corpse we found in the canal?'

For a second I thought she was talking to me, but the question was for Anand.

The doctor shook her head. 'I don't think so. The skinning was meticulous. This killing... this was a feeding frenzy.'

Maddox wiped his mouth. 'Great, so now we've got two killers on the loose.' He turned to me and shrugged. 'So...?'

'So what?'

'So, who did it? Who's our suspect?'

'Oh, right, yeah. Well, I don't know that just now. Not yet anyway.'

'And you're our psychic, are you? What the fuck are you even doing here, Fletcher?

'It's not that simple, I need time to make a connection,' I bullshitted.

'Bollocks,' he replied, smelling it.

'I told you who the first victim was, didn't I? Ingrid Vallens. Without me you'd still be trying to figure out how to dust a skinned body for prints.'

Maddox's lip curled. 'Yeah, I've been wondering about that. About where you get your little tip-offs. Tell me this, Fletcher, you ever hear of Occam's razor?'

I had, but I hadn't expected to find it living in his thick head.

Maddox answered for me. 'It's a principle that says the simplest solution is usually the best one. So, I keep wondering to myself, what's the simplest solution for the way you keep a step ahead of us? Is it that you can communicate with the spirit world, or is it that you know something about these dead bodies that you're not telling us?' His eyes bored into me like a pair of hate-rays.

Stronge put a stop to it. 'Will you two put your dicks away?' She smacked me in the chest with the flat of a clipboard. 'He's messing with you – we already have an ID on the heart donor.'

I took the clipboard and scanned the name at the top of the front page. Henry Carter PhD, retired theology professor. No criminal record, no known enemies.

'I don't get it. Why would someone bump off this guy?'

'That's what I'm hoping you can tell us.'

'Of course,' I said, except, thanks to the soul feaster, there was no ghost for me to question like there was after Ingrid's murder. I stroked my chin, stalling for time while I thought of something to say. I had nothing.

Dr Anand saved me. 'Could it have been a ritual? One of those blood sacrifices?'

Maddox snorted. 'Like in the films? Leave it out. What we're looking for is a lunatic with a sharp knife and a head full of wrong.'

I suppose he was half right. In any case, I wasn't going to correct the guy. What would I tell him? That there was a bona-fide demon on the loose? That there was black magic afoot in the city and that everything he knew was a lie? I didn't like the bloke, but I wasn't about to lay that load on him.

I turned to Stronge. 'I'll get a read on the killer soon enough, but in the meantime, what else aren't you telling me? Did he leave any clues? Were there any witnesses?'

'Just the one,' she replied.

I threw up my hands. 'Why didn't you say so?' I mean, talk about burying the lede. 'Well? Did you get a photofit?'

'We're waiting on that,' said Maddox.

'Waiting for what, for Christ's sake?'

'Waiting for the witness to come out of her coma.'

13

It was getting on for three in the morning, and I was wandering the streets of Camden in the pissing rain.

It was day four of my investigation, and I was no clearer about the identity of Ingrid's killer than when I'd started. I had to come up with something, and soon. Something solid to send her to the Good Place and clear some of that red ink from my account.

I passed a revolving door of tattoo parlours and kebab shops, thinking back to what Stronge had told me about the coma witness. Apparently, she lived in some big, glass, Grand Designs house overlooking the cemetery, and saw the murder go down through one of her floor-to-ceiling windows. Hazard of living in a transparent house, I suppose – sometimes you're going to see some things you wish you hadn't.

What she saw was recorded on her mobile phone, though not with enough clarity to be of much use. The video she captured was just about useless – dim, shaky, and worst of all, shot in portrait. What is it with some people? I swear to God, I could be filming the end of the world and I'd still have the sense to shoot it holding my phone sideways.

I was given a chance to review the video footage at the

station. It showed the silhouette of a slim, four-limbed creature crouching over its victim, head buried in his chest. True to Dr Anand's report, the vic was very much alive as it happened, thrashing about like a downed power line. It made for hard viewing, and I only got to see the blurry, happening-in-the-distance version. What the witness saw with her own eyes must have been far, far worse. No wonder it triggered the heart condition that laid her out.

After dropping Mark off, I'd headed over to Jazz Hands' place with the sample of black blood I'd sourced at Highgate Cemetery. If it really was the demon's blood, there was a chance —even if it was only a slim one—that it could be used to power a dowsing spell, except instead of looking for water, I'd use it to find the thing behind these murders.

Naturally, Jazz Hands had tried to talk me out of it, but I'd charmed her into helping me – by which I mean I'd begged her for close to forty minutes.

I know a thing or two about magic, but Jazz Hands? Well, she may not have written the book on it exactly, but she sure owns a fuck of a lot of them.

She took a scraping of the sample, verified that it was indeed demon blood—soul feaster blood to be exact—and diluted it with a potion that practically hummed with magical energy. After that, she took the stirred-together solution and smeared a dollop of it on the centre of my chest.

'Just follow the pull,' she'd told me. *'The blood will tell you where to go.'*

The dowsing effect wouldn't last long I was told, so the chances of it working were slim, but I was feeling lucky. I'd find that demon in no time, I was sure of it.

I tromped around Camden for something like three hours.

I wandered this way and that, up main roads and side streets, hopping from location to location, and each of them proved a bust. Occasionally, I had a feeling like my chest was tingling and the spell was working, shepherding me in a certain direction, only for the sensation to peter out and disappear.

I was about ready to call it a night and go back to my boxed sets when my chest suddenly broke out in tingles, like a family of ants was hang a party between my nipples.

And that's when I heard them. Screams.

Lots of them.

The noise came from up ahead, a little further down the high street and tucked down a side alley. What was it? Cries for help or just a bunch of drunks exercising their lungs? Had I finally found what I was looking for? I wouldn't know unless I checked it out, so I sprinted down the road and took the corner.

Terrified ravers were pouring out of an all-night fetish club called F*I*S*T. They were scared out of their wits, wailing like banshees, their faces chiselled with dread as they piled on to the pavement.

I worked against the tide, passing through the screaming clubbers as I forced my way into the building and past the empty ticket office. I phased through bodies dressed in studded leather, in rubber tuxedos, in gas masks, and, in the case of one particular reveller, a crown made of foot-long dildos.

Thrash metal blared from downstairs, loud as gunfire, jangling my senses like marbles in a tin can. I followed the noise-abatement-order-defying racket to the basement, bounding down the steps three at a time. The stairs bottomed out in the club's main room, and there, in the middle of the dance floor and lit by the frantic pulse of a strobe light, I found a dead body.

But that wasn't all I found.

A mirror ball shaped like a human skull swarmed the grisly scene with pinpricks of white light. Hunched over the dead body was a figure, head bowed and feasting noisily on the corpse's heart.

I'd found the fucker.

Stood nearby, her mouth agape, was a lone clubber dressed

like Tank Girl—all pink neon dreads and bovver boots—a peculiar specimen known as a cybergoth that you only find within a hundred square yards of Camden. She was frozen to the spot, knees locked with fear. 'W-what are you?' she squeaked, not at me—I was invisible to her eyes—but at the creature on the dance floor emptying out a dead man's chest cavity.

It was a fair question. I circled around the DJ booth to get a better look at the thing, moving silent and unseen. It was hard to make the demon out under the UV lamps and dry ice, but I soon found the right angle.

The demon wasn't what I expected at all. The soul feaster looked nothing like the woodcut in Jazz Hands' bestiary; all sinewy limbs and smouldering eyes and razor blade claws. It looked like a woman. A human woman with bad table manners and a real thing for offal.

She lifted her head and her blood-matted blonde hair parted to reveal a face.

It was a face I recognised. A face that made the room tilt and threaten to drop me to the floor.

The demon was Ingrid.

Ingrid Vallens.

But that couldn't be.

Ingrid was dead.

Wandering Camden's waterways as a ghost.

No way it could be...

...and then it clicked.

This wasn't Ingrid. This was Ingrid's *skin*—the same skin that had been peeled from her body—now worn by the soul feaster. It hung from the demon's bones like a badly-fitted suit, baggy and uneven. She looked beautiful still, but her features were like a death mask, lifeless and limp. The demon definitely passed for human though, which would explain how it had been able to walk the streets without drawing attention. I'd assumed it was using some kind of concealment magic, but this was a far more elegant solution. Gross, but elegant.

The demon sniffed the air and its hollow eyes darted my way and flared orange.

The cat was out of the bag.

I went inside my jacket and pulled out my gun.

Tank Girl shrieked, startled by the sight of a pearl-handled revolver materialising from thin air. It was invisible inside of my ghost clothes, but out of my pocket it was there to see, plain as day.

The demon saw the gun too and froze, caught in the open, uncertain of what to do next.

I didn't know what kind of damage a six-shooter was going to do a soul feaster—I might as well have been waving a fertility crystal at it for all I knew—but from the way it stalled, the demon was just as clueless as I was.

'Stay there,' I told it, cocking the gun's hammer.

Tank Girl screamed at the sound of my disembodied voice. Poor love. She really was having one of those days.

The soul feaster twitched.

'I said stay there!'

But the demon was having none of it. Quick as a flash, it darted behind a pillar then around the other side to grab the cybergoth. She screamed as the demon brought its arm around her throat, turning her into a human shield.

'Please,' she begged, 'whoever you are—whatever you are—don't shoot!'

I adjusted my aim but couldn't find a clear target. No way I could risk taking a shot without slotting Tank Girl. Besides, what do I know about firing a gun? I'm no marksman – the only firefights I've ever been involved in went down on Xbox Live.

The three of us stood there like human statues.

It was a standoff.

Or at least it was a standoff until the demon lifted Tank Girl off her feet and tossed her at me, sending her soaring across the dance floor like she'd been fired from a cannon. She passed through me but collided with my gun, taking it with her. The revolver spun from my grip and went clattering across the floor, lost beneath the dry ice.

I scrabbled around under the fog, desperate to find the one weapon I had to defend myself with, when suddenly I saw it.

I snatched it up and levelled the thing—

But the demon was gone.

I fouled the air with some choice profanities.

No one left but me and Tank Girl, out cold on the ground.

I scanned the room. The demon was fast, but it couldn't have gotten too far. I went looking for a trail and found a path leading through the dry ice, coalescing now, but distinct enough to show me the way the demon had fled.

I followed the path to the bar and found smashed pint glasses where the demon must have vaulted it. Sliding through to the other side, I saw an open trapdoor and a set of steps leading to the beer cellar. I leapt through the hatch, landed like a feather—easy enough when you're a phantom—and flashed my gun to every corner of the room.

I caught a blur of movement and popped off three rounds.

BANG.

BANG.

BANG.

The third one did the business.

The soul feaster squealed like a stuck pig.

I'd winged it.

I lined the bastard up in my sights and squeezed the trigger again—

But the demon was quick.

And desperate.

With no way to get past me, it hurtled pell-mell into a cellar wall.

CRUNCH.

It landed hard. Hard enough to bust through to the other side and leave me lost in a cloud of brick dust. By the time it had cleared, the demon was gone. All that was left was a trickle of black blood leading through a crumbling hole in the cellar wall.

I stuck my head through the opening and peered into the inky gloom. The demon had punched through to the city's old, Victorian sewer system. No way I was chasing it through there. The sewers were home to all manner of Uncanny – the kind that only walk the streets by cover of night. Creepers, lurkers, lurchers, not to mention fey folk. And I don't mean the Tinkerbell kind of fairies that frolic at the bottom of your garden; these are spiteful, evil little bastards. Vicious bottom-feeders who lay eggs in your stomach that hatch like a pound of Semtex.

I pocketed my gun and headed back upstairs. Tank Girl was starting to come around, woozy still from being ragdolled across the room. It didn't seem right to leave her head full of all the stuff she'd seen, so I stepped inside her and gave that blob of grey meat a good old scrub. I don't like to possess strangers if I can help it—least of all women—but it was that or a lifetime of nightmares for the lass.

After I was done scouring, I gave the girl back her body, along with a big hole where some bad memories used to go. Far as she knew, she'd had one too many snakebites and nodded off. She might wonder why she was the only one left in the club when she came to, but I doubted it would occur to her until she woke up the next day.

With that taken care of, I went to the mutilated corpse spread-eagled on the dance floor. The dead body used to belong to a man. He looked to be in his mid-forties, but that was just a guess. Ordinarily, I'd have confirmed the deets with his ghost, but once again, the demon had snacked on his soul.

The deceased was dressed in a latex catsuit, complete with a tasteful peephole for his unmentionables. Much like the last body, the rib cage was torn open and the heart taken out, except by the looks of things, this torso had been pried apart by the demon's bare hands.

It seemed the demon had decided to strike out on its own this time, without its summoner in tow. What was that all about anyway? I couldn't make sense of it. A demon and a magician in cahoots? It made no sense. What was the summoner getting out of this? And where the hell was he now?

I took a closer look at the victim, trying to get an ID. Brown hair, blue eyes, a cleft chin...

Huh.

One of the elders at the Magic Circle had a cleft chin. One of the Eternal Flame guys.

And then the obvious fell into place.

He was a member of the Order. Chin Dimple! And the body at the cemetery, the one with the weak chin; that must have been Glass Jaw. Why was I only figuring this out now? I was losing my touch. Bad detecting, Jake. Bad.

It looked as though Chin Dimple and Glass Jaw were the victims of a vendetta. The rogue magician must have been the empty spot on that pentacle they were all stood on.

I had no idea how he was doing it, but the tricky swine had figured out a way to talk his pet demon into bumping off his former colleagues.

Chin Dimple must have known what was going on though, surely? That someone had cored one of his buddies and left them laid out in a graveyard? It was on the front page of the Metro for crying out loud, and what does this genius do? Squeezes into a latex catsuit and heads off to a fetish club to air out his privates. I mean, come on, man. Priorities.

So, who was this guy laid out at my feet? I firmed up my ghost hands and patted him down; no easy task when the act of turning a door handle can leave me shaking like a washing machine on spin cycle. Still, I soldiered on, and after a little while I found a pocket sewn into the upper leg of the dead guy's latex outfit. Horny but practical – a winning combination.

Inside the pocket was a leather wallet, which I plucked out with a squeak and rifled for clues. His driver's license had his name as Timothy Martin Jones, DoB February 4th, 1969. Other than that, he had forty quid in cash, an expired rail ticket, and a creased-up library card. Nothing much of interest there.

I was about to return the wallet to its pocket when I noticed a zip on the side. I opened it up to find a condom and a half-empty blister pack of pills. I held the medicine up to the light to check the brand.

Ziagen.

I knew that name. A flatmate of mine at university used to take the stuff. Called them "Nukes." Used them to treat his HIV.

Guess that explained why Chin Dimple was living each day like his last.

Too bad for him that this was the one.

14

By the time I left the club the sun was coming up and colouring in a new day. The police would find the body I'd left at the club soon enough, in the meantime I'd check in on Ingrid and let her know how things were progressing. I made a mental note to keep the stuff about a demon running around in her skin to myself. That just struck me as an overshare.

When I got to the canal, there was no sign of her, though. I walked the towpath from Camden Lock to St. Pancras, checked under every bridge, inside every narrowboat, but Ingrid was gone.

Where the hell was she?

Had she drifted away and turned feral? Was she out there somewhere, haunting the streets, springing from alleyways and frightening the sensitive? Or had she gone full Bloody Mary, materialising from mirrors and scratching people's eyes out?

I thought about Ingrid's glowing smile. About how much I missed it already.

Then another theory occurred. What if the magician had gotten to her? What if he'd been down here, tying up loose ends while I was busy having it out with his demon at the club?

Did he rub her out? Did he obliterate her, like an exorcist cleansing a haunted house? Just like I used to do.

I should have been here. Should have protected her. I was so busy trying to scrub that red ink from my account that I lost sight of what mattered. I was thinking about myself, not Ingrid. About getting square with the Big Man. Typical me. Selfish to the end. Till after the end even.

It was all starting to feel like a lost cause, but then I had a thought. If Ingrid really had been obliterated, where was God's stooge? Why wasn't he here with a shepherd's crook, ready to yank me off stage and drag me in front of my maker?

I decided to keep my worst fears in check until I knew what had happened for sure. So long as there was a chance that Ingrid was still out there, I was going to fight for her.

I went to Frosty for the word on the street.

He occupied his usual spot, the patch of pavement under a Sainsbury's cash point, a stone's throw from Mornington Crescent Station.

'I need your help, Frost.'

He looked up at me with bloodshot eyes. 'My fee?'

I didn't have time for his bloody fee. It was day five of my investigation and the hourglass was almost empty. 'I don't have any booze for you, mate. Not right now.'

'Then you're shit out of luck, son.'

'Please,' I begged him. 'Sort me out this once and I'll have three cans for you next time. Scratch that, I'll have a whole bloody six pack. A crate if you want!'

His lips smacked like waves lapping against a rock. 'Promise?'

'Cross my heart and hope to die.' Again, not really a promise you could take to the bank, that one, but it seemed to convince Frosty.

'All right then,' he said, 'what do you need to know?'

'Ingrid Vallens. Where is she?'

'Ingrid Vallens the underwear model?' he asked, arching a frostbitten eyebrow. 'What are you up to, you mucky old bastard?'

'I don't have time to piss about, Frosty. She's dead and I need to find her. Can you tell me where she is or not?'

He flared his nostrils. 'You owe me one, Fletcher. Or six to be exact.'

He closed his eyes and did whatever it was he did. When he opened them again, his face was crossed with confusion. 'That's weird, I can't get a fix on her. I know I should be able to. It's like I can sort of smell where she should be, but I can't get to her. Like something's...'

'Blocking you?'

'Yeah.'

I filled a speech balloon with some swears. The rogue magician had figured out a way to cover his tracks. Of course he bloody had.

'What have you gotten yourself mixed up in this time?' Frosty asked.

'The Order I told you about. One of them's gone AWOL and started bumping people off.'

'And you think he's hiding his footprints?'

'Looks that way.'

He made a, *"We'll see about that,"* face and scrunched his eyes closed to seek out the errant magician.

A minute passed. Any other day, Frosty would have come back with a hit in about the time it took a roulette wheel to stop spinning, but he was struggling with this one. I watched his eyeballs darting about under their lids. His face screwed up and an axe-wound crease furrowed his forehead. Finally, his eyes flicked open.

'I don't see him. It's like someone went through a box of photos and cut the heads out of all of them. The bloke's a mystery wrapped in an enigma—'

'Dropped in a bucket of dog shit. Yeah, I know.'

I firmed up my foot and booted an empty can of Fanta across the street, surprising a couple of passing tourists.

Another dead end.

'Oh...' A smile cracked the crust of ice on Frosty's face. 'Your magician... I did manage to get one thing on 'em.'

'What?' I asked, in a pitch that came out just a bit too high.

Frosty showed me two rows of rotten teeth. 'I can't give you a name, I can't give you a face, but I can give you one thing.'

'What's that?'

'A place.'

15

I didn't have time to round up the authorities and take them with me. Three people were dead already, and I wasn't hanging around to let another one croak. Besides, if I could just find the magician, I was convinced I could get the whereabouts of Ingrid from him, even if I had to beat them out of him with my bare fists. Or Mark's bare fists anyway.

I took my mule to the address Frosty gave me. I needed Mark's body if I was going to deal with this magician; how else was I meant to get answers from him? With a couple of ghost arms and good intentions? I don't like to put Mark in harm's way, but without a physical form I'm about as useful as Aquaman in Iraq. Besides, if anyone deserved to get roughed up a bit, it was Mark "Kick me in the balls for shits and giggles" Ryan.

The pad Frosty steered me to was a plush three-storey townhouse in Primrose Hill, an area of Camden inhabited by people who give their kids names like Saskia and Rupert. Was this really the place? Was this where my rogue magician kicked up his heels? I bounded up the front steps and stopped at the entrance. I'd planned to pick it with an unlocking cantrip, but when I arrived there I found the door hanging off its hinges, which, you know, is a little ominous. And by *a little* I mean *a lot*.

I had a sneaky suspicion that this wasn't my rogue magician's house. This was just his last known location, or at least his last location as far as Frosty could figure it.

I drew my revolver and slipped inside, padding down the hallway as quietly as I could, and following a trail of something on the ground that might have been soot.

The interior of the house was a mix of industrial and bohemian—exposed brick and polished teakwood floors—but the decor wasn't the property's most notable feature. The thing that really stood out was the smell – a pungent, smoky tang, like someone had been cooking BBQ indoors. It didn't smell like any meat I knew though. It stank like burnt tramp with a top note of rotten eggs.

I reached the end of a hall and arrived in an open-plan living area: a lounge, minimally furnished with a loose scattering of tasteful Danish designs. No one was home. No one living anyway.

Sprawled across the floor and leaking its juices into an authentic bearskin rug was a body, its chest torn wide open, just like the others.

My man had been here all right, but I was a step behind him as always. This was starting to get old now. I was beginning to feel like an unwilling participant in the world's grimmest scavenger hunt.

I crouched down to get a proper look at the rogue magician's latest victim. He looked to be in his late seventies, with just a few wisps of hair clinging to his scalp and a pair of rheumy, blue eyes. Sat on his upper lip was a distinctive waxed moustache.

Mustachio.

I checked his arm to confirm. Sure enough, the limb was prosthetic. No doubt about it, this was the Order's chief elder. The leader of the pack—the one who lost a limb sending this demon back to Hell the first time—had finally met his match.

Only Cleft Lip remained now. Three magicians down, one to go. Christ, I was making a real balls of this job.

I cast a look at my surroundings. There, on a shabby chic sideboard, sat next to a Bang & Olufsen stereo, was a framed certificate: an award from the Royal College of Surgeons. It was a diploma in the specialty of cosmetic and reconstructive surgery. So, a dead theology professor, a departed HIV patient, and now a plastic surgeon. Three people sure to have a marked interest in the prospect of eternal life. No wonder they all belonged to their little immortality club. Ironic that it had turned out to be the death of them.

Searching the room some more, my eyes landed on a shape on the wall: the scorched outline of a silhouette spoiling a nice double-coat of tastefully neutral Farrow & Ball paint. Seemed I'd found the source of that BBQ smell. From the looks of things, Mustachio had gotten a last-second shot in before the soul feaster went to town on him. Fair play, old man.

Returning to the body, I saw something lying on the rug beside Mustachio's hand. A twig, one end wrapped in a length of blue leather twine. I stooped down to examine the thing closer. There were etchings running along its side. Magical runes. No, this wasn't a twig... this was a wand. A wand of lightning to be exact, which he'd used to blast the demon with. Magical wands and seraphim swords, huh? What *didn't* these guys have... I mean, except for their hearts.

I reached down and picked up Mustachio's wand. I wiped a smear of blood off it and ran my thumb along the runes, feeling for a magical spark. It seemed the enchantment had been good for one charge only. The item was spent. Those things don't mess around though; the soul feaster must have taken one hell of a whack. Along with the bullet I'd put through the thing, it should be pretty wobbly on its feet right about now. I just hoped I could get to it in time to take advantage of that.

I leaned across the body to set the wand down where I found it—

When something lashed out and seized me by the wrist.

A hand, gripping me like a vice.

I almost jumped out of my skin... literally.

Mustachio was still alive!

The guy was opened up from navel to neck and I was ankle-deep in his blood. Bright red arterial blood. How could he possibly still be kicking?

'I tried...' he choked, blood bubbling from his mouth as he pointed to the scorched silhouette on the wall. 'Tried... to kill it.'

'Easy,' I said, shushing him and making a face like everything was going to be all right, despite the wealth of facts indicating the opposite.

I could see his heart now, in his chest still and beating like a jackrabbit's. He must have blasted the soul feaster before it had a chance to chow down on him. Chased the thing off before it could chew out his vital organs.

'You did well, mate,' I told him. 'Played a blinder.'

He managed to croak out some more words. '...Has to be stopped.... promise... promise me you'll stop it.'

His bony grip relaxed and I took him by the hand. 'I'll stop it,' I told him. 'I promise I will.'

He smiled. His eyelids fluttered. And his heart stopped beating.

I set his hand down on the floor and bowed my head.

All was silent.

Until a sharp yell came from behind me.

'Put down the gun!' barked a voice I knew all too well.

Detective Inspector Maddox. Inspector Fuckwit.

I looked at the revolver in my hand. At that point I'd forgotten I was even holding it.

'This isn't what it looks like, Maddox,' I said, pathetically, like a teenage boy trying to explain away some questionable items in his browser history.

'I said put down the gun!' Maddox repeated.

I did as I was asked and placed the pistol gently on the rug. The blood-sodden rug that had soaked right through my trousers already. Into my hands, under my fingernails, pretty much all over me. I was marinated in murder. Doused in DNA.

I turned around slowly with my hands held high.

'Stay where you are! Down on the ground!' It was DCI Stronge issuing the orders this time. She looked as angry as she did disappointed.

A pair of laser sights dotted my torso. Both officers were armed with Taser guns.

Maddox grinned like the cat that got the cream. 'Look at all this. You've been a busy boy, Fletcher.'

Stronge remained the more professional of the two. 'Put your hands behind your head and lace your fingers,' she ordered.

'I didn't kill this guy, Kat. You must know that.'

'Is that right?' chuckled Maddox. 'What are you doing here then, reading the old man's entrails? 'Cause if it's the future you're after, I can tell you yours, Fletcher: life at her Majesty's Pleasure, no parole.'

'We don't have time for this!' I cried. 'You're letting him get away!'

'Who?' said Stronge. 'Who are we letting get away?'

At that point I heard a new voice. 'What's happening?' pleaded the ghost of the dead magician, who was sat up from his corpse and looking down at the giant pool of blood surrounding him.

'Tell them,' I said, forgetting myself. 'Tell them this wasn't me!'

'Who are you talking to?' asked Stronge, following my eye-line but oblivious to the old man's apparition.

'Going for an insanity plea, are you?' said Maddox. 'Good luck with that.'

He started walking towards me with a pair of handcuffs.

'I can't go with you,' I told him.

'Oh, yeah? What are you gonna do, Fletcher? Fight your way out of here?'

I froze.

'Yeah, I thought so,' he said, and started to robotically read off my rights.

He was inches from me, about to slap on the bracelets. I couldn't let him take me. Couldn't let him lock me up. And that only left me with one option.

I sprang to my feet and kicked Maddox square in the nuts.

Oof!

He went down like a bag of hammers, but I was quick to follow as a dart hit me in the chest, chased by about 50,000 volts.

My muscles convulsed and my teeth clamped shut as Stronge's Taser lit me up and dropped me hard.

As I lay on the ground, drooling on to the teakwood floor, a thought occurred.

Two electrocutions in this place in one day.

And they say lightning doesn't strike twice.

16

I was taken to the station and shoved into a cell. The cops were holding me on breaking and entering, assaulting an officer, perverting the course of justice, and possession of an unlicensed firearm. Oh, and there was that pesky multiple murder charge too.

They weren't just writing me up for the last batch of murders either. On top of Ingrid and the three dead magicians, they were trying to pin me with five years of homicides. Every case I'd assisted them on, every bad guy I'd steered towards the slammer, was being treated like a fit-up. As though I'd done the killing, planted false evidence, and served the police a patsy.

No doubt about it, things weren't looking great for old Jakey.

Apparently, Stronge and her trained monkey had arrived at Mustachio's house following an anonymous tip. I was beginning to get the distinct impression that I'd been set up. Taken out of the picture by the real culprit, the rogue magician. Was he working with Frosty? Had he paid that old lush off to feed me false intel? To speed up my trip to the noose?

'You really had me going,' said Stronge, as she locked the door to my cell. 'You really did.'

It broke my heart to see her so betrayed. So utterly beaten. 'I had nothing to do with this,' I told her. 'You really think I'm a murderer? Come on, Kat, you know me better than that.'

'I only know one thing about you, Fletcher: you're not a psychic, you're a fucking psychopath.'

I was ready to plead my case but she cut me short.

'A lawyer will be along shortly. If you've got anything more to say, you can say it to them.'

And she left.

My ex-wife, Ingrid, Jazz Hands, and now Stronge. I was getting to make a real habit of disappointing women.

A short while later, Maddox arrived on the other side of my bars wearing the kind of smile that belonged on the face of a Disney villain.

'You must have been laughing your arse off, Fletcher. Killing all those people and getting a pay cheque from us to play Nostradamus.' He slammed his hand against the bars of my cell. 'Well, you're not laughing now, are you?'

He was shaving with Occam's razor and making a proper meal of it.

I stayed schtum while he went on. No sense incriminating myself any more than I already had.

'We found the one you left at the nightclub,' he leered. 'That your scene is it, Fletcher? Getting tugged off by leather daddies with nipple rings and pierced cocks?'

'You haven't got a clue,' I spat.

Shite. Here I was, banged up inside someone else's body and about to be done for multiple counts of murder. I'd really dropped Mark in it this time. You could almost feel sorry for the guy... well, *you* could.

I had to get out of there. If I could just get to the rogue magician in time, if I could get some answers from him before he set his dog on the last man standing and dropped off the map, maybe then I could find out what had happened to

Ingrid. There was still a chance for her, and I wasn't quitting until I had the facts.

'Maddox,' I whispered.

'Yeah,' he said, leaning in close enough that I could see the network of veins on his eyeballs, but not so close I could grab him through the bars. 'What can I do for you, Fletcher?'

'Just one thing.'

'What's that?'

'You can bite down hard... 'cause I'm coming in dry...'

'Wha—' was about as far as he got before I made my move.

Jettisoning from my meat puppet, I shot through the prison bars and right into Maddox.

He flailed about like he'd been set on fire, jerking around, bouncing off the walls, clawing at his skin. He put up a fight, I'll give him that, but he was no prize bronco, and this wasn't my first rodeo. I took hold of his body, breaking him in, seeping into his bones and clamping down on his mind.

'Possession... for men,' I whispered, using Maddox's lips.

He was mine.

I ran a quick diagnostic to see what I had. I saw some things rattling around in that peanut Maddox called a brain. Things he wouldn't let me near with a barge pole: memories, passions, secrets. The whole kit and caboodle. No wonder he put up such a fight. I mean, for a card-carrying homophobe, he sure thought a lot about butt stuff.

There was one particular memory in there that flashed like a beacon. It came from his twenties, back when he was at university. To join the rugby team, he'd taken part in an initiation that involved him taking to the field and running from one try line to the other, buck naked and with a hotdog up his arse. And get this, every time the thing fell out he'd have to pick it up, take a bite and put it back where he found it. By the time he made it to the other end of the field, that hotdog was a stub.

So yeah, Maddox had some things to work through, but then so did I.

The first thing I had to deal with was Mark, who had come out of his stupor and started freaking out over his situation. It's not every day you wake up stone cold sober in a prison cell, and Mark had a lot to say on the subject. Before he could make too much of a fuss about it though, I thought it prudent to shut him up. I did that by using Maddox's key to get into his cell, then used my spirit arm to reach into his chest and give his heart the required squeeze to put him out for a few hours. He'd wake up feeling like he'd taken the ice bucket challenge in Antarctica, but he'd live.

Now to continue my investigation. Since I had access to Maddox's memories, I sifted past the butt stuff and had a root around for any info pertaining to the Vallens case. Anything the cops might not have shared with me. I found something noteworthy pretty quickly, from right back at the start of the investigation. It turned out that the warehouse Ingrid was skinned in belonged to a local businessman. Maddox had questioned him to find out if he was connected to the crime in any way, but the businessman had claimed the property had been broken into, despite not showing any signs of forced entry. Since the police couldn't prove any connection to the crime, the suspect was discharged and the matter considered an investigative dead end.

Here's the thing though, I know that businessman. He goes by the name of Vic Lords—an employer of mine from back in the day—and I can tell you this for nothing: Vic Lords is innocent of bugger all. The man's a gangster and an all-round bad guy, and on top of that, he's a closet Satanist. No surprise he'd be wrapped up in an occult ritual. Vic Lords and shady shit? The Venn diagram of the two is practically an eclipse.

17

It was early evening by the time I reached Lords' office, and a gentle breeze yanked low, grey clouds across the dimming skyline. It was getting on for day six of my investigation. After that I'd have 24 hours to make good on my promise, or I was toast.

I hadn't had the displeasure of Lords' company in a while, not since I'd died in fact. Before then I used to do house clearings for him. He'd buy haunted properties on the cheap then bring me in to exorcise the place so he could sell the purged estates on for a tidy profit. There weren't all that many gigs available to a freelance exorcist, so I tended to take whatever I could get my hands on. Of course, I'd always known Vic was dodgy, but I hadn't known the half of it back then. Or maybe I'd just chosen to ignore it. The prospect of ready money can play tricks on a man.

Since I became a ghost, I've become intimately acquainted with Vic's shadowy business practices: the illegal gambling dens, the drug smuggling operations, the sex trafficking rings, all of them nourished by his experiments in the black arts. Ever since he committed himself to mastering the occult, his power and notoriety have grown like a fungus, spawning in London's darkest, sweatiest corners.

I stood across the road from Vic's office and cracked my knuckles. Well, Maddox's knuckles. I'd been wanting to put that sack of shit Lords away for years, but the bloke's like Teflon. Pin whatever you like on him, he'd always have an alibi. Failing that, he'd grease some palms, or have his goons apply pressure to the arresting officer until he changed his statement. The cops could bring Lords in with a sawn-off head in one hand and a confession note in the other, and he'd still be back on the streets in the time it took to boil a brew.

I wasn't there to bring Vic to justice though, I was there for answers, and I was getting them with or without his cooperation. I marched across the road and arrived at the entrance to his premises, a nondescript door stood next to a set of battered steel shutters that hadn't been rolled up in years. I rapped on the door with Maddox's knuckle, and a moment later a hatch slid open. The eyeballs peering out from the other side caught the flash of my badge, and I heard a series of bolts slide open. The door swung inwards to reveal Vic's doorman, a giant slab of gristle in a too-small tank top.

'Here to see the boss man,' I told him.

The pituitary job flared his nostrils and reluctantly stepped aside. I brushed past him, maintaining eye-contact, then headed up the sticky staircase leading to Lords' den.

I didn't knock, but then I didn't need to announce myself. Vic had already seen me coming on the black and white security monitor he kept on his desk.

'Detective Inspector Maddox,' he said in the sleazy, phlegmy voice of a *Carry On* milkman. 'To what do I owe the pleasure?'

Vic Lords looked like a pile of spoiled luncheon meat with a layer of black mould on top: pallid skin and fish lips topped off with a head of greasy, coal-coloured hair and matching mutton chops. He sat sunk into a duct-taped, vinyl chair under a ceiling turned brown by decades of nicotine. His surroundings were the kind you didn't want to touch, even with the soles of your shoes. I got the feeling that if someone were to shine a forensics blacklight about the place it would flare up like the Milky Way.

'Vic,' I said, and watched his lip curl. No one called Vic Lords "Vic". I expect his own mother called him "Mr Lords".

'What do you want?' he asked, stubbing out a cigarette.

'I need you to answer some questions,' I told him, pacing around his desk like a gestapo officer, arms behind my back.

Vic refused to be intimidated. 'Anything I can do to assist your enquiries, Officer?' he asked, with the oily smarm of a practiced toastmaster.

I thought it best I establish my intentions, so I grabbed a fistful of hair from the nape of his neck and ploughed his face into his desk. He landed hard enough to loosen a few letters on his keyboard, not to mention a couple of teeth.

'Tell me what you know about Ingrid Vallens!' I demanded.

Vic's heavy was on the scene in seconds, crashing through the door, baseball bat in hand. He charged across the room and wound it up, ready to cave my head in, but Lords put up a hand.

'Stop,' he told him, wiping a dribble of claret from his chin. 'No need to be alarmed, Kojo. Me and the officer were just having a little conversation, that's all.'

Kojo lowered his weapon and looked me up and down. 'As long as you're sure,' he said.

The bouncer took his leave and headed back downstairs to his post.

Vic grinned with bloody teeth. 'It's good to see you again, Jake.'

I'll admit it, that shook me. I knew Lords was tapped into the Uncanny but I hadn't realised he could see me inside of my meat suit.

'An exorcist turned ghost, eh?' he went on. 'If I were a comedian I'd be feeling some real pressure to make a joke right now.'

I composed myself and wrested control of the situation. 'If you know what I am, then you know what I can do to you.'

I allowed my ghost hand to leave Maddox's body and rested my fingertips on Vic's chest. He flinched at the chill and held up his hands in surrender.

'No need to get nasty, Fletcher, I'm happy to talk.' He tutted. 'You know, I liked you much more when you were alive.'

I ignored him. 'You own a property by the canal. A warehouse—'

'Yes, an officer already questioned me about it – the one you're squatting in right now as a matter of fact.'

'And?'

'And I'm going to tell you what I told him: I don't know anything about what happened there. Not a single thing.'

'You better not be lying to me, Vic.'

He flinched as I raised my hand, but I wasn't about to strike him. I was doing it to get a read from the magic mood ring Jazz Hands had given me. I put the stone to him, and sure enough, it turned red. The man was talking out of his arse.

Putting my hand between his flabby teats, I reached inside his chest and closed my fingers about the black lump of coal he called a heart. He gasped like he'd fallen through an iced-over lake and seized up stock-still, his eyes the size of dinner plates.

'I loaned it out,' he hissed, his lips moving like he was trying to throw his voice. 'Gave them a key.'

'Gave *who* a key?'

'I don't know—'

'Give me name!'

'I don't bleedin' have one!'

My voodoo truth detector turned blue this time. He was on the level.

I plucked my ghost hand from Vic's chest and he let out a

great sigh of relief. He sunk back into his chair, panting like he'd crossed the finish line of a marathon.

'This guy, the one that rented the key, what did he look like?'

'Not a guy. A girl.'

True again. How about that? This whole time I'd been on the tail of an elusive, rogue magician, I'd assumed I was chasing a man, but no, apparently there was a woman under that balaclava. A woman stripping Ingrid Vallens of her skin. A woman in league with a demon.

So, the Order of the Eternal flame had accepted a female member, had they? Pretty progressive for an old boys' club.

I turned to Lords. 'The woman, tell me about her.'

'Hard to say, she was wearing sunglasses. The big movie star kind.'

Sunglasses indoors? Now I really disliked her. 'What else can you tell me about her?'

'I don't know,' he said, the corners of his lips twitching, 'women aren't really my thing.'

I once had the displeasure of eyeing some particularly illegal images on his computer, so I had a pretty good idea what Lords' "thing" was, the dirty bastard. I pulled back my arm and went to give him a taste of my ring hand.

'You're going about this all wrong, Fletcher,' he snapped.

'How am I?'

'If you want to find a killer you don't go looking for the killer. You go looking for their next victim.'

Damn it, he was right. I'd been going about this all wrong. The ID of the killer wasn't important right now. Catching her before she killed the last magician was what mattered.

I made for the door, but just as I was about to leave, Vic called after me.

'Oh, Jake?'

'Yeah?'

A splinter of sunlight caught his bloody grin. 'You ever want some work, son, you just let me know. It'll be just like the good old days.'

18

It was the dawn of day six of my investigation. I needed to track down the killer's next victim before she popped his clogs, and I had a pretty good idea where I should start. The man was a magician after all, and if it's a magician you're after, what better place to kick off than the Magic Circle?

If this were a movie, I'd be taking a pause right about now. Grabbing a quick breather before the climactic showdown and ruminating on what I'd learned so far. If I only had that luxury. I had an hour at most before Maddox's body rejected me, so the best I could do was put on my big boy pants and get cracking.

I was about to get going when I heard a ringing noise and realised it was coming from the inside pocket of Maddox's overcoat. I reached in and fished out a digital police radio, a communication device that was halfway between a walkie-talkie and your granddad's mobile. According to the read-out, it was DCI Stronge on the other end. I prevaricated for a moment, then decided to take the call.

'Hello,' I said, instantly wondering if that was the appropriate greeting.

'Where are you?' came the terse reply. She was expecting

her partner of course, and had no idea I was the one picking up the phone.

'Just... um, grabbing a bite,' I told her.

'Well, get yourself back to the nick. Our coma witness woke up and she's given a description of the suspect.'

'Is that right?'

'Are you okay, Maddox?' she asked. 'You sound weird.'

I coughed and deepened my voice, as if that was going to help. 'I'm fine, just a bit of a cold. What's she saying then? The witness.'

'She's saying our suspect's a woman for starters.'

'No way,' I replied, acting as shocked as my limited acting skills would allow.

'A real looker she reckons. Model quality. Not what I was expecting at all. Sounds more like a fit for our first vic than the Jack the Ripper I had in mind.'

This came as no surprise to me of course, not since I'd learned that the demon was running amok in Ingrid Vallens' skin.

'Bizarre,' I replied.

'*Bizarre?*' Stronge repeated, but with an inflection that told me she was growing increasingly suspicious of my Maddox impersonation.

I changed the subject. 'How's Mark doing? Jake I mean... You know, Nostra-bleedin'-damus. The man I really, really hate. The bastard.'

'Fast asleep in his cell. And you know what they say about the prisoner that sleeps soundly?'

'Guilty as fuck,' I sighed.

Great. On top of bringing a rogue magician to justice and sending her demon back to hell, I also had to find some way to clear Mark's name. The bloke's no angel—he's a bully who kicks his dog about and takes a pretty dim view on immigrants—but I couldn't let the tosser spend the rest of his life behind bars because of me.

'I have to go,' I told Stronge. 'Um... over and out...'

'What is going on with y—?'

I cut off the call before her pitch could get any higher.

Being as I was hitchhiking in Maddox's body, I wasn't able to do my Mr. Benn trick and zap inside the Order's HQ. Instead, I had to go the old-fashioned way, catching the tube to Euston, hoofing it to the Magic Circle on foot, and bypassing the magical cage surrounding the place with a spot of the old hocus pocus.

I made it into the building's ground floor lobby and took stock of my inventory. Being as I'd left my gun in my other trousers—so to speak—I had to work with what I had. Turned out what I had amounted to an extendable baton and some harsh words. Maddox must have checked his Taser in back at the station before I took hold of him. An arsehole to the end.

A noise drifted under the crack of a door marked STAFF ONLY. I stepped closer and pressed my ear to the door. I heard shuffling sounds beyond, accompanied by some kind of incantation. I went after the noise, pushing the door open and creeping softly down a corridor painted with murals of stage illusionists from days gone by. Rounding a corner, I found a man with a disfigured mouth stood by a door, frantically reciting the words to an unlocking spell.

Cleft Lip.

The last living magician of the Order of the Eternal Flame, and I'd caught up with him before the killer crossed him off her shopping list. At least I'd managed to save one of them. Hoo-bloody-ray.

I held out a hand. 'You've gotta come with me, mate. Right now.'

The magician ignored me and continued to chant, stuck inside of his spell.

'Pack it in, will you? We've got to get moving, sharpish!'

He placed his palm on the door and it began to glow. He wasn't leaving until he had that thing open. What could he be after that was so important he was ready to die for it?

I went to grab him by the elbow and yank him upstairs when he suddenly spasmed. A jet of blood blasted out of his mouth like an accident with a beetroot smoothie. After that came a hand, exploding through his chest and clutching a pulsating human heart.

The hand retracted and the magician's body flopped to the floor like a marionette with its strings cut.

Stood there in the gloom, a still-beating heart in its hand, was the demon, all dressed up in Ingrid Vallens' skin. The flesh hung off it now, loose and putrefying, a mockery of its former beauty. And it stank. Stank like a forgotten WWII death camp discovered in the mid-fifties.

The soul feaster dipped a pair of Prada shades, revealing twin hollows underneath that flared sulphur orange.

'Oh look,' it growled. 'A witness...'

The demon padded towards me with murderous intent. Its rotting skin-suit was scorched from its encounter with the wand-wielding Mustachio; feathered with a pattern of lesions that looked almost tree-like. It had a bullet hole in its left shoulder too—in one side and out the other—the shot I'd dealt it back at the fetish club.

The soul feaster grinned and sunk its teeth into the magician's heart, biting down on it like a candy apple. The demon's eyes rolled back in its skull as it swallowed and hoovered down the elder's eternal soul. It bowed its head, letting Ingrid's blonde hair cascade down its face like a golden waterfall. When it looked up again, I saw its stolen features had tightened and become symmetrical once more. The demon's second skin flushed pink, its wounds stitching together until they were gone completely. It removed its sunglasses to reveal a pair of perfect, husky-blue eyes.

There was Ingrid, just as she was the day I'd met her, only even more beautiful. Rejuvenated and in the prime of her life.

The demon drew its lips back in a snarl, tossed the sunglasses and crushed them underfoot.

What had I blundered into this time? I'd busted in, all ready to do battle with the forces of darkness, but stood before the enemy, I realised just how stupid I'd been. Not only could the soul feaster do me a mischief, it could take chunks out of Maddox too, and no matter how big of a tool he was, he didn't deserve to end up on a demon's dessert tray.

I decided to do a possibly very stupid thing. I decided to double-down and go on the offensive. 'So, come on then,' I yelled at the demon. 'Who's behind the mystery door? Who's pulling your strings?'

The soul feaster arranged Ingrid's perfect, Cupid's bow lips into a glowing smile. It wasn't just an approximation though, this was Ingrid's own smile, as beautiful and beguiling as it was on the bank of Regent's Canal.

'Hello, Jake. How lovely to see you again.'

That smile. That voice. And that's when it hit me. I took a wavering step backwards as the truth of the situation made my stomach drop. This wasn't just some demon running around in Ingrid Vallens' torn-off skin.

No, Ingrid was actually in there.

Ingrid's ghost.

The victim was the villain.

19

Everything I knew about Ingrid Vallens had turned to smoke, and I was choking on it.

'Surprised?' she said, blood dripping down her chin. 'Of course you are. You were my knight in shining armour and I was your damsel in distress. Just a dumb dead girl, waiting on a man to show her to the light.'

'That's not true...' I protested.

'Yes it is, Jake. You don't know me, but I certainly know you. All my life I've had to deal with your type. Men who see me as a thing. A commodity. A piece of meat on their casting couch. Well, I got tired of playing the victim, Jake. Tired of photo shoots that turned into porno shoots. Tired of fat arseholes telling me that size zero was too heavy and pushing drugs on me to keep my weight in check.'

My mind was racing. How? How could Ingrid Vallens be the soul feaster? 'Okay,' I said, 'you've been dicked around by men, I get it. That doesn't explain how we got here though.'

'*I* got here through hard work,' she said, her jaw muscles twitching. '*I* had to fight for my spot on the pentacle. Do you think this old boys' club wanted a catwalk model on their members list?'

I'd spotted a link between the rest of the elders already: a theology professor, a plastic surgeon, an HIV patient—the kind of people who'd be pretty keen to know the secret of everlasting youth—but only now was I seeing how obviously a former model slotted in there.

I still didn't get it though. How could Ingrid be a murder victim, the fifth elder, and a demon too? That was an awful lot of hats to wear.

Blood dripped from her chin on to the generous upper slopes of her breasts and down the runnel of her cleavage. 'Even when they accepted my membership I was a second class citizen to them. I'd studied magic for years, passed every test they threw at me, and still they treated me like a bimbo. I had ideas, Jake. Real ideas, to achieve what the Order was created for: to attain immortality! She lashed out and punched a fist through the corridor's plasterboard wall. 'But they wouldn't listen.'

'Easy, tiger,' I said. 'Don't give yourself a nosebleed.'

'You sound just like the rest of them,' she spat. 'Frightened. Scared of the unknown. For the rest of the elders the quest for eternal life had become academic. But they were men. This world lets men grow old. Not so for me. I was a woman, my looks fading, my best years behind me. I was ready to do whatever it took to get my youth back, and I wasn't about to wait for permission.'

Okay, I got the motivation, but I still wasn't seeing the whole picture. I still wasn't seeing how Ingrid wound up inside a demon.

'I don't understand,' I said. 'You died. I saw your ghost.'

In a flash, she leapt forward and seized my head between her hands, clamping down on my skull like a vice.

A riot of images washed through my brain.

I saw Ingrid, in the warehouse by the canal, stood before a chalk pentacle.

I saw a ritual, a summoning, a demon drawn from the Nether.

I saw a mistake. A flaw in Ingrid's ward. The demon crossing her protective barrier.

I saw the demon punishing Ingrid for her impertinence. Claiming its blood sacrifice.

I saw it drawing a fingernail across Ingrid's flesh. Stripping her of her perfect skin.

I saw Ingrid escaping. Fleeing before the demon could feast on her soul.

I saw her red handprint on a boat's porthole.

Saw her running until she could run no more.

Saw her topple from the bank of the canal and into its murky waters.

The images raced away from me, sucked from my head like water down a plug hole. I staggered and butted a shoulder against the nearest wall, clammy and hyperventilating. I had it all wrong. The rogue magician and the demon weren't colluding, they were one and the same. 'How though? How did you get inside a demon?'

She offered a high, brittle laugh. 'With your help.'

'Bollocks.'

But she wasn't taking *bollocks* for an answer. 'You've been helping me since the second you showed up, Jake. Ever since I first fluttered my eyelashes at you.'

'Except I haven't done a thing for you. I've been too busy for that. Too busy blundering all over Camden chasing the bodies you left behind.'

'Mostly, yes, but not entirely. My first victim was all thanks to you.'

'The body at Highgate Cemetery?'

'That's right. You're the one who gave me the idea to lay some bait.'

She grabbed me by the head again and I felt another deluge of pictures.

I saw the ghost of Ingrid Vallens at the cemetery.

I saw the elder with the weak chin—Glass Jaw—furtively picking his way through the tombstones.

I saw the two of them talking. Saw the elder tell Vallens that she'd deserved her fate. That she'd paid the price for meddling with demons.

I saw the knife in Vallens' hand. Saw it lash out and cut Glass Jaw from balls to sternum.

I saw the look on his face as he watched his innards slop on to the dirty ground.

The kaleidoscope calmed and my thoughts became my own again as she released her grip on my skull. I shook my head, trying to shake the images away, but they were seared into my psyche like a cattle brand.

Now I knew. While I was busy at The Beehive, laying bait for the mysterious rogue magician, Ingrid had taken inspiration from me and laid a trap of her own.

'You're good,' I told her. 'It took me years of being a ghost to handle objects like you did that knife.'

'Thank you,' she said, performing a smug little curtsy.

I managed to put together the rest. Vallens must have been lying in wait at the cemetery when the demon came sniffing around, eager to feed, hungry for a two course meal of heart and soul. When the off-brand Beelzebub went for the bait and tripped Vallens' weakening magic, she'd struck out, capitalising on the soul feaster's vulnerability and making its body her own. For once it hadn't been the demon that possessed the human. This time the person was on the inside.

That was certainly a turn-up for the books. I had no idea a reversal of that sort was even possible. The ghost of a dead magician possessing a demon dressed in the magician's original skin? We had a real Russian nesting doll situation going on here.

'So that wasn't the demon eating the heart out of the old

man's chest,' I said, piecing the last of it together, 'that was you inside the demon?'

'Got it in one,' she replied. 'I have to feed to stay in control of the soul feaster, and since those daft old codgers had already made my shit list, I thought why not kill two birds with one stone?'

I laughed. What else could I do, given the circumstances? 'You must be chuffed to bits,' I told her. 'You got your looks back and immortality to boot, and all it cost was four dead men.'

She shrugged. 'It's not the way I planned it, but it'll do. *C'est la vie*, or *Telle est la vie éternelle* if you want to get technical about it.'

She really had played me for a mug. I'd only taken the Vallens gig for the karma, but the whole time I thought I'd been wiping red from my account, I'd actually been helping out a psychopath. Something told me I wouldn't be earning any Brownie points for that little stunt.

'So where do we go from here?' I asked. 'I don't suppose you want to be a good sport and follow me to the cop shop, do you?'

'I'm afraid I can't do that,' she said, her face cut with a devil's smirk. 'See, I need one more soul to bond fully with my new body... and yours looks absolutely delectable.'

I could almost have taken it for a compliment if it wasn't for the fact that she was eying me up like a full English breakfast.

A forked black tongue emerged from her mouth and whisked around her lips. 'Goodbye, Jake.'

20

Vallens came at me fast, but I wasn't defenceless. Yes, she could hurt me, but then I could always hurt her back... or at least my host could. DI Maddox might not be too sharp up top, but he had a club on him and a meaty set of arms to swing it with.

I whipped out Maddox's police issue baton, grabbed it in both hands and battered Vallens in the neck as hard as I could muster.

Crunch.

The weapon broke in half like a piece of dry kindling.

The impact sent a shock coursing through my arm and into my shoulder, where it exploded like dynamite. I might as well have been hitting a marble statue for all the damage I did. It was as though Vallens' skin was draped over a tank.

I didn't stand a chance going against her toe-to-toe, so I made a tactical withdrawal that definitely wasn't a desperate, cowardly scramble for freedom.

I pushed through the STAFF ONLY door to the lobby and surveyed the area in search of something to defend myself with. Unfortunately, the best I could find was an old umbrella hanging in the lost and found section of the cloak room.

A thought struck me, a memory from the last time I'd paid this place a visit.

I remembered the elders talking about their previous skirmish with a soul feaster. Mustachio had sent it back to the Nether that time, and he'd done it using something called the seraphim sword, which I suspected, or really, really hoped, the Order kept in-house. The locked door the last magician had just died trying to open—that must be where they kept it—and now I was cut off from the bastard thing. Not that it mattered. The vault was sealed tight with magic, and by the time I was done cracking that, Vallens would have sucked down my soul like a pup on a tit.

She arrived in the lobby with all the hurry of a murderer from a slasher movie. Meanwhile, I was left panting and wheezing from all the running around – one of the unfortunate side effects of having to haul about a living body. Another is not being able to phase through solid objects—at least not without leaving one's host for dead—which meant I couldn't evade my pursuer by scarpering through the nearest wall.

I had to get out of there though, so, aiming for the only exit available, I threw Maddox's body towards the front door and went to give Vallens the old Irish goodbye. I already knew the combination to that lock, so I could bust through it in no time.

Unfortunately, Vallens had other ideas.

Springing into action, she dived into my path and cut me off, escape-proofing the place. I felt a gulp travel up Maddox's throat and back down again.

'Relax, Mister Fletcher,' said Vallens. 'No more being cursed to walk the Earth for all eternity. You're finally going to meet your maker.'

That's what I was afraid of. I had a lot of work to do before I was back in His good graces. A lot of wrongs to right before I returned to the mothership. A premature trip would undo five years of good deeds and leave a big, fat, *aided and abetted a demonic entity* shaped full stop at the end of an otherwise glittering career.

Vallens closed in on me, ready to twist the head off my meat suit and drink me down—

When the door behind her swung open.

Filling the frame was DCI Stronge, looking suitably confused. 'What's the bloody hell is going on here?' she asked, seeing her partner cowering before the bloody and surprisingly animate Ingrid Vallens.

'Shoot her!' I yelled, doing my best Maddox impression. 'Shoot the demonic cow!'

Ever the pro, Stronge whipped out her Taser and planted a couple of high voltage darts in my attacker's chest. Vallens convulsed, her legs locking as she keeled over backwards like a trust-building exercise gone horribly wrong.

Stronge took her finger off the Taser's trigger and turned to me. 'One more time... what the hell is going on here?'

I changed the subject with a question of my own. 'How did you find me?'

'You sounded weird before, so I used your phone to track you.'

And thank God she had.

'Come on,' I said. 'She won't stay down for long.'

Vallens was already beginning to stir.

I was about to grab Stronge by the wrist and steer her outside when something dawned on me. If Stronge had been able to breeze in here unhindered, that must mean the magic cage surrounding the building was down.

Of course it was.

The protection magic was the combined product of the four elders, and since they were all dead now, the spell was broken. That meant the vault must be open too, which meant the seraphim sword was ripe for the plucking. If I could get to that, I could put an end to Vallens *and* the winged monkey she was shacked up in. Two birds, one stone.

Speaking of the devil—pun most definitely intended—Vallens had recovered from the effects of the Taser and was hobbling to her feet already, her spine unfurling from a question mark to a very pointed exclamation mark.

'Isn't that our murder vic?' asked Stronge, her brain finally catching up with her eyeballs.

The sight of Vallens stood before her had understandably thrown Stronge's tidy mind into a degree of disarray.

'No,' I replied, weakly, 'it's her... um, evil twin.'

But Stronge's attention was already fixed on the threat, which was coming her way and seeking a swift retribution.

'Down on the ground, now!' Stronge ordered.

Vallens failed to comply, leaving Stronge no option but to pull out her baton and extend it with a deft flick of her wrist.

'I wouldn't do that...' I started to say, but Stronge was not to be deterred.

She pulled back her arm and clouted Vallens across the side of the knee with the intention of immobilising her. The effect was altogether familiar. Stronge cursed as her cosh snapped in two, then cried out in pain as the shock of the impact exploded in her arm.

By way of a thank you, Vallens grabbed Stronge by the face, lifted her off her feet and flung her across the lobby. Plaster rained down as Stronge struck the wall and rolled to the ground. I rushed in and dived on her attacker, but was back-handed flat for my trouble. When I came round, I saw that Stronge had somehow managed to find her feet and was facing off against Vallens for a second time.

She's a tough old bird, I'll give her that.

Shrieking like a Valkyrie, Stronge swung at Vallens, raking her claws down her face and peeling away a big, red flap of skin. It hung there, revealing what lay beneath: a demonic skull studded with one incongruous blue eye. The eye's partner had been punctured by Stronge's nails and was dribbling like a split grape.

'I'm going to make you pay for that,' Vallens snarled, plucking the ruined eye from its orbit and flicking it to the ground with a squelch.

The hollow socket flared orange and the jaw of her skull mouth chattered as she paced towards her attacker. Stronge wasn't even given a chance to freak out before her assailant pimp-slapped her to the ground.

DCI Stronge was out cold.

Vallens took a step backwards and cocked her head to one side to admire her handiwork. Satisfied, she pressed the heel of a Jimmy Choo boot to Stronge's throat and went to crush her windpipe.

'Oi!' I shouted, getting Vallens' attention. 'What am I, chopped liver?'

She removed her foot from Stronge's neck and turned to me, face flap swinging. Her eyes burned like a pair of hot coals.

I took off up the lobby's spiral staircase, running faster than a gambler from a bookie. With Vallens on my tail, I pegged it down a corridor I was already intimate with and pushed through the door marked PRIVATE.

I arrived in the Order's clubhouse. The room was lit by the familiar, flickering flame of witchfire that burned eternally in its hammered iron brazier.

Once again, I went looking for a weapon to defend myself with, but came up empty. I was hoping to find something of use in one of the room's musty old display cabinets, but all I found there were trinkets: crystal balls, a clutch of sinister-looking ventriloquist's dummies, and an Edison cylinder containing a scratchy sound recording of Harry Houdini.

Vallens appeared in the doorway looking like a supermodel that had stepped into a Brundle Pod with Skeletor's ugly cousin.

She had me cornered.

Nothing I could do now but plant my feet and fight.

'Get ready to die for the second time,' Vallens gloated.

'You know, I'm really starting to think twice about you and me having any sort of romantic future.'

She came at me whipcrack fast and landed a punch in my gut so hard I'm surprised Maddox didn't spew me up.

I managed to dodge the next blow, only for her fist to quest past me and through one of the display cabinets. I made an umbrella of my arms as glass rained down and all around. When I opened my eyes, I noticed a fan of circus throwing knives inside the busted cabinet. Seeing they were up for grabs, I reached in and plucked one out.

Vallens came at me again and I slashed her, sawing a wet flap of skin off her arm.

'Bastard!' she shrieked.

Beast mode activated, her fingertips split open and ten huge talons emerged from the ragged ends, absolutely devastating Vallens' manicure.

I took a couple of steps to the side, continuing to ward her off with the throwing blade as I attempted to skirt her to the exit. Vallens was smart though, and circled around to block me.

'You're not going anywhere,' she seethed.

Vallens tore the place apart, picking up whole cabinets and hurling them at me, smothering the place in glass and debris. At one point she managed to upset the Order's brazier, which tipped over and spread a pool of witchfire across the floor.

I ducked and weaved, stabbing and hacking whenever Vallens made it within arm's reach. I was quick, but compared to her souped-up demon body, I moved slower than a sundial's shadow. The fact is, all I was doing was buying myself a little time. There was no way I was going to come out of this one on top.

After a spirited bout of evasion, I found myself all out of puff, which gave Vallens all the excuse she needed to swoop in for the kill.

She lashed out, but I managed to throw an arm up just in time to defend myself from the blow. I heard a noise I mistook for a gunshot then realised she'd snapped one of Maddox's arms like a twig. His agony was mine to bear though, and I collapsed to the ground, clutching on to the broken limb.

Witchfire licked at the walls and smoke-choked the air, lending the room a distinct Hades vibe. As I lay on the floor, writhing in pain, Vallens leapt into the air like something from *The Matrix* and came down on me with one knee. I don't know how I managed it, but I succeeded in rolling on to my front just as she landed and put a crater in the ground beside me.

Undaunted, Vallens grabbed me by the scruff of the neck and clawed me across the back with her talons. The only reason Maddox didn't end up with ventilated kidneys was because of the stab vest he was wearing.

I squirmed and tried to roll over to face Vallens, but she had me pinned. I was about to give up the ghost—again, the pun is deliberate—when I saw the peephole Vallens' knee had put through the floor.

That's when I got an idea.

It was a risk, but at this point Maddox was dead anyway if I didn't at least try.

Leaving Maddox at the mercy of my attacker, I exited his body and phased through the floor to the room below.

Up above, I heard Vallens cackle. 'You really are a wretched coward, Fletcher.'

'Are you coming to get me or what?' I yelled back, as I scanned the room I now found myself in, desperately searching for the object I'd gone down there in search of.

'Of course,' she replied. 'As soon as I'm done gutting this pig.'

I was afraid of that. I needed to rile her up some to get her off Maddox's case and on to mine. Luckily for Inspector Fuck-wit, when it comes to pissing off the fairer sex, I am no slouch.

'Pretty good of the Order to take on a lady,' I said. 'Shame you had to go and kill them all – that's going to set the women's movement back a few years.' I could hear Vallens upstairs, growling like the devil's hungry belly. The heckling was working. 'Maybe you should have stuck with what you know,' I went on, 'keeping your mouth shut and looking pretty. You'd make a great magician's assistant, I reckon. I know *I'd* want to saw you in half!'

Vallens punched through the ceiling and came diving down at me, shrieking like a three a.m. car alarm—

Only to find herself skewered on the business end of an enchanted sword.

The seraphim sword, to be exact, with me holding the other end of it.

Face contorted like a gargoyle, Vallens slid slowly down the length of the blade until the sword's crossguard met her sternum.

Vallens' nose met mine and I grinned back at her.

'You... bastard...' she hissed.

'Sorry, Ingrid, no end-of-date kiss for you.'

It was only thanks to her cracking a hole between floors that I'd realised the Order's clubhouse was situated directly above the vault, and with no magical protection to stop me getting in there, I'd been able to slip right through. Leaving Maddox behind was a calculated risk, something I had to do so I could get to the sword and goad Vallens into coming at me.

'I'll kill you!' she screeched, and it was no idle threat.

Vallens' skull face ripped free of her skin and chomped at my throat.

Her teeth snapped down next to my jugular with nothing to spare. And I do mean absolutely nothing. If ghosts were able to collect dirt, she would have cleaned my neck. She gnashed at me again and again, eyes blazing, flecks of grey spittle flying from her skull mouth. If I didn't act fast, she'd bite my head off like I was a gingerbread man.

I widened my stance and white-knuckled the sword's hilt, straining to hold her at bay.

'...Kill you!' she said, as if it needed repeating.

I grunted and twisted the blade. Her mouth shot wide open – wide enough to swallow a baby whole. She let loose an ear-piercing scream that shattered the glass cases pressed against the room's walls, then the sulphurous fire burning in her empty eye socket guttered and died.

'Goodnight, Ingrid.'

Vallens went slack and fell to the ground, where she lay splayed and still. As I watched, her body began to flake and disintegrate, crumbling away like autumn leaves. Vallens was gone, and the soul feaster too, off on a tandem ride to Hell.

21

The thing about witchfire is that it acts differently to regular fire. The stuff the blokes with the yellow hats and hoses put out isn't known for being predictable, but compared to witchfire, it operates right out of a textbook. Magic fire spreads according to its own laws, unbeholden by such trifling matters as physics, least of all gravity.

When Vallens upset the Order of the Eternal flame's brazier, she unleashed a blaze that burned their headquarters down to the ground. It was only through quick thinking and good fortune that I tossed the seraphim sword, climbed back inside Maddox's body and scooped up Stronge before the place was razed.

The paramedics rushed the two detectives to the nearest hospital, where they were treated for smoke inhalation and various secondary injuries.

Not long after she was admitted, I went to pay Stronge a visit. I decided it was high time me and her had a talk – *real talk*, as the yanks are fond of saying.

Greeting her with a familiar face would have been my first choice, but since my usual mule, Mark, was still in pokey, I had to improvise. I arrived at the hospital with the intention of possessing a nurse and passing along my message that way, but the second I entered Stronge's ward, she sat up from her bed like she'd seen a ghost, which of course she had.

'Who are you?' she demanded, making a crucifix of some hospital cutlery.

This I was not expecting.

'You can see me?' I said, pointing at my face.

'Of course I can see you.'

'Well that's... odd.'

'I mean... I can see you, but... what are you?'

'I'm a ghost.'

It seemed Stronge could actually see me. The real me. I'd heard of this happening before. Sometimes, when people have a traumatic experience with the Uncanny, they've been known to develop The Sight. It's like it triggers something in their mind. Busts open a locked door.

I took a couple of steps towards her, hands held up in surrender. 'It's okay,' I said, 'I'm a friend.'

I took a seat on the edge of her bed and she swept a hand through me.

'You know, in the ghost community, that's considered quite rude,' I explained.

'I know you,' she wheezed, her lungs still feeling the effects of the smoke. 'I do, don't I? Where do I know you from?' she asked, studying my face.

'A few years back you solved my murder. My name's Jake Fletcher.'

I'll save us both some time and summarise how the meat of the conversation sandwich went down. I explained how I was a ghost that had, up until that moment, been carjacking a former bully to help her solve crimes. I explained the purpose of my investigation and broke down Ingrid Vallens' scheme, being extra sure to let her know that the guy she'd banged up in the model's place was in no way complicit.

It was a lot for Stronge to unpack, but she handled it well, all things considered.

'So, the person I've known all these years is really your... what do you call it...?

'My meat suit. Mark's just a vessel. I'm the genuine article.'

Stronge slapped her forehead. 'You didn't even change your name! Why didn't I make the connection before? Why didn't I realise you were the same Jake Fletcher as the one we had on the slab five years ago?'

I chuckled. 'It is a bit of a stretch: a dead man coming back as a ghost and setting himself up as a paranormal P.I. Don't be too hard on yourself about it. Even Quincy wouldn't have put those pieces together.'

'Really? *Quincy* is your go-to? Why not Sherlock Holmes?'

'What's wrong with Quincy?'

'Who goes with Quincy?'

We stopped and stared at each for a moment before breaking out in laughter. I'd just revealed the guy who'd been helping her out all these years was a ghost, and here we were arguing over fictional sleuths.

Stronge relaxed and rested her head on her pillow. 'So, what do we do now?' she asked.

'Well, the good news is that you're not one of the hoi polloi anymore.'

'How's that?'

'You've had a peek behind the curtain now, which means you've graduated from being a normal to what we call an "Insider".'

'And what's that supposed to mean? Like I'm in some kind of secret society?'

'Exactly. Really, really secret.'

'Let me get this straight; I'm supposed to stay quiet about all the things I've seen? About ghosts and magic and skull-faced demons?'

I aimed a gunfinger at her. 'Spot on.'

She shook her head. 'Forget it. People need to know about this stuff.'

'Trust me,' I replied, 'they really don't. People are scared of the dark. They freak out at the sound of their plumbing. Can you imagine what they'd do if they found out vampires were real?'

'Vampires are real?' Stronge screeched, sitting bolt upright.

I cocked an eyebrow at her. 'You take my point?'

She sighed and ran a hand through her bob. 'What about Maddox?' she asked. 'He'll know.'

'He won't, I've already seen to that, and I need you to help me keep it that way. Not a word to him about any of this. Your partner's had it out for me since day one – you tell him I'm a ghost and he'll be Googling proton packs before you finish your sentence.'

'What about my superiors then? What do I say to them?'

'Anything you like as long as it isn't the truth. The Order's HQ burned down, so you don't have to worry about evidence. Find a way to sweep the rest under the carpet. Case unsolved. One for the X-Files.'

She pouted and folded her arms. 'You're asking an awful lot, Fletcher.'

I smiled, made my hand solid and rested it on her shoulder. 'It could be worse,' I told her. 'At least you came out of this alive.'

I sat up and went for the door, then remembered I had one thing left to say. 'Kat,' I called back.

'Yeah?'

'Take care of yourself. You've seen the Uncanny now.'

'So what?'

'So that means the Uncanny can see you back...

I found Maddox in the ward next door with his arm in a sling. I crept in and waved my arms about in front of him, just in case he was able to see me too now. He didn't even blink.

'Oi, Maddox, you massive twat!'

Not a twitch, so I borrowed an abundantly-proportioned Nigerian nurse I found doing the rounds, and paid him a visit that way.

'How are you today, Mister Maddox?' I asked.

'Detective Inspector Maddox,' he corrected.

I ignored him and used the nurse's meaty paws to lift his egg-bald head and plump the pillow beneath.

'Do you mind?' he protested, squirming as I brushed his fragile wing.

I chuckled. 'You have been in the wars, haven't you?' I said, in an accent that was, to put it politely, a bit borderline.

'Yeah,' he replied, then looked at me quizzically. 'I mean, I think so. It's all a bit blurry.'

Just blurry? It sounded as if I might not have done a good enough job scrubbing that peanut brain of his. 'What do you mean, blurry?' I prompted.

'I don't remember much exactly. They're calling it a fugue state—some work-related stress thing—but I have these flashes... hellfire, a five-pointed star, some... *thing* with claws.' He shook his head as if to erase the memories like an Etch A Sketch drawing.

I changed the subject. 'I bought you something to eat, Detective,' I said. I put a tray in front of him, on top of which sat a plate of something the hospital canteen generously referred to as "food".

He prodded at a scoop of mashed potatoes thick enough to plant a flag in. 'Thanks, but no thanks,' he sniffed.

'I'll go back and see if they've got anything more to your

taste,' I said, and rolled the food trolley towards the door. 'Who knows, maybe they'll have some nice, tasty *hot dogs*.'

I gave him a wink that freaked him out more than the hell-fire and the demon combined.

Back at the nick, Mark Ryan was declared no longer a suspect and cleared of any wrongdoing. I managed to get to him before he woke up and walked him home for a nice, long nap. He'd be okay, even if he did find himself with another gaping black hole in his memory. Something told me the bill for his therapist was going to run pretty high this month, which was only fair. The way he'd treated me at school had given me plenty to talk to my shrink about over the years. Still, I'm not completely heartless, despite all the things he put me through as a lad. I decided I'd go easy on him for a bit, let a bit of time pass before I hopped back inside for another run around. I'm nice like that.

The shop bell tinkled as I arrived in Legerdomain to give my old pal Jazz Hands a debriefing.

'Still alive, I see,' she noted, peering through her magic spectacles.

'Yup. Well, after a fashion.'

'How did it go, then?'

'Piece of piss,' I told her. 'Never in harm's way.'

She arched a brow so high it practically lifted off her head.

'Okay,' I confessed, 'it did get a *little* bit naughty.'

I gave Jazz Hands an account of my confrontation with the Ingrid demon, making sure to gloss over the parts I knew she'd lose her tits over. In my version of the events I'd faced my enemy down with a no-fail strategy, not just blundered in there half-cocked and hoping for the best. In the end, my story was less a tale of derring-do than a tale of derring-didn't-really-do-at-all.

Still, Jazz Hands was not a happy camper. 'I told you, she grumbled, 'I told you you should have deferred to the London Coven.'

She had a point. I'd only survived this one by the skin of my teeth – next time I'd take whatever help I could get. 'Do you have a name?' I asked. 'A contact at this coven place?'

'Stella,' she said. 'Stella Familiar.'

I nodded and made a mental note.

After that, I gave Jazz back the magic ring she'd borrowed me. She placed it in the wall safe hidden behind the sage face of James Randi and asked after the revolver. The gun was a goner I explained, poached by the police and committed to an evidence locker. She groused some more and then, once she felt I'd been suitably chastised, returned to her celebrity magazine.

She was reading a particularly scintillating piece on Kristen Stewart's new haircut when a thought occurred. 'The sword you slayed the soul feaster with,' she said, 'did it happen to have a name?'

'Yeah, it did. The elders called it the seraphim sword.'

Her eyes widened. 'The seraphim sword is a tool of the angels,' she gasped.

'What are you saying?'

'The blade is forged from iron derived from the blood of a thousand fallen demons. What have you done with it? Where is it now?'

My face pinched. 'It kind of got burned up by witchfire.'

Jazz Hands' face turned as white as the proverbial ghost. 'There will be consequences for that,' she said.

I shrugged. 'Aren't there always?'

I made good on my promise to Frosty and brought him the six pack of Special Brew I owed him, blessed by Jazz Hands for his drinking pleasure. He genuflected as I presented it to him, then glugged the beers down one after the other. I felt a bit sorry for him, watching the bloke sink six cans of bruiser juice, but it's hard to grieve for someone who looks so damned happy.

And what about me? What did I get out of all of this? Nothing I could lay my hands on, that was for sure, but then I stopped caring about material things the day I died. My reward was a spiritual one, a real one, not the bullshit kind the door-knockers with the pamphlets and fake grins are shilling.

I watched the end of my *Ghost* DVD. It's not such a bad film really; the ghost gets to be the good guy for a change, and Swayze smashes it as always. It was somewhere near the end of the movie that Whoopi broke the fourth wall again. Acting as a mouthpiece for whatever jobsworth it was throwing his weight around Up There, she begrudgingly let me know that I'd performed my duty and that I was off the hook. At least for a little while.

For once I'd done some real good in this world – the kind that buys Brownie points with Him Upstairs. The kind that rubs a little red out of a man's account. Maybe even a whole lot of red. This wasn't sending down a pickpocket after all, or solving a little light fraud. This was big boy stuff. I'd sent a soul feaster back to Hell, and I'd brought a demonologist to justice too. No wonder the Big Man was so keen to have me send Ingrid's soul His way, He must have known what she'd done and been champing at the bit to punish her for it. Would have been nice of Him to put me in the loop too, but what the hell.

The important thing was that I'd completed His little assignment and bought myself some time before He came calling again.

I stood and looked out of my office window at the messy sprawl of Camden Town beneath me. It was almost dawn. I watched the sun peek over the horizon and laser off the morning fog before settling in the sky like a great, molten coin. When you don't sleep, you get to see a lot of sunrises—it's one of the nice things about being a ghost—but this sunrise was special. A new day was coming. A brighter one than before.

If I could defeat a rogue magician and win a fight with a demon, who knew what else I was capable of? What other kinds of Uncanny I could bring to justice. Vampires, werewolves, mermaids (just kidding), they were all on my shit list now. Sure, it might end up being the end of me, but it would hardly be a premature retirement. Besides, I owed it to them. Owed it to every soul I'd unwittingly scrubbed out of existence. Owed it to myself, too. To my future.

My name is Jake Fletcher. Ex-exorcist. Departed do-gooder. Phantom on the run. And when the Big Man finally pulls me in to judge my soul, I'm going to be ready.

The End.

MAGIC EATER

M.V. STOTT

1

I suppose this all started when I woke up without a single clue as to who I was, where I was, or why I was bleeding from so many different and interesting places.

My name is Joseph Lake, or at least that's what I've decided to call myself. Not the most inspiring of choices, I know, but I couldn't find anything else that felt comfortable, so Joseph Lake it was. The fact that it stuck made me wonder if the name meant something; like maybe it was a family member's name, or a good friend's, or even a good enemy's, but I Googled that thing down to a nub and ended up with nothing. Just one of many deader than dead ends I've chased aimlessly ever since I woke up next to that lake.

That was ten years ago. At the point this story kicks off proper I was stalking the streets of Carlisle in the middle of the night, dressed head-to-toe in black. This was my first time following a stranger at a discreet distance, but I'd seen enough movies to know the best colour outfit to wear for a good stalk. To begin with I'd even been wearing matching black shades, but it soon became apparent that this was not my brightest idea. What with the whole nighttime thing. Yeah, I didn't feel too smart as I shoved those in my pocket, I can tell you.

The stranger I was following was a homeless woman who looked like a charity shop threw up over a passing Helena Bonham Carter. Or in other words, like Helena Bonham Carter. She'd been tossing up red flags in my head for the last two months, so a bit of following seemed in order.

Anyway, back to my mysterious origin story. I was found by a fisherman named Joseph (hence the forename), face-down, and very, completely naked, beside Derwentwater, which is one of several bodies of water that make up an area known as the Lake District in the far north of England. Yup, you got it, from thence derives my surname.

Wait, that's a lie, I wasn't completely naked, I still had one sock on. I still have that sock, it's the only physical evidence I have of my past life and who I really am. Though it's difficult to extrapolate much from a sock, other than "I wore socks." Even Sherlock Holmes would need more to go on than that; unless I've skipped over *Sherlock Holmes and the Man Who Wore Socks*.

It was chilly out. I pulled my long coat tight around myself as I did my best to keep a discreet distance from the tramp, who seemed to be aimlessly wandering here, there, and nowhere in particular. She'd been showing up a lot recently. Not just hanging out by the cash machine I passed on my way to work, or pushing a trolley full of tin cans past me on the high street. No, she'd been turning up all over. I'd look out my bedroom window and she'd be sat across the street. I'd get to work and she'd be lurking in the car park, going through the bins. It felt a lot like she was following me. In the end I thought, well, two can play at that game.

So, there I was. Following a homeless woman around the streets of Carlisle—Cumbria's only city—in the middle of the night. No, *you* have too much time on your hands.

I'm sure most would brush it all off as coincidence, but when you have my kind of strange and stunted history, you tend to see the weird shining out from the ordinary and coincidental. No, this wasn't one of those situations where you buy a pair of red trousers and suddenly you start noticing people wearing red trousers everywhere you look. This woman was following me, I was sure of it. Keeping tabs on me, for reasons yet to be ascertained.

A little part of me even hoped it was because she recognised me. Maybe I'd been a tramp too before... well... before whatever happened happened and I wound up unconscious by a lake wearing nothing but a sock and an all-over bruise. Maybe that's why it had been so difficult to find anything out about my past; perhaps I'd been on the streets for years, away from polite society, living off the grid.

The tramp stopped and turned, so I ducked into the doorway of a betting shop that stank sharply of piss. For a moment it looked as though she was going to walk back the way she came and discover me lurking in my not-too-discreet, urine-scented hidey-hole, but then her head twitched to the left and she darted off down an alley. I counted to five then sprinted after her, coat tails flapping, heart pounding, grinning a lot more than I should have.

I didn't want to bust out of the alleyway and find myself smacking into the back of my quarry, so I slowed down to a walking pace, one hand trailing along the old, crumbling brickwork that lined the narrow crack between two shops.

And that's when the first strange thing happened.

As my fingers traced the old bricks, a strange mood descended on me like a heavy blanket. It was... *fear*. No. Not just fear, fear mixed with hunger, mixed with pain, mixed with desire. It felt like it was washing over me again and again, a multitude of disparate emotions and memories, like I was pegged to a beach and the sea's waves were battering against me, over and over, and if I didn't get away quickly I might just drown in all the intoxicating, terrible feelings of dread and—

—A scream.

My hand snapped away from the bricks of the alleyway and my head dropped back into the here and now.

There had been a scream, not in my head, not in whatever weird thing it was that I'd just experienced, but out there, in the night. Not a fun scream. Not a *playing around and being young and boisterous and drunk* scream. No, this was a blood-curdler. A real, *"For God's sake, won't somebody help me?"* scream.

I ran at the sound.

As I burst out of the dark of the alley into the comparatively bright square, my foot kicked something heavy and I found myself sprawling over the obstruction and tumbling to the cobbles, my head bouncing painfully as it connected with the ground.

I lay there for a few seconds, getting my breathing under control and trying to decide whether to throw up or not. I went with not. I pushed myself into a sitting position, the world tilting, and gingerly fingered my throbbing temple. I could already feel a lump rising like I was a cartoon cat who'd been struck over the head with a frying pan.

Feeling stupid for not looking where I was going, I peered behind me to see what I'd tripped over. I was expecting to see a bag of rubbish, or perhaps a tree root pushing up from a crack in the cobbles. What I was not expecting to see was the body of a woman with her throat torn out.

No, I wasn't expecting that at all.

2

The pain in my head forgotten, I shuffled over to the prone body laid out flat on her back. I swallowed, throat dry, a metallic tang in my mouth that made me want to gag.

'Hey...' I said, my voice emerging as an arid whisper. 'Are you... are you okay...?'

Yes, it was a stupid question, but I think I can be forgiven for it, bearing in mind the circumstances. After all, it's not every day one happens across a violently murdered woman.

She looked to be in her early thirties, her eyes still wide and staring blankly up at nothing. What was the last thing those eyes saw, I wondered. At what point had she realised her life was about to be given a savage, painful full stop? I felt a fist of anger clench in my stomach.

Now I was closer, I could see that not all of the blood on the ground was made up of random splashes and sprays. Some of it looked as though it been arranged in patterns. Deliberate shapes. Symbols written in an occult-looking language that made me feel strange to look at. It was almost like the shapes quivered. Like they buzzed with a dark energy. Impossible though, surely? I concentrated again on the blood and found it static this time. I must have been imagining things. A product of bashing my skull on those cobbles no doubt.

Had the tramp murdered this woman? She'd come this way, but surely she couldn't have had time to do this. But then where was she? Who carries on running after stumbling across a dead body?

Hand shaking, I reached out and tried for a pulse just in case I was wrong. I was not wrong. I shivered; not because of the cold of the night, but because her flesh was already cool to the touch, which was, well, wrong. This had happened recently. The blood was still wet, recently spilled. I looked at the ragged tear in her throat. At the blood pooling out onto the ground, mingling with her long, red hair. What could do that? A knife? Or—

Another scream.

Okay, this was too much. This was all much too much. It was dark and scary and dangerous, and it was stupid to even think about going anywhere near that scream. I'm no hero. I should have been getting as far away as possible and calling the police so they could get their arses into gear and sort this out. So why were my stupid feet carrying me smack bang into danger?

'Stupid, stupid feet.'

I crossed the little square in record-breaking time and raced down another alleyway. This time it didn't open up, but turned left, then right, before finally emerging onto a back street behind a row of shops. As I stepped out I had the forethought to look at the ground to make sure I didn't go tumbling over another dead body.

No dead body. That was a good start.

I looked around, eyes and ears straining for any indication of danger, my every nerve ending feeling like it was tingling, achingly alive. There were large, overflowing bins and big metal skips. Gates leading into shop backyards. Another alley in the distance, leading the way out. Plenty of places to hide. To lurk. To coil up and pounce on anyone foolhardy enough to investigate.

Everything was quiet, like the back alley was holding its breath to see what would happen next. I hoped it was something nice and not at all deathy.

Okay, Joe, get a hold of yourself.

Something moved: a shape, a dark patch of the world, something my eyes wanted to ignore.

It leapt from the shadows and barged into me, knocking me down. As I headed for the ground I reached out to grab hold of something—some clothing, a limb, anything—and my fingers brushed against something wet and cold and—

Hunger, Hunger, Hunger.

So many screams, so much blood, and Christ, the need, the need, it never stops, never ceases, it's just there-there-there, demanding more, and they scream as I approach and I like that, I exist for that moment, and then the feast! The feast! I can gorge on their fear and their... the fox waved, I could see his face smiling back at me. The fox wore a little helmet and seemed over the moon that I was—

It cut out as quick as it started, the terrible hunger, the taste in my mouth, the overpowering need to gorge on... on awful things, was pulled away and I was on my knees, teeth bared, fingers digging painfully into my chest. Wincing, I pulled my hands away and sagged, panting, glad that whatever had just happened was over.

But of course it wasn't over. There was more horror to come.

I looked to where the... the thing, the dark shape, had emerged from... and saw two feet sticking out. Another woman. Another corpse. What the hell was happening? All I'd been doing was a little light stalking and I'd stepped into a nightmare.

'Help... help...'

She was alive. Holy buggering shit, she was still alive!

I scrabbled over on my hands and knees to find her curled up, bloodied, but still breathing.

'Ha ha! Fuck you, you murdering twat!'

I must have surprised the attacker; spooked them before they finished the job.

'Please... please...'

'Hey, hi, it's okay, don't worry, it's okay.' I burbled these and other words at the woman, relief washing over me as my hands fluttered over her, trying to make sure she didn't have anything immediately life-threatening, like a cleaver sticking out of her neck. She flinched away at first, or at least tried to.

'I'm still in me. I'm still in me,' she croaked.

'What? What do you mean?'

'Don't take it, please, please, it's mine, it's...'

'It's okay, don't panic, you're going to be okay. What's your name?'

But that's all she managed to squeeze out before she shuddered and passed out. I yanked out my phone and dialled for an ambulance, praying to God, Buddha, and whatever those alien ghost things are Tom Cruise believes in, that she'd hang on until they arrived.

3

The chairs in hospital waiting rooms always seem to have been chosen with your discomfort in mind.

I sat, dog-tired and wide awake, in one such object of torture as the strip lighting overhead coughed and spluttered and did its best to tease out a fresh migraine.

'Chloe will be out in a minute, love,' said Big Marge from behind her reception desk. Big Marge was in her late fifties, with enormous barmaid hair and a neck that, through some optical quirk, appeared to be thicker than the head perched on top.

'Thanks, Marge.' I dragged myself up, headed over to the coffee machine, and got myself a disgusting styrofoam cupful.

'What exactly were you doing out there in the middle of the night, anyway?'

'Just, you know... exercise. General walky exercise. Leg stuff. Circulation is important. You don't want to clot. Never want to clot. Clots are killers.'

Big Marge looked me up and down, 'Mm-hmm...' There was a rumour in the hospital that Marge used to earn money traveling around unsavoury pub backrooms and beating all comers in arm wrestling bouts. Knowing her the way I did, I saw no reason to doubt that.

I was no stranger to Carlisle Hospital, or to Big Marge. I work at the hospital as a caretaker, cleaner, and all round handyman. It pays terribly, and the canteen lunches do nothing for my figure, but it pays the bills and allows me plenty of freedom. I used to wonder what job I'd had before I woke up with my life missing, but nothing sparked any sense of recognition, and I couldn't for the life of me find a stand-out aptitude in myself that helped narrow things down. As far as I could make out, I wasn't that great at most things. The idea that perhaps I was a homeless person, a drifter, like my mysterious lady friend, was starting to make a lot of sense

'You Joseph Lake?'

I jumped at the unexpected intrusion, causing piping-hot coffee to spill over my fingers. I swore and waggled my hand around like I was trying to fling off a piece of sticky tape. A woman in a sensible suit and a dark red leather jacket stood before me, screaming "police" from every pore. She was also black, which is a rare sight indeed in Cumbria. Around here you are about as likely to stumble across a troll under a bridge as you are an individual not sporting a pasty white face.

'Hi!' I said. 'Sorry, I didn't hear you sneaking up on me.' I held up my burnt fingers, which were already turning a nice shade of rouge. 'Good job we're in a hospital, eh? Efficient.'

'I didn't sneak up on you, I walked up on you.' Her voice was clipped and to the point. She seemed like the kind of person who didn't like to waste ten words when six would do the job just fine.

'Well, that is one light-footed walk you have there. You'd make a great thief, you could walk right into a sleeping person's bedroom and clear the place out without making a peep.'

'I'm not a thief.'

'Glad to hear it.'

'Nor a murderer.'

'Great, me neither. Messy business; plus not a huge fan of blood. I mean, I'm a big fan of it when it stays inside our bodies, in its proper, you know, "venue," but not when it gets out and about.'

'You Joseph Lake?'

'Of course, I do come across blood quite a lot, as you can probably imagine,' I said, gesturing around my place of work, 'I think that's actually helped me master the distaste a little. Otherwise, stumbling across the kind of thing I did tonight would have sent me into a puke frenzy.' I mimed puking. 'Which actually is great for another reason as I have a weird phobia about throwing up outdoors.'

'Please answer the question.'

'I am Joseph Lake,' I said quickly. 'Well, not really. Joseph Lake is what I decided to call myself. Sorry, long story.'

'Woke up by a lake, memory loss, I've already heard it.'

'Oh, okay.'

'So, you're Joseph Lake?'

'Yes ma'am.'

She looked at me with disdain, sniffed, and pulled out her regulation notepad. She had a natural, scary authority to her that was at once terrifying and deeply attractive. I was pretty sure she could beat the crap out of me with little to no effort.

'Are you new? I asked. 'I've not seen you around here before.'

'Been here a couple of months. Transferred from London.'

'Ah, that explains the accent, I was actually going to bring that up.'

'I know I have an accent.'

She looked at me as though she were a scientist peering through a microscope at a particularly troubling specimen.

'So, you know my name, and you are...?'

'Detective Maya Myers.'

'Ah, "Detective." A beautiful name for a boy or a girl.'

I gave her my best winning smile and she arched one

eyebrow slightly then looked down at her pad with a dismissive sniff.

'How is she?' I asked. 'The other one I mean? The not-dead one?'

'Still not dead, but it's touch and go.'

I felt my body begin to relax. I hadn't realised until that moment just how clenched up I'd been since finding the woman laid out in the street, so close to death.

'So, she's not dead and everything's great,' I chirped. I did a little twirl and punched the air like I was at the end of a movie, ready for my freeze frame and end credits.

'Everything's great?' repeated Myers.

'Yup. Great, tip-top; fine and dandy and randy. Not the last one. Nothing about this is randy.'

'One woman is dead, another close to it, and a psychotic murderer is loose on my streets. Everything is not "great."'

I squirmed a little under her glare, went to reply, then thought better of it. She was right, it was stupid of me to react that way, the euphoria had just overtaken me for a second. A woman had lost her life tonight; lost it to someone... to someone not altogether right. I still felt as though the aftertaste of the attacker—well, *aura*, or whatever you want to call it, whatever it was that I had experienced when the killer barged past me—was coating the back of my mouth.

'Mr Lake, what were you doing walking through Carlisle city centre at three a.m.?'

Stalking a woman.

'Me?'

'Yes, you.'

'What was I doing?'

'That was the question.'

'Just, you know... catching the night air. Nothing bad or illegal. You can count on that, one-hundred percent.' I gave her my best *I'm not at all suspicious* smile and attempted to lean against the coffee machine in a casual manner. The coffee machine turned out to be on my right, not my left, and as I staggered to one side, knocked over a chair, then just about managed to right myself before I crashed to the floor, I began to worry that I was not making the best of first impressions.

'You seem nervous, Mr Lake. Any reason for that?'

'Well, I did just break up a potential double murder, so yeah. I mean, he might come after me. He saw my face. Do I need police protection? Is there a safe house anywhere? Will I be safe in the safe house? Sometimes those things get compromised, I've seen movies.'

Detective Maya closed her notebook and pocketed it. 'You're in shock. I'm going to have a lot of questions for you, so come into the station tomorrow.' She turned and walked back into the ward. I had the distinct impression I'd made her "suspicious" list. Which is a bad list to be on when the list belongs to the lead investigator of a murder case.

'Will do! I'm looking forward to it!' Yeah, bit of a weird thing to say, that.

Big Marge watched Myers exit through the hospital's automatic doors, then turned to me. 'Now, *her* I like.'

4

I was sat on a wall in the hospital car park enjoying a smoke when Chloe finally came to find me.

'As a health professional I feel it's my duty to point out how bad and stupid that is.'

I smiled and passed it to her.

She leaned against the wall beside me and took a drag. 'Ah, sweet, sweet poison.'

We sat in comfortable silence for a few seconds, watching the sun come up. Chloe Palmer was a doctor at the hospital, and as near to a close friend as I had. She was also very pleasant to look at. Sometimes I got the impression that she was attracted to me, in a holding hands and skipping through a meadow sort of way, but I'm a bit of an idiot when it comes to romance so I hadn't taken a swing. Better to nurse an unrealised crush for the rest of my life than take a chance and face thirty seconds of acute embarrassment.

'How is she?' I asked.

'Still alive. She's been knocked around something fierce though. I had to stitch up a few nasty wounds.'

It suddenly occurred to me that if the assailant had been carrying a knife as they pushed past me, they could easily have sunk it into me on the way past. I'd taken a hell of a risk chasing after that scream. Being brave and doing the right thing were a bloody dangerous way to go about your day.

'What's her name?' I asked.

'Mary. Mary Taylor. I'm pretty sure her mum used to teach me French at school.'

'Est-ce vrai?'

'Oui.'

'Huh, small world.' I watched as Chloe leaned her head back and sent twin plumes of smoke streaming from her nostrils like a... like a.... sexy dragon? A sexy, non-scaly, wingless, person-shaped dragon. Yeah, let's go with that.

'Here,' she said, passing back the ciggy.

I took a pull. 'What about the, uh... the other one? The dead one?'

'A friend of hers, Janet Coyle. She's in a drawer already, ready for an autopsy in the morning.'

Janet Coyle. I hadn't known her, but having a name made her seem somehow more real. Which was stupid, but true. She wasn't just an anonymous slab of meat and bones that someone had tried to turn into confetti, she was a real person.

I closed my eyes and I was back in the square, knelt by the unfortunate Janet Coyle with her torn out throat and strange symbols scrawled on the ground in her own spilled blood. Maybe if I'd been a few seconds earlier she'd have been alive too. As the image stayed with me, Miss Coyle began to fade, and the scrawled shapes and squiggles began to sharpen. To glow, almost, in my mind's eye. I felt like I could see energy pouring from them, trails snaking up into the air. They felt familiar somehow. Like I should be able to read them, like it was a foreign language I'd once been fluent in, but had become lost to me due to neglect.

'Oi,' said Chloe, shoving my arm and making me stumble to the side a little. 'Not putting you to sleep, am I?'

'No! No, absolutely not. Just a little sleepy, not been to bed yet. Running on fumes here.'

'You know, it's a good thing you were there, otherwise we'd have two corpses in there rather than one. You're sort of... well, a hero, I suppose.'

'A hero?'

'Mm-hm.'

'Huh. Yes, I suppose I am really.' I passed her back the cigarette.

'What were you doing out and about in the middle of the night anyway?'

'Oh, you know, just stalking a woman.'

Chloe raised an eyebrow and let the smoke seep lazily from between her parted lips. 'Should I be jealous?'

I laughed, though it came out weirdly high-pitched, so I abandoned it as quickly as possible, hoping Chloe wouldn't notice.

'That was a very strange and high-pitched laugh.'

Damn.

And then I did it again by way of reply, turning it into a little cough for some reason at the end. Chloe cocked an eyebrow, then dismissed it.

'So, stalking, eh? Any particular reason?'

'Well, there's a very curious homeless woman who I'm pretty sure is following me and may be the key to unlocking my strange, unknown and very mysterious past.'

'A homeless woman?'

'Very homeless, and I keep seeing her everywhere. Sometimes three or four times a day. I'll be minding my own business—'

'—Perhaps indulging in weird, high-pitched laughs.'

'Right, and I'll turn around and she'll be nearby.'

'She's probably just a local nutter.'

'Ah, yes, that is a very distinct possibility, but on the other hand...' I opened my arms wide in a "who knows?" sort of a way. 'This could be it. A clue. A toe in the door.'

'If she pulls out an old syringe and jabs you in the eyeball, don't say I didn't warn you.'

'You have my word.'

Chloe raked a hand through her dark bob. 'Did the police woman talk to you yet?'

I nodded. 'Detective Myers, yes. I don't think she likes me. She definitely gave off a very heavy *I-don't-like-you* sort of a vibe. I'm very receptive to vibes.'

'I'm not surprised, you do tend to give off a spectacularly bad first impression.'

'Um, in what way, exactly?'

'The first time we properly met was when you crashed into my car.'

'There was a bee. I've explained all about the bee on numerous occasions.'

Chloe chuckled, took a drag, and handed a quarter-inch of cigarette back to me. Then, rather unexpectedly I might add, she turned, smiled, and wrapped her arms around me.

'You're hugging me,' I noted.

'I'm just glad you're safe, you big goon.'

'Right. Shall I hug back, or...?' She let go. 'Nope, good. Nice hug. Brilliant hug.' I gave her a thumbs-up. She smiled and shook her head.

'Okay, I'd better get back to the grindstone. Go home and sleep.'

'Will do.'

'You can put your thumb down now.'

'Yup.' I put my hand in my pocket and watched Chloe disappear back into the hospital. Now, that was almost definitely a signal of some sort, wasn't it? Almost definitely. Unless... friends hug too. I've seen them doing it in sitcoms. Hm.

I turned and made my way over to my battered little car, my head full of corpses and Chloe; which made for a weird cocktail. For a second I thought I saw the homeless woman staring at me from the far end of the car park, but in the time it took to blink, she was gone.

5

I woke up around midday from a muddled dream about torn-out throats, mystical symbols, and Chloe hugs, still feeling dog-tired from the previous evening's strange and awful events. I shuffled my way to the shower and let a cold blast of water smack the fug out of me.

Let me paint you a picture of my home:

I currently reside in a small, three-room flat in a scenic little town called Keswick, a good forty-five minute drive from Carlisle. I suppose it would make sense to live closer to the city I actually work in, but something about living within the boundaries of the Lake District just felt right. Spending longer than a couple of days outside of its boundaries makes me feel antsy, like I'm a baby in the womb who's become disconnected from its umbilical cord.

Also, it just looks nice out here. Keswick has all the picture postcard, countryside trappings you associate with this sort of place. Dry stone walls, hills, green bits, sheep, lakes. The awful stink of manure after the farmers muck-spray their fields. All that good stuff.

There's also a mother-fucking pencil museum within

walking distance, so don't for a second think this place isn't rock and roll.

The flat I live in might be small and losing a protracted battle with an aggressive creeping mould, but I'd come to think of it as home and couldn't bear the thought of abandoning it to some stranger. Plus it was really, really, really (really) cheap, and cheap trumps a funky smell and lack of sufficient insulation all day long.

Dried off and bowl of cereal in hand, I slumped onto the ratty couch (which I had liberated from a skip one fateful night) and brought my laptop to life to check on my site. It's a simple website: a large pic of my face with the words 'Do You Know This Man?' and a little message board to leave comments. I'd set it up a few months after I woke up by Derwentwater. At the time, I'd been something of a cause célèbre, with the police and journalists doing their utmost to try and figure out just who the hell I was. I even made a few appearances on the radio and telly, but it all came to nothing. A few people came forward, but they were either mistaken or just trying to snag a little of the limelight for themselves.

No one who really knew anything poked their head above the parapet. Any lead that was thrown up took us nowhere. Eventually the police told me I'd better get used to things the way they were. For a while I'd call in several times a day, but eventually they, pretty firmly, told me to stop doing that. Immediately. They would contact me if anything came up, but it was pretty clear I'd slipped to a low, low priority. Unless someone walked into the station and handed them a bunch of information, the investigation was done.

Not great.

I was meant to accept that I was a man without a past. Without history, family, friends, or lovers. Without memories good, bad or instructive. I was just this new, floundering, gangly beast; a newborn with the body of a man in his mid-thirties. I had a few dark weeks after that realisation sunk in, let me tell you.

Now all that's left is my dogged, some might say "heroic" (well, they might), determination, and this barely visited website. I clicked the link and my big face popped up. 'Hello handsome.' I checked the message board for fresh comments. As usual there was nothing new to see. Actually, that's a lie; there was a very helpful bot who wanted to inform me that their friend made $2000 a week working from home, but it seemed unlikely that this would lead me to my mysterious past, even if I could use the extra moolah.

I closed the laptop and tossed it to one side. I was checking it more out of habit than hope these days, I hadn't seen a new lead in over four years. I was beginning to accept that Joseph Lake was who I was: a hospital handyman with nice hair, a great coat, and an unhealthy interest in the strange. I suppose you could call that my second job—not having nice hair, that's a full time gig—but looking into any weird and wonderful goings on in the surrounding area. And it's no lie to say this whole area is bubbling with weirdness. Being one of those weird goings on myself sparked my interest, and I suppose gave me a distant hope that by exploring other strange happenings in the local area, I'd eventually bump into something useful about myself.

Yeah, so far that hadn't really worked out, but I live in hope.

I have a second website dedicated to my, well, occasionally paid hobby. It's for anyone who wants to hire me to look into something freaky going on in the neighbourhood. Such a request would be my first port of call today.

I slurped down the last of my bowl of Rice Krispies and got dressed. After that I slipped into my beautiful coat, gave my hair an expert hand-ruffle, plopped on my wide brimmed hat, and headed out the front door.

My poor little car coughed and spluttered as I headed at speed out of Keswick and off to my appointment.

Oh!

That was another thing I did know about my old self: I'm a driver. I had to pass my test again, but the moment I got behind the wheel it was obvious I knew my way around a gear stick.

So, for those of you keeping track, I'm a man who wears socks (at least one) and knows how to drive a car. How the police haven't been able to figure out who I am with those hot leads I'll never know.

The scenic Lake District opened up before me as I left behind Keswick and tootled down the Borrowdale Road, singing a Weezer song to myself (*Buddy Holly*, naturally). I had to make do with singing the lyrics solo as the car radio didn't, and never had in the time I'd owned it, work. I paid three different people money to rectify this situation, but within days of it being fixed, the newly refurbished radio would conk out again. Fed up of throwing good money after bad, I decided to soundtrack further journeys with my own mouth.

As I drove, Derwentwater—the lake I was discovered naked and bloody beside almost ten years back—slid up to join me. The road I was travelling on hugged close to Calfclose Bay, which was where I was prodded into existence by a fisherman's boot. I'd spent many evenings sat at the point I was discovered, looking out across the water, waiting for a spark of something to hit me. A memory. Just one. Some fragment of my life, of what had happened to me. Was I a criminal? Was I the victim of some strange and random attack? Was I a Tory, for Chrissakes?

But no memories or revelations ever came; just the silence of nothing. And sometimes ducks quacking, which really took the edge off my solemn brooding.

Shrugging off my morbid thoughts, I sang louder to cheer myself up (an Elton John number this time, *Saturday Night's Alright (For Fighting)* if you must know). I soon found myself at the pub I'd agreed to meet my prospective client in. I walked into the cosy bar and winced at the smell of stale beer. The ceiling was stained yellow still by the ghosts of smokers that had huddled beneath it, puffing away for decades.

I scanned the tables and booths. The clientele was thin on the ground and exclusively male. I purchased a glass of lemonade, a packet of crisps (cheese & onion) then settled down in a corner, swiping a copy of the previous day's paper to flick through. By the time I'd finished my fizzy drink and leafed through the paper for the third time, I was getting the feeling that I'd been stood up. I was just rising to leave when the door opened and a woman in her late fifties shuffled in, looking around for the person she was supposed to meet. Putting two and two together, I stood up and beckoned her over.

'Hey there, Mrs Coates is it?'

She looked around, a little embarrassed by my greeting, then rushed over, sliding into the booth to sit opposite me.

'I'll take that as a yes,' I said.

'Mr Lake?'

'In the flesh. Would you like a lemonade? I've finished mine so this would be an opportune moment to purchase one in for you whilst I refresh my own.'

She blinked twice. 'You what?'

'Lemonade? To drink?'

I returned a minute later with a glass of pop in each hand and another packet of cheese & onion between my teeth.

'So, Mrs Coates, why don't we get straight down to brass tacks? You know, that may be the first time I've used that phrase. I should Google where it comes from. "Down to brass tacks." Odd one, isn't it?'

Mrs Coates eyed me warily, as though she'd invited the

vicar in for afternoon tea, and only upon allowing him into her living room did she take a closer look and realise he was actually a wild mongoose with a switchblade.

'Don't worry, I'm not mad, I just make a poor first impression. I have that on good authority from a friend of mine.'

'Your friend is right,' replied Mrs Coates, swigging back a mouthful of lemonade.

I took a look at the woman sat opposite me—her tightly-permed, blue-rinsed hair, her smoker's mouth puckered like a cat's behind, her tired, lived-in body—and wondered what on Earth she was talking to me for. I was hoping for something juicy to distract me from all the recent murder business. It could be anything, anything at all. A haunting in her mews, a suspected vampire bite sighted on the lily-white neck of her favourite niece, the body of a deceased faerie fished out of her ornamental pond, anything! A potential gamut of weirdness stretched out tantalisingly in front of me.

'Mr Lake, my cat Boris has gone missing.'

Or it could be a missing fucking cat.

'Come again? It sounded like you said you dragged me all the way here because of a cat.'

'Yes. My cat Boris is missing.'

'Yup, that's what I thought it sounded like.' I swallowed a mouthful of pop and a crisp or two.

'I'm beside myself with worry, Mr Lake! My Boris is an inside cat! Oh, occasionally he'll take a little stroll around the garden, but he never crossed the garden fence, he doesn't like it out there! So for him to go missing, for days even, well, I imagine you can understand my distress.'

She placed a couple of MISSING posters down on the table. Boris the cat looked back at me, one ear white, the other black.

'Mm-hm,' I replied, tipping the rest of the crisps into my mouth and having a good chew. 'Mrs Coates,' I said, trying not to spit crisp shards into her saggy face, 'I'm not really in the beloved pet retrieval business. I'm in the weird, unexplained, and hopefully supernatural business. Unless your cat was of the witches variety, or perhaps resurrected from a pet cemetery, I'm not entirely sure why you decided to look me up.'

'Oh, well you see, Mr Lake, it's not just my Boris. There's Ginger, too.'

'Ginger?'

'Oh yes! And Cotton, Sooty, Nemo Bananapants; and that's just the cats from my street. All told, as far as I know, a good twenty-seven cats have gone missing, and all on the same night.'

'Twenty-seven?'

'Twenty-seven!'

'In one night?'

'In one night!'

Hm. Okay, maybe there was something to this story after all. It wasn't the village greengrocer levitating off the ground and speaking in ancient Babylonian I'll grant you, but that many cats going AWOL in a single night definitely strayed on the weird side. Chances were it was just some local nut with a cat compulsion, or maybe an increase in the local fox population, but what the hell, it would help take my mind off the previous night.

'Okay, I'll have a poke around Mrs Coates, see what's what.'

'Thank you! I do worry for Boris, he should be home and safe!'

'My fee is fifty pounds a day, with a minimum of four days payable.'

'Oh, okay. That's a bit steep.'

'A small price to pay for the hope of rescuing poor, lost Boris, is it not?'

'Of course. Of course, yes!'

I held out my hand. 'Those four days are actually payable upfront. In cash. Paper cash, no coinage, if you please.'

Mrs Coates dug into her bag for her purse.

Two-hundred quid! Even if the whole cat thing turned out to be a whole load of nothing, as very much suspected, two-hundred smackeroos was not to be sniffed at.

I sipped at my second glass of lemonade and had a think about what I'd like to spend my money on.

6

'You were supposed to be here thirty-three minutes ago,' said Big Marge, eyes fixed on the pages of her suburban infidelity and botched tit jobs magazine.

I strolled up to the hospital reception desk and gave her a wink. 'Aw, that's nice, you've been counting the minutes until I walked in here. It must be love.'

Big Marge raised an eyebrow then jabbed a meaty thumb in the direction of a mop and bucket. 'I'll tell you what you're not going to love; the three inches of shit up the walls of the second floor Men's.'

As I mopped up a stranger's abandoned anal deposits, I found myself musing once more on the previous night's terminal encounter. Someone had attacked Mary Taylor and Janet Coyle, and I found it highly unlikely that it was the mysterious tramp. No, whoever it was—*whatever* it was—had something of the unnatural about it. I'd felt it in that burst of... of whatever it was that washed over me when our skin briefly touched.

Something of the night had attacked those women. Something hungry. No, something *starving*. A patch of dark given life. A shadow that sought to kill and feast. Which sounds crazy I know, and probably wasn't going to fly too well when I was called in to answer Detective Maya Myers' no doubt numerous questions.

Whatever it was that killed that woman, I could only hope that Mary Taylor had something useful to offer the police so they could cage the animal before it struck again.

'You know, you really have a gift for cleaning up other people's shit,' remarked Neil Smith, doctor and all-round wank puffin, as he entered the toilets and made his way to the urinal to relieve himself.

'Doctor Neil—'

'Doctor Smith—'

'Doctor Neil, I'm going to take that as a strange yet genuine compliment as to do otherwise would make you seem like a tosspot, and I know you don't want to be thought of as a tosspot.'

Neil made to reply, stumbled as he tried to fully take in my reply, then gave in, zipped up, and began to wash his hands. He eyed me evilly in the mirror. 'I don't like you,' he said.

'Well, you've certainly kept that information close to your chest.'

He narrowed his eyes again, unsure whether I was taking the piss or not. For someone so educated, he really was quite slow.

'One day, turd boy, something horrible is going to happen to you. Something worse than horrible. Something just, ooh, awful. And when that happens, I'm going to be there front row and centre.'

'Something worse than this conversation?'

Doctor Neil grimaced, threw the paper towel he'd been drying his hands on in the bin, and stomped out of the room, swishing his white doctor's coat in a way that didn't at all scream *super villain*.

I finished up and washed my hands three or four times in scalding hot water, then complied with my stomach's grumblings and went off in hunt of a vending machine. Not every man can think of food after such a near-turd experience, but I have a surprisingly strong constitution for a person of such a remarkably svelte build. Besides, this wasn't the first present I'd been given from the bottom shelf.

'There you are,' said Chloe, rounding a corner as I bit down on the second finger of my Twix.

'Were you looking for me?' I asked, desperately hoping that the smell of excrement wasn't clinging to me like a poop wetsuit.

'In your dreams,' Chloe replied, grinning.

'You just missed another classic Joseph and Doctor Neil conversation.'

'You know he doesn't like it when you call him Doctor Neil.'

'Doctor Neil doesn't like it when I call him Doctor Neil? Did Doctor Neil tell you that, because Doctor Neil hasn't said a thing to me about it.'

Chloe grinned and gave me a playful shove.

'So, how's Mary Taylor?' I asked.

'Alive and awake.'

'She's spoken? Does she know what her attacker looks like? Does she know why he was attacking her, or what he was hoping to get?'

'Woah, woah,' said Chloe, raising her arms, 'I'm sorry but I haven't interrogated her to within an inch of her just-about-hung-onto life just yet, Columbo!'

'Right, yes, of course. Though perhaps more Sherlock than Columbo; I would never wear such a ratty coat.'

Chloe rolled her eyes and managed to look so adorable doing it that I practically swooned.

"Gis a bit of that then,' she said, snatching the last of my Twix and sliding it into her mouth in a way that may or may not have made my knees wobble a touch.

'Are you okay?' she asked. 'You've gone a bit pale. Well, paler than normal, so really, really pale.'

'I'm fine. All good in—'

'Please don't say "the hood."'

'—The corridor. All good in the corridor.'

Chloe smiled as she turned and headed away. 'Cheers for the choccy. See you later, Columbo.'

'Yes, but not if I, you know, see you first you won't. Not in a stalkery way.'

'Oh,' said Chloe, turning on her heel and walking backwards. 'I made a crap load of chilli last night. It's gotta go if you fancy tea at mine tonight.'

I want you to understand how much self control it took at that moment not to launch myself from the floor and go for another of those freeze frames.

'It's a date!' I said. 'Well, no, not a date, but another thing. A meal.'

Chloe shook her head and turned to face where she was going again, disappearing around the corner. 'Come round about seven, yeah?'

'Will do!'

Okay, was that a date? It could be. I mean, I said the word "date" twice. But Chloe didn't, she just said she wanted to get rid of some old chilli before it went bad. Then again, she didn't say it wasn't a date after I mentioned the word date. Twice. Maybe it was a date?

No.

Don't be stupid.

Or...?

I know I sound somewhat like a man who has never known the touch of a woman, and there's some truth to that. After waking by Derwentwater ten years ago, I was too preoccupied with just who on earth I was to really be interested in hitting on the ladies. Plus, well, in some respects it's like I am only ten years of age. I had no experiences stored in my head from my no doubt legendary sexual history. Not a kiss, not a hand-hold. After a few years I did make some tentative steps into the world of boy-girl stuff, but then Chloe came into my life and, well… I won't say I'd exactly been saving myself for her, but I hadn't been actively trying to give my equipment a thorough means-test either.

And now here we were.

With the maybe-could-be-date.

Chloe and me.

Or is it Chloe and I?

As I pondered the conundrum further, I liberated more chocolate from the vending machine. Once I was done with that I went to pay the surviving member of the previous night's horror show a visit. I wanted to check that she was well, but I had an ulterior motive. I wanted to be close to her, to see if any of that residual weird sensation I'd felt the previous night was still there. The strange feelings and sights that had washed over me. See if I could make sense of it. See if she was in any fit state to answer a soft question or two about exactly what, who, and why she was in hospital and her friend was in the morgue.

I was going to try and put it more delicately than that though. I may be an idiot, but I'm not an idiot.

I tapped softly on the door then stepped inside.

'Hi, Mary, are you awake?'

The only response was from her heart monitor, beep-beep-beeping a hello.

It was as the door closed behind me and I stepped towards the bed that I began to realise that something wasn't altogether correct. It was a sensation as much as anything I saw. My skin itched and I felt the gooseflesh rise.

'By the pricking of my thumbs,' I said, hushed.

It was at this point that I saw the markings on the floor. Strange shapes, daubed in what looked like blood, arranged in a circle around Mary's bed. The same sort of occult-looking symbols I'd seen around the first victim.

This was not good.

'Mary?''

Something dripped on my head, stopping me in my tracks. I lifted my hand and touched the spot, bringing my fingers before my eyes to see sticky red.

'Oh...'

I looked up to find a dark, quivering shape attached to the ceiling. Now I had a starker look at the thing, it was less person-shaped than I had first thought. It had a torso, legs, and a head, but the rest of it consisted of numerous octopus-like limbs that held the thing to the ceiling by row upon row of suckers.

At this point I should have been racing from the room, screaming my throat raw as I tried not to pee myself, but instead a strange calmness descended over me. A sense that what I was looking at was not a creature from a lunatic's fever dream, but vermin to be exterminated.

'You're done, ' I said. 'You've had your fill, now get the hell out of here!'

The creature's hairless head twisted sharply to look at me, its eyes giant, wide, and entirely yellow, its mouth a screaming beak that screeched with fury.

The strange sense of calmness suddenly left me to be replaced with a familiar, all-consuming terror. I staggered backwards, almost falling over the chair behind me. With little time to think about what I was doing, I grabbed the chair and launched it in the beast's direction. The chair struck it squarely on the head, causing it to scream in anger before its octopi limbs sent the thing swiftly towards the window, launching it through the glass and out into the car park beyond.

I gasped for breath for a moment or two, relief coursing over me that the thing had chosen flight over fight, then ran to the broken window to see where the creature was fleeing to.

I saw no sign of the beast, with its huge yellow eyes and numerous gross, sucker-limbs. Instead, I saw the homeless woman, sprinting away from the hospital.

7

Checking on Mary, I was relieved to discover that she was unconscious but otherwise okay. Some fresh wounds, but only superficial. For the second time now, I had been her unwitting saviour from Mr Octopus. Which no, is not the most fearsome of names to give to the dark, twitching horror I'd witnessed, clinging to the ceiling with its thick mollusc limbs, but it was the first thing that sprung to mind.

I pulled out my phone to snap a few pictures of the occult shapes daubed on the floor around her bed. As with the last time, I felt a strange sensation teasing at me as I looked at the symbols. A sense that they were imbued with an energy of sorts. With a meaning that my brain insisted I understand.

Mary moved and moaned in her bed, derailing my train of thought.

'It's okay, Mr Octopus has gone, you're okay.'

I patted at her arm like a worried aunt, then ran from the room, intending to tell Big Marge in reception to get the police on the blower. I then screeched to an almost-falling-over halt as I realised I was leaving Mary alone and that Mr Octopus might well take the opportunity to return and finish the job. Also, that I still had my phone in my hand and I could call the police myself and stay with her.

So I did that.

An hour later I was sat in the hospital reception, cradling a styrofoam cup of coffee and eating my third bag of crisps. My diet really was shocking, it was a wonder I still cut such a lithe, dashing figure. With great hair.

As police wandered back and forth, I went over what had happened in my head for the hundredth time. The beast, the creature, Mr Octopus. There'd been no sign of it after it launched itself through the window. The only thing I'd seen was the homeless woman who'd been stalking me, legging it out of view. A reverse of what had happened the previous night, when I'd chased after the woman, only for her to give me the slip and the dark shape to barge past me.

Was it possible this woman and Mr Octopus were one and the same? I'd read all sorts of interesting guff about shape-shifters in my trawls through the internet, although they tended to be from person to animal—human to wolf, mainly—and I hadn't read anything about people turning into half-person, half-octopus thingies. I was fairly sure I'd remember one of those.

'Deep in thought again, Mr Lake?'

Detective Maya Myers' matter-of-fact tone snapped me out of my thoughts. I looked up from my coffee to see her and a second detective stood before me.

'Ah, Detective Maya Myers, good. Good that you're here.'

'Is it?'

'Well, not good. Tragic, because of the earlier murder. And the new almost-murder. But now you're here I'm sure things will settle down.'

'Was that sarcasm?'

'Oh. No. I don't think so.'

Detective Myers raised an eyebrow. It really hadn't been sarcasm, I was glad she was on the case. I like to think I'm an okay judge of character, and something told me that no one as scary and no-nonsense as Myers could be anything other than a first rate detective. And judging by the case so far, that's exactly what this situation was going to require.

She nodded towards the man stood next to her. He was short, a little pudgy, and almost entirely bald, despite looking to be only in his mid-twenties. God can be cruel.

'This is my partner, Detective Sam Samm.'

'Sam Samm?'

He nodded. 'Two 'M's.'

'Where?'

'The second Samm.'

'Right.'

Detective Myers pulled out her notebook. 'So, the details.'

Ah, yes, those things. Tricky. I could hardly tell her the truth of what I'd seen, or at least what I thought I'd seen. I'd have sounded like a raving loon. People do not have beaks or rows of octopus limbs bursting out of their sides. Not in Cumbria, anyway. Maybe in London.

'Well,' I said, 'as I told the first officer on the scene, I entered the room to find a… a person was—how I would describe it now—leaning over Mary Taylor's bed. So, I said, "Hey now, you there, what's all of this about?" just like that.'

Detective Maya Myers' face slid from neutral into unimpressed. 'Mm-hm, go on.'

'Then, I sort of just ran at the bastard.'

'I'd have been cacking me pants,' said Samm. 'I don't really like confrontation.' He shivered and stuck his tongue out at the same time.

'Detective Samm,' said Maya, 'What made you want to become a police officer?'

'Hm,' he replied. 'I think it was the film *Dragnet*, with Tom Hanks and Dan Ackroyd. My favourite scene, if I had to pick one, would probably be the bit with the massive snake.'

Detective Myers gave him a long, hooded look, then turned back to me. 'Continue.'

'Right, yes, so, I sort of, put my head down, fists up, ready to, you know, box the fiend, and he turned tail and legged it.'

'Through a second story window?'

'Yup. Straight through, Superman style. And off he went.'

'I see,' she said, sounding as though she hadn't swallowed a word of it. 'Tell me, Mr Lake, would you have any reason to be lying to us?'

I sat back, eyes wide, feigning shock like a pro. Believe it or not, I've had no formal acting training. 'Every word is the truth, I swear it on my mother's grave.'

'You don't know who your mother is.'

'No, but I'm sure she's a lovely woman and I wouldn't want to say untruths around her burial plot. Assuming she's dead that is.'

'Can you give us a description of the attacker?' asked Detective Samm.

'Ah, well, no. A bit. Some. Not much.'

'To the best of your recollection.'

'A person. A human person,' I replied.

'A human person,' said Detective Myers.

'Yep, I'm very clear on that point.'

'Great,' said Detective Samm, 'you're being really helpful.'

'Anything beyond "human person," sir?' asked Maya.

'Well, dark. Dark clothing. Dark hair.'

'Dark skin?' said Detective Samm.

'Pretty dark.' Of course he was entirely black, but the last thing I wanted was for the police to start harassing the area's very limited stock of non-white people, so I fudged a bit. 'Let's say they had in-between skin. Average skin. A bit tan.'

Detective Myers sighed and wrote "In-between skin" in her

neat, efficient handwriting. Got to appreciate handsome penmanship – my own shaky scrawl makes Guy Fawkes' post-torture confession signature look neat.

'Did you get a look at their face at all?' asked Detective Samm. 'Because that would be really useful.'

'Ooh, ah, well, only a very quick flash. It was all so fast. Sudden. Speedy. Over in a heartbeat. But I'd say.... beaky. A beaky nose.'

Detective Myers flipped her notebook closed and slid it into the pocket of her red leather jacket. 'Thanks, that's all been very helpful.'

Now that was definitely sarcasm.

'Okay, Detective Samm, go grab the surveillance tape. Maybe we'll get lucky and the assailant shows up on the security cams.'

'Good thinking. That's London thinking, that is. I'd never have thought of that.'

'The bit at the end of the film," I said, 'where Dan Aykroyd says, "Twice," then raises an eyebrow and Hanks reacts... that's my favourite part of *Dragnet*.'

'Ha! Yes. That is funny. He means sex. Nice to meet you.' Detective Samm waved at me and headed off on his merry way.

'He's nice,' I said.

'Want to tell me why you think you can feed me a bunch of shit, Mr Lake?'

'What? No shit, no shit. All very non-shitty.'

Detective Myers stepped forward and looked down at me. 'I know when I'm being lied to. Normally that's a gift in this job, that sort of keen perceptive skill, but in this case the truth is bleeding obvious.'

'I promise you, on my maybe-dead mother's grave, I have told you all that I can.'

I shrank back as her eyes bored into me.

'I'll find out the truth, Mr Lake.'

'I believe it.'

She nodded. 'You still need to come in the station to make this and the previous statement official. Don't make me come and get you.'

'Understood,' I replied, my voice barely audible.

And with that, she turned smartly and headed out the door.

8

As my car headed towards Oldstone, the village from which all the cats I'd been hired to locate had absconded, I felt a mixture of unease and relief. Relief that Mary Taylor now lay safe in her hospital bed, with two burly armed officers stood outside of the door, and unease about, well, basically everything else.

A monstrous murderer with octopus limbs and a face only a mother could love was on the loose. A creature that may or may not also be the homeless woman who was stalking me. Occult symbols daubed in blood. My lying to the police about the truth of what I'd witnessed. All in all, it was adding up to the sort of episode that made the whole world feel as though it had been shoved off-kilter.

Whatever was happening, I was unwittingly involved somehow, that much I was sure of. The homeless woman, whether she was the monster or not, was clearly part of this, and she'd been keeping her eye on me for a while. How these things connected I hadn't a clue, but it certainly made me feel as though I was swimming in less than safe waters.

At some point, confessing everything to Detective Myers might be my only option, but for now, I'd only sound like a lunatic. Which was a real pain because I'd have liked nothing more than to pass this all over to the proper authorities and keep my head down. But then who are the proper authorities where octopus monsters are concerned?

It was all a little unnerving, so I decided to distract myself with thoughts of what might be waiting at Chloe's flat for our maybe-date. Twenty minutes later, as I completed my second full-throttle rendition of *I Wanna Sex You Up* by Color Me Badd (tell no one of this), I pulled to a stop on a leafy, pleasant street in Oldstone and unfolded myself from my little car, locking the door and patting her on the roof.

Yes, I am the sort of person who gives their car a name. Deal with it.

I turned from the Uncanny Wagon and looked around Oldstone's main square. A patch of grass with a single, giant tree in its belly sat at the centre of Oldstone, around which were situated the usual village fare: a church with a little steeple and a 'Jesus Created Adam & Eve, Not Adam & Steve' poster on the announcement board strapped to the gate. Obviously a very enlightened vicar ran the place. Then there was the village pub, named The Oldstone Arms, a post office, greengrocers, and lastly a general newsagents. All very normal, all what you'd expect of a small, northern village, right down to the backwards cleric.

Still, there was something strange about this little town. Something off in the air. Something that made me shiver. I couldn't put my finger on it, but it made me feel uncomfortable. Imagine brushing your teeth, reaching for the water and swigging down a glass of fresh orange juice. That would taste very weird. This was like that. Sort of.

I found the first MISSING poster shortly after, taped to a lamppost along with seven more. Each of them were the same; a black and white picture of some moggy with a name and contact details underneath, a plaintive request for anyone who might have seen their beloved pet to get in contact.

The posters were everywhere.

There wasn't a lamppost, telegraph pole, or car windscreen that hadn't been plastered. Whoever owned the photocopier around here was making a killing.

Mrs Coates had not been exaggerating when she hired me. Cats were becoming decidedly scarce around here.

'Hi there,' I said in as non-threatening a manner as I could muster to a girl, aged around seven with a pile of warm-from-the-copier posters under her arm. 'I wonder if I might ask you a question or two?'

'Depends,' she replied, stapling the poster for poor, beloved Nemo Bananapants directly over one asking for information regarding the retrieval of Mittens, who was new to the house, but still very much missed.

'Depends on what?' I asked.

'Whether you're one of them perverts me mam talks about.'

'I can assure you that I'm not. My name is Joseph and I'm a... detective. Of sorts.'

'Detectives can be perverts.'

'True, but not in this case.'

'What do you want? Come near me and I'll scream and gob on you.'

Charming.

'I see you're missing a cat. In fact, judging by the small forest of paper coating this village, it seems a lot of people are missing their cat.'

The girl sniffed wetly, than ran the back of her sleeve across her nose. 'Yeah, s'right. All the cats have buggered off.'

'All?'

She nodded, 'Nemo was the last one to go. After everyone else's went, I tried to keep him inside and safe, but he ran out when me dad set off for work yesterday and hasn't come back. Nemo never stays out for longer than half an hour.'

'And what do you think's happened to him?'

She shrugged. 'You're the detective, you tell me.'

'Do you feel... strange?'

She looked at me oddly. 'Well, I do need to wee a bit.'

'No, no, I mean, the air around here. Does it make you itchy?'

'I'm going to go now.'

The girl slid a poster under the wiper of the nearest car then headed off.

There was definitely something odd going on around here, and it wasn't just the tall guy in the hat and long coat talking to underage girls. Cats were going missing en masse and the air was tinged with menace. It was clear there was a mystery at play here worthy of my time. Had someone killed the cats? Someone with a cat grudge? Was that a thing? Or perhaps the odd sensation I felt had caused the cats to go missing. It's said that felines are sensitive to all sorts of different spectrums of reality, to the paranormal even. To things that us humans have no connection to. Perhaps the cats of Oldstone knew something bad was about to happen and made their escape early, like rats from a sinking ship.

For now, all I had were questions, it was my job now to try and find an answer or two.

I turned, intending to head back to my car to mull things over, when something small and black caught my eye. It was sat watching me from several metres aways, its eyes wide and unblinking.

A cat!

I began to slowly move towards it, one foot gently in front of the other, as though I was on a tightrope between two tall buildings and one false move would send me falling to my doom.

'Hey there, puss-puss,' I said, clucking my tongue. 'Where've you been, then, eh? Where've you been, little guy?'

I began to crouch as I approached, ready to grab hold of the thing, when it turned and bolted.

Coat flapping behind me, I sprinted as best I could after the fleeing cat, my boots slapping noisily against the cobbled road.

'I just want to talk!' I yelled after the fleeing moggy, as though that would convince it to reconsider its escape plan.

The thing about cats is, they're fast. The thing about me is, I'm not. Soon enough I found myself stood on a small road on the village's outskirts, hand against a wall, panting for breath. The cat had given me the slip, but it let me know one thing: the cats, or at least some of them, were still around here somewhere. Maybe they'd run from home, but they had yet, perhaps, to abandon the village completely.

It was just then I saw the fox stood upon a dry stone wall on its hind legs; a small, almost Roman looking helmet upon its head and an axe in its paw.

Yes, this came as quite a surprise to me, too.

It was a toy of some sort, it must be. A model left on the wall by some child who forgot to take it home with them.

The fox thrust its axe into the air, 'All hail the Magic Eater! All hail the saviour!'

The fox hopped off the wall and into the field beyond as I approached, a mixture of confusion and fear dampening my brow. When I reached the wall and looked over, the creature was gone.

I yelped and jumped to one side as something brushed against me, only to find the young girl placing yet another poster under someone's windscreen wiper.

'Did you see it?' I asked.

'See what?'

'The fox. The talking fox!'

'You're a bloody weirdo, you are.'

Given the circumstances, I found that difficult to argue with.

9

The sky was just starting to bruise as Chloe opened her front door with a grin.

'Hey!'

'I brought wine!' I said as I thrust out the bottle my sweaty hand was gripping tight enough to almost break the neck.

'Come in then,' she said, and with a quick, calming breath, I followed her inside.

We ate bowls of chilli slumped on her couch, the TV showing some old Cary Grant movie. Is it a date if you sit on a couch with a bowl of leftover chilli on your lap? Difficult to say, but whatever it was, I'll take it.

'Are you okay?' she asked.

'Hm? Yes. Yep! Tip-top and ready to rock.'

Christ...

'Cool. You just seem a little off tonight.'

Well, Chloe, I was chasing a cat earlier when an axe-wielding fox spoke to me.

'I am? Sorry, probably just all the, you know, bad stuff lately. The murders. Poor Mary Taylor. Lot of stuff on my mind and not much room up there to hold it.'

She laughed and my stomach released a box full of butterflies that it had been saving for just such an occasion.

'You always make me laugh, Joe.'

It took all my willpower not to fall to my knees and declare my undying love for her. Or, at the very least, my undying I-really-want-to-kiss-your-lovely-mouth.

'So,' I said, clearing my throat, 'I take it no further attempts were made on Mary's life by... the person. The murderer.'

Chloe dabbed up the remaining chilli with a slice of bread and shook her head, 'Nope. And there won't be, as long as the police do the right thing and leave those officers at her door. If you ask me, they should have been there from the start.'

To be fair to the police, they had no idea some sort of hellish octopus person was looking to tie up loose ends.

Chloe curled her legs up onto the couch, the ends of her toes touching my outer thigh. I griped the arm of the couch and did my best not to let loose a plaintive whimper.

She placed her now empty bowl on the floor and began toying with her hair. 'So, what d'you want to do now?'

A jumble of indecent answers arrived fully formed in my mind, barging their way to the front and causing my mouth to flap silently for a few seconds.

'Are you okay? You've gone all red.'

'Yep, just... toilet. Need a wee.'

'Right. No need to ask, you know where it is.'

I lurched up from the couch, feeling a fool, and headed towards the bathroom. Had that been flirting? What Chloe had been doing, did that constitute a flirt? The hair teasing between her fingers, the bare feet touching my leg, the invitation to take control of what happened next? It definitely seemed like flirting. Then again, it could also have been a tired person passing the time innocently with someone she looked at as a friend.

I locked the bathroom door and sat on the toilet, the seat still down and my trousers still up. I didn't actually need the loo, but this gave me at least a moment or two's respite from the idiot I was making of myself. A few deep breaths, that's all I needed.

If anything's going to happen, just let it happen, and if it doesn't happen, don't sulk about it.

It was then I felt a prickle dance across my scalp.

I was suddenly very sure that I was not alone in the bathroom.

I looked to my right, to the bath, with its shower curtain pulled across.

My head told me to get out of that small room sharply, my body, ever the traitor, reached out a hand and pulled back the shower curtain.

The axe-wielding fox, Roman helmet still upon its head, was stood on its hind legs in the bath tub.

'All hail the saviour of the Dark Lakes!' it said in its small, Cumbrian voice, waving its axe aloft.

I replied by yelling, 'Argh! Oh Christ, argh!' in a strangulated voice and falling off the toilet, landing on the tiles with a thump, my left elbow jarring painfully.

'She waits for you upon her throne of skulls, saviour!' cheered the fox.

I was closer than last time, and I could see the fox's fur was thick and messy, and its large, bushy tail cut short, the end missing. It was proportioned like a regular fox that had somehow learned to walk on its hind legs; it stood upright with confidence and poise.

A knock at the door. 'Are you okay in there?' asked Chloe. 'I heard noises.'

'Yes! Yep! I'm...' I looked back to the bath to find the fox had disappeared again.

'Are you sure? It sounded like you yelled *oh Christ!* in a high pitched voice.'

I crawled over to the bath and looked for any sign of the bizarre fox but didn't find so much a muddy foot print staining the white porcelain.

'Should I be worried?' asked Chloe.

I pulled myself up and opened the door, legs a little unsteady, 'Nope! No worry, just, thought I saw a... spider.'

'Okay.'

'A big spider.'

'Oh.'

'And then I fell off the toilet.'

'Right. You're acting a little oddly, even for you, Joe.'

I stepped out of the bathroom and headed back through to the front room.

'Yeah, sorry, just, blah, head all over the place.'

'Don't worry, me too.'

'Oh?'

'Today's the anniversary of my mum's death.'

I was very much not expecting that.

'What? Really?'

Chloe nodded.

'Right. Shit. Jesus. I'm sorry. I didn't realise.'

Chloe had mentioned her mum a few times. Usually after a few too many glasses of wine. Mentioned how she'd died when Chloe was only very young. How it was the entire reason behind her becoming a doctor. Every time she worked on someone, she was trying to save her mum.

'Joe?'

'Yes?'

'Do you want to do a bit of kissing?'

At least three silent seconds passed.

'I'm sorry? Come again?'

'Kissing. I'm sad, and I like you, and I thought I'd invite you over so we could try out a kiss or two to cheer me up.'

'Oh.'

'If that's okay with you.'

'That's okay with me.'

She looked at me oddly, and I suddenly realised I was doing a little jig.

'You're so weird,' she said, laughing.

'Afraid so.'

And then she reached up, pulled my head down, and pressed her lips against mine.

And we did some of the thing you Earth people call, "Kissing."

Oh yes.

As the Uncanny Wagon left Carlisle and Chloe behind and I headed back home, back to Keswick, I felt like a leaf on the breeze.

In other words, I was a bit happy.

The kissing had gone on for some time, enough time for a grope or two to occur before, grinning, she told me that was enough for now. We had plenty of time. No need to rush.

'Are you my girlfriend?' I'd asked, like a ten-year-old boy who'd just given the best girl in the school playground the last of his penny sweets in hope of affection.

'Maybe. Let's see how it goes, shall we? Thanks for making me feel better, Joe."

I was so happy and distracted that the fact a talking fox with an axe had greeted me on two occasions had, for a while, slipped my mind. A talking fox that could, apparently, appear and disappear at will. Perhaps the thing was connected to all the cats of Oldstone doing a runner? I supposed that, if I were a cat, I would run from a fox waving an axe at me.

There was also the fact that foxes can't talk, nor wield man-made weaponry, and that I might very well be losing my tiny mind. Then again, octopus men weren't real either, and I'd met that sucker (no pun intended) twice. Though, come to think of it, I was the only one who'd seen the assailant in that way. Mary Taylor had yet to give a statement to the same effect. Perhaps it was all in my head after all. I was a crazy, paranoid man in a fabulous, long coat, who thought tramps were stalking him, that foxes could talk, and that there was a killer man-octopus stalking the street of fair Cumbria.

That felt like it made a lot more sense than the alternative.

It was then that a thick, fetid octopus limb reached out from the back seat of my car, wrapped itself around my head, and caused me to swerve off the road and crash head-on into a tree.

10

The world swayed drunkenly before my eyes as I pressed my weight against the car door. It swung open and I fell onto the grass outside before throwing up my guts. I'd blacked out for a moment or two, and had barely clawed my way back to consciousness. My head felt as though a knife had embedded itself in my right temple.

I couldn't pass out again. I had to stay awake. If I blacked out and that thing was still close, I was dead. Which would ruin an otherwise lovely evening.

I looked up to see the windscreen was entirely gone, my seatbelt having saved me from launching through the hole as the tree brought the car to an abrupt stop. No such luck for the creature that had lunged at me from behind, it had been propelled through the glass and was somewhere ahead of me, hidden in the gloom.

It was almost pitch black out there on the small country road, and the thing could easily be close at hand.

I used the car door to pull myself up to my feet, my wobbly legs threatening to send me crashing back to the dirt. I could feel something wet dripping down my forehead and decided to pretend it wasn't blood gushing from an open head wound.

A movement in the shadows several metres away, a grunt and a groan.

'I have a gun!' I said, holding up my hand with two fingers extended.

Yes, Joseph, that'll fool them...

It seemed like I had two options: leg it, or clamber back into my poor car and see if I could bring the thing back to life. Well, actually, there was a third choice: try to tackle Mr Octopus and find out what it was like to be horribly murdered.

As I slipped back into the driver's seat I saw a smear of red on the steering wheel where my head had connected. The airbag had clearly failed to deploy. If the thing was even fitted with one.

I peered through the windscreen, or at least the expanse of air where it used to go. The creature was up on its feet and facing me. Its dark body had an indistinct shape, but its giant, yellow eyes cut through the gloom like twin suns.

I turned the ignition over and the Uncanny Wagon coughed, whirred, wheezed, then cut out.

'Come on, come on,' I muttered, trying again, but each twist of the key only achieved the same result. The car was dead, or at the very least, severely poorly.

I slapped my palms against the wheel in frustration, then stumbled back out into the night and tried to run. The sudden movement soon informed me that I was far from over my forty-mile-an-hour steering wheel headbutt. The world weaved before me, my knees jelly, my vision snapping in and out of focus. The world was grey and fuzzy around the edges and static edged further and further over my sight with each desperate step.

The thing was after me, I could hear it. I could hear the sound its beak made, the screeching fury. I could hear its heavy feet mashing the ground.

I risked a look over my shoulder. Bad move. Moving forwards and looking back was too much for my steering-wheel-bashed brain to deal with, and I tumbled hard to the ground, almost rolling completely over.

'Shitting shit!' I cried as I tried to right myself, tried to stop myself from giving in to my mind's insistence that we just slip into unconsciousness for a quick time-out.

I was up on my feet, almost bent double, trying to move forwards but mostly going sideways. A suckered limb caught my arm.

'No! Get off!'

I whirled round, swinging out a fist in the creature's direction, connecting more by luck than judgment. My knuckles met the side of the creature's head with a squelch and it stepped back, beak crying with anger.

I did my best to run some more but it was no good. I was exhausted, I was broken, I was moments from passing out. I leaned back against a tree, the only thing now keeping me upright, and watched with bleary resignation as the black, multi-limbed creature twitched slowly towards me, convinced it had its quarry beat.

'Fuck... fuck you...' was about as much as I could manage. 'Right up the rear end.'

Its octopus limbs began to dance, as though taunting me. I could see my face reflected in the large, yellow pools of its eyes, and it wasn't a pretty picture. My features drooped, my face splattered in blood, a large gash streaked across my forehead.

Was this how I would die? At the hands—or limbs at least—of some nightmare beast that shouldn't even exist?

It all seemed a tad unfair. I still didn't know who I was. Didn't know what was going on. Just a fool with great hair being buffeted from pillar to post, begging for a straight answer or two.

And Chloe had just started kissing me. I'd hoped for a bit more of that. Oh well.

'Well? Get on with it then!' I demanded.

The octopus man crowed, shrill and piercing in triumph as it prepared to do its worst—

—and that's when the front of its head exploded in every direction, splattering me in gore.

I'm not at all embarrassed to say that I screamed a scream only dogs would have heard. I swiped a handful of brains from my eyes to find the creature still standing, held up by the fist that was now jutting from where its face had once been.

Oh, and the fist was also glowing with what looked like fire.

The flaming fist then gave me the finger.

The creature twitched once, then the hand pulled free and it crumpled, wetly, to the ground, quite dead.

The homeless woman flicked chunks of matter from her now not-on-fire hand, then began wiping at it with her coat.

'Nasty bloody bastards, those things,' she noted.

'You… it's you…' I said pointing at her in case she was confused.

'I know.'

'And you just… just…' I pointed at the very dead Mr Octopus.

'You're welcome,' replied the woman, in what seemed to me to be a rather sarcastic tone of voice. She pulled at a cigarette, lit the thing, and inhaled on it deeply.

It was at this point that my body had its way and consciousness finally eluded me.

11

I was looking up at the sky, only it wasn't a normal sort of sky. It wasn't the daytime sky, azure blue with patches of white cloud, nor was it the nighttime sky, jet black and pin-pricked by stars. This sky boiled with fire. It roared and it raged and it spat great, flaming arcs down at the earth, as though it were trying to sterilise what lay beneath its endless, angry expanse.

I reached up a hand to my temple—to the wound I'd incurred in the crash—but I couldn't feel any gash, and my head had stopped throbbing.

I was laying in a small, wooden rowing boat, rocked gently by the surrounding water.

Gripping the sides of the boat, I sat up. I was adrift in the middle of a large lake. The Lake District has several large lakes, otherwise it wouldn't be called the Lake District, it would just be called the District. This lake didn't look familiar, though. I peered over the edge of the boat to examine the water itself, which, like the sky above, was far from normal. It wasn't clear, or blue, but entirely black. Blacker than the blackest black that you could ever imagine.

And then a bit blacker.

Was this a dream? The last thing I remembered was the mad homeless woman enjoying a ciggie after she'd punched an octopus monster right through the head. Life really had taken some turns of late.

I lifted the boat's heavy oars and placed them in the stirrups, or whatever the bits that you sit the oars in on a rowboat are called. I dipped the oars in the water and began to propel myself towards the water's edge, towards the shore.

I felt strange, and not just because of... well, everything. I felt a sense of déjà vu, like I knew this place. Like I belonged here somehow. Perhaps I'd had this dream before and just forgotten about it. People forget dreams all the time. They say you only remember a tiny sliver of the strange trips your sleeping mind takes you on as you lay curled up in bed and the night rolls by unseen.

The small boat buffeted against the shore and I stood unsteady as the thing tipped back and forth, threatening to throw me off balance. Getting my shoes wet, I leapt out and walked up onto the grass. All around me, hills rose into the roiling sky. There were no buildings to be seen. Just hills, mountains, trees, grass. But again, as with the lake water and the sky, the grass was not the sort you would expect to see. This grass was blood red. Crimson slashes that covered the ground and clung to the hills. I crouched and ran my hand through it and the grass left a sticky, red residue on my skin. This strange place was bleeding onto me.

I stood and decided to explore. If this was a dream, a fantasy my consciousness had retreated to after the car crash, then my brain was being very creative. I wondered what else it had in store for me.

It wasn't long before I found the first skeleton.

It lay on the grass before me, not a scrap of flesh or matter left clinging to it. I peered at the strange skull. It was large and held enormous, tusk-like teeth in its jaw. As I walked on, I found more and more bones, until it was difficult to find a path through them and I had to resort to trampling them underfoot. Which I felt somewhat guilty for, but something inside of me insisted I push on. Like my feet knew the direction I should be heading. And so my boots crunch-crunched their way over a field of bright, white bones that stretched as far as I could see, with eruptions of blood-red grass forcing their way into view here and there.

I stopped to catch my breath and wondered idly if I'd ever actually been out of breath in a dream before. Is that the sort of thing that happens in a dream? I was also sweating, rivulets of salty water irritating my eyes and causing me to wipe the sleeve of my coat across them to clear my vision.

Can you sweat in dreams? Feel pain?

As I swallowed and realised how dry-mouthed I'd become, I began to wonder if this really was a dream. Perhaps, instead, I was dead. I'd passed out after the crash, after the attack, and who knows what had happened to me after that. Maybe another of the octopus monsters had popped up and finished me off. That or the homeless woman had done the job. She did punch one creature's brains out. Literally. Maybe she decided to finish me off as dessert.

So, was this death? The afterlife? Purgatory? The sky was on fire, which had a definite Hell-y vibe to it. I mean, if I was going to design Hell, I'd certainly have plenty of that stuff around. And bones. Fire and bones. Your standard Hell jazz.

I climbed over a fence and walked on, thankful to be leaving the carpet of bones behind. As I walked on I became aware that I was making my way towards a particular hill. A bulbous hump in the distance. I lost sight of it as I entered a forest, but still, my feet seemed to know which direction to tread. I wouldn't get lost.

The trees were decorated with a red vegetation that matched the area's crimson grass. The leaves formed a canopy overhead, blocking the view of the furious, burning sky. As I walked beneath it, the unbroken red blanket rained lazy, bloody drops onto my head.

I left the huddle of trees for a moment and emerged into a clearing. In the centre was an old-fashioned wooden gallows, and from its noose hung a dead body. Steps led up to a wooden platform. The body hung above, a stool by its side, the corpse's feet a half-metre from touching down. It was a woman. She wore a black dress and had long, blonde hair that hung down to her waist. I ran towards her, bounding up the steps, but as soon as I touched her I could tell that she was dead. Cold and stiff and gone.

It was far from the most pleasant thing I'd stumbled across on a ramble through a wood.

The woman looked to be in her thirties, and fiercely beautiful. I sat on the gallows steps staring up at her, hoping this really was all a dream and that I'd hurry up and wake up already.

'All hail the saviour!'

I turned to see the fox with his axe held aloft, stood at the edge of the forest.

'You again! What do you want?'

'I've been looking for you. Looking for ages and ages.'

'Well, you've found me. Congratulations. I'm talking to a fox. I'm talking to a fox and there's a dead woman hanging behind me and the sky is made of fire.'

The fox shuffled from foot to foot, then scratched at his chin with his axe. 'You what?'

'Ignore me, I'm just going insane. Who's the woman?' I asked, pointing to the swinging corpse.

'Huh? Y'know who that is. It were your idea, after all. Good idea it was, too.'

'I think you've me mistaken for someone else.'

The fox took a step forward and peered at me. 'No, don't

think so. Then again, you all look the same to me. Sorry if that sounds racist.'

'Again, the dead person?'

'That's the Red Woman's sister, ain't it? Blonde Cathy. Was you that told Red to get rid of her. That she should rule alone. *Family stabs family in the back, so be sure to be the one holding the knife.* Your words, not mine.'

'That does not at all sound like something I would say.'

'Come on, then,' said the fox, gesturing at me with his axe as he turned and walked towards the treeline.

Not knowing what else to do, I stood and made my way down the gallows steps. 'Where are we going?'

'To the hill. She asked me t'come get you, so here I am, and there we'll go.'

I glanced back at the woman, twisting sadly in the light breeze, then turned back and followed the fox into the forest.

'Is it much further?' I asked. The fox licked its paw and held it up above his head.

'Naw, seems like it's pretty close. Always is this time of day, so it's lucky you dropped in now.'

'And where exactly is it I've dropped into?'

'Well, here. This place.'

'A less vague answer would be nice.'

'The Dark Lakes. The land of dread. The veil of anguish. Prison of the restless army of the dead.'

I nodded slowly. 'Right. That place. Got you.'

After what seemed like hours, we finally broke from the forest, and there it was, rising steeply before us; the hill.

'Come on then,' said the fox, 'Top's where you're supposed t'be.'

The hill was so steep I had to bend right over and crawl up the thing, its long, wild, red grasses leaving fresh ruby smears on my coat and trouser legs.

'Who would it be best to send my dry cleaning bill to?' I asked.

Finally, the hill levelled out as we reached the summit. On top of the hill was a chair. Well, more of a throne to be honest. A gleaming, white, very uncomfortable-looking throne made entirely of skulls. Which was creepy.

'Well?' I said, 'what now?'

'Now you take your throne,' came a new voice. She stepped out from behind the chair, a tall, lithe woman, with alabaster skin and the reddest of red hair. Her eyes were piercing green, the smile on her face vicious in its beauty.

Something told me I should be very, very scared.

'I have brought him to you at last, Red Woman,' said the fox, falling to his knees. 'As I were asked to, as I said I would. Now, shall I get my reward?'

The Red Woman approached the fox and removed his helmet.

'You have done well,' she said, stroking the fur on top of his head.

'Thank you.'

And then she tore his head from his neck and the body toppled aside.

'Jesus!' I cried. 'Why? Why did you just do that?'

She tipped her head back, mouth wide, as she raised the fox's head high and allowed the blood to pour into her mouth, over her face, and to splash down the dark green leather she wore from shoulder to toe.

She tossed the head aside, smiling at me, her perfect, white teeth stained blood-red.

'I'd very much like to wake up now,' I said.

'Wake up?'

I began to back away. 'This has to be a dream and I just want to wake up.'

'Oh, but you are waking up, don't you see? You are here again, before the throne, Magic Eater.'

The words made me pause. That name. That title. It meant something.

Magic Eater.

I looked down at my hands and bright red fire burst from them as the Red Woman laughed and the sky roared in anger.

'No.' I took a step back and the ground beneath my feet dipped suddenly and the world twisted away.

12

Sometimes, when you're dreaming, you feel like you're falling.

You can't remember how or why, but down, down, down you go, your stomach taking up residence in your mouth as you plummet to your doom. You don't know how this came to be, this endless fall, but you do know one thing with a crystal certainty: if the fall isn't endless, if there is a bottom for you to hit, then you will never wake up. You'll strike down and your bones will shatter, your organs pop, your meat splat. And that's when your eyes spring open and your whole body jerks, a sudden spasm, as though the mattress has broken your fall and saved you from a fate worse than death.

This was one of those times.

I looked around to see the familiar sight of a hospital room. No chairs made of bones or any of that jazz, just four magnolia walls, a weathered bedside cabinet topped with an empty vase, and an old TV set perched on a swing bracket. I took a wary peek at my hands to find that fire no longer seemed to be erupting from them.

Of course there wasn't.

I slumped back, my head now resuming its dull throb from the accident, and let out a sigh of relief as the door squeaked open and Doctor Neil, the epic wanker, stepped inside.

Never had I been more delighted to see the sod.

'Doctor Neil!'

'Doctor Smith, you prick,' he spat back.

I almost got up and hugged the man.

'Seems like someone gave you a right going over,' he said, grinning.

'Well, I'm glad my misfortune brings a little light into your horrific, empty life, Doctor Neil.'

'I'll tell you one last time, it's Doctor Smith, you piece of shit.'

'Don't think much of your bedside manner there, Doctor Neil. Real four out of ten stuff, that.'

The door swung open again and Chloe stepped in. 'You two boys aren't fighting again, are you?' she asked with a smile that dulled the throb in my head.

'Doctor Neil here was just telling me how relieved he was that I am fine and dandy and what a testament it is to my remarkable powers of recuperation.'

'Yup, that sounds like something he'd say.'

Doctor Neil looked at us in turn, malice in his eyes, then turned on his heel and stomped out.

'You know,' said Chloe, 'one of these days he's going to twat you one.'

'Oh, he loves me really.'

Chloe pulled up a chair and took my hand. A little shiver ran through me as flesh met flesh.

'What happened?'

A monster with octopus limbs attacked me, then a homeless woman punched its brains out, I took a detour through a hellscape accompanied by a talking fox, and then I went a bit on fire.

'Um. Accident. How did I get here, by the way?'

'Big Marge came back from the toilet to find you slumped across three chairs, unconscious and pissing blood out of your head. What sort of accident?'

I was found in reception? Huh. Well, there is no way I made my own way there. My car was wrecked and my head almost caved in. Could the homeless woman have brought me here somehow? Carried me here then done a runner? There seemed to be no other explanation, which meant I owed her twice now.

But why on earth was she looking out for me? What did I mean to her? Perhaps she did know me after all, from before I awoke next to Derwentwater ten years ago. I felt my heart flutter a little and sat up straight.

'A woman... did anyone see a woman drop me off?'

'No one saw anything; just there you were. Joe, what happened? Tell me.'

'Just, you know, I was driving back from your place, and... a cat. A cat ran out, and you know me, animal lover, so I swerved, had a bit of a crash, and bopped my head. Stupid, really.'

She looked at me, brow knitted, obviously not buying what I was selling.

'Is that the truth?'

'Of course.'

I hated lying to her, especially post-kissy, but what other option did I have? The truth made me sound like a lunatic, and very few smart, funny, successful, beautiful woman are up for kissing lunatics.

She softened. 'Please be more careful next time,' she said, then leaned forward and planted a gentle kiss on my lips. 'You twat.'

I grinned like a fool, cheeks flushing. 'You know, I could get very used to you kissing me.'

'Me too.'

Too agitated, too wired, too just plain ol' freaked out to sit still in a hospital bed when I felt fine enough, I dressed and, against Chloe's orders, checked myself out. Now true, I'd had a fierce bang on the noggin, so should stay in for observation, plus I'd been informed that the police would be coming by to ask me some questions, but off I went anyway. Telling the boys and girls in blue the truth about what had happened to me wasn't an option, so I'd only be wasting their time anyway.

Plus, I felt fine. Energised even. I was in the middle of a bunch of clashing, bizarre mysteries and I didn't want to lose time lying on my back eating hospital food and watching daytime TV. Even if there was an episode of *Quincy* on that I'd somehow never seen before.

I felt sure that my past was involved in this somehow. Or at the very least the homeless woman knew who I was. I left the hospital assuming I was due a rest from any shocks, at least for a few hours, but found that not to be the case as soon as I stepped outside to find the Uncanny Wagon in the car park with no visible evidence of ever having been in a crash. The front end wasn't crumpled and the windscreen was perfectly intact.

'What in the crap of all craps...?'

It was impossible. The crash happened. It actually, actually happened. My car had been wrecked.

I climbed behind the wheel, confused. The pain in my head where it had connected with the steering wheel was evidence enough that the crash really had happened. Not to mention the dried smear of blood from my head that was still on the steering wheel itself. So, well, what the hell had happened next? And why was my car not a squashed mess? I turned the key, which sat waiting for me in the ignition. The engine turned over and caught first time.

She's alive!

As I placed my hands on the wheel, I saw a flash of them engulfed in red fire, like they had been in... what had that poor fox called the place? The Dark Lakes? But that was a delusion, surely? My unconscious mind having a merry old time.

Then why had it seemed so real? So familiar, even. And why had the fox, who I'd encountered twice in the real world, also been there?

I pulled out of the car park and headed home, to Keswick, making very sure that there was no beast with suckered arms lurking low in the back seat.

After a hot shower and a change of clothes, I grabbed my laptop to check my who-the-heck-am-I website, more out of habit than expectation, only to find I'd been left a message. I sat up sharply and clicked:

Next time I might not be around to pull your arse out of the fire, you wanker.

The user name was just a string of random numbers and letters, but I knew who it was. The homeless woman. My fire-fisted saviour.

Who are you? I typed, hitting send, then stared at the screen for almost half an hour, hoping for a reply.

Yeah, no reply.

The woman's hand had been on fire, as had mine in my, well, vision, or delusion, or whatever you want to call it. Was that because I'd seen her hand on fire, or because we were connected in our... hot-hand abilities?

I closed my laptop and set it aside to focus on my hands.

'Um... flame on?'

Nothing.

I tried concentrating on them and thinking 'hot thoughts'. After that I hopped around the room, throwing dramatic shapes as though I were under attack and needed to unleash a fireball from the palm of my hand.

Nothing, obviously.

I sat back down feeling like a bit of a tit.

A lot of very strange stuff was going on, but I did not have superhero powers, and neither did the homeless woman, beyond one hell of a right hook. I'd barely been clinging to consciousness, deluded, my mind playing tricks, surely?

I mean, no one can really conjure flames from their fists, right?

13

It was just creeping into the late afternoon as I stepped out of my car and cast my eyes around Oldstone once more.

There it was, that strange, uncomfortable sensation I'd felt on my last visit to the village. It was worse this time if anything. It crawled and itched; a persistent static that prickled my skin. That wasn't the only thing there was more of, either, every available surface was plastered with missing cat posters now.

'Missing: Old Tom, ginger tabby, last seen on Friday.'

'Missing: Blackie, last seen Tuesday morning.'

On and on they went. Oldstone had been quite the cat haven before they'd all upped sticks and buggered off.

Actually, that might not be strictly true. I had, after all, spotted one of the elusive buggers on my last visit. Maybe they were all hunkered down some place safe, put off by the strange atmosphere of the place.

But how do you find a cat that doesn't want to be found?

I opened the back of the Uncanny Wagon and pulled out one of those boxes with a little cage door on the front that you force an unhappy mog into when it's time to go to the vets, plus some other bits and pieces. It was time to lay a trap and see what came a-sniffing.

Twenty minutes later I was sat on a park bench, the cat box resting on the ground several metres away, with a trail of cat biscuits leading inside. No, it wasn't much of a plan, but at least I was working for Mrs Coates' money.

I retrieved my buzzing mobile from my pocket and saw a message from Chloe: *Are you okay?*

I smiled, the little butterflies in my stomach swirling anew, and set my thumbs to work: *I'm fine.* Send.

Perfect. Enigmatic. Too enigmatic?

Another buzz:

C: *I was thinking... (emoji of a light bulb)*

J: *Ooh, dangerous, never leads anywhere good, thinking.*

C: *Shut up. We should have a date.*

A bit of a pause in replying there as I jerked forward, throwing my phone to the ground. I fell to my knees and scooped the thing up.

J: *Oh?*

C: *A meal. A meal out. (emoji of a chilli)*

J: *Yes. Me and you. Out. Eating. Sounds good.*

C: *Maybe try some more of that kissing. (lips emoji)*

It was very difficult not to just type back with a pathetic *Thank you, thank you, thank you.*

J: *It's a date.*

C: xxx *(heart emoji)*

(Man alive, that girl is partial to an emoji).

And that was that. A date. An honest to goodness date. We definitely weren't just friends now. I mean, the whole kissing bit was one thing, but a date? A date was girlfriend territory. A date was the sort of thing an honest to goodness *couple* did. Now, it was true that we hadn't nailed down specifics. Time, day, place. Still, no point rocking the boat at this stage. Get out while the going's good. The fact was, Chloe was into me, and I had the emojis to prove it. She was digging me. Digging the vibe that I was... secreting? That doesn't sound right. Well, whatever it was, she had the hots for me. The kissing and eating food in a restaurant kinda hots.

The look on my face at that moment was insufferable, I can tell you. It was just as well there was no foot traffic passing by as they'd have been compelled to slap me silly.

So caught up was I in my new bubble of warm-heart-swelling-loveliness, that I almost failed to see the cat that was creeping towards my trap, munching up one carefully placed kitty biscuit at a time.

I stood, nonchalantly pretending that I had no interest in what the cat was doing as it edged ever closer to the cat box.

'Go on, there's a good kitty,' I muttered under my breath.

The cat poked its head into the box and took a step back. I'd filled that box with enough food to test any cat's willpower. The cat glanced back once, then finally stepped into the box.

Victory!

I darted forward while the cat chowed down inside and fell to my knees, throwing the cage door shut and securing it.

The poor thing twisted, startled, and began to claw against the secured door of the cat box, against the sides, against the roof. Eventually, it stopped fighting as it resigned itself to its situation. I peered in at the thing, making friendly noises, willing the poor sod to calm down.

'Hey there, little guy, don't worry, I'm nice, me,' I said, then squinted at the thing I'd caught. 'Wait a sec...' I reached into my coat and pulled out the Missing posters Mrs Coates had given me. Sure enough, one black ear, the other white.

'Well, if it isn't Boris the cat,' I said. 'I know your owner. Small world, eh?'

A few minutes later I was rat-a-tat-tatting at her front door, feeling rather pleased with myself. When Mrs Coates opened up and saw me holding Boris aloft in my cat box, she was so overcome with joy I thought she might faint.

'Boris! Boris, my Boris!'

'As promised,' I said, proudly.

I stepped into her home and placed the cat box down on a sideboard in the entrance hall.

'How did you find him?'

'We private detective sorts have our ways, Mrs Coates, but what it truly comes down to is dedication. Dedication and a supreme attention to detail. Nothing gets past these eyes, Mrs Coates. Nothing.'

I opened the cat box to allow Boris the cat to emerge and hop over to his owner. It was then that Boris saw his chance and bolted from the box, out of the house, and off into the distance.

'Ah,' I said. 'Probably should have closed the front door before I did that.'

The look Mrs Coates gave me almost broke the skin.

14

I tried the same cat-catching trick at various locations around Oldstone before finally admitting defeat.

I was annoyed, but as I made my way back to Keswick and home, I at least knew that the one cat I'd seen previously was no fluke. No random stray left behind as the rats fled the ship. The cats were somewhere, either in or close to the town. It was just a case of locating their hideaway now. And, perhaps more to the point, understanding just *why* it was that they'd all felt the need to make themselves scarce, and whether it was connected to the sense of prickling dread the place gave me.

I'd attempted to raise the matter with Mrs Coates, but she wasn't too keen on chatting after I'd allowed Boris to leg it again.

Back home, I made myself a strong cup of tea, grabbed a packet of Rich Tea biscuits that I was delighted to find behind a rapidly decaying loaf of bread, and flopped wearily onto the couch.

Biscuit in one hand and another in my mouth, I reached for my laptop to see if any further messages had been left for me. There was nothing new. I polished off my tea and headed to the bathroom, parking myself on the toilet for a sit-down wee and a good old ponder.

A village fizzing with a bizarre atmosphere that seemed to be driving out its cat population.

Creatures with octopus limbs, murdering people and surrounding their corpses with occult looking symbols, daubed in blood.

A talking fox. Let's not forget the talking fox.

Had I gone mad, or had I always been this way? It was the first time I'd explored that option since I came to on the shores of Derwentwater, nudged awake and mind empty. Maybe I was just crackers. Maybe that's why I was suffering from amnesia in the first place. Perhaps my mind had decided it couldn't take anymore and wiped the hard drive clean. Factory settings reset.

That sounded like something that could be true. Maybe. I mean, I'm a believer in the weird side of things, of the paranormal, of there being more to this world than the everyday person generally experiences; but all of *this*? I thought there was something in hauntings, in undiscovered creatures, but octopus men and talking foxes? That was a little out there even for me to accept.

So maybe that was it.

Maybe I was as mad as a box of tits and I was seeing more and more of this oddness as I barrelled towards another hard reset.

It was only as I finally stood up from the toilet, flushed, and washed my hands that I became quite sure that I wasn't alone in my bathroom.

The room was small, just large enough to squash a toilet, sink, and a small corner bath into. The shower curtain was currently pulled across, hiding the small bath from view, but something was in there. Some dark shape; a black hump, that was now dimly visible through the curtain.

This again?

'Hello? What sort of a talking animal is waiting for me this time?'

My heart was now beating loudly in my chest, banging a coward's tattoo against my ribcage, and yet there went my hand, reaching towards the shower curtain. Being generally afraid but also incurably curious was a damned curse.

'Just so you know, whoever you are, I have a gun. A big gun. Just brim full of shooty bullets that will turn you into... a dead person. So, no funny business.'

One breath. Two breaths. Three breaths.

I yanked back the shower curtain with a little cry of aggression, to find a dead body squashed into the small corner bath. A body with a large hole in its head. A body with numerous octopus arms that had left smears of dark blood all over the white plastic.

Mr Octopus.

The creature that had attacked Mary Tyler.

The creature that had tried to kill me.

I stumbled backwards out of my bathroom with a pinched cry of surprise, and staggered into my living area.

'Finally,' came a voice from behind me. I whirled round, almost falling to the ground, to find the mad homeless woman sat on my sofa. 'Where the fuck have you been, I've been waiting hours!'

I stared at the woman in silent astonishment.

'Very rude way to treat a guest, and I should know, I always treat guests terribly.'

'You!'

She lifted a plastic bag and gave it a shake. 'I just went on a beer run, d'you want one?'

She placed the bag next to her on the couch, pulled out a can, cracked it open, and downed it in one.

'You!' I cried. 'Here! In my home!'

She reached into the bag again and retrieved a fresh can of very cheap-looking lager.

A thought struck: 'My car. Did you fix my car after the crash?'

The woman shrugged. 'Maybe. Needed to get your heavy arse to the hospital and I wasn't going to carry you the whole bloody way. I'm not as young as I was, you know.'

'How? How did you do that? Because the Uncanny Wagon was wrecked. And now, it's, well, not!'

'You know,' she said, before burping and carrying on, 'I think there's something I'm forgetting.'

'What?!'

'Oh, yep, got it.'

That's when I felt the mad woman's knuckles connect with my left cheek, followed by the floor connecting with my right cheek.

'Ow.'

'Too fucking right,' she replied.

I sat up, clutching my face. 'I think that's a first. I don't think anyone's ever hit me before.'

'Not true,' replied the woman, opening her second drink. 'I've hit you before, you piece of shit. Here,' she tossed a cold can my way. 'Press it against your cheek. Or drink it. Or both.' She cast a look about the room. 'You know, this is a very small flat. You must be doing terribly; I can't say how much that pleases me. Did I call you a piece of shit already?'

I nodded. 'You also punched me.'

'Oh yeah! Ha, good times, you piece of shit.'

I stood, keeping my distance as I opened the can and took a sip. 'You save me, you attack me, you fix my car. You're a very confusing person.'

The woman flopped on the couch then grabbed the remote and turned on the TV.

'So...?' I said.

'D'you get the wrestling? I like the wrestling. D'you remember Big Daddy? Now there was a fighter. And Giant Haystacks. Of course, these days it's all about the American wrestling. Sure, they bring a little extra polish and razza-ma-tazz to the thing, but for my money, you can't beat those classic, Seventies and Eighties British wrestlers. Kendo Nagasaki! I met him once. Odd feller. Had me ejected from his home on account of the fact I'd broken in and shouldn't have been there.'

'I can empathise with that,' I replied. 'Can we please get back on topic though?'

'Ha, that's me, wandering all over the shop. I've yet to meet a tangent I didn't love, you know. Now Rowdy Roddy Piper—if we're talking the American wrestling world—there was a man I *did* have time for...'

It was more than a little exasperating. I tried my best shot to bring the conversation back on track. 'Me, Joseph, you...?'

'...A woman fighting an overwhelming urge to squeeze your neck until that head of yours pops like a balloon.'

A mad homeless woman in my front room and an octopus-person corpse in my bathroom. That mental reboot was looking to be right around the corner.

'Listen,' I said, 'I don't mean to be rude, but there's a dead monster in my bath – a dead monster that you killed with your fist.'

She raised her right hand, which was now engulfed in blue flame. 'Right hand of doom.'

'How... how are you doing that?'

'With ease,' she said, and winked at me.

'Yup, I've gone mad. That's all there is to it.'

'No. Not this time. Not yet, at least. And if you do, I'll twat you one.'

'What do you mean, "not this time"?' The woman fell silent. 'Look, you break into my home, dump a body in my bath, drop all sorts of hints about who I am... I think I'm owed an explanation!'

The woman gently placed down her can of beer, then stood, fixing me with darkening eyes. 'Owed? There's only one thing you're *owed*,' she replied, her left fist igniting with blue flames too now.

I backed up until the front door pressed against my rear end, 'Now, come on, let's not get out of hand here. Hulk Hogan! He's a wrestler.'

I yelled in surprise as a sudden, hard knock landed on the front door.

The woman shook her hands and the fire sputtered our. 'See who it is.'

I peeped through the door's spy hole. It was detectives Maya Myers and Sam Samm.

'Well of course it is,' I said, then added a, 'Shit shitting shit,' for good measure.

15

As the door was knocked again I did the dithering from one foot to the other, dancing on the spot thing you only ever see in old, farcical sitcoms.

'Mr Lake?' came Detective Maya Myers' voice.

'Maybe if I stay quiet they'll go away?' I hissed at the homeless woman.

'I can hear you,' replied Maya.

'No, you can't,' I said. It was worth a shot.

'Yes I can.'

Damn.

This was bad. I had two detectives behind one door and a weird corpse behind another. It might have been the corpse of a monster, but a corpse nonetheless.

'Yes, sorry, just a... joke?'

I heard Detective Samm with two 'm's' laugh, then stop. 'I don't get it.'

'One moment, just need to make myself decent,' I said.

'What?'

'Decent, I'm completely naked, stuff flapping all over the place!'

I turned to the homeless woman and gestured wildly, unable to find the words to accompany the hands.

'Just don't let them in the bathroom,' she said, then shuffled in there, closing the door behind her.

Right then. Crap.

I smoothed down my clothes, gave my hair a quick ruffle, and opened the door sporting the largest and fakest of fake grins ever committed to a face.

'Detectives! What a pleasure!'

'Hm,' replied Maya, walking in, Detective Samm at her heel.

I closed the door and turned to the two detectives, my eyes involuntarily flicking to the closed bathroom door.

'I like your home,' said Detective Samm. 'Cosy.'

'Yes. Thanks. Thank you.'

'I have a really big, four bedroom place in Carlisle. Huge.'

'Well, that must be awful.'

Detective Samm nodded, sadly.

Maya was eyeing me. She must have blinked at least once but it didn't feel like it. Could she sense something was up? Could she smell the corpse on the other side of the bathroom door?

'You seem nervous, Mr Lake,' she noted.

'Me? Nervous? Am I nervous? I don't feel nervous,' I replied, nervously.

'Your voice is all high-pitched, you're sweating, and you're breathing heavily.'

'Um... yup. That's because... because of this thing that I am about to say...'

'Go on.'

'Right, well, it's because I was just... jogging? Jogging.'

'Jogging?'

'Jogging.' I performed a little jog on the spot by way of illustration, then stopped as that's obviously an insane thing to do. She knew what jogging was.

'So you've just been jogging, naked, inside your tiny flat?'

'Yep, in here. Forty laps around the front room. I'd jog outside but... all those car fumes, and the hard paving stones are murder on my ankles. My body's a temple, Detective.'

Maya narrowed her eyes then turned away. I think I'd gotten away with that. Pretty slick, Joe.

'Bullshit,' barked Myers.

Pretty, pretty slick.

'Is there a reason for this very welcome visit?' I asked.

'Yes,' replied Detective Maya Myers. 'Firstly, you have yet to come to the station to give an official statement about the incident involving Mary Taylor and Janet Coyle. Any reason for the delay?'

Monsters, cats, talking foxes.

'Just busy. Work and stuff. Slipped my mind. Sorry.'

'And then we were informed that you were involved in an accident.'

'Oh, yes, that was just... a cat. As I told Chloe. Just swerved to avoid a cat. My own fault.'

'Hm. Well, we're going to accompany you to the station and get that statement off you now, Mr Lake.'

Ah, good. Going to the station meant leaving; leaving the mad woman and the monster corpse in my bath tub. This was very, very good.

'Great! Off we go then, can't wait, a trip to a police station, always a pleasure.' I slipped my coat on ready to skip out of the door.

'Your bathroom.'

And there went my heart, diving into my stomach.

'I'm sorry?' I replied.

'Your bathroom, is it through there?'

'Why? Shall we go?' I said, pointing to the front door.

Maya headed for the closed bathroom door. 'I just need to quickly use your toilet, too much coffee.'

'No!'

'No?' she replied, turning to me, hand on the door handle.

'It's just, I haven't bleached it in months. I'm... embarrassed to have a lady use it.'

'I'm not a lady right now, I'm a detective.'

She turned the handle and stepped in. I darted across the room and joined her inside.

'I can usually handle a piss on my own, Mr Lake.'

I looked around, bewildered. There was no sign of the homeless woman, and no sign of any monster corpse in the bath tub. There weren't even any blood stains left on the white plastic. I did a little turn, peering around the tiny bathroom in astonishment.

'Mr Lake?'

'Hm?'

'Why are you in here?'

'I just... I thought I'd used up the last of the loo roll, but nope. There it is, hung the right way and everything.'

'I see it, Mr Lake.'

We stood in silence for a few seconds.

'Mr Lake?'

'Yes, Detective Myers?'

'Get out.'

'Yes, Detective Myers.'

With a final, confused look around the bathroom, I stepped out, the door closing behind me, and re-joined Detective Samm.

'She's just peeing,' I said. 'By herself. No one else in there at all. Which is not strange, or scary, it's very, very normal.'

16

I wasn't exactly a stranger to police stations, but I can't say I'd ever felt exactly at ease inside of one.

For a while there, after first waking with a blank history next to Derwentwater, this station had been a regular haunt. Numerous questions on the part of the police, and numerous visits from myself, desperately hoping for an update on my situation. A crumb of hope I could gobble up.

I hadn't visited for several years now due to a terminal lack of movement on my case, which I presumed was still, technically, open. The station looked exactly the same. From the looks of things, they weren't planning on renovating the place until it started raining down on their heads.

It was evening now, fast approaching midnight, and I was sat in a small, grim-looking room with Detective Sam Samm sat across a table from me.

I feigned looking over my written statement, nodding, and *hmmming*, then nodding some more.

'Does that look about right?' asked Detective Samm.

'Yup,' I replied as I grabbed the pen and scribbled my name on the dotted line. 'That sounds about right.' Apart from not mentioning monsters with a beak for a face and giant, haunting, yellow eyes the size of teacup saucers.

'Well then, that's that,' I said, sliding the signed statement back across the table.

'Great! Very helpful of you.'

'So, any leads yet?' I asked.

'Yes. Well, no, not exactly. Just the strange wiggles painted in blood, but we don't know what those mean. And we've put them through the computer and everything.'

Hm, that was a good idea, I should have done that. If the police computer had found nothing, that meant they weren't your everyday occult symbols. These were something else. Or just gibberish.

'I'm sure something will turn up,' I said. 'I have the utmost faith in you, Detective Samm.'

'Thank you very much. I know I'm not the best detective on the force, but I'm learning a lot working with Detective Myers. She really knows her stuff.'

'Yes, she seems very nice for a scary woman.'

Detective Samm laughed. 'Oh, don't mind that. She likes to put on a front but she doesn't fool me.'

'Hey, why is she working here, anyway? Why would a detective from London relocate to this backwater station?'

'All I know is her last partner was killed on the job and shortly after, here she was.'

Well that was interesting. And sad, of course. Sounded like she'd left behind a few ghosts.

Detective Samm sat forward suddenly, his brow knitted. 'Wait, I probably shouldn't have told you that. Oh dear.'

'That's okay, Detective Samm, I won't tell anyone.'

'Phew, thanks,' he replied, relaxing back into his chair. 'She's the best partner I've ever had. The only one who doesn't make fun of me. Well, doesn't make too much fun, anyway. I think she's making me better.'

The door to the interrogation room opened and Maya stepped in, a styrofoam cup of coffee in hand. 'All done?'

Detective Samm waved the signed statement at her.

'So, am I good to go?' I asked.

'Good to go. Unless there was something else you wanted to let me know,' Myers replied.

'Like…?'

'You tell me. It's obvious you have something on your mind. Something that scares you.'

She was one perceptive woman.

'Nope. Nothing going on up in this noggin.'

She placed the coffee cup down on the table and leaned over until our faces were so close I could feel her breath.

'I don't like it when people lie to my face, Mr Lake, and I don't like it when people keep things from me. You're doing both.'

I went to speak but she cut me off.

'Don't bother denying it. You have a piece of this thing that you're not ready to hand over for some reason, but hand it over you will. You want to know why?'

I nodded.

'Because people are dying, and it's my job to stop them dying, and that means I will not stop until I have what I need. Do you understand me?'

'Understood.'

She straightened up, lifting her cup to her lips and taking a sip of vending machine coffee. 'Well? Are you going to tell me now or are you going to continue to piss me off?'

I stood and pulled my coat off the back of the chair, sliding it on. 'I'm really a bit bushed. Need to get home, I'm on an early shift at the hospital.'

She grimaced at me. 'Get out of my sight.'

I nodded and headed for the door.

'Mr Lake?'

I paused.

'You will tell me. Sooner or later, you'll tell me. People are dead and I have a bad feeling that more deaths are going to follow.'

I pulled my coat closed and strode out the door.

To say I felt like a glob of sputum hawked out of some drunk's throat was something of an understatement. Maya was right. People had died, maybe more would, and I was keeping my cards under the table. But what else could I do? There was no way she or anyone else in authority was going to believe what I had to say. I wasn't even sure I believed all of it.

The dark outside matched my mood as I steered the Uncanny Wagon home. Maybe it was all over. The murders at least. The thing that had attacked Mary Taylor and me, and that had murdered Janet Coyle, was dead. A crazy woman had punched her fist through the thing's head, and the last time I saw it, its leftovers were curled up in my bath tub, more than a little dead. Maybe that would be it. Maybe it was all over.

No, I didn't believe me either, but I was trying to perk up my gloomy spirit, okay?

The first thing I did upon arriving home was dart into the bathroom and check the tub. It was still empty. No monster corpse, no blood, no nothing. I leaned close, even clambered inside the thing, looking for any trace that it had been there.

Not a trace. Not a clue.

This was rapidly returning to the "I'm crazy and about to have a breakdown" idea. Because the only time the body had been there, the only time the homeless woman had been there, was when I was alone. As soon as someone else entered my world, the strange stuff that nobody would believe, disappeared.

I saw the plastic bag sat on the couch, three cans from the six-pack still inside.

That didn't prove anything, I told myself. As part of my delusion, maybe I'd gone out and bought the beer and then, you know, forgotten.

I sat next to the bag, pulling one out and taking a swig of warm beer, before firing up my laptop and heading to my website. The mysterious reply, and my responses, remained unanswered.

Again, what did that prove?

I typed *Hey, if you're real, you left your beer behind.*

I waited for a few minutes to see if the woman would reply, or suddenly stride back into my flat with a few choice swears to toss in my direction, but I sat alone and silent. I closed my laptop and slumped back, slowly working my way through the rest of my drink. I touched the can to my cheek where the woman's knuckles had connected. There was a bruise there alright, but still, that wasn't proof of anything. I could have walked into any old door frame.

I needed to talk to Mary Tyler, if she was up to it. She was the only one besides me that I knew for a fact was real and had been face to face with the killer. Maybe she could settle this, one way or another.

I worked my way through another can, then went to bed, where I dreamt about the woman with red hair and her throne of skulls.

17

Far too early the next morning, I strode into the reception of Carlisle Hospital, ready for another shift of poop and puke mopping, bulb-changing, and general dogsbody work.

'Morning, Big Marge,' I said, cheerily. Big Marge greeted me with a grunt, not looking up from her magazine.

'Not really a morning person, are you?'

'I'm not really an any-time-of-day person, Joe,' she replied.

'Mary Tyler,' I said, 'is she okay for a visit, d'you think?'

'Let's say she is; why would she want to see you?'

'I saved her life, remember? I don't like to throw the word "hero" around, but, you know, I have heard others use it. About me.'

'The people you see in the mirror don't count, Joe.'

Early morning banter seen to, I headed up to Mary Tyler's new room. After the aborted attack, and the broken window, she'd been relocated to a new private room at the other end of the hospital, with two uniformed officers sat outside, bored out of their minds. I thought I might need to talk my way past them, but it turned out they knew who I was. Most officers around here knew about me. The mystery man. The bloke in the clapped-out car with all the questions. They waved me through.

As the door swung closed, Mary sat up, startled.

'Who are you?'

'It's okay, I work here. I'm sort of a caretaker.'

'Oh. Okay, sorry.'

'Not to worry, I'd be a little jumpy if I was in your shoes. What happened to you was...'

'Not good.'

'Very not good.' I grabbed a chair and sat beside her.

'What is it you want?' she asked, still a little unsure of me.

'My name's Joseph Lake.'

Her eyes widened. 'Oh, it's you. You're the one who found me.'

'Yes. I'm sorry I was too late to do anything about Janet.'

Mary bit her lip and nodded, her eyes turning to shimmering pools.

'Oh, God. I just don't understand it. It's so crazy. So horrible. How can Janet be dead? She's the most alive person I ever met. I know that sounds stupid.'

'No. No, it doesn't.'

A smile twitched at the corners of her mouth for a moment, before the grief pulled them back down again and a tear slipped down her cheek.

'Mary, I'm sorry to ask, but... what do you remember about that night?'

Her hands gripped the covers, knuckle-white, and she chewed at her bottom lip.

'Was there anything... anything at all that seemed, off?'

She looked at me again, a realisation dawning.

'You know, don't you?'

'The person who attacked you. Who attacked Janet. It wasn't really what you'd think of as a person, was it?'

Rivers ran down each cheek now. She shook her head. 'You saw it?' she whispered, her breath ragged.

'I saw it. More than once.'

'Monsters don't exist, Joseph. Monsters don't exist. I'm not some stupid little girl afraid of things under the bed, but that monster that attacked me, that.... that did that to my friend... that monster exists.'

'What did you tell the police?'

'Something that wouldn't make me sound insane. I just, I'm so sorry, Janet. So sorry. But I couldn't say the truth of it. I thought.... thought maybe it wasn't even true. But you've seen it too.'

There was no point pretending I was mad anymore. No point in trying to brush this aside, or tell myself I was, I don't know, hallucinating this conversation or something. It was real. It was all real. I only had to look in Mary Tyler's eyes to know that.

Monsters were real.

I placed my hand over hers. 'Don't worry. You're okay now. You're safe.'

We spoke a little more and I tried to distract her from thinking about how scared she was. I think maybe it even worked a little. I left, promising to pay her another visit, loaded with chocolate and a book or two to keep her busy. If almost-deadly encounters with monsters weren't enough to drive her insane, being trapped in a hospital bed and suffering a non-stop diet of daytime TV definitely would.

I'd worked in the hospital long enough to know the computer logins that I shouldn't, and so after leaving Mary Tyler behind, I found the nearest unmanned computer, slipped behind the desk, and gave myself access to the hospital's medical records.

I had a sudden, sure feeling that the attack on Mary and Janet couldn't have been the first of its sort. Searching for anything that looked similar, I soon found at least two cases in the past couple of months that might fit the bill. A man first, Geoff Smith, forty-two, dead three months ago. And there, Angela Carter, nineteen, died seven weeks back. Both had suffered severe throat lacerations.

I wondered if that would be all, or if there were more. More that hadn't been found. Dead bodies taken someplace else. Some "monster's lair," or even just dead out of view of any common foot traffic. Dead bodies surrounded by strange, occult symbols, painted in their own blood, waiting to be stumbled upon by a holidaying rambler in the hills. Here to take in the best sights the country had to offer, only to find the worst kind of sight anyone could see.

A hand gripped my shoulder and span me round.

'What on earth do you think you're up to?'

Doctor Neil, the Lord of Wank-ville, stood there fuming, his usually pallid skin a trembling puce.

'I was only browsing for porn, I swear it, Doctor Neil,' I replied, quickly closing the session so he wasn't able to see what I'd been up to.

'You're not authorised to access these systems, you're only authorised to push a mop across a shit-smeared floor.'

'I'm sorry, I've seen you using the hospital's computers and just assumed that meant any old arsehole could have a go.'

Doctor Neil's face moved rapidly between many different expressions as he took in what I'd just said. Doctor Neil and I had always had this sort of antagonistic relationship, though I couldn't say for sure why. Sometimes another person just rubs you up the wrong way. At times I did think it might have something to do with the closeness of mine and Chloe's relationship. Perhaps he was jealous. That would make sense. I'd seen the way he looked at her.

A flurry of noisy activity caught our attention as a trolley holding a body burst through the double doors at the far end of the corridor. Doctor Neil switched instantly into work mode and left me behind.

Chloe and Jim, one of the nurses, were working frantically on a body as they moved. Blood poured from a wound on the patient's neck. As they passed me by I got a closer look at the person on the trolley and recognised him at once.

It was Detective Sam Samm.

18

I found Chloe in the car park half an hour later.

I sidled up and leant against the wall next to her, and she passed the half-done cigarette she'd been smoking. I took it, inhaled, and handed it back.

'You did everything you could,' I offered, quietly.

Chloe rested her head against my shoulder and continued to smoke in silence. The number of times I'd comforted her when she'd failed to hold back death numbered in the hundreds at this point in our years together. It never seemed to get any easier for her. I'd heard most doctors manage to somehow step away from it, from the reality of all that death, for the sake of their own well-being. I don't think Chloe had ever learned that trick.

Detective Sam Samm was dead. That nice, odd man had been murdered and every part of me was screaming that it was connected to what had happened to Mary and Janet, what had happened to me. The octopus creature. It had gotten to Detective Samm somehow. Either the creature had somehow renewed itself, or there were more of the things out there. Neither option was appealing.

'You know,' said Chloe softly, breaking my chain of thought,

'I don't remember everyone who I've failed to save. It happens, you know? That's part of the job, death. Happens all the time. All the time. Sometimes more than once a day. One goes after the next and you're just there, frantically trying to hold onto their hand as they slip under the water. There goes another one. And another. And another. And I'm just desperately trying to keep hold of them as they're dragged away. There have been so, so many. But I still remember the first person I lost on the job.'

She paused, stomping out the butt of her smoke before pulling a fresh one out of the packet, lighting it, and carrying on, her eyes focussed on something I couldn't see.

'It was my second day at work. I'd been allowed one death-free day, then a few hours into day two, in she came. Seven years old. Alice Madders. She'd hit her head playing at the park and her parents had brought her in. Over-cautious is what I thought. She seemed fine. Kids fall, they hit their heads, they shake it off. I did a cursory examination, gave Alice some sweets from the vending machine, assured the parents that everything was fine. Their daughter was just going to have a little bruise on her temple. I even felt vaguely annoyed. Annoyed that they were wasting resources and time that could be better used elsewhere, all because they were nervous parents, wrapping their child in cotton wool. Five minutes after telling the parents everything was fine, Alice Madders began fitting. Her body bent back like she was trying to snap her own spine. Her eyes rolled into her head, her mouth started foaming. I didn't know what to do. The whole world slowed to a crawl. Just a blur. I found out later that the knock on the head had caused a bleed on the brain. There was nothing I could have done about it. The moment she'd hit her head, she was dead. Alice Madders. Red hair in pony tails and her front two teeth missing, a gap for adult teeth that never got to grow.'

We sat and smoked in silence after that, her head on my shoulder, our hands clasped together.

I had no intention of visiting the morgue, but my feet took me there anyway.

I pushed quietly through the double doors and the lights flickered on, triggered by my presence. The room was empty and the chill of the place prickled at my skin. Against one wall were twelve metal doors, hiding gaps long enough to slide a body in. Detective Samm hadn't been placed in one of the drawers yet, his body lay on the mortuary slab in the middle of the room. I approached his body slowly, placing each foot gently in front of the other. A childish fear bubbled up that if I were to make too much noise, I'd disturb the corpse. It would sit up sharply, its eyes black, dead hands reaching for me, clawing at my throat.

I looked down at the poor man. Like Janet Coyle, his neck had been severely damaged. Having seen the creature up close, I had to assume it was the large beak that had done the damage. But why? Why were they murdering people? They didn't seem to be eating them. They weren't draining them of blood like a vampire. They were just killing them and leaving their bodies surrounded by strange, cultish symbols. For what purpose? What was the point in it all? Just for the thrill of killing? Some gut instinct told me it had to be more than that. There had to be some reason behind it all.

At first I didn't even realise that my hands were moving to touch the deceased Detective Samm. It wasn't until the tips of my fingers connected with the chill skin of his temples that what I was doing became clear.

I wanted to *see*.

It was like a locked door in my mind had opened a crack and muscle memory was taking over. I didn't quite understand what was happening, but my body did, as sure as I could tie my shoelaces without thinking about it (most of the time).

I held my breath, and—

I feel fear.

Fear so strong I can taste it. Smell it. Hear it, beating in my ears. A tribal drum beat telling me death is near, death is near, death is near.

I am Detective Sam Samm and I am afraid. I am Detective Sam Samm and I am Joseph Lake. I am both. I can't hear Detective Samm's thoughts, but I feel what he feels, the emotions at war within him. I see what he sees.

I am in a house. This is my house. Detective Samm's house. It judders past like a film with frames removed. I can hear my breath, the air sucked rapidly into my lungs and expelled.

I am scared.

Terrified.

I am prey and I am being hunted.

I know this without seeing who's doing the hunting, without hearing Detective Samm's thoughts. The way my heart is beating, my eyes pinned, unblinking, the pure fear powering my limbs; these things tell me everything.

I am prey.

I am being hunted.

They will catch me and I will die.

I'm upstairs, in a bedroom, looking desperately to escape. The way downstairs is cut off. Only one option; the window. As it stutters towards me, my fingers reach for the handle, but then, as though the window had suddenly, impossibly, been pulled away from me, it retreats. I realise then that I am the one who has been pulled away. Something cold and strong is wrapped around my ankle and is pulling me from my exit point.

I twist, a scream on my tongue, to see the black shape of a monster, its beak clicking and screeching, its octopus limbs twitching, ready, eager, desperate. I'm going to die, I'm going to die, I'm going to—

I staggered back, pulling my hands away from Detective Samm's forehead, gasping for air. Falling to my knees, I clutched at my heart, convinced I was about to die. Which was not the most pleasant of feelings.

'Hail, Magic Eater!'

I fell back with a yelp at the sudden intrusion. I looked up to see the fox, its axe held high and proud, stood upon Detective Samm's chest.

'Saviour of the Dark Lakes! Eater of worlds!'

'Shut up,' I replied.

The fox blinked twice, then lowered its axe. 'Bit rude.'

'How are you back? I thought that woman with the red hair tore your head off.'

'Well, aye, she did.'

'Then...?' I gestured at his head, which was very much attached to his body.

'She'll let my death stick at some point, so she will. It's just I have yet to fully make amends for my past errors, that's all.'

I stood, shaking slightly from what I'd just experienced. From what Detective Samm had experienced.

'What's happening to me?'

'How d'you mean?'

'When I touched that dead body—Detective Samm, the man you are standing on—I felt things. Saw things.'

'Course you did. The doors are starting to open, y'see? Open they go and the real you's peering out.'

I was past the point of questioning this creature's existence by now. What had happened just then, that was no delusion. I'd touched Detective Samm's corpse and been given a glimpse of his final moments. That was *real.* I knew it was. I remembered the flash in the alley before I'd stumbled across Janet Coyle's dead body. The moment of insight into the creature as it had brushed past me, our bodies briefly touching, before I'd discovered Mary Tyler.

Wait a gosh darned moment—

The fox waved, I could see his face smiling back.

'I saw you!' I cried. 'When this all started, just before I

found Mary Tyler. I had a… feeling. An episode. Like I could sense what the monster was feeling, and then I saw you. Just for a moment. I saw your face.'

'Finally, a flare shot into the dark,' replied the fox. 'I've been trying to find my way to you for so very long. I was starting to think I never would. But I'm patient, me. I wait. And I wait. And I keep these eyes peeled and my axe sharp, so when the moment comes, I can use it to chop my way through to you. Ten years, it took. Ten years before you finally used your powers again. And there I was, eyes as sharp as knives, waiting on behalf of the Red Woman. And now here I am again.'

Ten years? Ten years since I woke next to Derwentwater with no memory.

'You know who I am.'

'Of course I do. All of the Dark Lakes knows you. All hail our saviour! All hail the Magic Eater!'

I lunged at the fox, grabbing him by the scruff of his neck and shaking him. 'Tell me who I am!'

'What are you doing in here?' asked a voice.

I turned in surprise to find Detective Maya Myers. I turned back, but the fox was gone. Only Detective Samm's corpse remained.

'I said, what are you doing in here?' Myers demanded.

'Nothing. I'm just, working. Cleaning.'

She grimaced and walked towards me. For a moment I thought she might be the second woman in as many days to punch me in the face, but at the last moment she stepped past me to look down at her dead partner.

'I'm sorry,' I said. 'For your loss.'

She snorted once.

We stood in silence for several heavy seconds.

'Do you think…' Detective Myers started, then hesitated, then carried on, 'do you think death can follow you?'

I went to answer, then found myself unable to think of anything.

'Doesn't matter,' she said. 'Now get the hell out of here.'

Perhaps I should have told her. Told her about what it was that had killed her partner. But what would be the point? Why would she believe me? She'd just lost her second partner in the force – for me to suggest the culprit of poor Detective Samm's demise was a creature with octopus arms would be insensitive at best.

'Really, Maya. He was a good one.'

I wanted to say more, to console her in some way, but I felt there was only one thing she wanted from me at that moment.

I walked for the exit and left her alone with her dead partner.

19

I had planned to find Chloe, to suggest we go out and eat something fatty and drink liquids designed to render your brain a trainwreck the next morning, but before I could find her, my phone rang.

'Where's my Boris!' screamed Mrs Coates.

'Ah, yes, fear not, I am on the case. Boris is my number one priority.'

'You found him once, find him again. Today! Or you're off the case. I want my puss puss back!'

I opened my mouth to reply, but she'd already hung up.

I carried on looking for Chloe, but Big Marge informed me that she was in one of the nurse's rooms having a nap, so I decided to leave her to it and find Mrs Coates' damned cat once and for all. Yes, the world was tilting on its axis, but I was a man of my word. I'd been hired to do a job, and I couldn't afford another bad review. My service was already down to two stars on *Yelp*.

I slipped into the Uncanny Wagon and sped along the empty roads, pulling to a stop in Oldstone some thirty minutes later. Missing posters blew past me across the tarmac, a paper tumbleweed.

Unfortunately, my plan for finding Boris—or any of the cats for that matter—had not progressed any from last time. I mean, how exactly do you find a cat that doesn't want to be found? I retrieved the cat box and cat food from the back seat and readied myself for a long, dull wait while I watched my cunning trap.

The fox knew who I was.

That was the thought at the front of my mind. As I looked for Chloe, as I drove to Oldstone, as I placed a small pile of cat treats inside the cat box.

The fox knew who I was and he'd been looking for me.

I'd often fantasised about someone from my past turning up to say they knew who I was, but not once had that person been an axe-wielding fox. Was he telling the truth? It was hard to say as I hadn't had much experience telling whether a talking animal was lying to me or not.

Then there was the homeless woman. She too seemed to know more about me than I did. The old me, at least. A talking fox and a fighty mad woman were, maybe, at last, the keys to unlocking my past. Now, if only they wouldn't keep disappearing, maybe I could get a straight answer out of them.

I felt my phone vibrating in my pocket and pulled it out to see Chloe's name.

'Hello! Hello there. You. Hello you. It is me,' I said. Smooth as mother-fornicator.

'Hey, where are you?' she asked.

'On a cat hunt in Oldstone.'

'Are you getting a pet?'

'No, just helping out an old woman. How are you? I came to find you before heading off but Big Marge said you were having forty winks.'

'Yeah, I just needed to crash for a bit.'

'Are you okay?'

'Of course. Will you come over later?'

Hello...

'Yeah, I can come over. There. To yours. Where you live.'

'You don't mind?'

I will literally crawl on my belly across poop-smeared shards of broken glass for this.

'Of course not. I had a thing, but I can probably move it.'

'You can?'

'I can move it. Consider it moved. It was here, now it's over there. Moved.'

'Thanks. Thank you. I'll be back a little after seven. Be there waiting for me?'

'Absolutely.'

'Cool. Oh, and Joe?'

'Yep?'

'Bring a toothbrush.'

And then she hung up.

I stood statue-still for several minutes, the phone still glued to my ear.

Perhaps her own toothbrush was broken and Chloe was asking for a replacement? A friendly favour?

'Will do,' I replied in a tiny voice, several minutes after she'd hung up.

Well then. Well, well, wellity, well.

My cheeks ached from over-grinning. I had a few hours before I was due to loiter hormonally outside of Chloe's front door, so I began to set my cat-nabbing trap at different places around Oldstone. I'd put the food-laden cat box down, watch from a discreet distance for half an hour or so, then move on to somewhere else. My mind should really have still been focussing on the talking fox and the fighty mad woman, but instead my mind was full of Chloe and my eyes full of hearts. So much so that, at the final place I rested the cat box, it took me almost twenty minutes to notice that I was sat, cross-legged on the grass, in front of a dead cat.

I might not have noticed at all if I hadn't decided to stretch back, and found myself resting my head on a tiny, furry corpse.

After a suitable amount of yelping and shuddering, I got down on my knees and gave the deceased moggy a closer look. I wondered how many of the hundreds of missing cat posters pasted all around Oldstone featured this poor cat's mugshot.

'Bad luck, fella,' I said.

It was sad, but a dead cat was not what I'd been looking for. I was looking for, well, alive cats. Boris specifically, but really any live cat would have done. I felt for sure that if the cats had all disappeared over the space of a few days, then it seemed likely all or most had ended up in the same place. For whatever reason. Be it the strange, uneasy atmosphere that hung over the village or, well, some other reason.

It was then that a thought struck.

'Oh.'

The strange feelings during the aftermath of the attack on Janet and Mary.

The things I saw when I touched Detective Samm's corpse.

Maybe a dead cat wouldn't be so useless after all. Maybe it could tell me exactly what I needed to know.

The fox had said the real me was peeking out. *You finally used your powers again.* I didn't feel powerful, and I'd no idea how I'd managed to make what had happened happen. Worth a shot though.

I looked down at the dead cat and let out a hard breath, preparing myself.

'Okay, magic brain, I am your master, please do your insight thing.' I punctuated my command with a little hand flourish that felt suitably mystical, then placed my hands onto the dead cat.

Which was gross.

Of course, a little earlier I'd been touching a dead man, but that had been an almost unconscious decision, this time it was all me. Really there. Choosing to put my hands on a dead thing.

Nothing happened.

I raised my hands to the sky. 'Show me your death!' I commanded, then grabbed the cat again.

Zilch.

Not a thing.

I didn't have powers, that was absurd. There had to have been some other explanation for my earlier "insights." The fox, perhaps. A talking fox is a pretty magical thing, maybe he had the powers and that's what affected me.

But then why would he say that I was using my powers at last?

I grunted in frustrated confusion—not an unfamiliar emotion for me—and placed my hands on the deceased family pet without thinking. No daft commands, no great thought behind it or hand gestures, I just touched the thing with no expectations.

And that's when it happened.

Scents, sounds, everywhere. A new world of information, so vivid, a feeling of poise, of strength, of hunger of...

Show me where, show me where...

I am low to the ground, moving at speed, need to hide, need to go back, fear. I feel fear. My heart is beating so fast. It's not safe, not safe. I see the streets rush by. People, sounds, smells, the giant world around me, and something else, something else. I don't like it. I don't like it. Run, run, run. Back to the safe place. This is not safe. Back to the safe place—

I gasped as the connection was broken, my eyes blinking rapidly as I found myself in a different place to where I'd started. I was out of breath. I think I'd been running. I could see Oldstone a good half-mile away, and in front of me a large barn.

For a moment or two I let the fact that I'd just experienced the emotions, sights and smells of a cat wash over me. Because that's weird. That's very, very weird. And no fox around, so... it was me. I'd done that. I'd touched the dead body of a cat and been given a glimpse into its life.

That was exciting. Or terrifying. One of the two. I wondered what else I might be capable of.

The barn in front of me didn't look like it was in use anymore, in fact it looked as though a strong gust of wind might reduce it to kindling. The door screeched a rusty-hinged complaint as I opened it and stepped inside to be greeted by a hundred glowing pricks of light. It was like I was looking into the night sky and stars were twinkling back at me.

I blinked, and as I became more accustomed to the gloom, I saw that these weren't impossible stars, they were eyes, shining bright. The barn was absolutely packed to the rafters with Oldstone's missing cats.

'I don't suppose any of you are talking cats and can tell me just why it is you're all hiding out in this stinky barn? Daft question I know, but I have recently made the acquaintance of a very talkative fox.'

None of them answered.

Maybe they didn't feel like a chat.

20

I was able to spot Boris amongst the crush, but having failed to bring my cat box with me, I settled for taking a picture or two as evidence. Of Boris, and of the rest of the cat-filled barn.

I still didn't know for sure why the cats had run away from their homes, or why they'd felt the need to huddle together for safety, but at least I knew where they were.

I told the cats to stay put and headed off towards Mrs Coates' home to bring her the good news.

I'd been an investigator of the peculiar for years now, but my ratio of solved to unsolved was pretty poor. By which I mean I rarely ever came out on top. That's the thing with the bizarre and inexplicable, it rather likes to stay that way. So here I was with a genuine "solved" under my belt, and I'd done it all by myself. Just me and my brand new superpowers.

I walked towards Mrs Coates' home with a spring in my step, I can tell you. Cats located, things of an adult nature waiting for me at Chloe's later, the gratitude of a village of cat lovers, this was turning into quite a day.

So of course something had to come along and turn it all to dung.

It was Mrs Coates' front door that did it.

As I pushed open the gate to her well-tended garden, bursting full of brightly coloured flowers and expertly manicured bushes, I saw that the door was slightly ajar. Now, this in itself shouldn't be a cause for concern. Perhaps she'd been doing something in the garden and had stepped back inside for a moment. That's a normal enough thing to have done.

So why was my heart starting to increase its rhythm? Why was a knot forming in my stomach? My body knew something was wrong, even if I had no real evidence for it.

'Mrs Coates?' I said as I reached the door. 'Hello, Mrs Coates? It's Joseph Lake, here about your cat. Well, all the cats.'

A cold, empty silence.

'Mrs Coates?'

I pushed the door open and stepped warily into her home.

'Hello, Mrs Coates? I'm just coming inside now. Is there any reason why my brain is telling me to turn tail and run for the hills?'

Staircase to my right, two doors on the left, and a third at the far end. Which way to go? Dealer's choice.

I made my way towards the nearest door and stepped inside.

The front room was neat, but a riot of clashing floral patterns. The carpet, the wallpaper, the furniture. This woman liked her flowers. And a headache, if the way it was all affecting had anything to do with it. Perched on the fireplace was a picture of a much younger Mrs Coates and a beaming man. Ex-husband? I hadn't noticed a wedding ring.

I left and made my way to the second room. This back room was more subdued than the first, and contained a couch, plus a desk with an old foot-pedal powered sewing machine on top.

Kitchen next.

'Mrs Coates?'

There was a cup of tea on the kitchen table. I placed my hand against it. The porcelain was still warm.

I turned back and made my way to the staircase, peering up into the dark second floor.

'Hello? Please say something reassuring so my stomach will stop doing somersaults, Mrs Coates.'

I began to make my way up the stairs, each one creaking under my weight. This was an old house. Well, all the buildings in Oldstone were old. Old Oldstone.

It was halfway up that I noticed the smudges of dark red on the stairs. Splatters against the pristine white of the staircase carpet.

Blood. Crumbs leading me up and up.

I stepped onto the landing and saw the door to one of the bedrooms was open. A foot poked out into the corridor, its sole facing me.

'Mrs Coates?'

I ran to her, pushing the door open to find her stretched out on the carpet, her throat torn out and the strange occult-looking symbols daubed onto the carpet around her.

'Oh, Christ...'

I crouched, feeling for a pulse as if the truth of the matter wasn't self-evident. Mrs Coates was very, very dead.

I stood, reaching into my pocket to retrieve my phone and call the police, then froze as a dark shape twitched in my periphery. The thick, lined curtains were drawn, lights off, and much of the room was in shadow. A perfect place for a monster to lurk.

I backed away as an octopus limb curled out of the shadows.

'Bastard. You bastard,' I said, my anger at Mrs Coates' death trumping my legs' demands to turn and run. Instead, I stepped further into the room as though I'd meant to fight the creature that had killed this poor woman.

The monster screamed and lunged out of the black at me. I stepped back, my heel catching something, and realised with horror that I'd been tripped by Mrs Coates' prone body.

I landed hard, bones jarring, wind jerked out of me, but there was no time to count my bruises. I scrabbled backwards on my hands and feet as the creature bent to grab at me, my boot kicking out and catching the thing in the head.

It reeled back, limbs thrashing in fury. Meanwhile, I turned, stood, and ran. The door at the other end of the landing erupted in a blizzard of wooden needles as a second octopus man burst from inside.

'Shit—'

I bolted for the staircase. I was closer, I could make it, I could escape, I could run from the house and not stop running until I was back in the Uncanny Wagon, stomping on the accelerator.

The stairway greeted me. I placed one foot down, then a fleshy limb struck my back foot and the world turned over and over, hard edges assaulting me, until my painful whirl of a journey was brought to a sudden stop. My vision blurred and spat stars.

'Up, get up, move,' I said, my voice a slur.

I looked up, time now moving at a crawl, to see the two octopus creatures descending towards me, beaks snapping hungrily. One walked down the stairs, the other clung to the wall with its suckered limbs, making its way down.

'Get up!'

Body aching, knees treacherous, I pushed myself to my feet and opened the front door to find a third monster stood in its frame.

I rocked back on my heels, one octopus man before me, another behind, the third now slithering obscenely across the ceiling above. I was a fly, caught in a web, as three spiders raced to claim me as their dinner.

'Get back!' I yelled, a pointless cry of defiance, as I knew full well I was dead. I was dead and that was that. There was no way out. This was it, three live monsters and one soon to be dead me.

The creatures were in no rush. Beaks wide, throats clicking, they moved incrementally towards me. Towards my death.

This wasn't fair. Wasn't right. None of it was. Who were these things to take my life from me?

'I said, get back!'

The creatures jerked back as though I'd pulled a weapon. At first I was confused. What did they have to worry about? Here I was, a nice, fleshy, easy kill, just waiting to have my throat torn open.

It was then that I realised my hands were engulfed in bright, blue flames.

Flames meant fire.

Oh shit, I was on fire!

I stepped back, waving my arms around, trying to extinguish the flames and wondering why I didn't feel any pain.

Apparently over their uncertainty, the creatures rushed me. My world became blue flames and writhing, suckered limbs, as death's guillotine came crashing down on me.

21

I assumed I was dead.

Well, you would, wouldn't you?

I was on fire and about half a second away from having three blood-thirsty creatures tear me to pieces.

I was dead.

I was an ex-Joseph Lake.

Which meant that I wouldn't be going round Chloe's later with a fresh toothbrush tucked into my coat pocket.

Damn.

In that moment, that was the thing that stung the most.

Not my death, not my murder at the tentacles of three complete bastards, but the idea that something just beginning, something potentially wonderful, was about to be cut off at the knees.

I'd been infatuated, or in love, or in lust, or all three, with Chloe Palmer ever since I'd first laid eyes on her. It was a Tuesday. Just a normal, boring, run-of-the-mill Tuesday, and Doctor Alex Kurd was showing a couple of the new recruits around the hospital. I was up a ladder prodding at a light fitting as they passed by.

As *she* passed by.

We met properly the next morning, when I drove my car directly into the back of hers. She was stationary in the car park at the time.

She could have been furious. Should have been. But as I waved my arms around, trying to desperately inform her of the bee that had distracted me and caused the accident, she did the strangest thing. She began to laugh. She didn't shout at me. Didn't swear at me. Didn't report me. She just laughed, and I found myself laughing with her.

I was too much of an awkward fool to ever do anything about it of course, so the years rolled on and I set up shop in the Friend Zone. Which was not at all pleasant at times, particularly when she'd choose to confide in me about her latest man. Her current bedfellow. Those times really slid a shard of ice in the old heart, but then I'd feel guilty for how happy I was each time those short relationships spluttered, coughed, and died. She'd be on the couch, red-eyed, stuffing ice cream into her face hole, and I'd be nodding sympathetically while my insides did a vigorous interpretation of *Riverdance*.

From time to time I got the feeling she was waiting for me to ask her out. To finally make my feelings known. But the longer time went on, the harder it became.

And then at last.

At last, at last, we'd gotten past all that. She liked me. She *actually* liked me and knew for sure that I liked her.

We'd done the kissing!

And now here I was, dead and massively annoyed that the great romance of my daft life was over before it could begin.

What rotten, shitty luck.

It was all coming together nicely, and now I was just another dead person.

Damn, damn, and double-damn with a cherry on top.

I realised I wasn't actually dead when something prodded my side and I opened my eyes to find the fox looking up at me, axe in hand.

'All hail, the saviour!'

'Oh, not you again.'

I tried to move but realised that I was affixed to a giant tree by thick chains.

'Wait, I'm alive. I'm alive, aren't I?'

'All hail, the Magic Eater!'

'I'm alive! Chloe Alison Palmer, I am alive!'

This was possibly the happiest anyone who had just awoken to find themselves chained to a tree had ever been.

'I have him chained to the Tree of Anguish, do you see him, Red Woman?' said the fox, projecting his words at the rolling red fire of the sky.

I was back in the strange place. What had he called it, the fox? The Dark Lakes? With its fields of bones, fire for sky, and bloody grasses.

'Is this my time? Shall death be my friend at last?' said the fox in a small voice.

'Why am I here again?' I asked.

'Twas your choice, not mine,' he replied. 'I did not bring you here, you brought yourself as doom descended.'

I wriggled beneath the chains, but they only seemed to tighten as I fought them, as though they were alive and resisting my struggle.

'That's because they are,' said a voice I recognised. I twisted my head as far as I could, to see the woman approaching with her bright, red hair.

'Living chains? Right. Do they have a name? It's rude not to introduce yourself to someone, you know.'

The chains gave me an extra squeeze that momentarily prevented me from breathing.

'Point taken,' I said, wheezing. 'No more trash talking the magical chains.'

'Look, here he is again,' said the fox, pointing at me with his axe. 'Surely now? I have done my duty, yes? Done and done and done and my weary body craves its prize.'

The Red Woman crouched before the fox and extended a pale hand, scratching at him under the chin affectionately. 'Your time will come. Your time will end. But not yet.'

The fox was close to tears.

The Red Woman stood and turned to me, walking slowly forward.

'Do you know who you are yet?'

'In a lot of trouble?'

A small smile. She was truly stunning, but something about her made my stomach squirm.

'It is starting to become clear though, yes?'

She reached out, her long, elegant fingers like feathers of ice across my cheek.

'Am I... magic?'

Her thumb stroked my lower lip.

'Oh, you're so much more than that. Shall I show you your future?'

'Depends. Is it a nice future?'

She smiled again. 'Oh yes. It's... delicious.'

She placed her right hand against my forehead and—

I stride across the face of the earth, a giant, a beast. My skin ripples with flames, my eyes black holes that see and judge and own all.

Screams caress my ears. This is my music. The music of fear. Of pain. Of the world bending to me. This is my food. I swallow it down but my stomach is never full. Never satiated. Never satisfied.

The Uncanny rise to block my path, and I eat them. I tear them in two and drink their power. I feel their bones crunch between my teeth and I think that this is good.

The end, the end, I am the end. And I am the beginning, too. A new, dark beginning. From the ashes I sow shall rise a new world. My world.

At my side is the army of the dead. My army. We step from the Dark Lakes and shake off the water, and all the world burns and fear and fear and fear and—

'Stop!' My head hung loose and I gasped for air.

'Was it not beautiful?' asked the Red Woman.

'What was that? What was that... thing?'

'It was your choice. You will remember that. You wanted it. You want it. Become the Magic Eater.'

What was this? Besides terrifying and perplexing, obviously. A trick of some sort? What was it the Red Woman was trying to get me to do? I wished someone would just give me a straight answer.

'I don't know what you're talking about. Also, these chains really chafe, could you just let me down? And your hands are freezing. A sign of poor circulation; I'd see a doctor if I were you."

'Look what you have become. A chattering fool, blind to your true purpose. Your true destiny.'

'All hail the saviour,' cried the fox, and the sky of fire roared its approval.

22

The buzz of a strip light.

I sniffed and caught a smell I knew all too well. I was laid up in a hospital bed again.

My eyes creaked open. Someone was sat on a chair at my bedside.

'Chloe?' I said, my dry throat cracking.

'Afraid not,' replied Detective Maya Myers.

I sat up in surprise. Maya handed me a plastic cup of water, which I took after a moment's hesitation and downed in one.

'Thanks. Thank you.'

Maya remained leaning towards me, her eyes narrowed.

'How about now, Mr Lake?'

'How about now, what?'

'Don't you dare give me that bullshit,' she replied, with venom. 'People are dying. My partner, Detective Samm, has been murdered. And now you're discovered, unconscious in an old woman's house, and the old woman it belongs to is dead upstairs. Same MO as the others. As Sam. So why don't you start giving me some answers before I start knocking teeth down your throat.'

Well, that was certainly to the point.

'I didn't do it. I didn't kill any of them,' I replied.

She snorted, kicking back her chair as she stood. 'I know that. You might be many things, but a killer you are not.'

'Well, thanks. Thank you. Just as long as that's clear.'

Maya lunged forward, grabbing me by the collar of my hospital gown and pulling me forward.

'Tell me what you know.'

'I can't!'

'Tell me!'

She shoved me back and turned away in disgust.

'I don't know what I can say.'

'Why? Who's got something on you? We can protect you.'

'No one has anything on me. It's just that you won't believe me. Even if I tell you everything I've seen, or think I've seen, you won't believe a word of it.'

Maya sagged and slumped back onto her chair.

'Just tell me. I lost my partner. Lost another partner. Just tell me something. Anything.'

For the first time since I'd met her, Detective Maya Myers looked small. Uncertain. Defeated, even. It didn't look right. This wasn't her. She was strong. I found myself telling some of the truth without even making the decision to do so.

'Do you believe in monsters, Detective?'

She looked up at me, eyes wide. 'Monsters?'

What was that I saw in those eyes?

Was that... recognition?

'You *do* know, don't you?'

'Joseph, tell me about the monsters.'

It was at that moment that the door to my private room burst open and a woman I'd never met before stormed in. Her hair was pulled back, the smart suit she wore, fierce, and the briefcase she clutched, shiny.

'Stop talking,' she said. Well, ordered. Every sentence she spoke was a blunt instrument.

'Who are you?' asked Maya, and the woman handed her a card.

'Belinda Washington. I am Mr Lake's lawyer.'

'You are?' I asked, quite flummoxed.

'I am. Detective Myers, have you been questioning my client without proper legal representation present?'

'I just—'

'I'll take that as a yes. Do you intend to charge my client with anything?'

Maya looked at me. I shrugged.

'No, I do not,' she replied.

'In that case, Mr Lake, I suggest you get up out of bed, collect your belongings, and follow me out of this building.'

Maya looked at me again, clearly not done with questioning me. In all honesty, I wasn't done with her either. When I mentioned monsters I'd seen a look of recognition, not a look of confusion, or anger. What did Maya know about monsters?

I really wanted to find out more, but Belinda Washington hustled Maya from the room as I dressed. When I stepped into the corridor, only my mysterious lawyer was waiting for me.

'Let's go,' she said.

'Yeah, I don't know who you are, so forgive me for not just following blindly on, it's been a strange few days.'

'Come along,' she said. 'I'll fill you in on the drive. Your car is outside, you can drop me off.'

'My car? How did my car get here...?'

I watched, bewildered, as she turned sharply on her black heels and strode away. Now a smart person, after all he'd experienced, would not have followed her quite so willingly, fearing some sort of trap might be looming on the horizon. So what did I do?

'Hey, wait for me.'

I threw my long coat on and chased after her.

As we pulled away from the hospital, Belinda Washington sat silently staring out of the windscreen.'

'Sorry, but when did you take me on as a client? Did Chloe hire you, or…?'

'No one hired me, you tool.'

I turned to her in surprise, only to find that smartly dressed Belinda Washington was no longer sat next to me, her briefcase balanced on her lap. Instead, it was the mad homeless woman, a can of strong lager balanced on her lap.

I did a little scream and jerked the steering wheel.

The Uncanny Wagon swerved this way and that, almost hitting a tree, and then I parked up and turned to the woman, my back pressed against the driver's door.

'It's you!'

'You're welcome. I just saved your miserable hide from a prison cell.'

'No. No, you didn't. Maya wasn't going to arrest me, we were just talking.'

'Oh.' The woman opened her can, took a sip, and shrugged. 'We all make mistakes.'

I looked at her warily, trying to find any hint of the person she'd been moments before.

'How did you…?' I waved my hand in front of my face.

'With difficulty. A little illusion magic, a little confusion magic. It stings like a fucker to keep it up for that long. I'll be pissing blood tonight.'

'Magic? That was magic? *Magic-magic*?'

The woman sighed. 'Well, duh.'

'Okay, I'm just not overly accustomed to really-real magic, is all.'

'Well, what d'you think you did to those three soul vampires earlier? Tickle them to death? Idiot.'

'"Idiot" seems a bit uncalled for.'

'How about I punch you in the face again?'

'No, that's okay, I'm fine with idiot.'

'Too fucking right you are,' she replied in a low grumble, turning her attention back to her cheap can of lager.'

Wait a minute.

'I'm sorry, "soul" what now? Did you say "soul vampires"? Was that the thing that you said that I'm just now fully registering? Soul vampires?'

She nodded.

'You don't remember me yet, do you?'

'Yes. I do. I've been seeing you all over the place for weeks.'

'No, you *don't* remember me. My name's Eva Familiar, and it's really very, very shitty to make your reacquaintance.'

'Right. Okay. I sense a lot of hostility in you, Eva. I'm Joseph.'

'No, you're,' she paused to burp, 'not. But idiot will do just fine for now, idiot. Now, shut up and drive me home.'

'You know, you're a very mean lady.'

'Thanks, I do try.'

She collapsed her empty can on her forehead and threw it out the window. Only the window was closed, so the can bounced off and fell in my lap, leaking its remaining contents onto my crotch.

'Right then,' I said, and started up the car.

23

Shortly after setting off again, the woman, Eva, fell asleep.

When she'd announced her intention to take a nap, I'd pointed out that I was supposed to be driving her home, and as I had no idea where that home was, a few directions might be in order. She'd assured me that I'd find the way if I just drove, and then promptly fell into a deep snooze that no amount of shaking, shoving, and shouting could rouse her from.

And so I drove.

At first I felt a fool.

I just drove blindly out of Carlisle and into the belly of the Lake District, taking turn after turn at whim. And then a strange sensation began to creep over me. I felt like I wasn't taking random turns at all, but like my hands and feet knew exactly where we were going. As though they were making my decisions for me, and that I just had to leave them to it and we'd get where we were supposed to be going.

I felt like if I thought too much about it, I'd throw off the trick and drive us into one of the region's great lakes, so I tried to distract myself. It wasn't difficult, considering all of the recent calamities I'd suffered.

I thought about the Red Woman. The thing she had shown me. The thing that had felt like me, but couldn't be. The monstrous beast with skin of fire and dead eyes that sought to lay waste to everything it saw and replace it with something terrible.

The Magic Eater. That's what she'd called it. That was what the fox had said, too.

Magic Eater.

'Stop!'

Eva's voice snapped me out of my musing, and I stomped my foot on the brake, bringing the Uncanny Wagon to a screeching halt.

'Jesus Christ, don't do that! This poor car has been through enough.'

I stroked the Wagon's steering wheel gently, as though soothing a frightened cat.

'This is it, we're here,' said Eva, pushing the door open and shambling out.

I peered through the windscreen to see nothing.

Well, not nothing, there were hills and trees and all the rest, but nothing that looked like a dwelling.

I got out of the car and looked around for something I might be missing.

'Exactly where is this home of yours, Eva? Is it a home or more of a bivouac sort of a situation?'

Eva turned to look at me strangely. 'Christ, don't tell me even your eyes are fucked.'

'My eyes are just fine, thank you. AI vision, sharp as a sharp thing.'

'Nope, you can't see shit, idiot.'

'Tell me then, what exactly am I missing?'

'The blind alley in front of you.'

Oh god, not only was she magic, she was insane.

'We're in the middle of nowhere, there are no alleys. You need buildings for alleyways. Streets. All there is around here are hills, fields, rocks, trees, and lakes.'

'Is that so?'

'That is absolutely so.'

'Look again,' said Eva, and then she touched my arm, causing me to yelp as a static shock pricked my flesh.

'What d'you call that then, idiot?' she asked, pointing in front of us.

The entrance to an alley was open in front of me. A gap between two other things that you could walk down. Only, the two things weren't other buildings, this alley was like a gap in, well, in reality. It's sort of hard to explain as it's impossible. But there it was, and it was only visible if I looked directly at it. If I twisted slightly, there was nothing, twist back, and oops, a wrinkle in reality. A crack in nothing.

'If you've finished gawping and rubbing your eyes like a cartoon mouse,' said Eva, 'follow me.'

She stepped into the fault in reality and began to walk down the impossible, insane alleyway. I suspect most people would have fallen to their knees at that point. Collapsed like an overdone flan as their brains objected to this obvious glitch in the matrix, but I'd been attacked by octopus men and held conversations with talking foxes, so weird really was my wheelhouse now.

'Okay. Okay then. Impossible alleys nestled between nothing. Of course.'

I walked in after Eva.

Inside the impossible alley itself, the "walls" to either side of me were just the surrounding countryside, but warped. Twisted. Stretched. Ahead of us lay a two-storey building made of large blocks of stone. Eva paused at a green metal door.

'Here it is then. Home sweet home.'

I felt odd looking at the place. Like it was trying to whisper things to me that I once would have been able to hear. Which I know makes little to no sense, but then most of the last few days had been a confusing whirl of nonsense.

'I'll be honest,' I said, 'I kind of assumed you didn't have a home.'

'Why's that?'

'Well...' I tried to find a tactful way to say, "You look like a tramp," then gave up and gestured at her general mad, homeless person appearance.

'It's really very hard not to keep punching you,' she said, unlocking the door and stepping inside.

'And what is it with all that?' I asked. 'The punching and the name calling? Eva?' I made my way in after her, wary that a fist might erupt from the gloom and break my nose.

It was warm inside. Warmer than I'd expected. I'd prepared myself for a tomb-like chill, but it seemed the ancient place had pretty decent heating.

The floor was bare, dark wood, and a staircase to my left stretched up to the next floor, its steps nude but for an inch of dust. It seemed that Eva didn't venture from the ground floor often.

At first I thought someone had thrown pots of dark paint randomly against the walls of the corridor, then, upon closer inspection, realised that the large blotches more resembled scorch marks. Fire damage?

The atmosphere within the building was... well, I'm not really sure what it was. But it was something. Not unpleasant, but almost as though the air inside was *thicker* than outside. I felt as though I'd stepped into an invisible river, and that I could feel the currents rushing past me. I also felt something else.

I felt like I'd been there before.

'Come through to the main room,' said Eva from further inside the house. 'And close the fucking door, were you born in a barn? Wait, scratch that, I think you actually were. Near some pigs, wasn't it?'

I closed the door as requested then moved down the corridor and into what she called the "main room." It was large, with an open fireplace dominating one wall. An old metal cauldron hung there, and a large, square piece of slate was fixed to the floor before it. Eva stumbled through from another door that looked like it led off to a very rudimentary kitchen.

'Here,' she said, tossing a can of lager my way, then she flopped onto one of the tattiest, rankest smelling couches I'd ever laid eyes upon.

'Thank you,' I replied, opening the can and taking a sip.

Eva retrieved a remote control from between the sofa cushions and pointed it at the far wall. A click, and a screen parted to reveal a truly ginormous TV screen. A *Fawlty Towers* repeat came on. This place was literally a burnt-out hovel, but the TV was worth more than my car.

'So,' I said, breaking the heavy, heavy silence, 'I like what you mostly haven't done with the place.'

Eva snorted.

I perched on the end of the couch and we both watched as Basil crouched, holding his head and hopping around in anguish.

'I've been here before, haven't I?'

Eva nodded. 'Say hello to the Cumbrian Coven. Used to look a bit grander in the old days, but it's still standing.'

'Coven?'

'Coven.'

'That's a witch thing, isn't it?

'Yup.'

'Are you a witch?'

'Nope.'

'Oh.'

'You're a witch,' she said.

There was quite a bit of silence then as my face did some rather spectacular expression gymnastics.

'Or warlock, if you like. Some of you male witches prefer that. All the same thing though. Except for the tits.'

A witch. Or warlock. Okay. Well. Hm.

'So I'm a warlock witch thing?'

'That's right, idiot.'

'Okay, I see, and tell me why I should believe a word you say? Who even are you? You're just an admittedly quite magic-savvy mad woman. How do I know you're not feeding me a load of old crap, like that fox?'

Eva turned to me, her eyes wide. 'Fox?'

'There has been a talking fox, yes.'

'And a woman? Have you seen a woman with red hair?'

'Yes. Why are you looking at me like that?'

She moved fast, did Eva. Before I'd had chance to blink, I was on my back on the floor, looking up into her furious eyes, a hand around my throat.

'What did she offer you?'

I choked and burbled a bit until she loosened her grip so that I could actually breathe.

'Rubbish,' I squeaked. 'She just talked rubbish, and I'm pretty sure it was just some sort of weird dream, anyway.'

Eva bared her teeth. 'If you ever see her again, you tell me. You tell me everything. And if I find out you haven't told me everything, I'll fucking kill you. You understand me, idiot?'

I shrank back, which was difficult to do as the floor prevented me from going backwards even an inch. 'Got you,' I said.

Eva grunted in anger, stood, then flopped back on the couch. I sat up, rubbing at my neck.

'That's one punch and a partial strangulation now,' I said. 'Just keeping a tally of abuse there.'

'Get out,' said Eva.

'But if you are telling the truth, then tell me more. What's my real name? What happened to me? Why can't I remember my life?'

'I'm going to sleep now,' she replied, and lay back. Within seconds, she was snoring like an overweight truck driver after a three-day haul.

'Eva? Eva!'

But it was no good, she was dead to the world.

It was at this point that I remembered an earlier invitation.

'Oh shit.' I looked at my watch. It was almost ten. 'Oh shit with some extra shit on top.'

I looked back at Eva, wondered if I should continue to try to wake her up and attempt to get some clear answers to my questions, then thought about how many times she might punch my face if I disturbed her. I had a feeling there'd be plenty of time for more of that.

I ran from the house. From the Cumbrian Coven as Eva had called it. I sprinted down the crazy wrinkle in reality and back into the solid everyday, the Uncanny Wagon there to greet me.

I was supposed to be at Chloe's place by seven. Eva had the right name for me.

I was an idiot.

24

After leaving the coven behind, my phone sprang to life and vomited up a tide of messages and missed phone calls it had been hiding from me.

Chloe was more than a little confused as to why I seemed to be avoiding her.

'Hey, Chloe, it's me. Joseph. An idiot, I've been reliably informed.'

'Where have you been? I thought we had a date, Joseph. And what's this Big Marge said about you having another stay in a hospital bed?'

'Fine. It's nothing. I just found another dead body and, I suppose, passed out. Manly.'

'Jesus, are you okay?'

I nodded furiously, then realised that this was a phone call and head movements in the affirmative were not going to move this conversation along any.

'Yep. Yes. I'm oh so good.' Which was a clear lie, but I think I sold it well enough.

'You don't sound good, you sound weird.'

Damn.

'Just, you know, finding another dead person. It's sort of,

weirded me out a little, that's all.'

'Are you coming over?'

'Yes. I am on my way.'

'Good.'

And through the country roads towards Carlisle and Chloe's home I sped.

Okay, so, it seems my tardiness had not put the mockers on things. I was still allowed to darken Chloe's door. This should have made me happy, but I was currently full to the trembling brim with all the new information I'd been given, jostling with all the other weird-to-the-point-of-insane sights and sounds I'd collected over the last few days.

I've investigated the paranormal for a long time, but this was the first hand evidence I'd seen that any of it was true. Finally, the weird had decided to pay me a visit, and it had brought the whole family.

Monsters.

Witches.

Magic.

My past life.

Alternate worlds.

Talking animals with a fondness for battle axes.

Any one of those would have been enough to make a man question his sanity. Question how real this so-called reality really was. And here I was trying to cope with all of them at the same time. It's a wonder I wasn't curled up in a ball on the ground, babbling in tongues.

It was like life as I had known it, as I had accepted it, had revealed itself to be only one part of the story. *Look here, under this sheet, see all of this other secret stuff, some of which is going to try and chew your face off with a large fucking beak?*

I realised I was sweating, my heart was beating too fast, my hands white-knuckling the steering wheel.

I needed to calm down.

Everything was fine.

Well, everything wasn't fine, everything was on the terrifying side, but I was going somewhere normal. Somewhere that magic didn't exist and I was plain old Joseph Lake: a gangly, well meaning doofus with terrific hair and the hots for a very nice woman.

Thirty minutes later, as Chloe opened her front door, I could see in her eyes that I must have looked insane.

'Joe, what's wrong?'

'Nothing. Nothing's wrong, do you have water? Ha! Of course you have water, who doesn't have water? Actually, that's insensitive of me, there are many countries in this world where on-hand, potable water is a problem. Thoughtless of me, I apologise.'

Chloe ushered me inside and I tried my best to get my shit together.

'Get your shit together,' I actually said.

'What was that?' asked Chloe, who was stood right next to me.

'Just a normal thing. Normal words.'

She handed me a glass of water, which I gratefully accepted, then downed in three large gulps.

'Ah! Okay, that's better. Now I am calm. And relaxed.'

Chloe looked down at my right leg, which was jiggling like a loon, as though trying to beat out a machine gun rhythm on a bass drum. I gave it a little slap.

'Joe, where have you been since you checked yourself out of the hospital?'

'Just around. Driving. Trying to clear my head after all the unpleasantness. Did Big Marge mention the latest victim was the woman who hired me to find her missing cat? Because she was. That was the woman who died.'

'Shit. No, she didn't say that.'

'Well, it was. So that's shit. Well, even if it hadn't been her, it would've been shit. Because dead person. Murdered person.'

I felt Chloe's hand slip into mine.

'Joe, calm down, you're okay.'

'Not really, for many reasons that I can't really divulge at this moment.'

Jesus, was I screwing this up. The past few days had been building an unsteady pile of bricks on top of me, and I thought I'd been handling things reasonably well, but nope, down fell the bricks, and there I was, sweating and trembling in the front room of the woman I was hopelessly in love with.

'Joe, I'm here. I'm your friend. You can tell me anything.'

She looked up at me with those big eyes. Eyes full of empathy and understanding. Eyes that made me feel weak at the knees.

It was at this point I did a very stupid thing. I began to tell the truth. Well, not tell as much as *purge* the truth in one eruption.

'Okay, okay, well, it's just been.... you know! These last few days, with the murders, and my being attacked—'

'You were attacked?'

'Yep, attacked, lied about that, said I just crashed the Uncanny Wagon, but no, attacked, and then there were the monsters with big floppy octopus arms that I haven't told anyone about, and a talking fox with an axe!'

Chloe pulled back, alarm on her face at my crazy unloading.

'Talking fox? Did you say a talking fox?'

'With an axe! And that homeless woman isn't actually homeless, but she is magic, and she lives in a big old house hidden in a wrinkle in reality and she tells me that I am, apparently, a witch.'

'A witch?'

'Or warlock. Witch warlock, that's me, that's apparently what I was before Joseph Lake, I was a witch or a warlock, or whatever, and life is very strange, and very frightening, and, oh dear, you're making a very not good face at me. Shit.'

Shitty shit.

Chloe let go of my hand and walked slowly over to the couch, then sat down.

'Chloe?'

She didn't answer, didn't look at me.

'I didn't mean any of that. That was all a joke. Ha! Fooled you, you big, you know, idiot.'

I squirmed on the spot, heartbeat loud in my ears.

Moron, moron, moron.

'Look, I'm sorry. I'm just a little... overwhelmed by recent events. Been hit on the head one too many times and I'm talking rubbish. I'm sorry. End of rubbish. I'm not a witch and foxes obviously can't talk and they certainly don't wear helmets. Can we start again?'

Chloe looked up at me, then at her feet, then back up at me.

'I'm actually feeling pretty tired.'

'Oh. Yes, of course. Me too.'

'I'll see you tomorrow.'

'Tomorrow it is. Not tonight, tomorrow.'

'Tomorrow.'

'Beautiful.'

Beautiful? Christ, I'm an idiot.

'I'll just be off then. Here I go. Off.'

I turned and headed for the door.

'Get some rest, Joe,' said Chloe.

I turned, saluted by way of an answer, and wondered why I'd just done that. Who salutes? A tool salutes. I then left Chloe's home, got into my car, and drove home, loudly calling myself some very impolite names.

25

I woke the next morning with a groan.

It's not often I wake feeling quite so thoroughly depressed, but then it's not every day I wake from having made myself look and sound like a basket case in front of the woman I want to like me in a sex way.

I reached for my phone and checked to see if she'd sent me any messages.

No messages.

I checked three times just to make sure I hadn't gone message-blind, which I decided to pretend might be a thing in order to make myself feel better.

I stared at my message stream with Chloe for several minutes, debating what to send. And if I should send anything at all. After typing out numerous different possibilities, and then deleting each before I had the chance to hit 'send', I finally went with 'Hey'.

Send.

I waited for a reply.

Twenty minutes.

No reply.

Damn and also bugger with a side dish of balls.

I dragged myself up out of bed and shambled miserably into a hot shower, hoping to blast the worst of my mood away. You always feel better after a shower.

So. The big question that I still needed to try and answer for myself. Did I believe what Eva had told me? Did I believe that I was some sort of a witch? A man-witch. A warlock. Eva certainly had abilities that were out of the ordinary. She also lived in a house hidden in a wrinkle in the fabric of reality. Or something. So, either she was messing with me, or she was telling the truth and I was a magic man. Or, third option, she *thought* she was telling the truth but was in fact wrong about me, because although she herself *was* magic, she was also completely bonkers.

Three options.

I've always hated options.

Too much choice turns me into a ditherer.

But the fact was, I did feel something at her home. At the coven. Like I'd been there before. Like I belonged there. Like the very air inside the place knew me. And then there was the fire. Not the sort I'd seen in the Dark Lakes, in what may have been a delusion, but the fire that erupted from my hands as the three octopus men readied themselves to pounce and sucker me to death. Or beak me to death. Or a combination of the two. I'd seen Eva do that sort of a thing when she'd punched her fist through one of the creatures' skulls. She did it, she was magic. I did it, somehow, so maybe I was magic too. Maybe Eva was telling the truth. Maybe I really was a warlock.

And then there were the strange visions and feelings after touching Detective Samm. After touching the dead cat. More evidence for the prosecution.

One thing was for sure, I needed to find Eva again and wrestle some answers out of her.

I turned off the shower and pulled back the curtain to reveal Eva, stood looking at me.

'Morning, idiot.'

I may have screamed, jumped back, slipped, and crashed down into the bathtub, jarring my bum-bone something rotten.

'Ha! I like that, because you fell and hurt yourself. That's just good stuff, love,' said Eva.

'Why!' I said, then added a few more for good measure. 'Why, why, why?'

'To make you scream like a girl and fall over. Mission a-fucking-ccomplished.' Eva high-fived herself, then left me, still curled nude in the small corner tub, covering my genitals with a wash cloth.

'Too late, I saw everything,' said Eva from the next room.

I towelled off and dressed before joining Eva, who I found stretched across my couch watching an infomercial about a new set of exercise DVDs that combined tap dance with the power of pole dancing for an easy twenty minute routine you can do daily in your own home. If your home happens to be equipped with a handy stripper's pole.

'Have you heard of knocking? Ringing a doorbell? Not breaking into people's homes while they're wet and naked?'

'You're out of cereal, love.'

'No I'm not, I have a box of Bran Flakes in the cupboard.'

'Had. Now have not.'

'Why are you here? Do you plan on attacking me again?'

'I never plan that, it just sort of happens. When the muse takes me, know what I mean?'

I poured myself a glass of orange juice, 'Want any?'

'Do you have any vodka or tequila to make it tankable?'

'Afraid not.'

'Then don't waste my time.'

'You're welcome. Is there a reason you're here, Eva?'

'Just curious to know how you're taking the news.'

'That I'm a warlock?'

'Ah. Decided on warlock over witch, have you? Why doesn't that surprise me? Yes, you're a warlock.'

'Then how come I don't know how to do magic?'

'Because you don't really remember being a warlock. Your brain's a blank, which, believe you me, is a good thing.'

'How is not knowing anything about my past life a good thing?'

There was a heavy silence as Eva's eyes seemed to lose focus, like she was seeing something that I couldn't.

'Trust me, love. It's a good thing.'

'How did I get here, Eva? Why can't I remember who I am?'

'Why are you in such a rush for bad news? First things first, soul vampires!' Eva hopped up onto her feet, went drunkenly sideways, and almost crashed into my TV set.

'That's the octopus men thingies, right?'

'Those ugly fuckers, yep. They're doing all sorts of nasty shit that they shouldn't be. Thought we'd dealt with them, but here they are. Need to find where they're holed up so we can take them out. That's why I brought that body here, so you could feel it up and see if it sparked anything in that noggin of yours.'

'Oh. I can do that. Maybe I can do that.'

'No, been dead too long now.'

'It worked with the dead cat.'

Eva blinked at me silently for a moment.

'I beg your pardon?'

'I've been on this case. A village of cats went missing and I was hired to find out where they were.'

Eva slapped her forehead with the heel of her hand and staggered back, which I'd never seen anyone in real life actually do before.

'Of course! Don't you see?'

'I see a lot these days but understand very little.'

'The cats, you wretched, foul, puke! The cats!'

'The cats?'

Eva stepped forward, grabbing me by the collar and pulling me toward her wildly smiling face. 'The cats know, idiot! The cats always know!'

Eva shoved me aside and bolted for the door.

'The cats always know what? Eva?'

Apparently, this day wasn't going to be any less insane than the one that had gone before it, so I grabbed my coat and ran off in pursuit.

26

As we sped towards Oldstone in the Uncanny Wagon, I peered at Eva in the rearview mirror as she stretched out across the back seats, eyes closed.

'You know, you could sit up front like a normal person.'

Eva gave me the finger.

I gave my phone a quick glance; no reply to my *Hey* from Chloe. Damn. I was really in the poop there. Made a real fool of myself. Well, a fool and a loon of myself.

Shit.

'Okay, let's say I'm a witch.'

'I thought you went with warlock, Mr *Look-at-me-I-have-a-penis*.'

'For the record, I have never referred to myself that way.'

Eva snorted. Then burped. Delightful.

'You're magic,' I said. 'You're very magic. But you said you're not a witch, so what are you? Besides violent, terrifying, and gaseous?'

'I already told you. I'm Eva Familiar.'

'That doesn't... oh...'

Familiar. A witch's familiar.

'Are you my familiar?'

Eva opened one eye and glared at me with it: 'Un-fucking-fortunately, yes.'

'Oh. Well. Right then. Righty-right.'

'Give me strength...'

'Okay, well, where have you been for the last ten years?'

'Around.'

'Where? Doing what?'

'I forget. Though I know I spent a really cracking fortnight as a French Bulldog in Devon.'

'A dog? Really?'

'Sure. Probably. Why not.'

One thing was very certain, Eva was not a fan of straight answers, nor filling in the whole picture. I wondered what it was she was holding back, and why she was so keen on my not mixing with the Red Woman.

'What does that actually mean, by the way? That you're my "familiar"? Are you sort of, my magical servant, or...?'

'Oi! I'm nobody's lackey, got that, love? I am my own person and I'm the one in charge here, and if you forget that, I'll deck you, got it?'

Sounded like a sore point best left alone.

'Wake me when we get to the cat place.'

And with that, her head nodded down and she was sound asleep (the "sounds" being a collection of snores, sleep-talking, and violent, gassy eruptions).

I'm a warlock. A witch. And I have a coven and a familiar and I am a magic person. Who doesn't know how to do magic. Okay. Well. Big few days. On we go. Despite the fact that the answer seemed to be "something that only exists in fiction," it felt rather wonderful to be filling in a blank or two on the real me.

A warlock. That's one avenue I definitely hadn't considered. Because that would have been nuts.

I drove on, glancing down at my phone every few minutes, trying to will the thing to drag a reply out of Chloe.

I pulled into Oldstone and parked up without receiving said longed-for reply, so I cracked again and decided to send another message. This time I upped the ante: I sent a smiley face emoji.

As soon as it said "delivered," my insides clenched in horror. I was a moron. No, no, no; I was King Moron. An Emoji? Yes, she obviously loved the things, but I'd just unloaded a whole pile of crazy-bananas on her. A "hey" and a smiley face were hardly going to erase that.

I was done.

It was all over.

Wave the white flag and embrace a life of quiet contemplation, celibacy, and—

My phone vibrated and I snatched that thing up quicker than The Flash. A reply from Chloe. She'd replied with a smiley face of her own. A yellow circle with a big, toothy, mother-flippin' grin. I hopped out of the Uncanny Wagon and punched the air, followed by a tight, circular strut, chest puffed out like a champ.

'Tosspot,' came Eva's voice, as she rolled out of the back seat, shielding her eyes from the morning sunshine.

I pocketed my phone, relieved at Chloe's response. Okay, I could work this. I'd just tell her, I don't know, after the incident with Mrs Coates, that I ended up in a pub and I think someone spiked my drink. She'd believe that. That's the sort of thing that happens. I certainly acted like someone who had been completely off their tits. Okay. Cool. All was well.

I turned to find Eva down on her hands and knees, sniffing and licking at the ground.

'That is disgusting.'

'I've sniffed worse. This is the place,' she said, pushing herself back onto her feet.

'You still haven't actually told me why we're here.'

'Yes I have, you just don't listen.'

'No. Okay, true. Often true, but not in this particular case. You just had a snooze instead for most of the journey.'

'Are you sure?'

'Very.'

'Huh. Well isn't it obvious? Can't you feel it?'

I knew what she was talking about. It was the same sensation I'd felt each time I'd visited Oldstone. That creeping prickle across my skin. The sense that something wasn't right with the place.

'I feel it. What is it?'

'Bad news, that's what it is.'

'I hypothesised that it's why the cats made themselves scarce. The cats could feel the oddness of Oldstone.'

'Cats and soul vampires. They don't get on. It's the magic the soul vampires secrete into the world around them. Messes the cats up, so they move away from it. And that's why we need to catch one of the little buggers.'

'And how are we supposed to do that?'

Eva smiled. 'We need a canary.'

I lead us to the barn I'd found the cats huddled inside of, expecting them to have flown the coup by now, but there they were.

With very little help from Eva (by which I mean no help at all), I managed, at length, to herd one of the unwilling mogs into my cat box. Which is not a euphemism. We then spent the next hour strolling around Oldstone, holding the furious cat-in-a-box in front of us, Eva using each twitch, hiss, and flick of the cat's tail to decide which way we should go next.

The theory was that as we approached the point where these soul vampire thingies were holed up, the cat would become increasingly agitated. The theory was successful in practice, and was also successful in encouraging many a passer-by give us a wide berth as we speed-walked randomly up and down streets with a cat that was doing its damnedest to pull off a jail-break.

'This feels a bit predictable,' said Eva, as we found a narrow opening in the small hill lurking behind Oldstone's Church, hidden by decades of overgrown foliage.

'I thought vampires hated churches, and crosses, and things of that holy, blessed nature,' I said, as I placed the cat box down and opened the door.

The cat erupted from within and out into the world at such speed that it resembled little more that a furry blur.

'You're thinking of ordinary vampires,' she replied, and kicked aside the scraggle of bushes hiding the thin entrance. 'Those are bloodsuckers, these are a completely different kettle of twats.'

'I take it they don't drink blood, judging by their name?'

'Nope. They eat your essence. Paint an incantation around you in your own blood to trap your soul so they can catch and eat the thing.'

'Oh,' I pulled out my phone and showed her the picture I'd taken of the symbols around Mary Tyler's bed.

'That's them. I'm surprised that didn't clue you in. They literally say, "*Soul, you are mine to feast upon.*"'

I squinted at the picture, 'They do?'

'Jesus Christ, you don't even have the basics in there anymore, do you?'

'Well, no, I thought that was pretty obvious. Why is that? If I'm a warlock, why can't I remember any of it? What happened to me?'

'Come on,' said Eva, and began to squeeze into the narrow opening.

'Fine, but you're going to have to tell me at some point,' I said as I followed after. Something told me that if she was so eager to keep the answer to herself, then it wasn't going to be anything good.

I'm not generally the claustrophobic type, but I admit to

sighing in relief that after a few metres the tight entrance opened up considerably and I could walk head-on as we moved further into the gloom.

'Hey, it's getting a bit dark,' I said, 'I'll use the light on my phone.'

'No need.'

A click of her fingers and Eva's right arm was a torch, her fist wreathed in rippling orange flames.

'Neat,' I said. 'I actually did something a bit like that earlier. Somehow.'

'It's not a competition, love. Come on, and be prepared to run, because these things will happily tear you into a hundred wet pieces.'

'Fear not, running away is something of a speciality of mine.'

Eva grunted and pushed on, her heavy footsteps echoing off the wet rock around us. After a few minutes we found ourselves in a large cave, the walls dotted with hundreds of holes. It reminded me a little of the mortuary back at the hospital. The openings were of roughly the same size, but there were no shiny metal doors hiding the bodies within. No bodies, either.

'Well,' said Eva, poking her glowing hand into hole after hole and then leaning in to take a look, 'this was the place alright.' She ran a finger around the interior of one of the spaces and licked it. 'They were here up until a day or so ago. Still reeks of them, yes?'

It did. A smell like the sea, mixed with blood and rot. I can't say I was super upset to find the place empty. One of those things was bad enough; who knew how many had been stuffed down here? Looking at the number of empty spaces across the cave walls, the answer was: A LOT.

As Eva moved the light from her hand around the cave, it revealed symbols painted all across the walls. More of the occult shapes.

'That is not good,' said Eva.

'What? What do they say?'

'Just stuff about being ready to rise up and feast on the souls of all of Great Britain.'

'Yeah, that is definitely not good.'

'Not good, and weird. They're usually the sort that likes to stick to random snacks, but this sounds like something bigger. Something more ambitious.'

A pack of ambitious, soul-eating vampires? That did not sound pretty.

'Maybe it's time to tell the police?'

'This has nothing to do with police. This is our job. The Cumbrian Coven's domain. Fuck up monsters and protect people from the Uncanny turds that want to chew on their insides.'

'Oh, so we're, sort of, magic police? I like that. Magic Police! You have the right to remain unmagical, all spells cast can be held against you in a court of law.'

Eva sagged and groaned. 'Don't say that again, it sounds oh so very shit.'

27

I pulled out of Oldstone in the Uncanny Wagon and headed for Carlisle Hospital, leaving Eva behind. She hadn't been too impressed with the fact that I needed to show up to my job to earn money and function in normal society, and called me a number of colourful names, complete with accompanying hand gestures.

I'll be honest, I wasn't really sure how I was talking to Eva Familiar. She claimed to be my familiar, my partner, but seemed like an obnoxious, gassy mess. Not to mention the fact that she'd recently punched me in the face for reasons she'd yet to divulge. What could the old me have done to be worthy of that kind of treatment? Seemed like if anyone should know it was me, and I was increasingly peeved off that she was keeping so many of the puzzle pieces to herself.

Still, for the last ten years my history had been a complete blank, now, at least, I saw a sliver or two of the truth. Even if the truth seemed a mite tricky to fully buy into.

I was going a little too fast down an empty country lane when it happened.

I turned a blind corner, only to find a person stood blocking my path. It was a woman with pale skin and long, red hair.

I yelped, twisted the wheel and hit the brakes, the world spinning as my poor car screeched and span, before coming to a halt with its rear end in a hedge. Not so much as a near thing in the last ten years of driving and now two accidents on the trot.

'I'm okay. Not hurt. Okay.'

I stepped out of the car and looked for the Red Woman, but she was nowhere to be seen.

'Okay, that's not funny, or clever, right? You could've bloody killed me!'

'All hail the saviour!'

My shoulders sagged at the voice, and I turned to find the fox stood on the roof of my car, little Roman helmet on his head, axe held aloft.

'You know a text message would be fine if either of you ever want to get in touch again.'

The fox slid down the windscreen, shuffled along the bonnet, and landed in the road.

'So, now you know,' it said.

'Know what?'

'Who you really, truly are.'

'Some of it. Hey, have you got me bugged?' I ran my hands over the fabric of my coat in search of a listening device.

'Ah, but she did not tell you all, that tricksy familiar.'

'Maybe she did, maybe she didn't.'

I felt a cold arm around my waist, then a pair of lips at my ear: 'She didn't tell you about the others, did she?'

I turned to see the Red Woman. 'You know... that was shocking road-sense. I could've hit you. You could have ended up a flesh bag full of bone shards. With red hair on top.'

Her smile could have sliced into flesh.

'She wouldn't like you talking to me, your familiar, because she knows I tell the truth.'

'Oh? What sort of truth?'

I felt a hand tug at my coat and looked down to see the fox.

'The truth about the other witches of the Cumbrian Coven. Didn't think it was just you and her, did you?'

'Other witches?'

The Red Woman shook her head sadly. 'It pains me that Eva feels the need to keep you so in the dark. You are one of three witches that looked over this county. Now why would she keep that information from you, Magic Eater?'

It was a fair question.

'Maybe she has good reason not to tell me.'

'What sort of a reason?' asked the Red Woman, her hand trailing lightly across my chest.

'You know, a... good one. Sort of thing.'

'Ah, now it's all clear,' said the Red Woman, pulling me close and planting a kiss on my lips. 'I never lie to you.'

'Okay,' I squeaked.

'I only want the best for you. Only want you to reach your full, glorious potential. Destiny is waiting for you, Magic Eater. I am waiting for you.'

I blinked and I was alone.

It's fair to say that the rest of the journey to work found me deep in troubled thought.

Three witches.

Was that true? And if so, why wouldn't Eva have told me? Perhaps the other witches were like family. I deserved to know about family. I'd often wondered about siblings, about who my parents really were. Perhaps this was it. I was a warlock, and these other two mystery coven members were what passed for my family.

I confess to feeling a little burble of excitement in my stomach. Warlock told me what I did, but other people, family, that would tell me who I *was*.

'You're ten minutes late,' said Big Marge as the automatic doors hissed closed behind me and I strode towards her reception area, brow creased, hands plunged deep into the pockets of my long coat. 'It looks like you've got a load on your mind, Joe.'

'A thing or two rattling around upstairs, yeah.'

'You're not built for deep thought, you're built for cleaning up shit. And lucky you, there's a fresh batch waiting for you on the third floor Ladies.'

With a heavy sigh, I headed for my locker to change into my work things, only to have Chloe push open the reception area's double doors as I was about to push my way out.

'Oh,' she said.

'Yes, oh, sorry, did I hit you with the door?'

'A bit, but that's okay.'

'Good.'

'Yep. Good.'

It felt like awkward had given birth to twins.

'About last night...' I started.

'That's okay, Joe.'

'No, it's not, I was just, all messed up, you know. From the murder! And I was in a pub, and I think my drink was spiked. Someone definitely spiked my drink. I think.'

'Okay. So that's why all the...'

'Crazy faces and witch talk.'

'And the talking fox. It was a talking fox, yes?'

'Mentioned that, did I?'

'Yes you did.'

'Right. Bloody... spiked drink..'

I could practically see the tension escaping from Chloe's body. I hated lying to her, but the truth would scare her silly, so a lie would have to do for the time being.

'I should've known,' she replied. 'I am a doctor, I should have rationalised how weird you were acting.'

'It's not your fault.'

'Yeah, you always act a bit weird.'

'Ouch, but valid.'

'But not like that. You really had things turned up to eleven.'

She laughed and touched my arm and suddenly any guilt at having lied to her skipped out of my brain to be replaced by a cloud of chirping love birds. So it was a pity that the moment had to be broken by a terrified Doctor Neil half-running, half-falling towards us down the corridor, his face even paler than usual. And his usual face was almost Casper-white.

'Neil, what is it?' asked Chloe.

'They're dead. They're all dead!'

Like I say; moment broken.

28

There's nothing unusual about death in a hospital. People pop their clogs almost every day around these places, and it's always sad.

But it's not every day someone is *murdered* in a hospital.

And murdered by people with octopus arms? I'd say the odds on that one would be so long you'd end up taking home the GDP of the entire northern hemisphere.

I'm not trying to encourage anyone to gamble here, fyi. Unless you're onto a sure thing of course.

We took the stairs two at a time, Chloe ahead, me behind. She was nippy, that's for sure.

We heard the room Doctor Neil had made his grim discovery in before we actually reached it. A high-pitched, electronic whine sliced down the corridor towards us. We both knew what that sound was. Multiple heart monitors flat-lining.

We burst into the small ward that currently housed six people. It now housed six corpses, with nurses milling round, some trying to help, others just looking in blank shock.

'Oh my God,' said Chloe, stopping so sharply that I almost ran into the back of her. Instead I swerved at the last moment and stepped on something damp that caused my foot to slip and send me crashing to the floor.

Blood.

Around each of the deceased patients beds were those same occult symbols, painted in their own blood. The soul vampires had paid the hospital another visit.

Chloe ran between the beds, obviously overwhelmed at what she was seeing, frantically looking for any signs of life, trying to help the nurses in attendance. It was no use, they were all dead.

I could sense the creatures in the room. They'd gone, but that magic scent that had so infected Oldstone was present. It itched at my skin and made me want to blow my nose.

Eva had been right, these things were stepping up their game. Six people in one go? And inside a room that was so public? They clearly had no fear. They no longer felt the need to stalk vulnerable people through empty streets in the dead of night, or hide in the back seats of cars to lurch out and surprise. Anyone, anywhere, was in danger.

My heart bounced angrily against my rib cage as a thought landed—

'Mary...'

I ran from the room, desperate to be wrong, desperate that the protection that had been put in place by Detective Myers had made the things think twice. Or maybe they'd just forgotten about her. Surely one victim was as good as another?

I received my grim answer as I turned the corner to find both of the officers who had been left to protect Mary Tyler slumped on the floor, windpipes torn out.

'Mary!'

No thought for my own safety, no time to allow fear to infect me, I leapt over the deceased officers and shoulder-barged the door to Mary Tyler's private room open.

The sight waiting for me was something I'll never forget.

Blood was daubed in thick strokes around the bed, but

there was something different to the symbols painted, something unlike the other ones I'd seen. The word that sprang to mind when I saw them was *active*. An impossible black "light" was leaking from the occult symbols like smoke, accompanied by a low hum.

Stood around the bed were three of the octopus-limbed creatures. Soul vampires. And for the first time I was getting to see what that really meant.

On the bed there were two Marys. One was physical. A body, eyes still open, rolled back so that only the whites were on show. Her windpipe hung from the tear in her throat, glistening with fresh, wet scarlet.

The second Mary was floating just above her corpse. A ghost. An apparition. Mary Tyler's soul. She thrashed, her semi-transparent form twisting and spasming, clearly in horrific torment as the three creatures began to feast on her soul.

It was too late for me to do anything, though what I would have done if it hadn't been, I still don't know. In her final moments, Mary Tyler opened her eyes and saw me. My mouth flapped dumbly, words failing to appear, as she reached towards me, imploring me to do something, to do anything.

I did nothing.

And then, with a sudden, piercing scream that made me tremble, she was gone. Multiple octopus limbs wrapping around her pulling a piece free for themselves to gorge on.

Mary Tyler was dead.

Her soul feasted upon.

'Bastards!' I yelled, my fury overriding any sense of personal danger. I'd saved Mary from these wankers twice, and it still hadn't been enough. Police protection hadn't been enough. They'd marked her and they'd taken her. I hadn't really saved her, I'd just delayed the inevitable. Made them work a little harder for their supper.

They turned to me, their huge, unblinking yellow eyes

bulging from their sockets as though on some sort of high from swallowing the essence of Mary Tyler.

'You stupid, dumb, ugly, fucking bastards!'

They opened their beaks and screeched at me, each taking a step forward. It was at this point a little clarity worked its way through the haze of anger, and I realised I was in very, very, huge and immediate danger.

I wanted to attack them, wanted to wreak immediate, terrible revenge for what they had done to Mary. To the other six dead bodies down the corridor. To Detective Sam Samm. To Mrs Coates. To all of them.

Eva claimed I was a warlock, and considering all I'd experienced recently, I thought she was very likely telling the truth. She'd said we were the people who stood against things like this. The monsters. The mythical, the monstrous, the unbelievable. The things that you wake from as light filters through your curtains, content in the knowledge that such awful things could only exist in nightmares.

I was the thing that protected them from the horrible truth.

And I had no idea how I'd done it.

No idea how to do magic, how to utilise whatever powers I apparently had. Oh, I'd had flashes of my ability, in Mrs Coates' house, for example; but I had no clue how to manifest such abilities when I actually needed them.

As the creatures stalked towards me, I was hopeful of something just happening. And quickly.

'Jesus Christ...'

I turned to find Chloe stumbling into the room behind me, staring at the monstrous creatures, their limbs weaving, beaks chittering. I saw her eyes, so disbelieving, so huge, they almost put the octopus men's dilated peepers to shame.

'Chloe, no, get out—'

'Oh,' said Doctor Neil, stood between the two bodies of the police officers, looking past me at the monsters.

I grabbed Chloe and tried to bundle the both of us out the

room, but the door slammed shut. Some invisible hand had thrown it closed to prevent our escape. I turned the handle, shook it, pulled desperately, but the door refused to budge. The creatures had somehow locked the thing and cut off our escape.

'Neil? Neil! Help me with the door!'

'This can't be happening, can't be, this isn't real,' stammered Chloe.

I could feel her retreating into herself, not able to cope with this sudden incursion into how she thought the world to be. 'Chloe, stay with me, I need you to be able to—'

A limb wrapped around my waist and the room streaked and twirled as I span through the air and crashed against the far wall, the floor catching me and knocking the wind from my lungs.

I reached out, tried to call Chloe's name, but only a dry rasp escaped my throat.

'Joe!'

The creatures loomed over Chloe as she slid down the wall, hands up protectively, uselessly.

Gulping down air, I pushed myself to my feet unsteadily.

'Get your filthy octopus limbs away from her!'

I felt a crackle in the air, as though something in the room were flowing towards me. To fill me. It felt almost like I was some sort of computer game character who had just levelled up. I felt sharper. Stronger. Focussed.

I had no idea what I was doing. Not really. But some instinctive part of my brain did. It had done this a thousand times before. It didn't need me to know, because my inner self knew. The part of me that had lain dormant for ten long years.

'Leave her alone!'

I clapped my hands together and the room shook, my hands erupting in flames.

One of the creatures broke from the pack and ran towards me. I punched out a fist and the flames exploded from me, catching the creature in the side and sending it smashing straight through the window and landing with an audible, painful-sounding crash in the car park outside.

I'd done that.

Me.

Joseph Lake.

Toilet cleaner and cat-catcher extraordinaire.

I had made fire surge from my fists and knock a monster clean through a window. And because I was suddenly so aware of that fact, it was as though I lost a grip on whatever it was I was doing, and the fire I was emanating spluttered and died.

'No, come on,' I shook my hands, clapped them together, willed flames to appear, but it was no use. Lucky for me, it seemed my demonstration had convinced the remaining creatures that it might be time to make themselves scarce.

Unlucky for me, they decided to take Chloe along for the trip.

Before I could attempt to do anything, one of the creatures wrapped a limb around the bed and tossed it in my direction, as the other grabbed the screaming Chloe, then all three disappeared through the broken window and after their fallen comrade.

29

Ordinarily speaking, I'm not the sort of person who drops out of a second storey window. I respect stairs. That's the way to get from one level to another as far as I'm concerned. On this occasion, though, three octopus monsters had abducted Chloe, and I was fairly certain that taking the conventional route and letting them get away with her would result in my friend ending up dead as a dead thing.

So there I was, casting a fearful eye at the distance I was about to drop, my hands starting to ache.

'Joe! Please!'

And with those two words, any uncertainty evaporated. I let go, the hospital's outer wall streaking past me before the ground met the soles of my feet and my ankles made their complaints loud and clear.

This was no time for pain though. For hobbling around, or curling up in a foetal position and tenderly patting down any sore area to see if bones were jutting through the flesh, white and angry.

No time for that.

No time for me.

The creatures had Chloe, whose eyes were still on me, reaching out imploringly.

'Chloe! I'm coming!'

I ran-hobbled after the three creatures, who were rapidly making their escape through the almost-empty car park spaces at the back of the hospital.

If I lost sight of them, that was that. I knew it. What reason would they have to keep Chloe alive? Either I somehow rescued her, right here, right now, or Chloe was good as done for. Her throat ripped out, her soul shredded and feasted upon by these beaky fucks.

But what could I do? I wished Eva was with me. She actually knew how to wield her magic with purpose, it wasn't an unconscious bubbling up that she couldn't control. I remembered her fist bursting through the skull of one of the soul vampires, and sorely wished I'd asked her just how the hell she'd managed to do it.

'Hey, where are you going?' I yelled as I ran after them. 'There's three of you and one of me! Don't you want a snack for the road?'

The creatures paused and turned to look at me, a sharp hissing sound escaping their beaks. Maybe I'd just given them an idea.

'Come on flamey hands,' I said, shaking my fists, willing them to hurry up and get magical already, but they stubbornly refused to unleash even a faint spark.

'Oh shit,' seemed a reasonable response as one of the three octopus-limbed creatures broke from the pack and charged towards me, using its extra arms to give it extra propulsion, its beak wide and screeching.

I had no clue as to what to do, so, screaming like a loon, I put my head down and ran right at the thing. A second or two later I stopped tumbling painfully across the car park surface and lay blinking up at the sky in a daze. Despite my state of "about to be killed-ness," I found time to notice that one of the clouds above me was shaped like a horse. Strange, the things you notice when death is almost upon you.

I pushed myself up, ready to dodge out of the way, only for the creature to descend on me, its limbs like the bars of a cage, slamming down all around me to block my escape.

'You probably don't want to taste my soul,' I stammered, 'I think it's gone off.'

The beast threw back its head, beak stretched wide, and let loose a bowel-loosening scream as it prepared to tear out my windpipe.

My life did not flash before my eyes.

Instead, I thought about Chloe, and how I'd failed her. I was going to die, which means she was, too. I hoped they wouldn't hurt her too much.

The creature's noise ceased and I prepared for the strike, eyes tightly shut, body a hard nugget, only to open an eye when the expected deadly attack didn't come. The creature was no longer looking at me, it was looking over its shoulder.

It was at this point that a car engine registered.

I peered past the bulk of the creature to see a vehicle hurtling at speed towards us. One way or the other, it seemed the world was determined to put an end to me today.

As the soul vampire lifted some of its limbs, I seized the moment, kicking out with a scream and a swear word, before rolling over and over until a parked car brought my journey to a stop. I looked up just in time to see the speeding car strike the soul vampire square, and carry the thing—its limbs thrashing furiously at the vehicle's bonnet—straight into a wall.

Wham.

The car reversed, and the creature flopped forward, its torso partially crushed, the yellow shine in its eyes weakening. The car idled as if to savour the moment, savour the knowledge that the creature knew what was about to happen and there was nothing it could do about it. Then the back wheels spun, the creature screamed, the car lurched forward again. The soul vampire reached out defensively with its many limbs, and then the car struck, metal crushed, and the beast screamed its last.

I climbed to my feet, searching for the remaining creatures, for Chloe, but neither were anywhere to be seen. I ran in the direction they'd been heading, but there was no sign of them. They couldn't have escaped in such a short space of time. They should still be in sight.

'Chloe! Chloe, where are you?'

Silence.

She was gone.

Whatever trick the creatures had pulled to hide from view, I was too late. They may have lost one of their number, but they had their prey. They had Chloe. Which meant she was dead. Which meant her soul would soon be eaten and there would be nothing left of her but a rotting carcass.

Then a thought struck.

Stupid warlock.

Stupid, stupid warlock!

I'd already done this a few times, maybe I could do it again!

I turned and ran towards the dead soul vampire to find the driver stood looking down at its squished corpse. It was Detective Maya Myers, no doubt answering the call Big Marge would have put through when Doctor Neil stumbled, ashen, into reception.

'One of the things I never anticipated when I started this job,' she said, 'was all the damn monsters.'

I fell to my knees and laid my hands on the thing, its blood soaking through my trousers, which was disgusting, obviously.

'I'm pretty sure it's dead,' said Maya.

'Yes, I know, but that's okay, I did this with a dead cat already.'

'Did what?'

I closed my eyes, thought about Chloe, about where she could be, and grabbed hold of the dead creature.

'Please,' I said. 'Please show me. Show me something!'

I pushed, I grabbed, I hugged, I even clenched at the pile of spilled intestines, grunting in frustration as I tried to will the darkened corners of my mind to just shine a little light. But it was no good, I wasn't getting a thing.

'Mr Lake, what the hell are you doing?'

Distracted, angry, I looked up at Maya's confused face. 'I want to make the dead thing show me its home—'

The world was whipped away and—

A road. There is a road. Hills. Grass. Walls. Home is close. New home. New home that we have moved to. Bring her back here. Bring her back here. Bring her back here—

I gasped and fell backwards, the connection broken, Maya looking down at me.

'Are you okay?' she asked.

I laughed, and leapt to my feet, cradling her face in my hands. 'You distracted me! Thank you!'

'You're welcome. Now get those gore-soaked hands off my face before I knee you in the crotch.'

'Yes, right, sorry!'

I wiped my gory hands against my coat, then immediately regretted doing so. Hopefully monster goo comes out in the wash.

'You were driving the car,' I said.

'Yes.'

'You could have hit me!'

'That was a risk I was willing to take.'

'Good to know.'

I had a place. An image of an area. It might just have been a road, some scenery, but it was something. It was hope. And right then, that was all I needed to convince myself that I might be able to find Chloe before the creatures murdered her. It was something to hang onto.

I turned to run for the Uncanny Wagon, only for Maya to grab me by the arm and throw me back against her totalled car. She was, it came as no surprise to find out, really quite strong.

'I have questions,' she said.

'There's no time! They have Chloe, and if we don't find her very, very, very fast, they will kill her. So either help me, or get out of my way!'

I half expected Maya to stop me. Instead, she looked at the dead soul vampire, looked at her smashed car, then looked back to me and nodded: 'Let's go monster hunting.'

30

It was only once we were in the car and speeding south out of Carlisle towards the Lake District, that what Maya had said actually filtered through.

'Wait, monsters. You know about monsters?'

'I would think that was obvious. The question is, how do *you* know about monsters?'

I ignored the question. 'How do you know about monsters?'

'I asked first.'

'Yep.'

'I'm also the police.'

'Indeed.'

'So answer my question.'

'Okay. Well, it turns out that secret past of mine involved being a warlock. A male witch. Magic. Fighting weird stuff and generally protecting the public from freaky supernatural turds.'

Maya nodded slowly. 'You're a witch?'

'I know, I can't say the knowledge sits too comfortably with me either. Now go on, your turn.'

Maya bowed her head and began to toy at the hem of her leather jacket.

'What is it?'

'My partner.'

'Detective Samm?'

'No. My partner before that, in London. Her name was Allie Sanders. We were investigating a drug ring operating out of Hammersmith. We thought we'd tracked down the head of the operation, went to investigate. Got split up. I heard her screaming and when I found her, she'd been torn apart by… by something I can't even describe. Something that couldn't be real. And… I ran.'

Maya's voice was cracking, it was the first time I'd ever seen her being vulnerable, her armour slipping.

'Go on,' I urged.

'I filed a report. They thought I was crazy, of course. Monsters don't exist. I went to find proof, bumped into a lot of scary shit. Once I'd seen one it was like the truth was everywhere. Monsters live among us. But I couldn't make my superiors hear me. They made me go to a psychiatrist. Eventually, I pretended it had all been a mini-breakdown caused by Allie's death and they transferred me up here. Out of the way. Out of their hair.'

I wasn't sure what to say by way of response, so I patted her leg.

'Do I look like the family dog?'

'Um. No.'

'Then don't pet me again or I will break that hand clean off and beat you unconscious with it.'

'Righto. Sorry about your partner. Both partners.'

'Two dead partners, both murdered by things that can't exist. Maybe death is stalking me.'

'It's possible,' came a voice from behind us. 'Death is a well known stalker.'

I yelled, twisted the wheel, and yelled again as a truck thundered past, swerving just in time so as not to turn us into a leaky, crushed can.

I glared at Eva in the rear view mirror. 'Where did you

come from?'

'Ah, well, geographically, organically, or metaphorically?'

'My car! Why are you in my car?'

'Oh, I came to find you. Couldn't find you. Broke in here and took a kip on the back seat.'

That was it, after the octopus monster and now this, I was going to make a habit of giving my back seat a mighty thorough once-over before setting off for a drive again.

'You were not in the back seat, no one was in the back seat.'

'You're not too bright these days, are you?' She waved her hands around. 'I'm magic, love.'

'Who is this?' Maya asked.

'Difficult question,' I replied.

'I'll take a simple answer.'

'Who am I? Is that what the bird in blue just said?'

'Yes, who are you?'

Eva snorted. 'We met the other day, bit of a short memory there, love. A bit of a worry that Cumbria's finest have memories like goldfish."

'I can assure you, I have never met you before in my life.'

Eva looked at Maya like she was insane, then realisation dawned. 'Oh. Oh! Sorry, that's right, my mistake. We did meet, but I had a different face on. Not your fault, love, my hands are up on that one.'

'Different face? Did she just say she had a different face on?'

'It's... tricky to explain.'

'Try me.'

'What are you talking about?' said Eva. 'Piece of piss to explain. I'm magic. He's magic. You're not magic, though somehow you're really pulling off those sensible trousers. Where did you get those anyway? And where are we going? I'm up for pizza.'

'They took Chloe,' I said. 'Those soul vampire things, they killed a bunch of people at the hospital and they took a friend of mine and I need to find her before they... well, do things I don't want to think about.'

'Right,' said Eva. 'She's probably already dead.'

'Not helping!' I said, turning almost fully around, before Maya shoved my back.

'Hey, driving, remember?'

'Right. Yes. Sorry, Detective.'

'So what happened?' asked Eva.

'Does it matter?' I replied. 'Those things killed people and kidnapped Chloe, and Detective Myers appeared and squashed one dead with her car, and now I'm trying to find out where they've disappeared to, which is really very difficult with you two nattering on.'

There was a brief, strained silence.

'You squashed one with your car?' asked Eva.

Maya nodded.

'Rammed into the thing twice. It died screaming.'

'Christ. That is cold-blooded. I like you. You're now my favourite person. Wait, no, second favourite, I'm still number one in my eyes. Drink?'

Eva pulled a can of cheap lager from her coat pocket and offered it over. Maya stared at it for a few seconds, then shrugged and took it, settling back to suck the can dry. 'I know I'm on duty, but monsters.'

'I'm not judging,' I replied.

'So what's the plan?' asked Eva. 'Just drive aimlessly? We still don't know where these arm-heavy bastards have moved on to. I traipsed all over the place, even got a replacement canary-cat, couldn't find a sniff for buggery.'

'I know where they are.'

'Well, then why don't you lead with that?'

'I mean, I sort of know. I don't know where it is exactly but I know where they are.'

'Does he always talk in riddles?' asked Maya, wiping her mouth with the back of her sleeve.

'He's an idiot and a twat, you'll soon come to realise that.'

'Ladies, you're going to make me get a big head here.'

'Just get on with it, idiot.'

'I touched one of them. The dead one. The squished horribly one. And used my, you know, magic warlock man-witch powers somehow. Not entirely sure how. But it showed me a few images, a few thoughts. It showed me where they were, it's just, I'm not entirely sure where that was as it just looked like, you know—' I gestured at the countryside spread out around us. 'It all looks kind of the same.'

'Oi, racist,' replied Eva.

'What? How? I... what?'

'Do you have another drink?' asked Myers. 'This one was only about ten-percent full.'

Eva produced a full can from somewhere and handed it over. 'So, you have the image. You have the place. Now, use your powers to hone in on it.'

'How exactly?'

'How did you see the images in the first place?'

'I don't know how, it's just whenever I'm distracted, whenever I'm not really purposefully trying, it just happens. If I come at the thing head on, I get nothing. If I don't think about it, if I keep it sort of just to the side of my conscious mind, the muscle memory takes over and gets on with it.'

I slammed my foot on the brakes and the car screeched to a halt. Eva tumbled into the footwell and Myers spilled her can down herself.

'What's with the emergency stop?' she asked, pissed off.

'I don't know, it's like my foot took over for a moment.'

'I know,' said Eva as she scrambled back up into a sitting position. 'We distracted you.'

'What do... oh...'

I looked out to where we'd ended up. I recognised it. 'Oh!'

'Yeah,' said Eva. 'This ain't my first rodeo, love.'

We were there. We were at the soul vampires' lair.

31

I stepped out of the Uncanny Wagon and turned in a circle, taking in my surroundings in wide-eyed surprise.

'This is it! This is what I saw, this place! I did it!'

'Alright,' said Eva, shambling out of the back of the car, 'I was the one that did most of the distracting. And on purpose, I might add. I'm due the credit. Also, have yourself one of these —' She waved a middle finger at me.

'Can we please get past the strange, abusive aggression, Eva? We're meant to be comrades, right?'

Eva snorted, then as Maya joined us, snatched the can of lager back from her, downed it, belched, and tossed the empty receptacle into a bush.

'That's public littering,' said Maya. 'I could have you for that.'

'Just try it,' replied Eva, 'I fancy a bit of girl-on-girl.'

There it was again… that tingling sensation itching its way across my skin. The same feeling I'd noticed in Oldstone, but, if anything, even stronger.

'This is it. This is definitely the place.'

Chloe was somewhere near. I'd gotten there as fast as I could, my only hope was that they were still full up from all the food back at the hospital and maybe, just maybe, they'd shoved Chloe into the soul vampire pantry to snack on later. I thought that extraordinarily unlikely, but I had to hold onto something.

'Okay,' said Maya. 'Forgive me being non-magic and everything, but it looks to me like we're just stood in the middle of nowhere. All I see is a dirt road, fields and hills. There's nothing here. No house, no building, no secret monster hide-out. Where exactly are we supposed to be?'

Before anyone could reply, the ground shook, a giant octopus tentacle burst from under the road, wrapped itself around a still pretty nonchalant-looking Eva, and dragged her beneath the ground.

'Shit!' I cried. 'Oh, Jesus-crapping-shit!'

'I hear that,' replied Detective Maya Myers. 'That was... a big monster.'

'Very big monster.'

Detective Myers nodded.

I edged tentatively towards the fissure that had been created in the dirt road. 'Eva?'

A fresh opening led down at an angle into the dark.

'That seems unlikely,' said Maya.

'How d'you mean?'

'Why hasn't that collapsed in on itself? The giant octopus arm has left behind a perfect tunnel for anyone stupid enough to want to explore.'

'Yes. Ah. A trap, perhaps?'

'Seems likely.'

'Still. That's where they must be. Where Eva now is. Where, presumably, Chloe is.' A hopefully not-dead Chloe. 'They're in some sort of cavern, or cave system, underneath our feet. So...'

'You're not serious.'

'I really, really wish I wasn't.'

'If you go down there, you're almost certainly dead. Did you see the size of that limb? That thing must be ten times as big as the one that lost a fight with my car. Twenty times the size even! And you're going to crawl down into its conveniently created tunnel, right onto its home turf?'

'Believe me, I know how stupid this is. I have, for much of the last ten years, been very comfortable in my cowardice, but I am from the Cumbrian Coven, and I think I'm starting to understand what that means.'

'That doesn't mean anything! I'm an officer of the law. We should get back-up.'

'You do that, see if they believe you. Meanwhile, Chloe is down there, so I'm going to walk—well, crawl—right into their trap and see what sort of trouble I can get into.'

Maya threw her hands up, then walked away. Then back. Then away again.

'Stay and call for backup,' I said. 'You don't need to risk yourself too. Those are my friends down there, not yours.'

Maya sighed, her head hanging limp for a moment. 'Fine, but if I die down there, like I probably will, I am going to kick your arse.'

'Fair enough. Shall we then?'

I peered into the tunnel, down into the fathomless black, then had a quick think back to the happy days of a week ago when I had no clue who I was and that monsters were actually real. You don't know how good you've got it until you're crawling into the underground lair of an octopus-limbed nightmare that wants to eat your soul.

And down we went.

With the way partially illuminated by the light from Maya's phone, we crawled for what seemed like hours, but was actually closer to three or four minutes.

This was—I think it's fair to say without risking my image of staunch macho-ness—really poop-your-pants terrifying. The only thing that pushed me on was the knowledge that

Chloe was down there somewhere, and if she was still alive, she'd more than likely have given up. There was no way she would expect help to appear. She was underground, hidden away in a monster's lair, waiting for the end. There was certainly no way she'd expect someone as daft as me to show up, but I was a-coming, and I was prepared to take whatever happened, as long as I went down knowing I'd done everything I could to help her.

'I take it you really like this Chloe then?' asked Maya, shuffling down behind me.

I shrugged. 'She's okay,' I said, cool as a cucumber. A cucumber with really nice hair. Which would be disgusting. Scratch that, I'm not eating a hairy cucumber. Also, scratch *that*, as it's just put another image in my mind.

Then all thoughts of salad—hairy or not—slipped from my mind as my hand met nothing and I tumbled out of the end of the tunnel and hit the dirt several feet below.

'Ow.'

Maya stepped on me as she climbed down.

'That's another ow.'

I stood, brushing off the worst of the loose muck from my clothes.

'Shouldn't it be a lot darker down here?' asked Maya, turning off the light from her phone and pocketing it. 'It should be pitch black.'

'That'll be my doing,' said Eva, causing me and Maya to jump and make high-pitched noises.

'You're okay!' I said.

'Always am, love. After getting dragged down here, I bit the fucker and it let go. No one likes getting bit, you know. Not even tentacle monsters.'

'So you're doing the illumination?' asked Maya.

'You better believe it, sugar tits.'

'Do not call me that.'

Eva gave a little salute. 'Understood, twinkle tush.'

Detective Myers sighed and rubbed at her eyes. 'So, this is magic. Us being able to see down here... it's down to magic.'

'You're catching on,' replied Eva. 'Shall we head down here then, see if we can pay a home visit?' She lit a cigarette and made off.

'I don't suppose I could bum a smoke, could I?' I asked.

'I'm all out.'

'That tin was full.'

'You are mistaken.'

I was not.

Me and Maya followed on.

'So, that was a big one,' I said. 'Bigger than the others.'

'Probably the queen. Big bitches, the queens. The rest just work for her. Go out, chomp down a few souls, then bring the nourishment back to ol' fatty to help propagate the species.'

'Do we have a plan at all?' asked Maya, 'besides sticking our heads in the lion's mouth?'

'I've got a plan, don't worry,' replied Eva. 'Well, a bit of a plan. Well, no exact plan, technically. We'll improvise.'

Myself and Detective Myers shared a look that was not at all confident.

As we moved forward, a noise started. A sort of droning hum. It was more than a little unnerving.

'What is that?' I asked.

'Hm? Oh, that's probably just a whole bunch of soul vampires harmonising,' replied Eva.

'It's times like this I wish I was a gun-toting, U.S. copper,' said Maya.

'I've got a gun,' said Eva, pulling one from her pocket.

'That's a plastic water pistol,' said Maya.

'Oh! Holy water, is it full of holy water? Does that kill these things, just like normal vampires?' I asked.

'No. This is my vodka gun. It's full of vodka.' She fired about three shots into her mouth, then pocketed it.

'That's going to be really useful, I'm sure,' said Maya.

'Depends,' replied Eva. 'Maybe they like to party.'

The sound was huge now, echoing around and around, bouncing off the stone walls. There was an opening ahead.

This was it. Time for the big final showdown.

We stepped warily through the opening and into a space the size of a cathedral, packed full of the octopus creatures, maybe a hundred of them, all on their knees, arms aloft, worshipping their queen. Their queen was, indeed, a big bastard. She looked like Jabba the Hutt's bigger, uglier sister, with huge, thick limbs twitching and weaving out of the trembling, oozing flab.

'You see that?' said Eva.

'Yes?'

'That's your mum, that is.'

For now, all of the creatures' attention was away from us. None of them seemed to have noticed our arrival. I craned my neck, attempting to catch sight of Chloe, but all I could make out were the dark, twitching shapes of the soul vampires.

'Okay,' said Maya as quietly as she could whilst still being audible. 'Nobody make a sound. Let's just scope the place out and come up with a plan of action.'

'Agreed,' I whispered back.

Eva stepped forward. 'Oi, wankers, over here!'

Around a hundred pairs of giant, saucer-sized eyes turned our way.

Bollocks.

'My name's Eva Familiar. I believe I bit your Queen earlier. Hello again to you, tubbs.'

Myself and Maya shuffled in behind Eva. I was desperately looking for a way that this might turn into a win for team Not Octopus Monster, but I was coming up blank.

'Right then,' said Eva. 'We're here to kick seven shades of shit out of you. Who's first?'

A hundred beaks opened wide and screamed in fury, the sound amplified by the vaulted ceiling of the cave, deafening the ears. Any second now they were going to charge us and kill us and eat our souls.

'Hold on.' A voice.

A voice I recognised.

'Chloe?'

And there she was, stepping out from the shadows. Chloe Palmer.

'Hey, Joe.'

'You're alive!'

She was definitely alive. I felt my grin grow so huge it was almost of cartoon proportions.

'Shit, quick, run!' I yelled.

Chloe didn't move towards us. Not even a little bit.

'Chloe? What's wrong?'

'Yeah,' she replied, 'this might break your heart a little. Sorry.'

'What are you talking about? Let's go!'

'Joseph,' said Maya, 'I think your girlfriend is a bad guy.'

I laughed, then turned back to Chloe and saw the look on her face.

'No.'

Chloe shrugged, then nodded.

Shit.

And big, hairy man-balls.

32

'No, no, no. No. No, no, no.' I said. Which seemed reasonable given the circumstances. All sense of immediate danger had evaporated and I stood rooted to the spot, my limbs useless, my face slack.

'What is it then, love?' asked Eva. 'What're you getting out of this exactly?'

'What am I getting?' replied Chloe. 'I'm getting what should rightfully be mine, and I'm going to do something wonderful with it. Something important.'

Maya stepped forward and showed off her badge. 'Chloe Palmer, you're under arrest, I'm going to have to ask you to accompany me to the station.'

'Really?' replied Chloe, disbelievingly.

'Yeah, I had a feeling that wasn't going to fly,' said Maya, stepping back and putting her badge away.

'Chloe,' I said, 'I don't understand. How can you be the bad guy?'

'I'm not the bad guy, Joe. What I'm doing is for the good of everyone.'

I shifted, trying to ignore my body's desire to crumple pathetically into a melodramatic heap of boo-hoo in the dirt.

'Look at them all,' said Chloe, turning and waving at all the surrounding soul vampires. 'Aren't they beautiful?'

'Not really my type,' replied Maya.

'Boring!' said Eva. 'Come on, love, cut to the chase already, I'm zoning out here.'

'When I was seven, I had to watch as cancer ate away at my mum... As death took her, piece by painful piece, and there was nothing I, or any doctor, could do about it. I can still hear her screams, Joe. Still see the agony etched into her face. And then I was alone. I never knew much about my dad. I was told he'd died when I was just a baby, but that was about it. Then I got a job at Carlisle Hospital and I started to learn the truth.'

'What truth?' I asked.

'That I'm special. That I'm meant for something more.'

'And who told you that?' asked Maya.

'A fox,' she replied.

Oh...

'That little bastard,' said Eva.

A fox. A talking fox.

'He's said things to me, too,' I explained. 'It's just bullshit, Chloe, that's all. Come on, you can still walk back from this. Please.'

She smiled, almost sadly, and shook her head.

'It's not bullshit. As soon as the fox told me, as soon as the Red Woman showed me, I knew it was true. Felt it. My father was from the Dark Lakes. He came here and he fell in love with a mortal woman, and I was what came from that love. My father, with me and my mum by his side, was going to lead an army to conquer Great Britain. This,' she said, arms wide, gesturing to the creatures surrounding her, 'was his army.'

'Shit army,' said Eva, 'Fuckers don't even have swords.'

'Being told the truth opened something up in me,' said Chloe. 'I found them. I found the army that my father was meant to lead. They were asleep, waiting for orders. I woke them up. I was terrified, I wanted to run away, but I couldn't. It was as though I was *meant* to be there. I thought they might attack, but they didn't hurt me. They saw who I was. Who my father was. And they've been growing stronger ever since. Getting ready to emerge from the shadows, with me at their head.'

'Bad luck, love,' replied Eva, ''cos you've got three problems there.'

'Oh?'

'Me, him, and her. I know it doesn't sound like much, but I am fucking scrappy.'

This was too much. It couldn't be real. Couldn't be true. I'd come here to rescue Chloe, to rescue the woman I'd been not-so-secretly in love with for the last several years, and now... what? She was part-evil, on her dad's side?

'Chloe, you're a doctor,' I said, 'this goes against everything you've ever worked for!'

'No. Because I haven't told you the best bit yet. We're going to save this country.'

'From what?' I asked.

'From death.'

'Yep,' said Eva, 'she's gone full loon.'

'My dad, yes, it seems like he wasn't altogether nice. He was going to use this army to lay waste to this country. But I've found a different, better use for them.'

I stepped forward, desperate to hear something good from Chloe. Something that would make me understand.

'What d'you mean,' I asked.

'These beautiful creatures, they don't have to just eat the souls. Imagine a person, close to death, beyond the help of any doctor. Just not enough time. Not enough tools, or the right medication, or the right knowledge. One of these creatures can remove and hold the sick person's soul. Cleanse it, with my help. With the magic I have inside of me, from my dad's side of the family. Infuse the soul with elements of the Uncanny so that when they deliver it back to the body, the patient will live. Will fight against what's killing them and win! Don't you see? They'll cheat death! Isn't that good, Joe? Isn't that worth doing?'

I had to admit, that did seem, well, sort of noble, maybe? Good, sort of?

'One teensy problem; these things need to kill people and eat their souls to survive,' said Eva. 'They're not just going to chew on them, then spit them back into their bodies. How are you going to get round that?'

'Oh, they'll still feed. Only they'll save their feasting for people who deserve death.'

Yup. And there it was.

'And who decided who deserves to die,' asked Maya.

'Me of course. I'm in charge. It's my birthright.'

'What about the people your pets have killed so far,' asked Maya, teeth clenched. 'Were they all 'deserving'? Was my partner!'

Chloe shuffled, looked unsure for the first time since she'd stepped out of the dark.

'They need to eat to grow strong enough for what's ahead. They'd been sleeping for years. They were starving. There wasn't time to—'

'Save it,' replied Maya, almost growling with contempt.

'I remember their names,' said Chloe. 'I'll never forget them. I'll never forget a single one of them. They died so a better world could rise and they will be worshipped for their sacrifice. Millions will live because of them. Millions.'

'I'll be honest, Chloe,' I said, 'this is giving me real second thoughts about kissing you again.'

'Chloe Palmer,' said Maya, 'If you think everyone out there will just fall in front of you, follow you, allow you to decide who lives and who dies, then you don't know shit about people.'

'They'll accept whatever I say, because I'll give the gift of life. Don't you see? Don't you understand the wonderful thing I'm offering? I'm going to change Great Britain for the better. No more mothers crying over their sick, dying children. No more children left without a parent, all because of some mutated, evil cells. No more. Not ever again.'

'And those that deserve to die get fed to Mr. Octopus,' I said, quietly.

'Yes. Isn't that right? Isn't that a small price to pay for all the good I'll do?'

'Listen,' said Eva, 'all you are is a half-Uncanny and a pile of soul vampires. That's not nearly enough magic, not nearly enough *power*, to do the sort of thing you're… oh…'

'Oh?' I said.

'Oh,' repeated Eva.

'Oh what?' replied Maya.

'Oh *you*, Joe,' said Chloe.

'Me? What about me?'

'Besides being the biggest knobhead this side of Manchester,' said Eva, 'you're also a source of crap-loads of Uncanny power. I mean, you're just a potential volcano ready to fire that shit out in every direction.'

'Well, it's not as though I know how to access any of that, and even if I could, I'm not going to help her.'

'Yeah, not really a consent issue,' she replied.

'Joe,' said Chloe. 'I'm sorry, you don't know how sorry, but we're going to kill you and feast on your soul. Your special, special soul.'

'See,' said Eva, 'not a consent issue.'

'Right. Oh. Great.'

'And then,' said Chloe, 'we'll have more than enough power to change things for the better.'

'For your version of better,' I said.

I looked to Chloe, who had an almost sheepish expression on her face. She shrugged. 'Sorry, Joe. Sorry it has to be you.'

'You were using me.'

'No. Not at first. I've always liked you, Joe, you know that. But then I started to realise what you *actually* were.'

'It was the fox, wasn't it? When I mentioned seeing a talking fox.'

She nodded. 'That was the first clue, yeah. I'd been looking for something like you, something so incredibly powerful, that we could all eat and use. That could finally give us the power to take our place up above and *save* people. And there you were. There you'd always been and I had no idea. Strange thing, life, isn't it?'

'Getting stranger,' said Maya.

'I wish there was another way,' said Chloe. 'I'd hoped you'd be at my side when the moment came. That we could stand side by side as I beat death at last. I really did like kissing you.'

'Oh,' I replied, 'I've had better.'

'No you haven't.'

I slumped my shoulders. 'I really liked you, Chloe Palmer.'

'And I really liked you. But I can't wait any longer. People are dying up there. People we can save. People who need me. So now it's time to kill you.'

'Shit; heads up,' said Maya.

I turned to see the stone burrow that we'd come through was now packed with soul vampires blocking our way. We were trapped. Maya pulled out an extendable baton, ready to smack anything that came too close.

It had become painfully clear that Chloe's abduction had only been a ruse. A ruse to get me here so they could kill me, eat my soul, and do the whole take-over-the-country thing. And I'd fallen for it. To be fair, I'm not sure how I could've been expected to piece any of this together beforehand, but still.

The creatures began to edge towards us.

'One step closer,' said Eva as she pulled her water pistol, 'and you fuckers are going to have a hell of a hangover tomorrow.'

Maya yelled and swung her baton, backing the things up.

'Bring him to me,' said Chloe.

The bravest of the creatures descended on us, wrapping its limbs around Eva and Maya, and holding them back as I was shoved towards Chloe, towards the huge blob of meat that was the soul vampire queen.

'Chloe Palmer,' said Maya, struggling to free herself from her assailant's grip, 'I am an officer of the law; if you harm a hair on Joseph Lake's head you will have the entire force of the Cumbrian Constabulary to answer to!'

It was a nice try, but it wasn't much of a deterrent at this point. Chloe was now only a few metres in front of me. I felt like grabbing her by the hand and trying to pull her towards the exit. Maybe if I could just get her away from here, away from these creatures, I could talk some sense into her. She was still the Chloe I knew. That part of her must still be in there. And if that was true, and I really, really hoped it was, then maybe there was a chance.

That hope was quickly squashed by what happened next.

'It's time for me to become more,' she said.

'More what?'

'Just... more.'

She smiled and gave me what you could almost class as a cute, goodbye wave.

'Bye, Joe. Thanks for being a friend. Sorry you won't be able to see the wonderful world I'm going to build.'

Then the giant soul vampire queen split open and Chloe stepped inside.

'Chloe!'

The wound healed. The queen began to tremble, twitch, scream, her subjects crying out in reply.

She was changing.

She began to sprout up and up, fresh limbs erupting from her damp, meaty torso. When she stopped growing, she resembled a giant, thick tree of twisted, dark green meat, with twitching octopus limbs for branches. A pure, Lovecraftian nightmare made sloppy flesh, that screamed from its huge beak, causing the ground to quake.

I staggered backwards, looking up at the terrifying beast before me. Chloe had somehow merged with the Queen. There was no talking to her now. No convincing. Chloe was gone.

It was over.

'Hey, idiot,' said Eva, 'You kissed her. Ha!'

And now she was going to kill me and eat my soul.

My fists clenched as I willed something to happen. Anything. I was magic. A warlock. If what they were saying was true, I had enough power in me to stop this. To put an end to this abominable army before it emerged above ground.

I lifted my hands, screaming, willing the impossible to happen. For fire to burst from me and turn these creatures to ash.

Nothing happened. Instead, the Chloe Queen reached out with one of its limbs and plucked me from the ground, carrying me towards its giant beak.

This was it then.

Really, really it.

I can't say it was how I'd expected to go.

'Nope,' said Eva, 'He might be a dickhead, but he's my dickhead.'

I craned my head round to see her twist and headbutt the creature holding her, breaking free. She dashed forward, octopus limbs grasping at her, hands burning with livid, orange flames.

'Get your tentacle off my witch, fucker!' She punched out a fist and a ball of fire shot from her hand and severed the limb holding me. I fell to the ground at her feet as the Chloe Queen screamed in fury.

'Thanks,' I gasped, kicking the dead limb off of me.

'Don't thank me yet, you might still be horribly dead in a minute.'

Eva pulled a piece of chalk from her pocket and drew a quick circle on the rock at her feet.

'Inside, now!'

I didn't ask why, I just hopped in.

'You too, Detective.' Eva reached out a hand and gripped Maya with some unseen force, pulling her towards us and inside the confines of the chalk circle.

'What use is a chalk circle gonna be?' Maya asked.

'What she said,' I added.

I soon got my answer. The soul vampires swarmed, desperate to grab us, to pull us apart, to feast on our souls. But some unseen barrier prevented them from getting within the chalk circle.

'Magic force field?' I said.

'Technically, it's a ward of protection,' replied Eva, 'but yeah, "magic force field" will do.'

'Are we safe?' asked Maya.

'Yep. Well. No. Well, yes. For a bit. I'm not very good at these protection circle jobbies, so sooner or later—and I'm guessing sooner—the spell's gonna break and they're gonna get in. And there's only so many of them I can deal with before they swamp us.'

The Chloe Queen raged at us, her giant limbs as thick as tree trunks, beating against the magical shell Eva had constructed with her chalk circle.

'So what now?' I asked. 'Can we move the circle? Just shuffle right on out of here before it breaks.'

'Nope.'

'Ah.'

'Then we're still going to be dead, just in a minute or two, rather than immediately,' said Maya.

'Pretty much,' replied Eva.

'Well, shit,' said Maya.

'Exactly. That is of course unless Magic Joe here pulls his finger out.'

'Me? What the hell can I do?'

'I need you to fuck these twats up.'

Delicately put.

'How?' I cried. 'I don't know how to access the power I have! It's still all locked up and hidden away and I can't get at it! Not when I actually want it, anyway. It plays very hard to get.'

We ducked instinctively as a fresh barrage of limbs assaulted us, the sharp sound of whatever magic shell it was that was protecting us straining and complaining, stabbing at our ears. It didn't sound like it could take much more punishment.

'Wait,' said Eva.

'Wait?' I cried, 'I think we're about all out of waiting time!'

'I... No... yes! I've got an idea. Bound to happen, that. Never doubted me for a second.'

'What idea?' I asked.

Eva grinned and waggled her eyebrows. 'Amplifier.'

'Amplifier?' replied Maya, stumbling back against me as the ground began to shake beneath our feet from the relentless onslaught.

'Ampli-shitting-fier! He might not be able to use his magic himself properly, but I can try and force my magic through Mr Idiot here, and he'll act as a booster, whacking up the volume to burn these fuckers to a crisp, and leaving us all nice and safe and alive and ready to party. Sound good?'

'Sounds good to me,' said Maya.

'Will that work?'

'Yep. Definitely work. Well. Maybe. Possibly. It'll either work or it'll make your brain go off in your skull like an egg in a microwave.'

'What!'

'Don't worry, you won't feel it if it goes wrong. Well, you will, it'll hurt like an absolute bastard, but then you'll be dead and you won't feel anything at all.'

'How likely is the egg scenario?'

'Don't worry, it's an 80/20 chance of that happening.'

'80/20? Is exploding egg the 80 or the 20?'

'Absolutely,' said Eva, noncommittally. 'Now brace yourself.'

'Is it the 80 or the 20? Eva? Wait—'

Her hands gripped my skull, and suddenly I felt like I'd been dropped from a height into a freezing pool of water. I could still see everything around me. Still see Eva, still see Maya. Could still see the monsters, and the Chloe Queen monstrosity. But it was all in slow motion. Distant. A dot on the horizon.

There were threads of fire in my mind. Burning tendrils, flaming worms. They wiggled their way through my consciousness, forcing connections that no longer existed. Images flashed before my eyes. Terrible things. Confusing things. Faces and monsters and places and sounds that I knew must be things I'd experienced. Things the old me, the forgotten me, had lived through. Whatever Eva was doing was giving me access to my past. Would it last? Was it just a temporary glimpse that would be locked away again?

I was a witch.

A warlock.

But who was I?

Those things weren't the answer. Not really. It didn't tell me who I really was. What I was like. It didn't give me my memories, my fears, my loves, my hates. Then two faces, two women, women who I knew, loved, belonged with. Me and them and Eva and we had purpose. Strength.

And then all clear thoughts were lost as it felt like my whole body was being pulled apart. Fingernails dragged down every raw nerve ending and I heard a horrible sound that I think was me screaming in agony.

I was found. I was lost. My heart was broken, betrayed, scattered to the winds.

Chloe Palmer. I had loved her as much as I could remember loving anyone, and it didn't matter. It was nothing. I was nothing. I was just a means to an end. A tool to be used and cast aside.

Anger.

It swamped me. It fed me.

What had the fox said?

The Red Woman?

Become the Magic Eater.

I'd wanted that, hadn't I? I suddenly felt like I had once wanted that very much. Desired it. Coveted it. Obsessed over it. Was willing to burn everyone to the ground to get it.

A beast. I was a beast.

I could see the Red Woman looking at me, only it wasn't me, it was the other me, the forgotten me, and I was holding her hand and smiling. She was smiling back and the sky was on fire and a million-strong army of the dead raised their weapons to the heavens and screamed and hooted and cheered and they were all mine.

We will do such things together.

The Red Woman was right. I wanted it. The power, the power, the power, the power and I think I'm falling apart. I think I'm dying. It's not working. It's too much. I don't know how to handle it, and any second now it's egg in a microwave time and that's all she wrote. I needed to control this. Needed to use it. Needed to unleash it. Come on, please, just do it!

'Hey, idiot.'

A voice. Not out loud, in my head. Eva was in my head.

'I can't do it.'

'Yeah, I know, you're useless.'

'Shut up.'

'I never should have come back to the lakes for you. I was having a good time, but here I am, and look what I find. You're pathetic, love.'

'I am not! I am... I am the Cumbrian Coven. I am Joseph Lake.'

I am the Magic Eater.

'You're a twat, is what you are.'

Why was she doing this? Why now, when we were moments from death and... oh....

'Yeah. Distraction. You're welcome.'

And then the cave exploded.

33

I was lying back on something that felt familiar.

'Finally,' said Detective Maya Myers.

I opened my eyes. I was in the back of the Uncanny Wagon, and it was on the move. I sat up to see Maya driving, Eva beside her. 'I'm alive.' I gave myself a quick pat down to make sure. 'I'm alive. How am I alive? How are both of you alive?'

'We won, that's how,' replied Eva, lighting a cigarette and handing it to me.

I took it with a trembling hand and inhaled.

'It worked?'

'Yup. You shat out enough magic to turn every single one of the fuckers to dust. Almost killed us too. The whole place started coming down while you were sleeping it off. Me and sensible trousers here had to lug your dead weight out of there, sharpish.'

'We did it. We did it!' I laughed, exhilarated. We'd put an end to it. Avenged the murders of Mrs Coates, of Mary Tyler, of Detective Sam Samm and all the rest.

It didn't take long for the bucket of cold water to be thrown on my high as Chloe's face swam into my mind's eye.

My best friend for years. The person I'd been head over heels for. Who I thought I might have an actual future with. Dead by my hands. Okay, it turned out she was a half-monster, that she had allowed the deaths of numerous innocent people, but still. She hadn't been all bad. I didn't think I'd be able to just wipe away all the good memories. I didn't want to. They were real. She'd lied to me, but I don't think she had about that.

And now this was real. All of it. Monsters. Magic. What I was, and what I could be. I may not have most of the pieces, or any of my memories, but I knew more than I had done for the last ten years, even if the things I knew were a mix of crazy and wet-your-pants terrifying.

I wasn't just a half-forgotten local mystery. The man who woke up, naked, without a past, beside Derwentwater. I was *more*. And I was pretty sure this was only the tip of the iceberg.

'Listen, I'm part of this from now on, right?' said Maya.

'You?' replied Eva. 'You were about as useful as a chocolate teapot down there.'

'I'm a detective. I can be useful. Resources, information, access. Also, this isn't a request, it's a done deal. From now on, I'm part of this. I'm the police here, and that means I am involved in protecting people from whatever they need protecting from. Understood?'

'Yes Ma'am,' replied Eva. 'Besides, if it was just me and ol' dickless over there, I'd probably end up killing the fucker.'

'Hey, I have a penis. And balls. Two of them.'

'Seen 'em. Not impressed.'

'Eva, why do you hate me so much? I mean sometimes you seem okay with me, others you'd be happy to feed my tender, baby-making parts to a wolf. It's very disorientating.'

Eva snorted, but didn't reply.

We left Detective Maya Myers at the police station, then I drove Eva back to the coven.

I'd seen the place during Eva's invasion of my mind. Seen memories of my life there, I know I had. Just flashes, but real things from my past. Now they were like fragments on the edge of my vision. Just frustratingly out of reach, out of focus. But for a few brief moments, I knew something of my life here. Not just my life. I'd seen other people who belonged here too.

Other witches.

I thought back to what the Red Woman and the fox had told me last time I saw them. What they had said Eva was keeping from me.

I looked at her, slumped on the tatty couch, drinking from her vodka pistol, watching a woman try to convince a couple to spend £300,000 on a large detached house by the sea.

'There were other members of this coven, weren't there? Others besides me and you.'

'That house is completely overpriced,' said Eva, before shooting vodka into her mouth.

'Eva.'

She watched the TV in silence.

'Eva, tell me!'

'There were others, yeah. Two of them.'

'So, it wasn't just me. What happened to them?'

Eva sat up and rubbed her eyes with the heels of her hands, then she looked at me and sighed.

'Eva, tell me, what happened to the other witches?'

'Well, to put it bluntly, you murdered them, love. Shall we go hit the pub then? You're buying.'

The End.

LEAVE A REVIEW

Reviews are gold to indie authors, so if you've enjoyed this collection, please consider visiting Amazon to rate and review.

READ THE NEXT UNCANNY KINGDOM COLLECTED VOLUME

The *Uncanny Kingdom Collection, Volume Two* is out now. Get your copy on Amazon.

MORE STORIES SET IN THE UNCANNY KINGDOM

The London Coven Series

Familiar Magic

Nightmare Realm

Deadly Portent

The Spectral Detective Series

Spectral Detective

Corpse Reviver

Twice Damned

The Dark Lakes Series

Magic Eater

Blood Stones

Past Sins

The Branded Series

Sanctified

Turned

Bloodline

The Hexed Detective Series

Hexed Detective

Fatal Moon

Night Terrors

Strange Stories

Apocalypse Hill

BECOME AN INSIDER

Receive **FREE UNCANNY KINGDOM BOOKS** by signing up below. Also, be the **FIRST** to hear about **NEW RELEASES** and **SPECIAL OFFERS** in the **UNCANNY KINGDOM** universe.

WWW.UNCANNYKINGDOM.COM

37189333R00283

Printed in Great Britain
by Amazon